*"Riveting. An enjoyable read from beginning to end and you'll love the strong characters as they fight to survive against great odds, against an enemy filled with vengeful hatred."*

—Tom Johnson, Fading Shadows, Inc.

*"Incredibly suspenseful!"*

—Writer's Digest

# OSGUARDS: GUARDIANS OF THE UNIVERSE

## By

## Malcolm D. Petteway

Homecoming
Revelations
Armageddon
Revenge

# REVELATIONS

## BOOK TWO
## OF
## OSGUARDS: GUARDIANS OF THE UNIVERSE

# MALCOLM DYLAN PETTEWAY

Rage Books LLC
www.ragebooks.net

# Osguards: Revelations

Edited by:
Karen M. Petteway
James Barnes
Harvetta Colvin
Michael Colvin

ISBN: 098436451X
EAN-13: 9780984364510

Printed in the United States
Rage Books LLC
www.ragebooks.net

*"The power of excellence is overwhelming. It is always in demand and nobody cares about its color."*

—Gen Daniel S. *"Chappie"* James, USAF

# Prologue—The Night Prior

The mugginess blanketed the city, trapping the heat and humidity like a body bag on this hot summer night. It was almost midnight. And in the distance on Texas Street in Shreveport Louisiana, where a row of one room nightclubs thrive, the blaring of different music and sounds wafted through the air in a strange cacophony.

The still night air cracked with gunshots. Two nine millimeter bullets rang in the air followed a split second later by three thirty-eight caliber rounds. Then the rattle of a semi-automatic pistol, spurting out its deadly load, cut through the dark.

Nelson Ford cowered against the bridge pillar in the midst of the city's Festival Center Plaza. Sweat glistened from his baldhead. Nelson shot a quick glance over to the next pillar. There he saw his friend, John Carter, better known as J.C., returning fire with his own nine millimeter. Under his breath, Nelson cursed J.C. for getting him into this situation. What was he thinking? What the hell did he do to deserve this? Just then, a bullet cracked the white pillar inches above his head. Nelson ducked and hugged the pillar closer, praying for a way out.

"J.C." a voice called from the other side of the plaza. "You might as well put the gun down and come on out."

"Why?" J.C. yelled. "I ain't going out like that!"

"Come on man! My bad...I thought you were trying to rip us off." The voice explained from the shadows.

"No, man. I was being righteous with you. You assholes are trying to rip us off. It ain't going down like that," yelled J.C.

"Oh yes it is!" a different voice yelled from the shadows. "You might as well kiss your ass good-bye...because you aren't getting out of here alive."

"Neither are you," J.C. screamed.

1

Nelson's face dropped with surprise. He'd never seen this side of J.C. He always thought of J.C. as a wannabe gang-banger. He never knew he had the die hard core to his personality. In fact, he always considered J.C. a joke, a clown—sort of a punk. Now J.C. was talking tough, and he had a gun to back it up.

Nelson shook his head in disbelief. He didn't know whether he was scared of dying, or just angry with J.C. for putting him in this situation. He looked over at J.C. with angst. He wanted to beat his brains in. Right now, he had to get out of here. He turned and looked behind him. There was a short open area before reaching the abandoned train station. If he could get to the building, it could be used for cover. However, the area was in full view of the Dallas boys chasing them. They couldn't make it before getting shot in the back. Nonetheless, it was their only chance.

"J.C.?" Nelson whispered. J.C. shot a glance at Nelson. Nelson pointed toward the abandoned building. J.C. nodded. Then J.C. jumped from behind his pillar, with his gun pointing into the shadows where the voices originated. And with a tremendous yell, he squeezed the trigger, spitting out a barrage of bullets into the darkness.

Click…click…click. J.C.'s gun clip went dry. J.C. turned toward Nelson, "Run!" he screamed.

Nelson's heart jumped as his adrenalin pushed into his muscles. He bolted down the dark path toward the left, putting the old train station between him and his assailants. He heard J.C. behind him. With each strike of his foot against the pavement, he became angrier and angrier. He wanted to trip J.C. and let the Dallas boys have him. However, he knew any energy used to do anything but run away would be a waste and may cost him his life. So he ran, having some solace at the sounds of J.C.'s footsteps behind him. They reached the end of the old train station and ran down the park stairs toward the lower parking lot.

Just as Nelson thought they weren't being followed anymore, a bullet clanged against the metal railing; close enough for him to feel the heat from its friction. He jumped the rest of the stairs, crawled to the next flight and slid down the stairs on his belly. At the bottom of the stairs was the wide and open lower parking lot—nothing he could use for cover. Fright gripped his soul. Panic grabbed his gut. He whimpered as he looked back.

J.C. came crashing into his legs as he slid on his stomach down the stairs. Both crumbled to the ground and against the wall leading to the restroom. Nelson shook J.C. off of him and crawled down the short corridor to the bathroom doors. He tugged at the doors to the men's room. The metal lock of the doors clanged but they did not open. Nelson pounded on the doors with his fist in frustration, and then he kicked it. The kick echoed in the stone hall.

2

"Shit!" Nelson sighed. He looked up and saw J.C.'s shadow. "What the hell are you doing?" he whispered.

"Shut the hell up!" J.C. whispered pointing above him.

The sound of footsteps coming down the stone stairs echoed in the hallway. There was just one of them. Originally there were three. That was some good news, Nelson thought. Nelson also knew the man only had to turn and peer down the hallway and they would be dead. Nelson prayed for it to be too dark for him to make them out in the shadows.

Then he saw the man. He stood about six feet tall, skinny and dressed in sweat pants and a Los Angeles Lakers basketball jersey. It was too dark for Nelson to distinguish any features, or read the number on the shirt. Nelson crept against the wall, hoping to blend his shadow into the wall.

The man turned, as if he heard Nelson move. He pointed his gun into the hallway and fired three quick rounds. The bullets hit the metal door, and ricocheted against the stoned walls. The man lowered the gun, stretching his neck into the hallway.

On the far side of the parking lot, a scream bellowed through the air. The man spun toward the scream. There were more nightclubs on the other side of the parking lot and the noise started to echo into the lot. However, the man didn't know that, he thought his prey had somehow got to the other side. He dashed out of sight and ran across the parking lot.

Nelson counted to two hundred while still gripping the wall. He had pushed his back so much into the natural stone wall, his skin cracked and blood began to run. He dared not move for he did not know if the man was gone, or waiting for any movement in the dark to single him out of the darkness.

In the distance, Nelson could hear the sirens blaring, indicating the cops were nearby. He had to leave now. He knew he couldn't let the police catch him—not now—not ever.

"J.C.?" Nelson called. Nothing… "J.C.?" he called again. Still nothing. Nelson took a deep breath and blew it out. "J.C., where the fuck are you?" Nelson listened, trying to filter out the noise floating on the still warm midnight summer air, coming from the other side of the parking lot. He heard a slight moan this time, the moan of death bestowing its unwelcome visit. Then he heard a thud, like a body crashing to the ground.

J.C. had fallen; face first, onto the cement floor. Nelson released the wall and rushed to the sound. He groped in the darkness until he felt J.C. His hand plopped into a sticky warm liquid in the middle of J.C.'s chest. He pulled his hand back and wiped it on his shirt. It was blood. He couldn't see it, but he knew it. J.C. had been hit by one of those ricocheting bullets.

Once again panic clutched his stomach. The sour taste of fright occupied his mouth. He wanted to scream, but he didn't. He sighed. He knew J.C. was dead, or at least he wanted him to be dead. Because if he wasn't

3

dead, he wasn't going to carry him out of there. He did not need that type of baggage as he tried to escape. The sirens were getting louder in the distance. He knew his time was limited. He had to leave now.

Nelson emerged from the hallway and ran up the stairs, reversing his route. He knew the one guy was behind him and he hoped the sirens had scared the others off. He pushed his body as he flew down the alley and past the bridge pillars. He stopped in his tracks as he saw them at his feet.

The other two men lay on the ground in a pool of their own blood. He guessed J.C. must have hit them when he did his last barrage of gunfire. *Finally,* he thought. *J.C. did something right.* Nelson booted both men in the head several times, releasing his frustration, fright and anger with each kick.

The sirens wailed closer and closer, piercing his reality. He had to get moving. He had to run. The red and blue lights now framed the night sky around the Festival Plaza, bouncing off of buildings like glowing neon signs. Nelson estimated three police cars were waiting on the street above. He knew he couldn't go that way. He thought of going back the way he came. Yet, he was unsure if the last killer had left.

Nelson felt desperation tingle his body. The police lights and sirens were like an invisible noose around his neck. He swallowed hard and shook his head. He tried to breathe, but the air caught in his throat. He coughed a dry hacking cough. Nervousness now ruled his actions. He would be damned if he went back to jail; especially for some bullshit J.C. cooked up. One idea consumed him—escape.

He was running on automatic, no thought process involved. He turned to the far wall separating the area from the train tracks below. It was a long drop on the other side of the wall, but he had to do it. He pushed fear from his mind and sprinted toward the wall. He jumped, pulled himself over the wall and dropped into the night on the other side, disappearing from sight and from the cops. Nelson had escaped with his life—for now!

# Chapter 1—Funeral

Chaktun's sun, one-third bigger than Earth's sun and with a fierce orange glow, burned in the sky with unmerciful intensity. Juanita Genesis-Clark, Osguard Fifty-Five, the sire of the *Galaxy Protector Sharyla*, the protector of Galaxy Fifty-Five, known as the Bletherien Galaxy, had forgotten how intense the heat could be on her adopted mother planet. She had trained almost twenty years earlier on this planet with her relatives under this same sun. However then, the enthusiasm and the adventure of it all consumed her consciousness and blotted out the heat. Now she did not know how she survived in this environment. The one saving grace – it was pure heat with little to no humidity. Today was like other summer days in this hemisphere of the planet—dry and hot with the temperature above one hundred degrees Fahrenheit. For all intents and purposes, it was a moderate day for the average Chaktun.

The burial ceremony for her great-great-grandmother, Sharyla and her great-great-great-aunt, Kashara was complete. The attendees, mostly her relatives, made their way from their seats in the courtyard toward the palace, where the current Maxum, Reppus Osguard, a direct descendant of Vedar Osguard's younger brother, Akaher Osguard, planned a reception. Akaher assumed the duties of Maxum after his nieces, Nausona and Laurona, abdicated the throne in pursuit of creating the Universal Science, Security and Trade Association of Planets—USSTAP. Somehow, Juanita always thought Akaher received the raw portion of the deal. The Chaktun Republic dissolved; replaced by the newly formed and untested USSTAP.

That was almost a hundred universal years ago. Since then, USSTAP had driven back the Kulusks, discovered fifty nine other galaxies and incorporated over fifty thousand planetary governments into USSTAP. All this came to fruition from the dreams of two sisters who fled from Chaktun only to be enslaved, beaten and raped for their efforts. What a twist of fate...

"Aren't you coming?"

Her mother's voice rattled Juanita from her deep thought.

"Huh?"

"Aren't you coming?" Sarah Genesis repeated.

Juanita looked around and realized the entire courtyard was empty except for her and her mother. She had lost herself in thought far too long.

"Yes, mother. I am coming," she whispered.

Her mother turned to the freshly covered graves as a tear rolled from her right eye.

"Another funeral! I don't know how many of these I can take," she whispered. "At least this time they were dead before I knew them. Yet, I can't help feeling I still lost a loved one. Two loved ones," she corrected herself. "When I buried your father, twenty years ago, I thought I would die too. Then I had to bury your brother." She turned toward Juanita and held her face with her hands. "Now that I've seen what you do, I am afraid I will have to bury you someday. That is too much for one woman to bear. It's too much for a mother to bear."

"Mother, we have gone through this a dozen times this week..."

"I know, but you had to bury a husband also. Now you tell me, you aren't feeling a little dispirited over this," Sarah countered, pointing to the graves.

"Mother, I am more dispirited over the Kulusks and what they have done to us. You saw the holovidpics we recovered from their ships. After Nausona and Laurona left Earth, Nom Ritchen sent his sons Erif and Efas to

Earth to kill Kashara and Sharyla. Instead they found their daughters Betty and Shirley, and killed them. Ortho always wondered what happened to them. Now we know. The holovidpic was not pretty. What's worse is now our suspicions are confirmed. The Kulusks have been behind the majority of hate groups, including the KKK and the introduction of drugs into our society in a systematic attempt to kill not just us, but anyone on Earth, no matter if they had any trace of Chaktun DNA or not." Juanita pushed her mother's hands down from her face and placed her face within inches of her mother's.

The anger burned bright in her hazel eyes as the water began to soak them. "Mom, the Kulusks are responsible for the poison Conrad overdosed on. They may not have pushed the junk into my brother's arm. They may not have even sold the smack to him. Hell, I don't know if they even touched it in any way. Because of their master plan of using the inherent qualities of smack to destroy the genes of anyone with strong Chaktun DNA, my brother, your son, is dead. I always thought it, now I know it."

Juanita turned away as she felt a tear roll down her cheek. She raised her head to the sky in an effort to regain composure.

"I am an Osguard, I was born an Osguard and I will probably die an Osguard," she said with strength in her voice. She turned back to her mother, "But it won't be anytime soon—I promise. Death is not a concept I welcome or one in which I prepare for. My training, as you saw from this so-called Universal War, is for self-preservation and the preservation of my ship. I damn those who deem otherwise…especially the Kulusks."

Sarah gazed into her daughter's eyes and saw her conviction. She knew this look all too well. Her husband, Juanita's father, had this same look when he wanted things done. Sarah knew it was a futile attempt to try to sway her away from her destiny. Yet, the pain still haunted her. She did not want to lose another loved one. She did not want to lose her daughter to death—not before it came for her—and she wasn't planning on death for a long time yet.

"Well?" Sarah asked.

"Well what?" Juanita replied.

"You never answered my question," Sarah continued. "Are you coming or not?"

Juanita looked puzzled for a minute. Then a broad smile emerged on her face. Her mother diffused the situation by changing the subject. Or did she win the situation? For now, it did not matter and she did not care. The reception was in the palace and they were late. She took her mother by the arm and strolled up the stone stairs into the palace courtyard entrance.

Inside the Steeple Palace entrance, the walls were blue marble with a shiny white floor. Sarah stopped for a minute to take in the beauty. She thought, technically, this was her husband's birthright. A birthright he did not live to see. A birthright he could have enjoyed if Ortho had found them before the cancer took him. Yet, it was no longer a birthright. The palace now belonged to the descendants of Akaher, not Vedar. Therefore, it was not her daughter's birthright either. USSTAP was her daughter's birthright. And what gave her the right to take that away from her daughter. Her daughter was born an Osguard and will remain an Osguard until her death.

She turned to Juanita, "I understand it now, but baby, I need time to accept it. Okay?"

"Okay, mother," she said with a smile. "I will pray for you."

"And I for you, baby. And I for you."

***

The reception hall was gallantly large and superbly decorated with paintings, statues and flowers. The walls were as blue as a tropical ocean with golden sand color marble floors and interspersed with several white columns stretching toward the ceiling. The garnishing was similar to USSTAP's diplomatic rooms. This was due to the common heritage and bond the two organizations shared. The room rang from the cacophony of the Osguards and their families, along with dignitaries from the Chaktun government mingling together recounting the events of the last couple of days—known as the First Universal War.

"That was a beautiful service," Maxum Reppus said to Michael Genesis.

Reppus held his glass of guild, a Chaktun type Champaign, made from paspers, a grape-like fruit, for Michael to tap in an unplanned gesture of a toast.

"Thank you so much my dear Maxum," Michael replied as he tapped Reppus' glass with his own glass of guild. "It was long overdue. Ortho had planned this over ten years ago. I thank you for your support in having our ancestors buried on Chaktun soil, next to their mothers."

"It was my pleasure," the Reppus replied. "However, I must admit, it took some doing to convince our parliament to approve the burial of non-Chaktuns on Chaktun soil. However, once I convinced them these were the remains of Osguards, it didn't mattered their blood was not pure Chaktun." Reppus' smile contained the glee of a hunter as he finished his statement.

"I see," Michael responded. "You mean to tell me, the people of my ancestors are as race conscious as our enemy?"

"No...no...no, my dear cousin," Reppus uttered, "not race conscious, but proud of their heritage."

"I see," Michael nodded. "Therefore my dear cousin, you have no pride in what I or my relatives have done for you and our adopted mother planet, because we are not pure Chaktun?"

7

Reppus leaned in closer to Michael's ear. "Michael, I have nothing but pride for you and all my cousins. You have taken a Chaktun dream and built upon it a mighty organization. No...not a Chaktun dream, but an Osguard dream. I for one, as an Osguard, have more at stake in the success of USSTAP than I do in the views of the Chaktun Parliament. With me, you always have an ally. Therefore, I request you do not take my non-diplomatic words and attempt to place hidden meaning in all I say. I am a cousin, your blood is mine and mine is yours. It does not matter what percentage is Chaktun and what percentage is not. We are who we are and Jus knows what is in our hearts."

"You're right," Michael apologized. "I have the diplomat in me on overdrive. It just seemed you took so much delight in the words 'pure Chaktun.'"

"That is not what gave me pleasure," Reppus whispered. "It was the fact I made the parliament see things my way on this issue that gave me pleasure. I am saddened by the arrogance of our people, yours and mine, in hiding intolerance inside the term heritage. I am sure you have not come across such mannerism before."

"Unfortunately, yes I have. Heritage, nationalism or culture, whatever term you use, it reflects the same thing—a feeling of superiority, which eventually conceives the wickedness of bigotry. It is insidious and infectious. We all have it, and sometimes we need it to define our own self-worth...I dare say in some cases, to validate our own self-worth. It is only the strong that can prevent it from advancing our own self-worth over others' individual rights." Michael turned to check who was around him. "This very concept is what I fear drives the Kulusks to destroy us. We need to subdue our own feelings of superiority and widen our nationalist fervor to include all of humankind—even the Kulusks."

"I understand, Michael," Reppus said as he looked down. "However, I am afraid it won't happen in our lifetime … not after this universal war."

"I am afraid you may be right. Nevertheless, we still must try." Michael looked down as well. "However the discovery of Kulusk's holovidpics has widened the canyon between us even more than this war. I am not sure I can offer them the olive branch of humankind anymore."

A few seconds of silence lingered in the air between the two men. Reppus frowned in thought as Michael gazed into Reppus' eyes. Michael was searching for a hint of understanding between him and Reppus, but saw none. Reppus responded to Michael's statement with indifference, a politician's shield.

"Enough, Michael," Reppus suggested. "It is time to celebrate our victory and honor our fallen comrades."

They both raised their glasses of guild and drank the entire contents in one swallow. When they finished a bond of trust emanated from their eyes.

With this, Michael thought Reppus understood and supported the need to include the Kulusks into the USSTAP ranks. However, Michael also knew Reppus was in no position to espouse those sentiments aloud, today or anytime soon. They smiled and separated into the crowd to mingle, celebrate their victory and honor their fallen comrades.

# Chapter 2—The Killing

"Tyree...you stay on the sidewalk...do you hear," shouted Yolanda Smart to her only child.

The heat of the Shreveport Louisiana July day had dissipated enough for Yolanda to let her five-year old son go out and ride his bike. She didn't want him to go outside today, because of the violence, which seemed to grip the city during this unusual heat wave. The temperature had hit triple digits for the tenth day in a row ... and as she suspected, when the temperature rose, so did the tempers. She had read in the *Shreveport Times* of the city's tenth killing in as many days. It wasn't safe to be out at night on the streets these days. She wondered if the people were going crazy or if she was.

Yolanda smiled as she watched her son, from the living room window, ride his bicycle to the stop sign and back. She soaked her thoughts in her son's smile and laughter as he showed off for his mother. His father had just taught him how to ride a two-wheeler and Tyree thought he was a big boy now.

Yolanda paused at the thought of Nelson Ford, her baby's father. They had dated the last two years of high school. He was the big basketball star and every girl wanted him, but Nelson chose her. Something at the time she was so thrilled about, but her mother, Jessica Smart, was not. Nelson introduced her to the wild life—drugs, alcohol and sex. Sometimes Yolanda got so high, she did not know whom she was, or where she was. Nelson had turned her into a prostitute, and she began selling her body for drug money to sustain both of them. Fortunately, Yolanda's mother, Jessica, did not give up on her.

Jessica got her daughter the help she needed—got her cleaned and back into school. Yet, Yolanda was a mother by the time she graduated high school. Paternity test proved Nelson to be the father, but he did not want anything to do with his son. Unlike Yolanda, Nelson was able to stay in school and graduate. Nelson went to Grambling State University, sixty-five miles east of Shreveport, on a basketball scholarship. However, he flunked out and returned home to Shreveport for life on the streets.

When he returned he would frequently stop by to see Yolanda and Tyree. Yolanda even imagined they would be a family someday. Jessica still did not trust Nelson, but she allowed him to see his son whenever he wanted to. They had become close in the last two years, as evident by the bicycle Tyree was so proud of riding.

Yolanda started to think life was looking up for her. Her man was back in her life, she snagged a job as a blackjack dealer on a casino boat docked in the Red River, and she was about to get off welfare. Yes, things were looking up for her. Soon, she imagined she would be able to get her own apartment, and take her son away from Cooper Road. She had grown up in Cooper Road, one of the roughest neighborhoods in Shreveport. However, she did not want her son to grow up here.

"What you smiling about?" Jessica bellowed.

Yolanda turned from the window to see her mother in her favorite easy chair hanging up the phone.

"Nothing mother; I'm just watching Tyree ride his bike," said Yolanda. "Who was that on the phone?"

"Oh, that was your Aunt Sarah."

"How's she doing? I know you've been worried about her since her phone was disconnected last week."

She was concerned for her aunt, but a tinge of jealousy in her had hoped something had upset her perfect world in Virginia. Yolanda was jealous her cousin, Juanita, made such a good living; she could uproot and place her mother in a distinguished house in Virginia and then care for her every need. Yolanda wished she could do this for her mother. However, she thought herself a complete failure and an utter disappointment.

"She's fine. Juanita took her out of the country for a vacation and in her absence the phone bill must've not got paid."

Yolanda shifted her body on the couch to face her mother in the two-bedroom house.

"So, where are they?" she asked.

"You know...she didn't say," said Jessica in amazement. "All Sarah wanted to say was that she was alright, and not to expect her back home for another month. Other than that, we talked about you and Tyree."

"That's odd," remarked Yolanda.

Yolanda turned back toward the window and saw Nelson entering the front gate.

"Mother, Nelson is coming," she shrieked. Yolanda turned to her mother with a cold stare. "Now Momma, I want you to be nice to him. He is trying his best."

"Girl, it takes all that I have not to throw him out on his ear," Jessica roared. "He has not been anything but the devil in your life. I can never forgive him for what he did to you."

"Momma, that's the past. He's a changed man," said Yolanda trying to defend her baby's father.

"Once a devil; always a devil," answered Jessica.

"Now momma, be nice…I beg you to be nice."

"Aren't I always," said Jessica with a smirk.

Three hurried knocks banged at the door. Yolanda jumped off the couch and rushed to the door to the side of the couch. She brushed off her yellow tank top and blue jean shorts. Another quick three knocks echoed from the door. Yolanda swung it open without hesitation. Nelson was in the doorway, sweaty and somewhat nervous looking. He had a shaven baldhead and stood six feet tall. His muscle shirt accented his frame, which made Yolanda weak for him. He cut her his patented smile, pushed her aside as he made his way into the compact living room.

"Well, hello to you too," Yolanda snapped.

"Yolanda, I am in big trouble. I need your help," replied Nelson.

"That's my cue to go start dinner," Jessica interrupted as she stood. She looked Nelson up and down with disapproving eyes, shook her head and turned in a huff toward the kitchen.

Yolanda closed the door and moved toward Nelson. Nelson lowered his head and raised his knuckles to his mouth. He was biting on his trigger finger knuckle. He turned toward the kitchen to see if Jessica was listening. He saw her moving about the cabinets in search of something. He thought this was good. He knew Jessica was a busy body, but she was not interested in his troubles this day.

"Okay, what kind of trouble are you in now?" Yolanda asked.

"Did you hear about that shooting last night?"

"Yeah…why?"

"That was me," Nelson whispered.

"What…what do you mean…that was you?" asked Yolanda who was now shaken.

"That was me," he repeated. He grabbed Yolanda by the arms and stared into her eyes. "J.C. and me were in the middle of this deal. It went bad. People started shooting. J.C. shot back. Before I knew it, J.C. was dead and two of the other people shooting at us were dead."

"What…what the hell are you talking about? What deal?"

"A drug deal, baby…a drug deal!"

"What do you mean a drug deal?" asked Yolanda, breaking free from Nelson's grip.

"J.C. had a cousin in Dallas who hooked us up with these dudes. We were going to score some stuff. J.C. thought we could double our money in a week, but something went wrong. The Dallas dudes went crazy. They thought we were five–oh. They pulled guns on us. Baby, I was so scared. Then J.C. pulls his gun. Next thing I know everyone is shooting. I duck…I hide…I don't come out until the shooting is over. That's when I saw they were all dead. Now the word on the street is some more Dallas dudes are in town looking to settle the score. They're out to kill me. That's why I got to get out of town—now!"

Yolanda looked at Nelson for a couple of seconds. Her mind was racing between disbelief and denial. Her golden brown skin tightened around her jaw. Her eyes widened with horror at what her mind couldn't conceive. She brushed her right hand through her silky brown hair. Then she shook her head as a final gesture of disbelief.

"What the hell do you want me to do?" she said.

"I need money; I need your mother's car to get out of town."

"No and no!" she screamed without hesitation. "My mother was right all along. You are the devil. I be damned if I let you drag my mother, me or my son into your shit." She turned, walked toward the door and then opened it. "I want you to leave!" she demanded.

"What, no baby…you can't mean that?"

"Oh the hell I can!" she yelled. "I want you out of here and I don't want you to ever come back."

"What about Tyree? What about us?" he asked.

"Tyree has no father and there is no us. Now I asked you to leave. Or do you want me to call five–oh?"

"Can I at least say good-bye to my son?"

"Make it quick."

Nelson walked outside onto the porch. Tyree saw his father about to leave, dropped his bike on the sidewalk and rushed to him. Nelson felt for the first time alone and ashamed. He was about to say good-bye to his son and he would not know when he would see him again. He watched Tyree race toward him. With every step his son took he searched his mind for what he was about to tell him.

On the street, a blue Pontiac Firebird with Texas plates slowed to a crawl. No one noticed it. The driver's widow electronically rolled down. A silver barreled nine millimeter pistol flashed through the window's opening. When the car was aligned with Yolanda's doorway, five shots rang out, piercing the summer day and overshadowing the laughter of children playing in their yards.

Nelson fell back into the house on top of Yolanda. His blood splashed against the wall and onto Yolanda. She screamed. Jessica ran from the kitchen to see Nelson with blood all over his chest lying on top of Yolanda. His eyes were stiffened wide open in death. She knew right away, Nelson was dead.

"Lord…no…no…not my baby!" screamed Jessica.

Jessica bent down grabbed Nelson's arm and rolled him off Yolanda. Yolanda was still screaming from the top of her lungs. Jessica could not tell if the blood was her daughter's or Nelson's. She patted her down, but could not find any holes in her clothes.

"Baby...baby, you're alright. Baby, you aren't hit," Jessica said more to convince herself than to calm her daughter. "Where's Tyree? Honey, where is Tyree?" she asked.

Yolanda kept on screaming. Jessica lay next to her and held Yolanda's head on her lap. In the distance she heard the police sirens responding to the shooting. She glanced out the doorway and looked on with horror. She dropped Yolanda's head to the floor as she sprinted up and out the door with poetic movement surprising for a woman her size. Her eyes welled with tears as she dropped to her knees. She looked down on the ground at the bloody body. She saw the bullet had tore part of the top of the head off. She saw the same death stare in the eyes as she did in Nelson's eyes. She raised her fist to the air and screamed a wretched scream that shook the neighborhood.

"No Lord...No Lord...No Lord...No Lord...not my grandson! Not my grandson! Lord ... no! Lord ... no! Lord ... no! Lord...no! Not my baby!"

# Chapter 3—Reclaiming the Bodies

A forty-ship convoy of USSTAP morgue ships, sailing in a three tier inverted 'U' formation dropped out of MOP speed to hyperlight, then to hypersonic, and then to subsonic speed. The morgue ships, with the characteristic convex engines running the length of the starboard and port side, carried the Kulusk dead from the battle, which occurred a week prior. Intense negotiation led to this moment in which the Kulusk's dead soldiers were to be returned to their home planet. The automatic pilot system on each ship registered their position as being in the Kulusk's solar system. A confirmation signal originated from Kulusk, as negotiated. If the ships did not receive the confirmation signal within five universal minutes of reaching the Kulusk solar system, the automatic pilot would reverse course and set sail for USSTAP Capitol Station. However the signal did come. It reached the ships within three minutes of its deadline. The signal, carrying coordinates for the planet's surface, activated the USSTAP ships' micro portals. One-by-one, the micro portal's yellow energy beam engulfed each casket. The light flooded the caskets, mapped their micro-cellular structure, disassembled them into cellular pieces and shot them through the cold vastness of space toward Kulusk's surface. Using the coordinates provided in the confirmation signal, the micro portal began restructuring the caskets and their contents on Kulusk. The gruesome automated task of transporting 85,394 bodies to Kulusk took thirty minutes. With only 25,603 listed as prisoners of war, the missing in action totaled 49,003.

# Malcolm Dylan Petteway

This venture cost Kie Ritchen eighty percent of his military and the life of his only son, whose body was not found. The picture of the wreckage of his ship told Kie his son's body would never be found. Xer had died in a vain warrior's death. He gazed on with dread as the cigar shaped brown caskets phased into the area, one by one. With each casket his heart sank deeper and deeper and his anger mounted higher and higher. He had stopped counting after the first thousand caskets materialized. The caskets filled the landscape of the chosen area. The brown slick cigar shaped caskets sat in formation. The carrier signal had provided the direct spot for each casket. However, there were some caskets containing no identification; and there were some caskets carrying only identification tags. Kie remained in his command hovercraft, surveying the area with mock intensity. His eyes swelled with angst as the caskets continued to materialize.

When the ships registered their cargo holds empty, the automatic pilots on each ship reversed course and set sail at MOP thirty for Capitol Station. The unmanned, unarmed morgue ships had accomplished their duty. They had carried the dead of an enemy back to the enemy's home without risking another confrontation between forces.

Kie exited his hovercraft and began to walk amongst the caskets. His cape dragging behind him, brushed up against the caskets as he walked by. The cape seemed to gesture a passionate pat on each casket it touched. Kie walked for ten minutes in a straight line and still saw coffins as far as the horizon. He stopped and turned his head to his right, still he saw nothing but coffins. Then he turned his head to his left; still he saw nothing but coffins. However, he now could make out the light of his troops on the boundary's edge.

His troops, a derisory four dozen, remained on the outskirts to secure the area from the populace. They watched their leader, their commander pay his last respects to the soldiers who died for his cause. The Kulusk sun descended behind the far mountain, as the sky turned burnt orange. The soldiers watched in awe as they studied the silhouette of their commander floating amidst the dead. The scene was too surreal for the soldiers who saw their commander as a harsh, rigid and uncompromising leader. The trance of the moment pushed their anger for this leader to the back of their minds. For a fleeting instant, the soldiers felt a kinship with the man they feared. They felt a connection they never felt before—the mourning of dead comrades in arms.

Kie continued to walk. As far as he could see, there were coffins. To him they appeared endless. The formation stretched into eternity, as did his hate for the Osguards. He became overwhelmed with emotion and sank to his knees. He placed his head on a casket and read the name before he closed his eyes—Epah Joam. Death never mattered to him before. He had ordered the death of over a hundred men, women and children. He dared to think the

14

count to be in the thousands during his thirty universal year reign. Although, for some reason, the death of these men had touched a heart he never knew existed. It was because these men died with and under the command of his son, Xer. He could not grieve properly for his son, because there was no body, but here lay over eighty five thousand bodies—bodies of men he never knew or cared for ... until now.

"The revenge is set my friend...the revenge is set," he whispered to Epah's casket.

Soon his thoughts of grief clouded his conscious mind and overtook him in slumber. He lay with his head on Epah's coffin, not moving, not seeing, but only breathing in the deep slumber of night called sleep. The night soon blanketed his body, consuming his soul into pitch darkness as the Kulusk sun paid its final tribute to the slain and the Kulusk moons dare not appear.

"Wake-up Kie," the voice came as Kie felt a kick to his boot. "Wake-up I say," the voice urged again.

Kie's head popped up from the coffin as saliva escaped from the corner of his lips. The grogginess of sleep still confined his mind as he fought for his awareness.

"Wake up, you pig," ordered the voice as Kie received another kick.

Kie turned toward the voice in the night but only could make out the figure of a man—a man pointing a pagenay to his face. Kie moved his hand toward his belt.

"No...no...no, my dear cousin," the voice said. "I wouldn't do that if I were you. I have no qualms about killing you here, and I'm sure your men on the perimeter would not mind either."

"Cousin? What manner do you speak of me as cousin?" Kie questioned in his most commanding voice.

"Oh yes, you do not know of me," the voice confirmed. "I am Opel, the great-grandson of Efas, your great-uncle; or is it great-great-uncle? I could never keep it straight." The voice now seemed pleasant, almost joking.

"It is true, Efas was my ancestral-uncle," Kie confirmed. "Except he died without bearing an offspring," Kie continued as stumbled to his feet.

"Yes, that is what dear old great-grandfather Nom stated. However, it's not true."

"What are you talking about?" Kie demanded.

Opel activated his PGP. The white light from inner space illuminated behind them, like the sun. The guards who saw the light assumed their Maxum was stepping back to his palace and dismissed the phenomena. Opel pointed for Kie to step into the portal opening. Kie saw the demeanor on Opel's face from the light and decided to do as he was told. Kie stepped into the light, followed by Opel and the invisible door of darkness slid down closed behind them.

# Malcolm Dylan Petteway

\*\*\*

Commander Terilela surveyed her console. Her red crystal-like eyes darted back and forth between screens. The yellowish skin of her face was drawn from worry and paranoia. She knew the morgue ships should be returning at any moment. She had worked the computation, what seemed, several hundred times. She calculated the distance, travel time, time to complete the transport and the time of return. She had one unknown variable left—the confirmation time of receipt. However, she knew the maximum time of wait was five universal minutes and using this factor would have the ships within scanner range in another three minutes. Deep down inside her mind, she wondered if the Kulusks would attack the ships, or worse use the morgue ships as a Trojan horse. She pushed back her golden hair from her eyes and bit her lower lip in anticipation.

She was never amazed at the ruthlessness of the Kulusks. She anticipated the Kulusks would commandeer the morgue ships, step an invading force on them, wait for them to dock at Capitol Station, and then launch an attack. This is why she insisted in firm time control. If the ships did not reach Capitol Station within the prescribed time window, then her orders were to destroy them upon reaching range. She knew a five-minute window was stringent. Yet, any larger window would allow time for the Kulusks to board the ships prior to the ships return journey. She also knew the Kulusks could be capable of stepping to the ships while the system conducted the body transport. Technically, the window did not assure her the Kulusks would not be on-board anyway. Yet, the window did make it difficult for such a deception. If it were her decision, she would have had the ships self-destruct after they completed their mission. Nevertheless the parliament thought this to be an affront to the Kulusks. She tilted her head to the right as she wondered if it mattered at this point in the game.

Then the signal caught her attention. Station twenty-five reported scanner contact. The mathematical display flooding the screen indicated the mass and speed of forty USSTAP morgue ships moving at MOP thirty. Terilela slewed her console to station twenty-five and watched with intense emotion. She was so tense, if anyone had touched her at this moment, she would have literally jumped out of her skin.

She tapped her console once more to connect to each ship's sensors. She thumbed through the log as each ship reported *'NO LIFE SIGNS.' This was good*. However her paranoia would not let her rest. She thumbed through the sensors once more for each ship. This took approximately two more minutes. Again each ship reported *'NO LIFE SIGNS'*.

The massive black ships, with rectangular shape hulls, slowed to a stop at the designated rendezvous point. Terilela directed her crew to dock each ship, using remote control unto the morgue station. There, she had arranged security to board the ships and search for stowaways or explosive devices.

Personally, she detested the entire mission. In her eyes, the Kulusks did not deserve the return of their dead. She wanted to incinerate the entire populace in the garbage station. However, the Osguard Senate had agreed to do the honorable thing and return the dead. The Osguards seldom let emotions rule their decisions. It was part of their training, and hers as well. Yet the Osguards were more capable of adhering to the training than she was. The entire situation begged, in her mind, for retaliation and no mercy. Yet the Osguards continued to show mercy during the entire episode.

The ongoing negotiations over the prisoners captured during the battle were a prime example of the Osguards' mercy. Kie Ritchen was still intransigent as ever over any palatable solution. It appeared obvious to all who studied the matter. Kie Ritchen began the battle on the sheer objective of galactic conquest and domination. Kie pleaded pre-emptive strike based on self-defense. To Terilela, Kie's reason for self-defense was unfathomable and enigmatic.

Kie claimed the Osguards were planning to attack the signatory planets of USSTAP and overthrow their individual governments. However, Kie was unable to produce any sort of evidence to back up his claim. Presently, the congress and parliament gave Kie thirty universal days to present such evidence.

Terilela shook her head to shake the cobwebs from her mind. The thought of the congress and the parliament giving credence to Kie's accusations angered her. Yet, the Osguards took it in stride and agreed to the legislative bodies. She understood why the Osguards agreed. There was no such evidence, but she did not agree with it. Speaking of affronts ... this reeked of an affront to the leaders of USSTAP, and she did not like it one bit.

"Commander Terilela," the voice in her earpiece thundered.

Terilela's eyes widened as her mind returned from her profundity. She checked the screen and saw the incoming transmission was from Centurion Gloria Katrengin, head of station security.

"Yes Centurion Katrengin," she answered.

"We're ready to conduct our security sweep of the morgue ships."

"Acknowledged...proceed with caution," Terilela ordered.

"Tiah," Katrengin replied as she tapped her communications collar off.

# Chapter 4—The Pledge

The heart and hub of the Universal Science, Security and Trade Association of Planets (USSTAP), Millmum Capitol Station, was an amalgamation of seventy self-contained black-coated stations, peeking out of the shadows of space through thousands of distant stars. They were diamond shaped and of different sizes, placed asymmetrically surrounding the biggest station. The bigger stations including the main one in the middle had large docking rings around them. The main station dwarfed the others and was eight miles wide at the base and two hundred decks long from point to point. The nearby sun of the Chaktun solar system framed the beauty of the station, which had a mosaic arrangement of window ports of different sizes and shapes decorating the black energy absorbent skin, called slitanium. Some ports were oval, some square, some rectangular and some shapes only Picasso could have invented.

Juanita sat in the main station's clubroom reading the damage report for the fiftieth time. She still was amazed at all the damage the *Sharyla* sustained in the fight. No one knew of the destructive power the Kulusks had obtained in their new shockdel gun. She never guessed anything could shred through a chromerion field like the melenai pulse. If it weren't for luck, and the slitanium energized hull, her ship would not be just damaged; it would have been destroyed.

She reached for the glass of wine she had been nursing for the last hour and drained it of its last drop. She pushed the sensor to highlight a section of the report she did not quite grasp. She made a mental note to ask her engineering and maintenance departments about it. In the report, engineering, which was responsible for the ships engines, ARITs and other mechanical, electronic and computer subsets, had estimated the time for repair on the intergalactic portal engines as two weeks. However maintenance, which was responsible for the ships outside structure, infrastructure, cleaning and other cosmetic items, stated the hull structure was damaged near the IPEs and needed refitting … a task requiring the ship to be in space dock for a month. Juanita wanted to ensure the two departments spoke to each other and no task was done out of order. She imagined engineering repairing the engines only to have them ripped from the hull because they were too weak to withstand the strain of the thrust.

It was bad enough; she would be without a ship for almost a month. Additional accidents adding to the time, especially if the accident could be avoided was unconscionable. Now she questioned her choice of leaving it at Millmum Capitol Station for repair instead of stepping to Bletherien Capitol

Station. The MOP engines were in good order and her ship was space worthy enough to make the travel. Yet, she needed an excuse to stay, and this was just as good as any.

"Juanita," boomed Michael's voice from behind her seat.

Juanita turned to see Michael smiling for the first time in a week.

"Yeah, cuz...what's up?"

"Two galaxy cruisers from Galaxy fifty-five will be here in two weeks, after the Osguard Senate meets, to pick you and your crew up and take you back to Bletherien Capitol Station," Michael said taking the seat next to his cousin. He stared into her hazel eyes to catch some kind of relief. All he received was a blank stare. "Well, I'm sure you can't wait to get back to your own territory," he continued.

"Yeah...can't wait," she mumbled.

"What's wrong, lady?"

"I don't know," she admitted. "I feel like this business with the Kulusks is unfinished." She paused and set her tablet down. "Look, we both know, Kie Ritchen is bluffing. Nevertheless, I feel he is buying himself some time to try something else. I'm not sure I want to leave until I know what."

"Thanks, but I can handle Kie Ritchen from here," Michael asserted. "You and the others gave your ships to defend the home galaxy while yours was under attack as well. I can't ask you to stay. You have an entire galaxy waiting for you."

"Michael, the blunt of the attack was here. What happened in my galaxy and the others was a weak show of force. Those battles were easily turned back. The Kulusks came out with this shockdel gun. It was only in this galaxy they fielded the weapon. Therefore, I believe it is this galaxy where he will continue the fight. You need our help." Juanita stopped and waved for the waiter to bring her another glass of wine. Then she turned toward Michael and placed her hand on top of his. "With your concurrence, I plan on sending the ship's compliment back home, but my defenders and their pilots stay here—at least until I am satisfied Kie Ritchen is no more."

"Jeez...I don't know what got into you guys—"

"—What do you mean you guys?"

"It seems I receive the same offer of help from all the others. And those with working galaxy protectors plan on staying awhile as well—at least until the congress and parliament rule on Kie Ritchen's accusations."

"Then why do you think I would do any different?"

"I guess I didn't," Michael said smiling with shame. "I just needed to hear it from you."

Juanita reached over with her right hand, pulled Michael's face toward her, and kissed him on the cheek.

"When we were kids, you always looked after me," she whispered. She stopped and swallowed hard. "Now it's my turn to look after you."

"There is no need for that. We all looked after you. I mean…you were our baby cousin."

"I know, but you didn't have to. You had your own baby sister to watch out for and I was only a second cousin."

"Cousin is cousin. Look at the Osguard family. I don't know how we are related to half the Osguards. Shit, I didn't even know half of them until Ortho put us together. Now look at us. We are willing to die for each other in a heartbeat." Michael looked into Juanita's eyes. "We could not let anything happen to you. We screwed up with Conrad. We did not try as hard as we could have to bring him back. Your father's death hit him too hard. We could not let you down."

"Conrad was Conrad. You could not tell him anything. I'm afraid he was on drugs way before daddy died. He was too far gone for any of us to do anything." Juanita placed both hands on Michael's cheeks. "It's not your fault Conrad overdosed. Conrad was weak. The drugs made him weak. His willpower was gone. His self-respect was gone. His spirit, his motivation, his moral compass were all gone." She paused to take a deep breath. "Michael, Conrad was dead long before he overdosed, and there was nothing you or I or anyone else could have done about it." She let Michael go, picked up the tablet and feigned reading it. "It was the Kulusks that did this, Michael. I tell you, the Kulusks did this in an effort to eliminate us before we knew of our birthright. Look how many of our cousins; our relatives, our people got hooked on that junk. The Kulusks wanted to kill the entire African American population just to get us and they didn't even care how many of the other races they took out either. Look, they almost wiped out the entire planet just to get us. These mothers are sick…real sick. We need to stop them now. Stop them forever." She looked back at Michael. "I'm here to help you—that's right. However, I am also here to stop Kie Ritchen once and for all."

The waiter returned with the glass of wine she had ordered.

"Osguard Fifty-Five," the waiter interrupted. Juanita looked up at him.

"You have a communiqué. Shall I have it transferred here?" the waiter queried as politely as he could.

"Yes, please," she said picking the glass of wine up.

"Very well," the waiter replied as he retreated to the bar again.

She sipped on the wine glass once more. Michael looked somewhat puzzled, but kept quiet as he digested Juanita's motives for staying. The red light in the center of the table blinked twice. Juanita activated a hidden sensor and a monitor lifted out from the middle of the table. Sarah appeared on the monitor.

"Mother, what are you doing calling me here. I will be back on Chaktun in two hours," Juanita said a little ashamed and disgusted at the same time.

20

"Juanita, you have to get me back now!"

"What mother? Why?"

"It's Jessica!"

Juanita's heart sank. She knew the next words wouldn't be good. She knew this call was to convey bad news.

"Her grandson was killed in a drive-by shooting yesterday…today…whatever." Sarah was confused with the time and date difference she had experienced on the station and now on Chaktun. She had no idea what day it was on Earth—especially in Louisiana. Her confusion triggered her emotions as she started to sob. "I need to get back to be with my sister," she blurted.

Juanita digested the information and stared at her mother's face on the screen. She was stunned. The reality of her mother's words drilled into her head like a jackhammer, but her mind fought not to accept it.

"What? Are you sure mother?"

"I called her again this morning after I spoke to her last night. It happened right after I hung up with her. One of her neighbors told me. She said Jessica needed sedation and Yolanda was out of it as well," Sarah replied as she attempted to control her sobbing.

"Okay, mother. I will be there in two hours with a startram. I'll pick you up and we will be back on Earth in ten hours." She activated the sensor to close communication and the monitor slid back down into the table. "Michael—"

"—Don't worry. Go! We will be alright here."

"Thanks," she said as she hopped up from the table and rushed out the door.

Michael looked at the two glasses of wine on the table and made a quick mental calculation about his cousin's state of mind, bearing the news she just received. He tapped his Communications Collar, commonly referred to as a CC.

"Control Bridge, Osguard zero–one." He waited for the protocol to synchronize.

"Control Bridge…Commander Terilela here."

"Commander, send a startram pilot to alpha bay and rendezvous with Osguard five–five. She needs to fly to Chaktun, pick-up her mother and fly to Earth. There has been a death in the family."

"Tiah," replied Terilela and the communications link went dead.

Terilela looked at her duty roster and noticed Sentinel Rican was onboard filing her report about what happened at Osguard Gardens. She was due to return to Earth in an hour. It was a perfect solution.

"Sentinel Stelana Rican, Commander Terilela."

***

Katrengin monitored the progress of her forty teams through a video cam hooked to their delta belts. The first team to go into a morgue ship was team Alpha. Alpha One, the team leader's camera recorded all movement.

Alpha One pushed the outside sensor to direct the control room to pressurize. The morgue ships were all depressurized due to no human life onboard. The cold and unpressurized environment of space also kept the bodies from decomposing during the trip.

After the meter read pressurized and the temperature read two-zero chimes, Alpha One opened the hatch to the control room. He stepped through the boarding hatch and swept his rifle around in an arch. The lights blinked in a normal standby mode. Two of his members took position on his flank. They stepped in unison in an inverted 'V' formation. Alpha One stopped at the cargo door, behind the control room. The cargo door led to ten decks of body racks, which lay end-to-end and stacked four high. Alpha One's team consisted of forty men. They would divide into ten groups of four and search the two hundred and twenty racks on each deck. Alpha One's group planned on searching deck one; Alpha Two's group would search deck two and the others would check their corresponding decks.

Alpha One activated the sensor for the cargo hold to pressurize. This took ten more minutes, due to the vastness of the cargo hold. Once Alpha One was satisfied the cargo hold contained the proper environment for his men, he ordered the door opened. Again Alpha One and his men entered with their weapons held at the ready. The ARIT sensing human life turned on the lights and a sea of silver metal racks displayed before Alpha One and his group. Alpha One could not imagine the ship was filled with caskets just hours prior. His concentration faltered for a moment as he heard Katrengin's voice over his earpiece.

"Get moving Alpha One."

Alpha One responded without acknowledgement. Katrengin saw the movement on her screen and was satisfied he was carrying out her orders. Alpha One's group shimmied up the ladder the ten decks to deck one, with their rifles slung across their back, as did Alpha Two through Alpha Nine to their respective decks. Alpha Ten remained on the bottom deck and proceeded to walk through the fifty five rows of steel shelves using hand held sensors looking for explosive devices. Usually the ship's internal sensors would register such a device, but the validity of the sensors was now in question.

Each team member scoured the shelves with intensity. Yet as they made their way toward the aft of the ship, the intensity lessened as fatigue set in. Their ARIT sensors registered nothing out of the norm. This only hastened their complacency to the assigned task. Each black clad member held a rifle in one hand and the sensor in the other. They would point each to the shelf they were examining. Thirty minutes into the search, their helmets started to weigh on them like cement. Their backs began to ache from the bending and stretching to get to the lower shelves. Their breathing became unusually labored and sweat began to form on their faces.

Katrengin dismissed these unusual symptoms as nerves. Even though her people were trained for such a task, actually doing it, especially after the battle that occurred last week, put tremendous stress on them. Nonetheless, she was proud of how they handled themselves under such stress. Alpha One stopped to take a break. He became light headed for a moment and signaled his three team members to hold their position. Katrengin took notice of the situation. She did not know why Alpha One called for the stop. Then she noticed her other team members were taking more frequent rest stops as well.

Something wasn't right, she thought. However, she could not place her finger on it. She connected to Alpha One's sensors and scanned biological readings. She saw nothing out of the ordinary, but her team leaders' hearts were racing more than usual. She made a note to have everyone medically checked soon afterwards. For now the mission was almost complete.

One hour later, Alpha One checked in with Katrengin.

"All clear," he told her

"Acknowledged, tell your people they did a great job," she responded. "Alpha One, I want you and your people to get a med check before your next rotation," she added. "Your heart rate was elevated a little more than usual. Of course it could be my ARIT malfunctioning. Nevertheless, to be on the safe side, please run by med lab as soon as possible."

"Tiah," he responded.

As each of the other thirty-nine team leaders checked in, Katrengin prescribed the same advice. Each leader promised her they would do so. Then Katrengin gathered the recordings and sent the biological readings to med lab with a note, 'Please check for anomalies.'

# Chapter 5—Revelation

In the light of inner space, Kie Ritchen thought he could overpower his abductor. However, curiosity begged him off from attempting any rash moves. There was something odd about this man, besides his brazenness to abduct Kulusk's ruler. This somehow intrigued Kie. He wanted to find out more. Therefore, he decided to wait, gather intelligence and then he would look for a way to escape.

In front of Kie, the white light gave way to darkness as the PGP door lifted open. Kie took the nudge in his back as the sign to step through. Kie raised his foot to move and then stopped. The nudge became a shove as Kie stumbled across the PGP threshold into a cold dark place. He fell to the hard dirt floor as his cape flew over his head. Kie threw the cape from his head and rose to one knee. He turned his head around in time to see the silhouette of his abductor exit the white light of the PGP. He rose, never taking his eye off the figure. Then he turned to face the outline. The light disappeared when the PGP door slid shut. Kie stood in complete darkness.

"Lights," Opel commanded.

The lights illuminated the area. Kie looked around in awe, twisting his neck and body to survey his surroundings. To the right he saw a sophisticated communications array system. Next to it, on the left, lay an advanced space and geographic early warning and tracking system. The rest of the area contained other ARIT systems, which he did not recognize. Even though it was Kulusk in character, the technology of the systems suggests a newer generation of equipment than he was accustomed to in the Capitol's station in the city of Renard. His jaw dropped. His mind calculated his abductor was far more advanced than he.

Yet, this command center, as he surmised it to be, was in the heart of one of the most cavernous caves he had ever seen. The dark gray and brown jagged edged rock suggested he was still on his home planet of Kulusk, somewhere near the southern polar cap—probably the continent of Taiole, where the Kulusks have exiled the enemies of the state for over a century. However, Kie stood dumbfounded as he measured the erudition and knowledge buried in this cave.

Who? Where are..." Kie's voice stammered, while trying to take in the awesome scene.

"Chair," Opel commanded.

Next to Kie, a haze of sparkling black light blossomed like a flower. Several seconds later, the black light faded and a black leather-like chair materialized. Kie recognized the phenomena as a micro portal, but the intensity and strange sparkling was different. The MP was different than any Kulusk MP. It had a USSTAP flavor to it. Kie's mind diagnosed it as a USSTAP trap.

"Sit, my dear cousin...have a seat," Opel said, using the pagenay to emphasize it was a command and not a suggestion. "Oh, I need your pagenay," he added.

Kie reached for his pagenay, which was holstered in a small pocket near his right waistband.

"Slowly, my dear cousin...I don't want anything to happen...you know," said Opel, smiling and pointing his pagenay in Kie's face.

Kie slowed his reach and pulled his pagenay from its pocket holster, using his thumb and index finger. He raised his hands over his head, with the weapon in sight and pointing to the ceiling.

"Toss it over here," Opel commanded.

Kie pitched the weapon, which landed in the dirt at Opel's feet.

"Good...now take a seat, my dear cousin," Opel commanded as he reached for the discarded weapon while keeping his own trained on Kie.

Kie sat in the seat, still surveying the equipment in the cave. He tried to figure out each piece of equipment he studied. Nonetheless, his mind kept concluding this was USSTAP technology.

"As I was saying back at the casket reception area, I am Opel, the great-grandson of Efas," Opel continued.

"Again, I say, Efas had no heir," Kie responded looking him up and down. Opel stood about six feet tall and was approximately half his age, with no sign of gray in his dirty blond shoulder length hair.

"Oh yes, he did! I am living proof," Opel yelled moving two feet in front of his quarry.

The fierceness of his voice quelled Kie to listen and leave his comments unsaid. Opel realizing he had lost his temper took a deep breath to regain his composure.

"Restrain," Opel ordered. Metal clasps pierced from hidden openings in the chair and bound Kie's wrists and ankles. Kie was shocked. He pulled and tugged against the bindings to no avail. Then he examined his captor and saw a gleam of satisfaction sparkle in Opel's eyes.

"Chair," Opel then commanded with a grin. The MP materialized another black chair to Opel's right. Opel stepped aside and took a seat in the chair facing Kie. He holstered his pagenay and crossed his legs. He watched the confusion dance in Kie's face. He had dreamt of this moment his entire life and now wanted to savor it. The taste of the victory was sweet in his mind. His joy was hard to contain as it escaped moment by moment on his face. His eyes widened and his smile seemed to cover his entire face.

At that moment, Kie saw the Ritchen trademark dimple in his captor's face. His heart raced as fear pierced his conscious mind. Sweat began to bead around his forehead and he began to breathe a little heavier.

"Well, is that fear I smell? It's about time. I thought for a moment the stories about you were true. That you had ice water for blood and feared no man," Opel said peering into his prey's eyes. "Are you afraid?" he asked.

Kie took a deep breath to calm down. He had never tasted fear before, and it was a soiled taste. His training had taught him to embrace death. He never quite understood the concept, but he was ready for death if it came today. He told himself not to show any signs of fear. He replayed his father's words in his mind over and over again; *Embrace death for it is the final reward of victory*. It appeared to work. His heart rate slowed down and he stopped sweating around his brow.

"No, I am just a little warm," countered Kie. "It appears you have a great heat source for this cave. I guess we are sitting above a hot spring."

Opel saw he lost his edge. He had played his cards too soon. However, he still had a couple of tricks up his sleeve. Opel made a mental note, *Round one to Kie.*

"Because if you are not, you are a fool," Opel added. He turned from Kie and scanned the room with pride as a physical gesture of changing the subject. He let out a heavy sigh.

"Welcome to Taiole, the command center of the resistance...or as you know it, the land of the exiles." Opel turned back to Kie with fury stemming from his eyes. "For generations, your family has sent the greatest minds into exile here ... starting with my great-grandfather. The maxum thought they would not survive the cold and ice. Doctors, philosophers, scientists and other free thinkers, who questioned the great Maxum Ritchen, followed him. Soon we had a society of our own. He thought they would die from hypothermia or starve to death."

Kie's eyes widened as he drank the information in. Opel saw he had his victim's attention and played the tense moment with a pregnant pause. He directed Kie's attention to a spot on his left. Holovidpics, HVPs, displayed several people one by one.

"Dr. Moranel, the inventor of interstellar communications—exiled. Professor Whome, who introduced upgrades to PGP travel—exiled; Dr. Truleel, inventor of transcendent technology—exiled; Dr. Suil, who discovered cellular bonding, the mainstay of MP technology—exiled. The list goes on and on. You idiots sent the greatest minds into exile. If you had only nurtured their talents, the Kulusk Empire would have been ruling the universe instead of USSTAP."

Opel let the HVPs continue to flash as one hundred and fifty men and women paraded through the spot. Opel allowed each figure to turn three hundred and sixty degrees as a written notation appeared in front of them stating their identity, their contribution to Kulusk society and the Kulusk year they were exiled.

Kie had never heard of them. The names meant nothing to him. However, the list of contributions seemed impressive. Yet, to Kie, these contributions were accomplished in the laboratories in Renard by the maxum's special team.

Kie shook his head, "This is a lie. I never heard of these people."

"Of course not! When they were exiled, their identities were erased from official record...recognition of their contributions were given to someone else...someone else more loyal to the Ritchen Regime. But of course you have heard of these people."

The HVP showed a man and a woman dressed in royal gear.

"Oh yeah...my great-grandfather and his wife were the first in a long line," Opel continued. "He was sent here to die, but instead he found these caves, sitting on top of a hot spring, as you so promptly noted. On the lower levels, he grew his own food. And outside, the placons are plentiful. So he had meat. Then others showed up. Did you know Taiole is a great natural resource area for almost any type of metal?"

Opel studied Kie's face for a reaction. He received none.

"Of course you didn't," he concluded. "If you did, you would have been down here in a heartbeat." Opel laughed at the thought. "You see the metal down here is so plentiful and with the right engineers and scientist we could build, so we did. We built, we built, and we built. I dare say we out built the Ritchen Regime. You see, my dear cousin, we built a gate portal and escaped to civilization. However, we didn't like what we saw. So we commandeered items and technology and came back here…to our home. And we continued to build and build and build until we produced a civilization that rivaled any in the outside world. Now, we have a network of agents, descendants from the people your father and his father before him had exiled to this bountiful land, throughout the planet. They possess technology and weapons more advanced than yours or USSTAP. They are poised and ready for the beginning of the revolution, a revolution to destroy your empire. Now, thanks to you, we have the catalyst for the revolution."

"What do you mean?"

"The war…you idiot," Opel said trying to keep his fury in check. "You have dismantled your entire army over an age old rivalry that no one cares about anymore let alone remembers how it started. My ancestors died on this continent because of that rivalry." He stopped and leaned forward in his chair. "And so shall you, my cousin…and so shall you."

Kie closed his eyes for a moment and concentrated on his father's words once more. He realized his moment was at hand and he wanted to die with dignity. Still, he had first to check his fear.

"First, I have a little surprise for you," Opel continued. "I don't want you to die without knowing the truth about the Ritchen Regime."

Opel picked out a remote control from his waistband and clicked it. To his right was an open area like a stage. It was an HVP stage, a place where the holograms of an HVP were projected. It gave HVP a three dimensional effect, like watching a play in a theater. However, the play did not have to stop for scene changes. An HVP theater was the best of both worlds. It fully utilized the holograms so a person could walk amongst the action if he wanted to.

"Here is an HVP of the truth about Efas and Erif. The truth that got Efas exiled and gave Erif the throne of Kulusk. Watch my dear cousin. Enjoy it, because it will be the last bit of entertainment you will ever see."

The HVP began with Efas standing in the middle of the area, dressed in his royal attire, garnished with ribbons and medals. He wore the rank of general and the patch of the Ritchen Elite Guard, an entity disbanded long ago by Kie Ritchen's father. However, if it was truly a HVP of his great-uncle it was one of him long after he supposedly died. Efas died around thirty-five years of age, but this individual appeared to be in his sixties. Kie reminded himself HVPs are computer-generated holograms using data from an ARIT report. This HVP could be and probably was a total fabrication—so he thought.

"I am Efas Ritchen, the rightful heir to the Kulusk throne," the figure began. "My wife and I were banished to Taiole over twenty-five years ago. However, we have survived. We found shelter, food and water. We have been joined by the elite academia of our society whom the empire also felt was in the best interest of Kulusk to exile to this land. We have carved out our lives in this cold, icy tundra. And we like it. However, I feel it is my duty to tell my story for history's sake on how I became an outcast on my own planet."

# Chapter 6—The Beginning of the Truth

The Maxum of Kulusk, Nom Ritchen, was in deep thought when his sons walked into the palace office. The Maxum sat behind his desk resting his head in his hands. Efas, the oldest son realized his father did not hear them enter the room. He cleared his throat attempting to get his father's attention. The noise went unnoticed. Efas looked at his younger brother Erif. Erif shrugged his shoulders and then let out a blatant fake cough.

Nom looked up and gave a half-hearted smile to his boys. The boys saw the worry on his face and guessed this was not a social call their father wanted.

"Come and sit boys, I have something I need to speak with you about," Nom said in his harsh graveled voice showing his many years. Nom was almost seventy galactic years old. His father before him died at fifty and his father before him died at fifty-two. Nom was the oldest maxum ever in the Ritchen Regime. Yet, his face gave the appearance of someone in his late eighties. The war with Chaktun and now the constant confrontation with the new alliance called USSTAP had withered Nom down to a fraction of the man he was when he first assumed control of the empire.

Efas sat in the visitor's chair straight across from his father, while Erif sat on the couch closer to the entrance. Since Efas was the oldest and the next heir to the Empire, it was his duty to be close to his father in times of trouble. Erif knew his place was strictly support and nothing more. However, this did not sit well with Erif. He knew he could be a better Maxum than his brother. Yet, protocol was protocol, and he knew better than to challenge it.

"What is it, father?" asked Efas

"I just received this communiqué from one of our agents in the new USSTAP organization." Nom handed the tablet to Efas. "Erif, pull up the other chair, I think you should see this as well. That is why I called you both in."

Erif did as he was instructed and pulled up the chair sitting by the window next to his brother. They both began reading the message. Efas finished first and looked up at his father. A moment later Erif finished and shook his head in disbelief.

"You mean we have bastard Osguards on one of our former prison planets?" asked Erif.

"Looks that way, son."

"What do you want to do about it?" asked Efas, placing the tablet back on his father's desk.

"Well it is obvious...we need to kill them."

"Yes father, but how? This happened almost thirty-two galactic years ago. The trail is more than cold by now," Efas interjected.

Nom stood and stretched his arms to the ceiling, trying to work the kinks from his back. He yawned with a grunt so very common to older men. Then he reached behind his head with both hands and began scratching what little hair he had left. The job had worried him so his hair began shedding when he turned thirty and hadn't stopped yet.

"That's why I am sending you two to this prison planet," Nom said, plopping back down into his chair. "I trust you to take care of this. You have just as much at stake as I do."

"Great, when do we step?" asked Erif.

"No, you aren't stepping."

"What?" Efas questioned.

"No, you can't step," repeated Nom. "I don't trust the coordinates we have in the library, and I am not sure we have anything left on the planet to step you back with. Remember, the coordinates must align to the expansion of outer space and inner space. It is too dangerous for me to trust some math geek to come up with the proper coordinates. No...I want you to take a ship and go to this planet."

"But father, it is a fifteen galactic month trip there...that is a thirty month round trip. Plus the time it will take us to track them down. We may be gone for some time," Efas objected. "You may be ill and no one will be around to run the empire."

"Boy, I am as strong as a placon. No, I will be here until you return with the news of those bastards' demise." Nom hit his fist on top of the desk for emphasis. "Your ship is fueled and ready on launch bay two. I have given you a copy of the HVP sent by the agent. It is in the language of the planet. You will need it to learn the language. You have two galactic hours until launch. I suggest you get packing."

"Soli," Efas responded as he stood. He looked down at his brother who was still seated and in deep thought. He nudged his brother's chair with his foot. Erif looked up as he arose from his profundity, and then jumped to his feet.

"Soli," Erif responded.

The two brothers walked out of the office into the large corridor. Neither said a word as they continued to follow the winding corridor. They passed several guards and key personnel in their father's cabinet. Each person they passed appeared to look away from them as if they were giving the cold shoulder, or as if they thought them exiles from the palace.

Usually, Efas would demand eye contact and a greeting from his subjects, but this time he decided to keep a low profile. He wondered if this was a form of exile. What did he or his brother do to lose favor with their father? Or was it as it appeared? Was this a mission too delicate and too important to leave to members of the Ritchen Elite Guard? Nothing was too important for the guard. They vowed their undying loyalty to the family at all cost, even the cost of their lives or their family's lives. Yet, he and his brother were now the recipients of an impossible order—to find two women, on a barbaric planet, who were born almost thirty-five years earlier. Efas stopped and grabbed his brother's arm.

"You know these girls would be older than us. They may have children. They may even be dead by now," he lectured his brother.

"Yeah genius...I've already thought of that," Erif rebuked. "I was thinking that in the office before you embarrassed me in front of father. This may be a frivolous waste of our time. I just can't figure out why father is sending us to do this. Right now the empire is in shambles. We've been fighting the Chaktuns as long as I can remember and the advent of this Universal Science, Security and Trade Association of Planets is hemming us into a box. The empire is not as great as it once was and I dare say we are the weakest we've ever been and he is sending us out for revenge—on what—on who—for what—for who?" he said raising his voice.

Efas tugged his brother and pushed him forward to start walking again.

"Lower your voice," he warned. "Father would not hesitate to kill either one of us for treason if he heard us talk like that. I have the same questions. But there is no sense in asking them. The only one with the answers is our father, and he won't tell us anything more than he has already told us. So let us be dutiful sons and push on with the mission."

"I didn't bring it up...you did," Erif protested.

"All I asked was did you realize how difficult our mission really was," he said in defense. "Besides, you are the one that went off half cocked." Efas was now looking around to see if anyone had heard them or if anyone was following them down the corridor. He was afraid the large stone corridor's acoustics carried his brother's comments further down the corridor than he first had imagined. He hated these old palace walls. It was like talking in an echo chamber. The walls amplified every sound ten times and carried it further than speaking outside. He always thought that was how his ancestors spied on people. He had no doubt there were listening devices in the hallway. That is why he defended himself during the verbal debate with his brother.

Erif looked at his older brother with contempt at this moment. He realized his brother had just left him out to hang if someone had overheard his comments. In his mind, he no longer could trust his brother. Well, he never fully trusted his brother before, but now he knew he could not trust him period. Even though there was two years difference between them, Erif always thought of himself as the more regal type. More like his father, willing to do whatever it took to get the job done. To Erif, Efas was a compromiser, a weak man, and it galled him to know his brother would someday be maxum.

Then it hit him. They will be gone for over two galactic years. During that time, anything could happen—including death. Then he tried to shake the thought from his mind. It was not his place to think that way—protocol was protocol. And if for some reason his brother did not return, it would not be any fault of his. Honor in the family was the number one creed and he would not break it. Technically, he had already broken the honor by questioning his father's motives. He lowered his head in shame.

"Now what's wrong?" asked Efas.

"I am ashamed of what I said."

"I know," Efas confessed. I also know you did not mean any harm from it. Therefore, we will not speak of this anymore. Understood?"

"Soli."

The two continued to the residential section of the palace and went into their separate rooms. Each packed one piece of luggage for the trip. They felt they would not need much clothing. They packed some knick-knacks to remind them of home. They packed their uniforms and their small personal items.

Efas went to his brother's room. He wore his Ritchen Elite Guard Uniform with the rank of general. When the door slid open, he saw his brother in his uniform wearing the rank of Colonel. Each wore a combat belt with a pagenay holstered. Efas was left-handed, so his pagenay was holstered on his left side, while his brother, who was right handed, had his holstered on the right side.

"I want to say good-bye to mother before we leave," said Efas.

"I'll come with you. We have thirty minutes before launch."

Again the two brothers walked the long corridor toward the office arena. This time they took a right at the junction, which lead them to the East

Garden. They walked outside to the rear of the garden and both knelt at a tombstone erected in the shade of an ink tree. The tombstone read, *'Deelia Ritchen.'* The brothers remained quiet for several minutes each in their own thought paying tribute to a fallen mother they only remembered through HVPs. She had died when they were very young, during the war with Chaktun. She was sick with a rare virus, and the supply ship carrying the antidote was delayed behind enemy lines. Nausona and Laurona were in charge of Chaktun's military then. They had returned after two years in exile—so they thought at the time. However, now they knew where they were—on Earth. Until now, they always thought the Osguard sisters were in hiding, and only returned to ensure their mother's death.

Efas thought he now understood his father's motives. It was not that the mission was too important to give to an elite guard. It was that it was too personal to give to an elite guard.

"That's why Erif," he whispered.

"What?"

"That's why," he repeated. "Father wants revenge for mother. He always blamed the Osguard sisters for her death and he always vowed to see their destruction. He is old and now he is afraid he will never see their destruction. Except, by destroying their offspring, he will have some solace. He can't do it, so we must."

"Soli, mother," Erif whispered. "We will avenge your death."

The two brothers rose and retraced their steps back into the palace. They walked to the gate portal room. After a brief exchange of pleasantries with the gatekeeper, they stepped into the box, the steel door closed and a white light engulfed them. Seconds later, the steel door on the Kulusk transport and battle craft *Sisen*, opened. The brothers stepped onto the floor of the gate portal room, which was empty. They moved to the bridge, one deck up, and settled in for the launch. Fifteen minutes later, the *Sisen* moved from Kulusk orbit on a course to the old Kulusk prison planet called Ea rth.

# Chapter 7—Above the Earth

Efas studied his monitor as the gray square ship settled into orbit around Ea rth. He and his brother had practically memorized the HVP of Nausona, and Laurona's adventure on this planet. They studied the language and the customs to the best of their ability. Efas dreamt the story of the HVP for several nights. It was a lurid pictorial of a strange planet abusing a common foe. He did not know whether to be sympathetic to the sisters over their ordeal or to be angry they escaped it. Whatever his emotions should be, he knew at this moment he was anxious to get off the ship.

# Osguards: Revelations

They had traveled for over four hundred and eighty galactic light years in fifteen galactic months and he had more than cabin fever. The *TBC Sisen* held a crew of fifty and was made for deep space exploration. However, he and his brother were the only two onboard her. The ship was so large there were days in which he did not see his brother at all, which suited him just fine.

Since their departure from Kulusk, Efas and his brother had grown apart. Efas was now suspicious of his brother's motives. Certain words in Erif's language denoted more than sibling rivalry, but a deep hatred of Efas' status as the undisputed heir to the Kulusk throne. He thought it a dangerous jealousy and feared for his life on this mission. At first, Efas labeled it cabin fever, but the eeriness plagued his mind almost every day. This feeling caused a massive distrust between them, or at least on his part. That is why he stepped to the control bridge without summoning his brother this morning. He knew the ship would enter orbit around the target planet, but did not enlighten his brother on the matter. Efas felt he could accomplish more without his brother's interference or questions.

The ship's guidance was automated as well as its scanners and internal sensors. There was no need for him or his brother to ever venture to the bridge, other than to look on the view screen simulation of space and take in the beautiful black vastness of space, sprinkled with the white sparkle of light from the stars. There was a hypnotic calm watching the stars in space. It was soothing and tranquil, which somehow put the mind at ease. Efas enjoyed the scenery. He would gaze through the screen portal and watch one particular star, guessing how many light years it was and watching it grow either smaller or larger day by day, depending if they were moving toward or away, as they traveled through the cosmos at speeds faster than light.

Efas also wondered if the star he was looking at was in fact there or if the star had long since been destroyed and he was looking at the light of a ghost star long dead. It amazed him to know what he was looking at happened long ago. He imagined if he had a powerful enough telescope, and if he could point it to his home planet, he would see life as it was on his planet four hundred and eighty years ago. The thought that he had traveled faster than the light carrying his image had his conscious mind in a conundrum.

Now he was orbiting a planet four hundred and eighty galactic light years away. This was the furthest he or his brother had ever traveled from Kulusk…he felt alone and a little afraid. The task at hand was enormous and very intimidating. However, his brother felt confident and very assured of the mission's success. The thought of his brother's confidence shamed Efas. As the older brother and the lawful heir to the Kulusk throne, he should be the brother demonstrating the conviction befitting of a maxum. Yet, he could not. This added to the tension between them.

33

Efas danced his fingers along the sensor controls to get a sharper picture of Ea rth. He wanted to find the processing station the sisters depicted on their HVP. Because of the naivety of the sisters to Kulusk equipment, Efas understood the images on the HVP were not completely accurate depictions. Yet, they were close enough.

The scanner readout informed Efas the hydrosphere covered approximately seventy-one percent of the planet's surface. This was more than he expected. The old processing station was somewhere in the hydrosphere. The other factor complicating Efas' search was that the average depth of the planet's oceans was over four thousand rings. Unless he was either very lucky or very good, it would take some time before he could locate the processing station.

His determination was about to falter when he remembered the emergency locator beacon. He hoped the processing station contained an ELB. His fingers sailed over the smoky brown glass sensor plate of his station, hitting several color-coded spots. He entered the five-digit search code and closed his eyes in a silent prayer of hope.

The Kulusks used the ELB as a signaling device to either call the troops back or disband them from a ship, station or encampment. Depending on the situation, the commander of the ship, station or encampment would activate the beacon, which would appropriately signal the troops. Efas sent the royal code recognized by all Kulusk infrastructures. However, he did not know if the station was equipped with the ELB, and if it had one, would it still be operational after all these years. However he would not know unless he tried.

Efas hoped it was still operational, and according to the HVP, the sisters activated the station when they entered it. The question ... was it still activated. There were many unknown factors in Efas' hunch, but he could not ignore the chance. He continued the surface scan, hoping against the odds.

Ten minutes expired with no indication of an ELB. Efas smiled and waved his hand toward the plain smoky glass sensor control. He began to tap to turn the ELB code off when a red light blipped on his monitor. Efas stopped and turned his attention toward the monitor. The red blip flashed again. His focus narrowed on where the flash occurred on his monitor. Then it flashed again, about five seconds later. Efas maneuvered his scanners to tighten the search field of view closer to the blip.

"What do you have, big brother?" Erif had entered the control bridge, unbeknownst to Efas, and had been studying his brother's actions. "I guess we are there, big brother. Nice of you to come get me."

Efas cocked his head toward his brother, "I think I found the processing station."

"Yeah! What for?"

"If I can tap into the ARIT system, I might find the chamber they used to step to land. Then maybe I can find the coordinates they used to step on land. Then we—"

"Then we step to those coordinates, retrace their steps and maybe find their kids," Erif blurted, finishing his brother's thought.

"Yeah, that's right," said Efas, not hiding his agitation with his younger brother. "It gives us a place to start."

"What about the sensors? I thought we were going to scan the planet's surface for Chaktun life forms."

"I tried that already. This is a former prison planet...a planet we sent Chaktuns to. It is full of Chaktuns...mostly partial...but still Chaktuns. Besides, the Osguard sisters' children are bastards. They are not full Chaktun either. The ARIT could not discern them from anybody else with any amount of certainty. No, we have to get an actual blood sample to be sure. That means we have to step to the planet."

"Great! Just what I didn't want to do...go mixing with the savages..."

"Well, like I told you back on Kulusk—this job will not be easy. I fear it will take us years to accomplish. I am just hoping..."

The light on the console stopped flashing and illuminated solid red. This caught Efas' attention as he activated some sensors on the console.

"What...what is it?" Erif demanded.

"I think I got it."

"Got what?" Then Erif's face lit with understanding. "You mean you have the processing station."

Efas ignored his brother's outburst as he refined on the signal with the skill of a surgeon. He caressed the sensors as he watched the monitor with anticipation.

"Just a few minor adjustments," he told himself. "Yes, I have it," Efas announced. He turned to his brother. "Yes, I have it," he repeated.

"Can you get the chamber's ARIT? Can you get the coordinates?" Erif implored.

Efas pushed a sensor with his index fingers and then pointed to the monitor. Zero–one–three decimal eight–seven–seven, mark four–four–nine by four–nine–three decimal eight–eight–eight, mark zero–zero–two appeared on the screen.

"There it is brother...there it is."

"Can we trust it?" queried Erif.

"I am plotting the coordinates now. The ships scanners can give us a survey of the area."

Efas moved to another console and plugged in the coordinates. The ships scanners on the square bow of the ship rotated and shifted toward the planet surface.

"We need to set up a geo-synchronous orbit at those coordinates for the scanner to give us a good picture of the area. I am also deploying the imcam," said Efas.

"Soli," Erif replied as he watched his brother swing into action. He noted Efas was a natural. Efas felt right at home in this control room, manipulating the ARIT to do his bidding. The data stream poured across the screen. Efas was taking in the information at inhuman speed. His mind calculated the stream prior to the data converting it to readable text. Erif saw this in his brother's eyes and then in the smile that insidiously grew on his lips. His brother was on to something. Whatever it was, it was big. Erif decided to let him savor his own thoughts, because whatever it was, he was sure it could not be accomplished without him.

The readable text emerged on Efas' monitor. He tapped the sensors on his console. A duplicate readout appeared at the station in front of his brother.

"Look!" he demanded.

Erif sat at the station and read the content of the text. He too smiled. He understood this was the right spot. It fit the scene in the HVP.

The imcam imagery's complete light illuminated. Erif hit the smoky brown sensor to set the imagery on both monitors. He chuckled. Then the chuckle became a dirty laugh. Then the laugh became a shout for joy as he lifted his fist above his head in a victory salute. Efas just shook his head in awe.

"Damn, the area looks just like the HVP. There is the creek. There is the farm several rings to the north..."

"And there is that big plantation to the southwest of the coordinates," interrupted Erif. "But it doesn't look as ominous as the HVP depicted. It looks dilapidated...sort of run down."

"Well Erif, it has been thirty-five galactic years. According to the HVP, these people were on the verge of war. Maybe they are still at war," his brother hypothesized aloud.

"Perhaps. But where does that leave us?"

"I don't know," Efas confessed. "Neither one of us can risk stepping to the planet alone. Someone has to stay here to operate the gate portal."

"Maybe not," Erif interjected. "Maybe I can fix a timer on the gate portal to open up periodically. We can set the coordinates for the cave where the sisters tried to get the old portal to work. Maybe we can get it to work and then I can turn off the timer on the ship's portal." Erif looked at his brother for any sign of approval to his plan. "What do you say?"

"I say if you can do it, then do it. However, I want to test it first, before we place our lives in jeopardy here." Efas' distrust of his brother was evident in his tone.

"Soli"

"Well get going," he ordered his little brother.

Erif ran toward the exit, almost not allowing the door to sway open. It barely cracked as he slid his body sideways through the exit. Efas noticed the big smile on his brother's face and somehow began to feel better about going on the mission with him. Yet, deep inside he still wondered if his brother would display the right discipline and common sense to do this mission without putting their lives in peril. He was willing to ease up on his feeling about him, but only so far. This mission was too important, too valuable, for any sentiment, no matter how infused, to interfere.

Efas studied the monitor again, trying to aim his thoughts on the mission and on his brother's role in the mission. He needed to concentrate…he needed to form a plan. He chastised himself for not thinking the mission out during the fifteen months of isolation he endured on the ship. Still, there were too many unknowns to contend with. With the new data and the imcam imagery, the unknowns were not as scary. In fact some of the unknowns were falling in place and starting to become the known. Unfortunately, the more he discovered the more unknowns he produced.

"Efas, this is Erif in the chamber room," shouted the voice over the ship's intercom.

"Yes," Efas replied, snapping out of his thoughts.

"I think you should come down here. I have something to show you."

"Soli."

# Chapter 8—Welcome

Inside the murky cave between the old Gentry farm and the Pathgo plantation in Virginia, a white light pierced the darkness, illuminating the cave with a wash of blinding light. Two figures stepped through the light into the cold dampness that inhabited the cave. The darkness slid down as the door to the gate portal closed behind them. Erif activated his belt light, as did Efas. The light illuminated the cave with a circular pattern of the belt.

Efas saw the steps leading to an oval cutout at the back of the cave.

"This way," he directed, pointing toward the steps.

Erif followed his brother into the oval cutout. Efas moved toward the gate portal control panel. It stood waist high on a solid pole about four inches in diameter. An elliptical panel lay on top. He reached down below the rock next to the panel and activated a power switch. A red light bathed the cave as it chased the darkness away. The gate portal, a big black metal box, stood in the middle of the area. Other ARIT systems surrounded the walls of this part of the cave. An ARIT solar chart came to life on the wall opposite the control panel.

It displayed the Kulusk solar system, as it was several thousand years ago. It still displayed the tenth planet in their solar system, Sabith, which was destroyed during one of the earlier Galactic Wars with the Chaktuns. It was a Kulusk weapons storage planet that saboteurs destroyed in a daring raid.

It was a dark and gloomy time in Kulusk history. That was the end of the Maxum reign of the Ettep family. The populace executed them for allowing the enemy to get close to the home world. That was when the Ritchen family reign began. And the Ritchen reign has lasted for over two thousand galactic years.

"Is that Sabith?" asked Erif.

"Yes, I believe so."

"Rox, I had heard of it, but I never saw a display of it," Erif said in amazement. "It was so small."

"You know, if this star chart still has Sabith on it, this means this machine is from before the Ritchen reign," Efas commented.

"According to father, nothing was before the Ritchen reign of rule," Erif clarified

"Yeah, but how did our codes work on this, if it was before our rule?"

"Don't know, big brother…don't know," Erif responded shaking his head in denial. "But it worked. Maybe the sisters did something and reconfigured it to modern day Kulusk programming."

"If they did, then that would mean they know too much about our internal security."

"Yeah, you're right," Erif admitted. "Maybe it is a simple explanation…the codes never changed. Maybe the codes are the same as the Ettep reign."

"Yeah, that has to be it," Efas shrugged. "Let's take a look at what we have."

Efas did a cursory glance at the control panel and shook his head in disgust.

"The ARIT mini-recorder is missing."

"According to the HVP, the girls took that with them to the farm on their last night on this planet," Efas reminded his brother. "That is why the old antique of an ARIT mini-corder and other spare parts were in the cargo hold. Father knew we might need this machine operational. I can go back up and get the parts when the door opens again."

"When will that be?"

"Another two hours."

"Great. What do we do until then?"

"Well, I –

"Shut up!" demanded Efas holding his hand out as if to freeze his brother in a physical gesture.

A faint scream echoed in the cave. The sound originated from the entrance and bounced off the walls. Efas heard a fraction of a second of the sound, but it was enough to recognize as a female scream.

"Did you hear that?"

"Hear what?"

The scream echoed in the cave again.

"That…Erif, did you hear that scream?"

Erif played back the sounds of the last few seconds in his head. The sound he had ignored as white noise in a dark cave now registered as a female scream in his conscious mind.

"Yes, I think so," he admitted.

"Come with me," Efas blurted as he ran to the cave's exit.

The brothers peered out the cave's opening. At first the light from the sunny day blinded them. However, the screams were more prevalent now. They turned their heads in the direction of the screams. Both Efas and Erif blinked several times to force their eyes to adjust to the daylight. In the distance across the creek they saw a horse drawn buggy stopped. On one side of the buggy were two horses without riders. On the other side of the buggy it appeared people were struggling in the dirt.

The brothers stepped from the cave and moved toward the scene to get a better view. They waded across the stream not caring they were wet. Something drew them both to cross the creek and get a better view of what was happening. As they came closer, the screams became more shrill. The last scream activated their adrenaline as they sprang from a slow cautious walk to a rapid run toward the scene. The brothers ran up to the side of the buggy, jumped over the buggy with birdlike agility, and landed on the other side.

In front of them were two men accosting two ladies on the ground. The first man had his knee in one lady's chest with a knife to her throat. Her outer garment was torn from the neck to her stomach. Her undergarment was dirty with mud from the struggle. The second man had his victim lying on her stomach and he was attempting to lift her dress from behind. Both men were dirty looking with shaggy beards and tattered clothing. The ladies were both blond and formidably dressed.

Usually, according to Kulusk practice one would walk away from a scene like this. Kulusk men were overtly sexual and they would practice their needs anywhere and anytime. However, the brothers realized they had interrupted a sexual assault. Even a Kulusk man would not force himself onto an unwilling participant. Sexual assault was punishable by instant death—no questions and no chance for defense.

Erif looked into his brother's face as they both stood up. He read the same determination to defend these ladies in his brother's face as he had in his own heart. The sparkle in Efas' eyes ordained the action he was about to partake.

Erif tackled the first man, rolling his body off the woman. The two men rolled several times until Erif was on top straddling the man's chest with his knees. Erif then connected to the man's jaw with a right cross. The sound was thunderous as the pain shot through the man's face. He went limp as he fought for consciousness. Then Erif struck again with a left cross, and again with a right. Erif struck with such a force the skin of his knuckles tore. His adrenaline fueled his movements with fiery power. Soon the man's face ripped open and blood poured from the cuts on both sides of his chin. Each hit caused blood to spill from the victim's mouth. When the man slipped into unconsciousness, Erif ceased his assault. It was no fun hitting a man who could not feel the pain. It also was a waste of energy. For the Kulusks, the pleasure of the fight was in the agony one could inflict on one's opponent. An unconscious man did not give that pleasure.

Efas ran toward the second man, pulled back his left leg and kicked forward, hitting him in the chest. The man sailed up four feet and over onto his back. Efas hopped over the lady and landed on the victim's throat with his left foot, choking him. Then he shifted his weight and swung his right knee into his chest. The man coughed up blood, but could not breathe because Efas' foot was lodged on his throat. Efas saw the blood squirt from his mouth as the man struggled to catch air to feed his starving lungs. This excited Efas into a frenzy energizing his right knee to bang one more, two more and then three more times into the man's chest. Each hit caused blood to gush from the man's throat into the air like a geyser. With the last hit from Efas' knee the man crashed into unconsciousness. The pleasure of the fight was over. However, it was very therapeutic. It gave a source for Efas to vent his frustration about his brother, the mission and his father.

Efas grinned as he turned to the lady he'd just saved. She still lay on the ground, her head turned toward him with a frightful look in her eyes. Efas' smile dissipated as he saw how scared the woman looked. He slowly stood so he wouldn't frighten the lady anymore than she already was. He looked to his left and saw his brother standing over his prey, blood dripping from his knuckles onto the ground. He turned back to the lady.

"Are you alright?" asked Efas, not realizing he said it in Kulusk.

The lady appeared to be no longer frightened, but perplex.

"Are you alright?" he repeated holding his left hand out in an effort to soothe her tension.

She again looked confused. Efas turned to the other lady still on her back on the ground. She had the same look on her face. Then he turned to his brother once more. Erif was wiping the blood from his hands on the ground next to his opponent.

"What's wrong with them," he asked Erif.

"Maybe if you ask them in their language, they might answer you."

Efas shook his head in disgust with his eyes closed. He had forgotten the moment, the mission, the situation, and let his guard down. Anywhere else, this could have been a fatal mistake. He looked up again and saw his brother grinning at him. This burned the fuel of animosity deeper in his soul, but now he had to rectify the mistake.

"Are you ladies alright," he repeated in English. His annunciation was harsh and quick.

The first lady then began to sob. Then the second lady sobbed as if reacting to the emotions of the first lady.

"What did I say?" asked Efas to his brother.

"Don't know," he shrugged. "I really thought you said the correct thing. Maybe the HVP is in error about their language."

The first lady attempted to rise off the ground. Erif lurched over to her and lifted her by her elbow while supporting her back with his other arm. She took his help, with gratitude, as she stumbled to her feet. She rested her weight against his chest as he escorted her to the buggy. Somehow the feeling exhilarated him. This woman, so helpless and so much in need, who did not know him, trusted and relied on him at this moment in time.

Watching the silent bond between his brother and this woman confused Efas. He did not know what to do next. Then the sound of the other woman still sobbing broke his fog of confusion. He walked over to the woman who was still on the ground, knelt down next to her and supported her to her feet. She stood to his shoulders and tilted her head to look at her hero. She peered into his eyes. Her blue eyes melted something inside of Efas. He felt a lump in his throat and his heart rate accelerated. She was so beautiful, he thought. Her blond hair, although in a mess from the attack, seemed to frame her silky smooth tanned skin perfectly. Under her weight, he could feel the body of a slim fit woman befitting a Kulusk warrior. He smiled as he wiped her tears from her cheeks.

"You are fine now," he said in his best English. "They can't hurt you now."

"Thank you," she gasped out, trying to control her sobbing.

Efas just nodded in acceptance. They walked the few feet to the back of the buggy, where Erif was already attending to his newfound charge.

Erif was attempting to fix her dress by tying the torn pieces together while she sobbed nervously. In a veiled attempt to control her sobbing, she buried her face in his chest, and shook.

Efas lifted his newfound charge onto the back of the buggy next to her friend and allowed her to cling onto his arm. Her sobbing began to subside as she continued to stare into Efas' face. Her beauty hypnotized Efas. He could not move or speak. He just remained still allowing her to support herself with his body.

After several awkward minutes, Efas' charge began to talk.

"Thank you. I don't know what would have happened if you had not come along," she whispered.

Amazingly, Efas understood her. Yet he was more amazed at the softness of her words than the content of them. He just nodded once more.

"You aren't from around here, are you?" she whispered.

Efas now became scared. How could he explain his presence?

"No, we are not from here," he blurted out.

"I thought so, I could tell by your accent," she continued. "You are German or Prussian, aren't you?"

The question confused Efas, but it also alleviated his fear of trying to explain his presence. He would say he was just visiting.

"What do you think, my dear lady?" he said.

"I dare say you are German."

"I dare say you are correct madam," he lied.

"And your name sir? A lady should know the identity of her savior."

"I am Efas, Efas Ritchen, and this is my younger brother, Erif."

Erif shook his head in disgust. He thought his brother surrendered too much information during this chance meeting. How could an heir to the throne on a secret mission as sensitive as theirs was, give their true names?

"Definitely German," said the other lady, who now had regained her composure.

Erif looked at her, surprised at her rapid recovery. "Why do you say that," Erif inquired.

"Your names sure sound German to me," she half giggled and half cried.

This came as a reassurance to both the brothers. Somehow their assumed identity as Germans would work along with their real names. Erif gave a sigh of relief as he looked at his brother. His brother ignored his stare.

"And do we get the knowledge of your names?" asked Efas.

"I am Jenny, Jenny Pathgo and this is my younger sister, Ellen," the lady Efas helped said.

The name shot through the Ritchen brothers like a spear. Erif brokered a loud cough as Efas eyes widened with wrought surprise.

"Pathgo?" repeated Efas.

"That's right," Ellen answered.

"Any relationship to Phillip Pathgo?" he asked.

"What? What did you say?" asked Jenny

"I asked if you were any relations to Phillip Pathgo?" he repeated

"O my word, I haven't heard that name in a long time," Jenny confided. "Not since Aunt Jessica died." She stopped and looked into Efas' eyes. "Phillip Pathgo was our uncle, my father's brother. Sadly, he died several years before we were born...before the war." She lowered her head in a mourning-like gesture.

"Actually, he was murdered," Ellen added.

"Murdered? How?" Erif asked.

"He was beheaded by two nigga slaves. Our cousins, his sons were also killed by the same two slaves," Ellen answered in anger.

"What else?" Erif inquired.

"Nothing else...why? And how do you know of my uncle?" Jenny countered.

"Our father," blurted Erif. "Our father had dealings with your uncle...before the war that is. He asked us to look him up when we came here. I am so sorry about your loss."

"Don't be. It is ancient history. We never knew him," Ellen said showing her discomfort with the conversation. "I think we need to get going. It's getting late, mother will be worried," she added to change the conversation.

Pointing to the two unconscious and dying attackers, Erif asked, "What about these two?"

"Leave them; they are nothing but white trash anyway. They won't be attacking any more ladies. Let the buzzards pick their bones," Ellen said with disgust, "unless you want to fetch them a doctor or get the law out here for them."

Erif checked his timepiece. He didn't want to miss the next opening of the ship's gate portal. Besides, death was the appropriate sentence for what they did. A slow agonizing death was exactly what they deserved.

"Suits me fine," he said.

"Do you need us to escort you?" Efas asked.

"Why thank you. That is very gentlemanly of you," Jenny replied.

Erif pointed to his timepiece to let his brother know they did not have time for any more diversions. Efas made a face at his brother to let him know he didn't care.

"Erif, won't there be another opening?" he asked his brother in Kulusk.

Erif nodded his head in the affirmative.

"Then we should catch that one. It is our duty to see the ladies get back to their home unharmed," he added in Kulusk.

"The timer is only set for one more opening after this one. If we miss that one, we will be stuck on this planet for life," he reminded his older brother.

"Soli," he replied.

"We will escort you until we know you are safe. And I promise no more speaking of the past," Efas told the ladies in English.

The brothers mounted the dying men's horses and strolled up to the carriage. The girls moved toward the front of the buggy, Jenny took the reins, unlocked the brakes and gave the command for the horse to move.

"I'll send back a servant to take care of the white trash when we return," Jenny remarked. "If they are dead, they will bury them."

"And if they are alive?" asked Erif.

"Then they kill them first, then bury them," Ellen orated with ice in her voice.

When he heard that, Erif felt an immediate connection to Ellen. She had a Kulusk warrior heart.

As the horses picked up the pace, the Ritchen brothers, and the Pathgo sisters galloped onto the road and headed south toward the Pathgo Plantation.

# Chapter 9—Pathgo Plantation

The Pathgo Plantation was as large as the HVP had pictured it. The long dirt driveway was about one-fourth of a mile, which led up to the front steps of the house. However, the grass was not as neatly trimmed nor the bushes perfectly edged as the HVP depicted. The house looked like it had not been painted for quite some time. The white paint was dirty from age and wear. The gray trim was faded and sun bleached. However, the front porch with its four eighteen-inch pillars still gave the house the façade of wealth and status.

The carriage carrying Jenny and Ellen trotted up the winding dirt driveway, flanked by Efas on the right and Erif on the left, riding the horses commandeered from the would-be attackers. Jenny put the horse at a hurried pace. Somehow the sight of home brought the wrought emotions of their ordeal back to the surface and she had a panic attack. The attack placed one single and solitary thought in her head—home.

The carriage came to a halt at the front porch and a young black man appeared from the side of the house as if scripted to do so when the ladies returned. He grabbed the horse by its bridle to settle the horse down. It was excited from its hurried pace.

Jenny looked up at the young man trying to catch her composure and elicit an authoritative posture.

"John, will you take care of the carriage," she said more as a command than a request. "And will you see to our escorts' horses as well."

John just nodded his head in agreement. Efas dismounted and helped Jenny from the carriage, as did Erif with Ellen. Ellen was still holding on to her torn dress with more than a bit of embarrassment. She did not want John or any of the colored help to notice her appearance. When her feet hit the ground, she ran up the stairs and into the house without looking back or stating any pleasantry for Erif's help. Erif just followed her with his eyes as he was dumbfounded by her actions.

"Come, you must meet our mother and give us a chance to thank you proper for your assistance," Jenny said motioning them to follow her upstairs and into the house.

Erif turned to Jenny with a boyish grin, "Well if you insist."

"I do insist Mr. Ritchen...I do indeed insist."

"Please, call me Erif," he petitioned.

"Okay, then Erif...I insist you join us for some lemonade."

"Lemonade? What is Lemonade?" asked Efas.

"You never had lemonade before, Mr. Ritchen," she smiled. "I declare. Do all Germans only drink beer?"

"You can call me Efas," he said searching his mind for a response to her question. He decided to let it linger after several awkward seconds of silence.

Jenny just looked into his eyes and smiled. "Well you're in for the treat of your life. Nobody makes lemonade like my mother...and I mean nobody."

"Well, I guess we can't wait," Efas said, feeling somewhat naïve.

Jenny hooked her arm around Efas' arm and steered him toward the house. Erif fell back in trail as he took in the sight of the house and how accurate the HVP had depicted it. He turned around to an open area he imagined was the spot where the Osguard sisters were whipped. His mind overlaid the images he had studied for the last fifteen galactic months in the courtyard. The images played the entire scene in a split second. However, in that second a sweet pleasure washed over his soul. A peacefulness he never felt before calmed his spirit and excited it at the same time. He was standing in the spot where history was made, the spot where the Osguard sisters received their first beating. A chill ran through his body as he shook.

"Are you all right, Erif," Jenny asked. She had noticed his strange behavior when he turned to the courtyard. The gleam in Erif's eye frightened her just a bit, but it also made her more curious. She needed to know more about her saviors who appeared from nowhere to beat her attacker off her. They had no horse. They had no buggy. They were not in sight before the attack. Where did they come from? Who were these men dressed in their strange two toned black and white shirts? Something about their clothing was almost militaristic. They were in some type of uniform. They were the same except for the braiding around the collar. Were they as dangerous as the Smith brothers who had attacked them?

45

She had known the Smith brothers since she arrived on the plantation as a little girl. They were scary and creepy to her even at her young age. She knew they were of higher society, but the Smith brothers did not recognize that fact. They were sharecroppers, not people of society like she. Therefore, they did not warrant her attention, nor deserve it. They were white trash.

Yet, she and Ellen had made the dreadful mistake of announcing their sentiment on the road this morning with no means of protection against their wrath. A strategic mistake, she will never make again. Yet, the Smith brothers made an even more strategic mistake. They attacked them, ladies of society. She will see to it they never make that mistake again.

The thought solidified in her mind in a flash while she studied Erif. Erif did not hear her first question. "I say, Erif, what has your attention?"

The voice echoed in Erif's head for several seconds before he realized Jenny was addressing him. He turned and smiled, "This land…it appears it was home to many slaves at one time. What happened to them?"

Jenny reeled back from the shock of the question. "Why of course the war, silly," she chastised. "I'm sure you heard of our war between the states, even in Germany. The war my daddy fought and gave his life for, to advance the cause of the glorious South. Unfortunately, the Yankees won the war and have made my beloved homeland the north's personal outhouse. The slaves were given their freedom. And now we have to pay for the services we once faithfully received without question." Her voice turned cold and bitter as her eyes darted skyward in mental shame.

"Yes, but that was so long ago," Efas stated to draw her attention toward him.

"Sir, it feels like yesterday to me," she contested, tightening her jaw and demonstrating a devilish streak that excited Efas' Kulusk warrior instinct.

She turned and waved them to the front door of the house. They followed her direction. Inside the house the lighting was poor but the magnificent size of the house still came to life. It reminded Efas of the Kulusk palace in some Spartan way. Jenny directed them into the parlor, the same parlor where Mr. Pathgo talked to the sheriff. Yet the parlor was nothing like the HVP. It was understandable, Efas realized. The Osguard sisters never stepped inside the Pathgo plantation house. They only saw it from outside. They had to rely on descriptions from Mrs. Gentry and the sheriff on how the inside looked when they entered the data into the HVP. So there would understandably be errors. The parlor was somewhat smaller than the HVP depicted and it was not as foreboding. Yet, things could have changed over the years. Efas kept an open mind on what he witnessed this day.

Jenny asked them to sit while she freshened up. Efas and Erif sat on the couch, each not wanting to speak, but both interested in what they were seeing.

Jenny, Ellen and another woman finally returned after what seemed like an eternity. Jenny introduced the woman as their mother, Caroline. The Ritchen brothers extended their gentlemanly salutes as taught to them on Kulusk. The ladies were very impressed. They saw it as a witnessing of German culture, something they were never exposed to before, and something they could brag about later to the other ladies in the area.

Efas knew the gentle rubbing of the ladies hands and a soft delicate kiss on their wrist had a calming effect, which lowered the ladies' guards. The sisters sat next to their rescuers—Jenny next to Efas and Ellen next to Erif. Caroline sat in the easy chair. The chair was facing the couch and not the window overlooking the plantation as depicted in the HVP. The chair was not as large, but very plain and sensible for this parlor.

"My daughters tell me, you came to their rescue when the Smith brothers attacked them," Caroline stated.

Efas was somewhat shocked at the revelation the ladies knew their attackers. "I did not know you knew them."

"Yes we knew them," Jenny verbalized with no hint of emotion. They are sharecroppers from down the road. They have taken a liking to us, but we would never consider giving them the time of day," she continued.

The coldness in her heart while speaking of the poor wretched fools somehow awakened a spirit in Efas, he never knew existed.

"Well you don't have to worry about them anymore," Caroline interrupted. "I sent a hand out there to take care of the bodies. No one need ever know what happened today. No one will ever miss them."

At this point, Efas realized where Jenny got her cold demeanor from—her mother. The sharpness in her eye matched the sharpness of her tongue as she spoke of the Smith brothers. In her words, Efas knew Caroline thought of herself and her daughters as a special breed of humans—too special for the likes of the Smith brothers.

The black maid entered the room and served everyone a cool glass of lemonade. Efas studied the sparkling yellowish liquid with some trepidation. Erif, a risk taker, sampled the lemonade as soon as it was placed in front of him on the coffee table. He sipped it. The sweetness with a tart aftertaste surprisingly refreshed him. Erif smiled at his brother as to say it was safe to drink. Efas picked up his glass and held it in a mock toast. He smiled and took a sip.

Caroline watched with anticipation. When the brothers smiled at each other, she knew they liked her lemonade. However, she still had to be sure. Neither had offered a comment or compliment.

"Well?" she asked.

"Well what?" countered Erif.

"The lemonade…how is the lemonade? Jenny told me you never tasted lemonade before," she said.

"It is fantastic," Efas praised. "I'm not sure I have tasted anything as sweet and refreshing as this. It is the proper drink for this heat."

"Yes, it is," added Erif. "It is simply delicious."

"Thank you," smiled Caroline. She placed her glass down on the side table and observed her guests. Her eyes bellowed with curiosity and her mind raced with ideas. "So you are from Europe?"

"We are German," Erif countered realizing Caroline was interrogating them. He knew nothing about Europe or Germany and he needed to change the subject quick. "We are visiting your country on a vacation. Our father asked us to look up some of his old acquaintances. We were on our way to see Phillip Pathgo, but your daughters inform us he has passed. Tell me how did you come by ownership of the plantation?"

Caroline regarded the question with skepticism. She paused for a few minutes as she thought about answering the awkward intrusive question. Yet, they were foreigners and they did rescue her daughters from a fate worse than death. Her story of how she came to own the plantation was a small price to pay for what they have done for her daughters. She took another sip of her lemonade still watching her guests with curiosity.

"Phillip Pathgo was the older brother of two sons," she blurted. "Charles Pathgo was my husband and Phillip's younger brother. Phillip Pathgo inherited the plantation when their father died and Charles moved to Augusta Georgia to start a law practice. When Phillip was murdered, Charles offered to come back to the plantation to help sort things out. However Jessica, Phillip's wife, did not want that. She had two sons who were more than ready to take on the job of master of the plantation. Yet her sons were murdered soon afterwards on the Gentry farm, a few miles north of here. Rumor had it that two slave girls that lived with Mrs. Gentry, a neighbor farmer, killed the boys. However, that was never proven. Soon afterwards, Jessica went mad. Charles moved us to the Pathgo Plantation and took charge of its operation. The war started and Charles felt it was his duty to fight for the South. He entered the Virginia Cavalry as a Colonel but was soon killed in action. His death left me in charge of the plantation, my mad sister-in-law and my two infant daughters. Well the plantation slowly died during the war from union soldier raids and slave uprisings. After the war, the plantation was in financial trouble. I began leasing the land to sharecroppers to make ends meet. Several ex-slaves jumped at the chance to become sharecroppers, and the arrangement has been somewhat profitable. I also leased land to white families whom the war had displaced."

"I liked the arrangement, except for the help. I had no free labor to clean, cook and do the little odd jobs I had become accustomed to slaves doing. Now I had to pay wages, room and board for such menial labor. Although, I don't pay much, just the thought of paying anything sickens me. However, if I want things done, that's what I have to do. Yet, that didn't stop me from employing good white men to teach the nigga a lesson—to put them back in their place." Her anger frothed from her lips.

"For a while, the nigga thought he was equal, under the northerner's idea of reconstruction. Thankfully, the South put an end to that. That dark period in history only lasted a few years. Thanks to the Knights of the Ku Klux Klan and God-fearing Christians, the nigga is back in his place. He may be free, but he is poorer now than he was when he was a slave." She lectured.

The Ritchen brothers soaked it all in. They fed on the natural hatred the Pathgo family had for the darker skinned humans, who they knew were probably descendants of the Chaktun Republic. Unbeknownst to her, her hate was their hate and it thrilled them to hear her speak so eloquently on the nigga's status in life.

After the hour-long civics lesson, the Ritchen brothers joined the ladies for dinner. Erif and Efas enjoyed the fried chicken. They never had anything like it before. Chicken was not an animal on Kulusk or any other planet they knew of. In fact, the technique of frying food was foreign to them. They were accustomed to roasted meat. The crunchiness and the spices associated with this fried chicken awakened taste buds they never knew existed. The chicken was a sweet spicy explosion of taste that tantalized their tongues throats and stomachs. It was a true delicacy they had never experienced before. Caroline noticed how much they enjoyed the chicken and asked the maid, Tessa, to wrap some up for the brothers to take with them.

Also the sweetened tea rang in a new sensation of taste. The sugar, another foreign substance to the Kulusks, was exceptionally welcomed as the tea bit into their dry thirst. Each drank several tall cool glasses of the dark liquid.

With their stomachs full and their curiosity satisfied, the brothers bade the ladies good night, mounted their black horses and road down the long winding road out the tarnished white gate with the sign 'PATHGO PLANTATION.'

They traveled back to the cave, watching for any intruder following them. They saw none. They passed the spot where they had struggled with the Smith brothers. Their bodies were nowhere in sight. The dirt surrounding the area did not even depict a struggle had occurred. The hands Mrs. Pathgo sent out were very good at covering their tracks. They would make a Kulusk hunter proud.

They crossed the stream to the cave, dismounted and walked the horses into the cave. The task was hard, for the horses did not want to enter the cave. However, after several Kulusk horse-coaxing techniques, the horses obeyed. Five minutes after they entered the cave the white light from the ships gate portal appeared. The horses with their new masters stepped into the light and darkness soon swallowed them in the blanket of night.

# Chapter 10—The Gentry Farm

Eight miles above Virginia in a geo-synchronous orbit, the *TBC Sisen* hovered. The ships gray rectangular box figure pierced the blackness of space. The husky cylindrical port, starboard and the square stern engines hummed with hypnotic rhythm straining to keep the one hundred and seventy five metric ton structure from slipping into Earth's gravitational pull. The ARIT system adjusted the orbit using the ship's thrusters ensuring the orbit did not decay. Inside the gate portal room, Erif was adjusting the controls to add several more gate portal openings at different time intervals. He did not know how long they would need on this visit.

For the past two weeks, the brothers had visited the Pathgo Plantation, getting to know Jenny and Ellen as well as trying to gather information on where to begin their search for the Osguard children. Today, the sisters were taking them to the Gentry Farm. It was still part of the Pathgo Plantation, but Caroline had leased it to a white family as part of the sharecropping agreement she had explained to them when they first met. Efas wanted to search the secret cellar to see if they could garner any more clues to the Osguard children.

According to the HVP, this was the last known whereabouts of the children. And if luck stayed with them, no one had touched the place since that day. No one alive on Earth should have known about the secret cellar. When Efas questioned Caroline, she did not know about it. She didn't even suspect Mrs. Gentry was involved in the Underground Railroad. Efas was careful not to let on about the cellar, but he could still tell Caroline was unaware of its existence. So today, they were going to search the cellar.

The door to the gate portal room hissed open and Efas sauntered in with a big grin on his face.

Erif glanced up to acknowledge his brother's presence then focused his attention once more on the control panel. He entered several commands, which the ARIT processed. The control panel lit red, then yellow, and then green as it accepted the commands. Erif took pleasure at his handy work with a gloating smile.

Efas saw the self-recognition in his brothers face and made a mental note that Erif will be more of a pain to live with than ever, because of his manipulations of the portal system.

# Osguards: Revelations

"I added three more openings, two hours apart," voiced Erif, more to hear himself say it than for his brother to know it. "This gives us a total of eight openings within twenty four hours," he continued.

Efas nodded in acknowledgement without looking at his brother. Efas was ashamed he did not possess the technical knowledge to manipulate the gate portal system. However, he knew he was a better pilot than his brother; he just had not had an opportunity to demonstrate that skill during this mission. The ship remained on autopilot and there was very little maintenance to keep the autopilot operating within acceptable parameters. Efas' single claim of success on this mission was he pinpointed the area of the search. His efforts led them to the Pathgo Plantation which in turn, led them to the Gentry Farm. And he was sure he would find another important clue to set the search on its way.

"I'll get the horses," Efas said giving his brother the opportunity to celebrate his victory alone for a few more minutes.

Efas slipped back through the doors. The corridors he had walked so many times in the last fifteen galactic months seemed colder in nature today than ever. His mind wandered as he walked. He wondered if they would ever find the Osguard children. This planet was big. The nation was huge and the state of Virginia was not the area he suspected they would find the children. He was at a loss for what their next step would be. He hoped they would find something in the old Gentry house. What? He did not know.

He understood the Underground Railroad, Mrs. Gentry ran, was a secretive operation, and not one conductor had access to the entire route. He understood Mrs. Gentry or the Osguard sisters did not know the final destination of any of the cargo. Yet, he did know the next stop after the Gentry farm, and if the house turned up nothing, he and his brother would be traveling the route to that stop.

Before Efas knew it, he was standing outside Cargo Bay Two. He was so preoccupied with formulating his strategy he walked the corridor in a silent fog. He did not remember the path he took to get there. His body was running on automatic pilot. He turned and looked down the corridor, trying to remember his steps, but could not. He shook his head in disbelief and entered the security code to enter the bay.

The doors swished open and in the huge cargo bay he saw the makeshift stable he and his brother constructed for the horses. They had gathered several bundles of hay and manipulated some cargo boxes to simulate stalls. Additionally, the horses were not bound to the stalls and had the freedom of the entire one and a half ring cargo bay. It was plenty of room for them to roam and run. Yet the hard floor proved to be painful on their hoofs. Nonetheless, they did not seem to mind. It was the façade of freedom that kept the horses' spirits high.

The hard part of keeping livestock on board was the care and feeding. The ARIT system pushed the horses' food supply at specific times. And Efas had adjusted the ship's environmental ARIT to collect and recycle the horses' waste. However, the stench of the horses in the cargo bay was getting to be unbearable.

He whistled for them. They trotted to him. He ushered them toward the stall and mounted their saddles on each one. The horses neighed as he patted and caressed them. Then he grabbed the reigns and made a clicking noise with his mouth. The horses understood this to mean follow him. The horses stepped behind Efas as he led them through the cargo bay doors.

This was much different than the first time the horses had traveled these corridors. The brothers had to push, pull and kick them. They were so frightened, the old Kulusk horse coaxing techniques failed. No amount of cajoling seemed to help. Then suddenly, like a horse broken by a broncobuster, the horses obeyed the brothers' directions, especially after they'd used a Kulusk food supplement in their hay. The supplement calmed the horses and allowed the brothers to control them. Plus they loved the openness of the cargo bay. Yet, the lesson took its toll in damage to the corridor from the horses kicking and stomping it. The poor horses' heads hit the ceiling every time they tried to rise up on their hindquarters. The ceiling to the corridors was only nine feet high.

Efas returned to the gate portal room with the two black horses in tow. His brother was closing the access panel to the mini-corder ARIT control to the gate portal.

The panel snapped into place when Erif pushed on the corners. Then he ran his fingers along the seam to activate an invisible seal with the body heat in his finger. Erif looked up at his brother and smiled. He moved toward the chamber arches and stood there as his brother stepped toward him. The white light of inner space flowed from the arches as Erif stepped into the light. Efas followed with the horses in tow.

Several seconds later, the travelers exited the cave next to the creek. They walked the horses across the creek and onto the road. Jenny had instructed Efas, they would meet them at the Gentry farm at ten o'clock in the morning. He had some difficulty adjusting the Galactic time to the time used on this planet, but he figured it out. He looked at his timepiece and noted to his brother they were going to be twenty minutes late. Erif acknowledged his brother as he mounted his horse. Efas followed suit.

Fifteen minutes later, the brothers galloped onto the dirt road leading to the old Gentry farm. Jenny and Ellen's carriage was parked near the front porch. They were sitting in the chairs on the front porch enjoying a cool glass of lemonade. Mr. Jason Taylor, a tall slinky gruff looking man with a beard stood next to them. As he and his brother rode up to the porch, Efas concluded this was the farmer who to whom Caroline leased the farm.

The brothers dismounted. Mr. Taylor extended his hand toward Efas first.

"Good day, sir. My name is Jason Taylor," he said in a strong but low tone.

Efas shook his hand in the manner he'd learned from the HVP. Mr. Taylor's grip was strong and rugged, a sure sign of a working man. He attempted to squeeze Mr. Taylor's hand back in a show of strength, but he was unsure if he had succeeded.

"Mighty strong grip you have there, Mr. Taylor," Efas offered as a compliment. "Good day to you as well, I am Efas Ritchen, and this is my brother Erif."

"Hello, sir," Mr. Taylor directed to Erif. "Can I get you some cool lemonade to shake the trail dust from your throats?"

"Yes sir, I would appreciate a glass," Erif replied.

"Make that two," his brother added.

Mr. Taylor went into the house giving the gentlemen their first chance to speak to the ladies.

"Sorry, we are late," offered Erif as an apology. "We became disoriented."

Ellen began to giggle and a smile broke out on her face. She turned to Jenny who attempted to hold her stern look of disapproval, but soon gave in to the levity of the moment. She began to giggle as well, shaking her head in disbelief.

"What is funny?" asked Efas.

"You mean to tell me, two worldly gentlemen like yourselves, who have been in the area almost three weeks now, became lost on the only road from town?" Jenny teased.

Efas' mind raced for an answer. Could he say they came from a different town? That they stayed somewhere else last night? No, then he would have to name a town, and he didn't know the name of this town. Could he say they had trouble on the way? No, he dismissed that as a bad idea. He took in a deep breath in an effort to gather strength. He held his breath for a moment and turned to his brother, who was looking at him for an answer as well.

"Yes," he said as he exhaled.

The ladies burst out with laughter. Efas was confused now and the perplexing look was more evident on his face. His brother played along and began laughing as well, even though he did not know why he was laughing. Erif thought if he laughed it would ease the tension of the question, but it didn't.

"What are you laughing about," Ellen asked Erif through her laughter.

"I don't know, Erif stated as he faked trying to gather his composure. " I guess it is funny, we became lost on the only road from town, but we were unsure how far to go and we stopped a few times to make sure we did not pass it," he added as his laughter subsided.

"Oh I guess I forgot, you don't measure in miles like we do," Jenny added. "You use kilometers in Germany. I am so sorry, we didn't tell you." Her laughter stopped as she blushed with shame. "Now I understand your confusion," she added as she tapped her sister on the knee to signal her to stop giggling.

"Yes, we are sorry. We forgot. But as you are not use to the mile, we aren't use to the metric system," Ellen added, fighting her giggling.

"That is quite all right," Efas stammered, not understanding what the ladies were speaking of. He was just relieved that his brother somehow altered the ladies' suspicion

Mr. Taylor returned with two more glasses of lemonade and they sat on the banister exchanging pleasantries for thirty minutes. Efas and Erif learned about the weather and how the drought affected Mr. Taylor's crops this year. He called the crops tobacco. The brothers learned it was a leafy substance used for smoking. Erif compared the tobacco to wen; a substance on Kulusk used in the same manner to relieve tension and to lull the body to a calm state. Yet the effects of wen have been detrimental to the body. It caused dependency and was linked to several diseases. Fortunately, the doctors of his world could cure these diseases. This made wen more attractive to smoke, knowing the aftereffects were not permanent, if caught in time.

Even his father smoked wen once or twice a day. It always seemed to put him in a good mood. Erif knew if he ever wanted anything from his father, he would wait until after he had his pleasure with wen before approaching him. He liked him more when he was relaxed. He was more tolerant and more like a father than a ruler when he smoked wen. And the smell of it was almost hypnotic. It was a pleasure to the nose. Erif always wanted to try wen, but never did. He did not know why. It just never happened.

Mr. Taylor offered Erif and Efas cigars, rolled from his own tobacco. He warned them, the cigars were not of the usual caliber due to the drought, but they were still good. He cut the end of the cigars with his pocketknife, handed one to Efas and one to Erif. He motioned for them to put them in their mouths and he lit Efas' cigar. Efas puffed on his cigar as he witnessed his father do with wen so many times. The end of the cigar flared with fire and began to burn. Efas took in a long drag of smoke from the cigar and rolled it around his mouth. At first the smoke stung his tongue and clutched his throat. He let out a small cough and allowed some of the smoke to escape. Then he blew the rest of the smoke out away from his host and other guests.

"A bit sharp," he noted to Mr. Taylor.

"Ah, finally a connoisseur of tobacco," he added as he lit Erif's cigar. I thought this crop was not as smooth. But the people around here don't know the difference. This crop will sell at regular prices, even though it is not as good as last year's crop."

Erif took a long drag and coughed the smoke out.

"I say it is a bit more than just sharp," he coughed, "but I never had a cigar before," he admitted.

"Well give it some time, it will grow on you," said Mr. Taylor.

*It will grow on my lungs.* Erif flicked the ashes over the banister and into the dirt. During the rest of the conversation, Erif pretended to take drags from his cigar, letting it burn away. However, Efas was enjoying his cigar. He would blow the smoke, trying to make designs with his lips and tongue. Erif was amazed at the acceptance his brother had for the physically foul cigar. However, the cigar like the wen on his home planet seemed to put its consumer on a plane of serenity. And he liked that, at least for his father and now for his brother.

"You know, before the war, my family had a tobacco plantation on the other side of the county," Mr. Taylor commented exhaling the smoke from his cigar. "We owned about fifty niggas. I know it wasn't as big as the Pathgo Plantation, but it was larger than this." Mr. Taylor walked to the end of the porch with the cigar in his mouth and pointed out into the fields. "Yes, that's right…when I was small we had niggas work the land. Now I have to have my own sons work the land. What is this country coming to?"

"What do you mean?" asked Erif as he clamped his lips around his cigar without inhaling.

"I mean the niggas got uppity after the war…demanding things no nigga should have," he said with earnest. "My father died fighting the northern Yankees and they tried to make the nigga equal to me. My momma told me about the Reconstruction Act of 1867 and the Freedmen's Bureau. But those are things of the past. Thanks to the Ku Klux Klan we are about to put the South the way it was." Taylor turned to his guests. "Now that the northerners are involved in this war with Spain they aren't so interested in keeping us in tow anymore. It's time for us to make our move."

"Again, I don't know what you mean," Erif said.

"Tonight, the local boys of the Ku Klux Klan will be meeting right here on my farm. I thought you boys might want to stay awhile and hear for yourself what real American men are doing to win back the South."

"I don't know, I suppose we can stay," Efas wondered aloud checking his timepiece. He looked at Erif for a confirmation. Erif nodded. "When is this meeting?" he asked Mr. Taylor.

"Tonight at eight o'clock. You are welcome to stay for supper. My wife is making pork chops."

"Great, we'd love to," said Efas. Both brothers smiled, because now they knew they had time and the opportunity to search the hidden cellar while the meeting was taking place.

\*\*\*

Late that afternoon, Mrs. Taylor prepared a hearty meal and Efas and Erif gorged themselves on fried pork chops, collard greens and cornbread, another southern delicacy foreign but tasty to them. Erif thought the fried chicken was tasty, but something about the fried pork chops seemed almost heavenly. The closest thing to it on Kulusk for Erif was corg meat, an animal similar to Earth's pig, but smaller and more agile. He wondered how corg would taste fried. The collard greens were a little bland but something about the taste was also inviting. It tasted like cherite plant, a delicacy used for a Kulusk salad. Then the cornbread was a new experience. They had had some at the Pathgo plantation with the fried chicken, but every time Erif ate cornbread it was like eating it for the first time. Mrs. Taylor enjoyed her guests' appreciation for her cooking, something she very seldom received from Mr. Taylor.

However, the night had come and the ladies, including Mrs. Taylor left for the Pathgo Plantation. Men had started arriving wearing white robes and carrying white hoods. At first Erif thought them robbers, but Mr. Taylor corrected his misperception. The scene looked comical to the Ritchen brothers, but they kept their serious demeanor as each person arrived.

Mr. Taylor walked the Ritchen brothers and his two teenage sons to the barn where the Klansmen were congregating. Standing on a makeshift stage was a man they later discovered was the grand wizard of this particular Klan. His name was Joshua Bennett. Surrounding him, standing and sitting on bales of hay, were some of the members Mr. Taylor had introduced to them earlier. Efas counted twenty-five men ranging from teenager to barely breathing. Two lanterns, illuminating him in the darkness of the barn, flanked Bennett. Other lanterns flickered ghostly in the darkness giving the audience an inhuman aura.

Efas and Erif found a spot near the back of the barn and behind the crowd. They leaned on the barn wall hidden in the shadows of the flickering lanterns. They were already conspicuous as the only ones not dressed in the comical white robes; therefore, they wanted to limit their presence as much as possible. This they told Mr. Taylor, and he nodded he understood. But Mr. Taylor made them promise, they would listen to everything Bennett had to say. Both agreed, but neither intended to keep the promise.

Bennett's rhetoric was another history lesson for the brothers on how the North invaded the South and caused famine, depression and destruction to many good God-fearing white Christians. He blamed the nigga for their plight. His voice was strong and determined. Efas looked at the audience and

56

could tell they believed all he said. He witnessed a fire burning within the audience's heart and their rage exploding from their eyes as Bennett spoke. The frenzy he saw produced reminded him of his father's speeches against the Chaktun Republic. Then he thought; after all, these niggas are descendants of prison planet scum, but so was Bennett. Wouldn't it crush their world if they knew they were considered enemies of a more valiant society along with the nigga they so much loathed? That in Kulusks' eyes, they were equal to the people they opposed.

Yet, this was a very interesting lesson on events, which happened after the Osguard sisters escaped this prison planet. A civil war had occurred, a war between the states. Eleven Southern states had seceded from the union called the United States of America and formed their own nation called the Confederated States of America. Efas and Erif learned how the white man considered the Northern states interference as an invasion of their own self-determination. Now that thought was appalling to Efas and Erif. Under Kulusk rule, no one had the right of self-government. Only the maxum decided that. Therefore, Efas and Erif had to keep their own feelings submerged during this portion of Bennett's speech. Besides, even Bennett could not hide the real reason for the war. It was not self-determination; it was about keeping the nigga as a slave…free labor. Who could blame him? Who didn't want free labor? This area lived for over two hundred years with slavery; they just could not stop because their government said so. However, if they were on Kulusk and that was the governmental decree, they would have stopped, or they would have been executed…end of story.

Nevertheless the real fury in Bennett's rhetoric came when he spoke of the period called Reconstruction. Mr. Taylor had mentioned something about this earlier, but Efas and Erif elected not to pursue the issue. After this Civil War, in which the Confederate States of America lost, the president of the United States, a man called Abraham Lincoln was assassinated, and his second in command, Andrew Johnson became president. Andrew Johnson welcomed his enemies back into the fold, but he saddled them with the philosophy of reconstruction—a rebuilding. However, the rebuilding had to center around the nigga, or as the United States labeled them—the freedmen. This rebuilding came at a price, the ratification of the Thirteenth, Fourteenth, and Fifteenth amendments to the Constitution of the United States. The Thirteenth amendment declared slavery illegal. The Fourteenth amendment granted full citizenship. The Fifteenth amendment gave the male nigga the right to vote.

Erif thought the entire concept of allowing your citizens to vote was asinine. Yet, something in Bennett's speech was appealing and hypnotic. He saw the affect he had on the Klansmen in the barn. They were hanging on his every word, even though they had heard this before—or at least Erif thought so. Although, this was his first time hearing it and Bennett told it with the power of an Asher cell. He was enthralled and wanted to know more.

Bennett continued with his history lesson, filled with dramatic pauses and various pitch and tone changes to emphasize his points. He spoke of March 3, 1865 as a dark day in Southern history. It was the day that the United States established the Freedmen's bureau. "This new organization," he preached, "fed and clothed the nigga. It provided schools and managed former white owners' land for the nigga." The fury of distaste waffled over the crowd as Bennett's voice resonated in the barn, while recounting this period in their history.

"Yet it did not last long," Bennett related with glee, as he continued to recount how the North turned back the South's true representation in the thirty-ninth Congress in December of 1865. "These representatives, including the vice-president of the Confederate States, four Confederate generals, five Confederate colonels, six members of the Confederate cabinet, and fifty eight members of the Confederate Congress, returned to the South to block the enforcement of these new amendments aimed at helping the nigga."

The excitement was evident in Bennett's voice as he reminisced like an old warrior remembering his last battle. "The nigga could not testify in court and had to have a travel permit." However, he was most joyful when he spoke of the new slavery these men invented. "They arrested niggas without jobs and gave them to plantation owners, who bailed them from jail, to work off their debt. We put the nigga back in his place...we made him a slave again...just like the Almighty intended."

Suddenly his voice lowered as if he was in pain, "Then the Reconstruction Act of 1867 came. The North sent their army to occupy the South and uphold their damned Constitutional amendments. Soon, rich white Southerners lost their prominent positions in public office. The nigga became congressmen and senators. With this crushing setback came the carpetbaggers, men who came to the South to make money out of the state of confusion now reigning over the South, and the scalawags, the Southern whites who sided with the North. The white Southerners became angry—angry at the military occupation, angry at the nigga representing them—angry at the carpetbaggers and scalawags—angry at the niggas incompetence and their corrupt leadership—but especially angry at paying high taxes for the establishment of nigga schools and new roads in nigga areas. It was more than appalling it was atrocious."

Bennett spoke of how he whipped and murdered niggas, carpetbaggers and scalawags and how the Klan saved the South. Bennett praised the Klan for restoring the white man to his rightful place in America. The fear, the Klan gave the nigga, helped defeat the nigga in elections and gave the political control back to the white Confederates. The white

Confederates gained control of Georgia in 1868, Tennessee, the home of the Klan, in 1869, North Carolina in 1870, Texas in 1873, Arkansas and Alabama in 1874, Mississippi in 1875, South Carolina in 1876, and Louisiana and Florida in 1877. This coupled with the Republican deal of 1876, which brought Rutherford B. Hayes into the White House, sealed the death of Reconstruction in the South and destined the South to take back their heritage.

Erif nodded his head in slight agreement. His passion was ignited by Bennett's fiery speech. His eyes boiled for revenge for something he had no knowledge or stake in. His blood rushed through his veins as he felt his heart pump the flow faster and faster. He knew not what, but he knew he had heard something great this evening. The magnetism Bennett produced was enviable, uplifting and refreshing to Erif, particularly after their long trip and their failure thus far on their mission.

"Now my friends, it has been a long time since we taught a nigga a lesson," Bennett's voice boomed. "We have this county pretty much the way we want it. We have the nigga where he belongs. Except…"

His voice trailed off for what Efas suspected was dramatic effect.

"Except for Jeremiah Johnson," he blasted.

The crowd was silent, waiting on the next words from Bennett's lips. Bennett drank from a glass of water he had perched on a bale of hay next to him.

"I say…except for Jeremiah Johnson," he reiterated after his dramatic pause. "You know the boy…we all know the boy. He is Mr. Keith's delivery boy."

A man in the crowd raised his hands and started nodding as he turned around to let everyone know his presence.

"That's right…he is Mr. Keith's delivery boy down at the general store," Bennett continued. "Well it seems old Jeremiah Johnson has had his eye on Mr. Keith's daughter Rebecca for quite some time now. And that is understandable. Rebecca is a might pretty young thing. And we all know the nigga doesn't want his own kind, he wants a white woman. Well I'm afraid Jeremiah Johnson has become too friendly with Rebecca and we can't have that. We have to stop it before it becomes a problem."

"What are you thinking?" a voice echoed from the crowd.

"We have to make an example of Jeremiah," Bennett answered. "We have to show the nigga, he can't be eyeing our white women in that way. He is a threat to Rebecca and a threat to us all."

"How do we make an example of him?" the same voice echoed.

"I say we string him up," Bennett responded. "I say we string the nigga up from the nearest tree so all the niggas can see him and know that they best not mess with any of our women."

The crowd began cheering as if they had won money. The frenzy was at its most heightened point and the audience was drunk with hatred ... hatred Bennett stirred with the mastery of a Kulusk maxum. He worked this crowd like a concert maestro. His words were like musical notes. He knew the words to play and with what tone to play them.

Bennett jumped from the makeshift stage and grabbed a rope he had hidden behind some hay and raised it in victory.

"Who is with me?" he shouted.

The crowd roared with glee as they all lurched forward to get closer to him as if the proximity would give them angelic vision.

"Let's go," Bennett ordered.

The men dressed in their white robes, donned their hoods and raced to their horses. Efas and Erif saw Mr. Taylor and his sons also race for their horses. Efas thought this was good. With them gone, he could search the cellar without fear of being interrupted.

"How much time we have?" Efas asked.

"The next opening is in four hours," Erif stated. "It is the last opening of the night," he added.

"Fine! You go with them. Make sure they don't come back too soon. I will search the house. I will meet you at the cave in three hours."

Erif looked at him with distrust. He did not like the idea of being separated. Efas saw the concern in his brother's face.

"Don't worry, I'll be there. You just make sure you are there," he ordered as he pushed Erif toward his horse. "Now go!"

***

Efas looked around to make sure all had gone as he stepped onto the porch. He pushed on the door and it slid open. *Good it's not locked.* He crept into the house, placing the lantern in front of him for light. Although the furniture was different, old and more inferior than, depicted on the HVP, he could tell this was the right room in which to find the cellar. He walked over to the spot where he suspected the cellar door to be. A throw rug and a rocking chair stood there. He moved the rocking chair and slid the rug over. There was no handle. He wondered if he had the right spot.

He bent down and examined the cut of the wood. He placed his fingers along the ridge of each piece of wood on the floor until he came to a loose piece. He retrieved the mation from his belt and dug into the wood. The piece flew out. He peered down into the new crack in the floor he had just created. He saw the cellar. He reached in with his hand and pulled on the floor piece. The entire piece gave way and he pulled up and out. He placed the piece against the fireplace and looked into the cellar again.

Now he saw the steps that led to it. He shimmied down the steps and into the cellar, raising his lantern to illuminate his view. In front of him was a large pot with copper tubing stemming from the top. The tubing emptied into a bucket. Efas knew this was not depicted in the HVP. He surmised Mr. Taylor was using the cellar. Therefore, what he may be looking for was probably gone.

Efas walked over to the pot and kicked it. The echo told him it was hollow but not empty. He ran his hand over the round side. It was cool to the touch. Whatever Mr. Taylor was cooking in the pot, it was cold now. Efas studied the contraption awhile. Something about it was so familiar. Then he thought it reminded him of the contraptions on Kulusk for making counterfeit guild. He smiled and wet his finger with the liquid that formed in the bucket. He tasted it. It was not guild; it was harsher and burned the senses, but there were many taste sensations on this planet foreign to him. This form of guild was just another entity he must try later.

Efas turned his attention to the other side of the cellar. This part seemed almost untouched by human hands. Cobwebs decorated it like the leaves of fall. He brushed the cobwebs away and turned the lantern for better illumination. In the corner, he saw it...the ARIT mini-corder from the gate portal. Now he knew he was in the right place.

He picked it up and dusted it off with his free hand. The dampness of the cellar had begun its corrosive nature on the part. Efas wondered, why for centuries in the cave, the planet's elements hadn't attacked their machine, but in a few years in this cellar, the mini-corder fell to the powers of nature. He surmised the power in the cave kept the machines rejuvenated and protected them from the corroding, but down here, the mini-corder had no power and therefore, no protection.

Efas pocketed the part in his vest pocket and began sweeping the ground with his hands. The dust rose and crept into his nostrils and eyes. He began to tear up and cough, but he continued his work. He brushed the dirt to one side, and examined the new layer. When he was convinced there was nothing to see, he would brush another layer of dirt to the side and start the process again. After two hours of this, he began to regret ordering his brother to stay with the Klan. He needed his help in searching the cellar.

Then he heard it. First he ignored the sound, attributing it to the rustle of the wind through the opened door, but the sound was now too persistent and too regular. It was a rattle, like silver balls in a glass. He listened for it again. The sound was behind him. It was getting louder now. He turned and caught in his peripheral vision something dark and slithering on the ground. He jumped back in fright, but it was too late. The pain shot through him like fire. The two puncture wounds oozed droplets of blood. The rattlesnake had bit him in the right leg above his boot.

# Chapter 11—The Hanging

The Klansmen rode to the edge of town up to a little shanty of a house, some carrying torches, others carrying rifles. Erif remained in the rear, watching and studying what they were doing. Bennett dismounted first. He had his hood on and a rifle in his hand. He called out Jeremiah's name several times. There was no response. Erif dismounted and hid behind some trees about twenty five yards from the Klansmen. Again, Bennett called Jeremiah's name. The shanty looked abandoned, no light and no visible signs of habitation. Suddenly a light appeared in the window. The shadow of a women peering from the window emerged.

A female voiced called out, "My son ain't here." The voice was frightened.

Erif pictured the dark woman crying, tears of fright streaming down her cheek. Somewhere in his abhorrent mind, the thought pleased him. He had watched with awe on his home planet of Kulusk, his father's soldiers strike in the middle of the night a suspected terrorist house. They would drag the person out and step him away, leaving behind a grieving spouse, and sometimes grieving children—never to see or hear from their loved one again. At first his heart was saddened when he witnessed these acts, but that all changed when he was twelve.

*The soldiers had gone to the house of a suspected murderer. He watched from a hover camera stationed above the scene. The guards had trouble gaining entry into the abode. During this time, the suspect emerged on the house roof and jumped over to a neighbor's house, then another and another, like a rabbit. By the time the guards gained entry, the suspect was four-houses away and gathering more distance with every house he jumped. Erif smiled as he watched the guards bungle the capture. Up until now, Erif had silently cheered for the suspects. He had believed them innocent and his father's advisors paranoid and ill mannered.*

*When the head guard asked through T-Comm, if he had seen anything, Erif said he did not, thus giving the suspect a much larger lead and the opportunity to get away. For the next three days Erif was pleased with himself. He had allowed an innocent man to escape and he had probably saved that man's life. His joy was awkwardly visible, but his father did not mind. It was very seldom the Maxum saw his son in such a good mood. So, he did not question the aberration.*

*Then during a celebration in the capital of Renard, it happened ... the moment that turned Erif's character, the moment that defined Erif's mortal soul. That afternoon, the royal family was seated in bleachers overlooking the town square in preparation of Demoux, the celebration of the first and only victory the Kulusks had had over the Chaktun Republic. His father, the Maxum sat in front of him. To the Maxum's right was his older brother Efas and to his left was an empty chair in which his mother would have sat if she were alive. They always set a place in the celebration for Deelia Ritchen. It was a memorial ritual they wanted to do to assure their mother was always with them. On Erif's left was his uncle, Letel Ritchen, his father's younger brother.*

*Letel had become his very best friend and confidant during these years. His father was always busy with state affairs and whatever time he had to give to the family was spent on Efas, the heir apparent to the throne. If his mother had not died, she would have been occupying his time so he would not notice the neglect, but she was dead and he did notice. It hurt his soul as well as his pride. Letel must have recognized this. It made sense. Letel was the youngest brother and his father probably neglected him as well. Yet, he had his mother to bind his love. Erif did not.*

*Letel began spending more time with him. The time became precious to Erif. Letel would take him to sporting events, horseback riding and many times off world to other planets in the Kulusk Empire for studies. Letel had taught him all he knew about gate portal technology, weapons and the Kulusk battle fighting techniques. Letel was a mentor as well as his uncle.*

*He remembered smiling up at his uncle. His bright grin and sparkling green eyes always lit the day on fire and today was no exception. Letel was big, strong and rugged. He appeared more of a leader than his own father. That was because Letel spent time in the service of the Kulusk military. He had captained a battle cruiser in the last war with Chaktun, the war that kept the proper medicine away from his mother, and caused her death. While his father was safe and sound in the palace, too distracted to notice his mother was dying, Letel was out killing the bastards who did that to her. He had won numerous decorations and medals for bravery—half of them given to him by his father. Letel had won the second highest Kulusk honor—the Cross of Kulusk.*

*He had received this honor for saving a battalion from certain destruction on the planet Drow in the Drad system. The five Chaktun cruisers had the battalion pinned down and were about to open fire on the planet's surface when Letel attacked. Letel's ship, the Pride of Kulusk, destroyed three Chaktun ships and heavily damaged the other two. The damaged ships retreated into Chaktun space before his uncle's ship could finish them off. Letel lost a third of his crew that day, but he saved one thousand and four hundred Kulusks on the surface. His strategy and techniques were now studied at the Military Institute of Klyteth, the officer academy of the Kulusk Empire.*

*Erif remembered looking into his uncle's eye and beaming with more pride over him than his father. His uncle always had time for him ... his father did not. Then the blue glint, flash and searing heat of a pagenay blast whizzed by him. He could still feel the heat on his cheek today. The scarred flesh on his face was a constant reminder of that day. The heat, then Letel's eyes flashed in his memory like a bright light. His uncle's eyes, just a moment earlier beaming with pride and joy, went blank. Letel tensed up like someone punched him in the stomach. His eyes lifted then rolled back. Erif remembered looking into his uncle's eyes and seeing his life force ripped from his body.*

*Erif looked down. His uncle's stomach was charred and black. The flash of light was from a pagenay rifle. Erif went to grab his beloved uncle, but could not catch him as he rolled off the bleacher chair and onto the floorboard. Erif wanted to scream, but his years of training and his uncle's memory choked him and stifled the scream in his throat. Everything that happened after that was a blur to Erif. His memory blazed the picture of his uncle, crumbled up grasping at his charred stomach wound and his eyes rolling back in death.*

*Erif visited that picture in his dreams nightly, a reoccurring nightmare with no end. He had accepted the image's duty of keeping fresh in his mind the hate he bore that day, but he could never accept the image as the proper fate for his uncle.*

*Later the guards captured the man who assassinated his only friend ... his only true family. Erif visited the prison cell. He wanted to look into the eyes of the man who had forever changed his life. He wanted to inform the man of the horrid and wretched feeling he now had for him. It was more than contempt; it was more than hate ... it was loathing.*

*Erif mustered the courage to walk down the damp rock floor and long corridor of heavy chromerion closed cells to his uncle's assassin's cell. Each step seemed like a mile, but he kept telling himself he needed to do this. He needed to see the man who stole his life. Erif kept his eyes on the floor, counting the different designs in the rock. There were rose designs, geometric designs and mathematical designs. They were so intermingled it took Erif's mind off his task as he separated and counted them in his mind.*

*Then he was there. The guard escorting him stopped and pointed to the man, identifying him as the killer. Erif lifted his head. His eyes dared not look directly at the man, but he had to. It was what he came here for. He had to confront this monster and let him know, he will surely die for his actions this day. Erif's head faced forward but his eyes were still looking down. Then with a deep breath Erif directed his eyes onto him.*

*No, it couldn't be, Erif's heart exclaimed as he choked for air. He searched the man with his eyes from toe to head. His soul began screaming for clarity, but he received none. It can't be, his mind repeated over and over. It just can't be. The man stared into Erif's eyes. The pain was evident, but there was something more in his eyes. Erif stared back. He fought through the terror in the man's eyes but could not see a soul—a heart. Erif saw nothing but darkness. Erif only saw the man he let get away from the guards days earlier.*

*"Did you kill my uncle?" Erif whispered.*

*"What?" he barked.*

*Young Erif cleared his throat and with the voice of authority and determination, "Did you kill my uncle?"*

*"No, I didn't kill anyone. I've been framed," he snorted.*

*Erif studied his eyes--still nothing. Erif did not see remorse. Erif saw a man hiding the truth. The guards caught him on the roofs with a pagenay rifle. The scientist confirmed it was the pagenay that killed his uncle. The man's DNA was all over the pagenay. And Erif knew for a fact, this man traveled the roofs like a bird.*

*"You will die anyway. It is up to you how painfully you will die," Erif said.*

*The man straightened up and moved to the chromerion barrier. His face scowled with displeasure. He regarded his young interrogator for a moment and then he smirked.*

*The smirk told Erif what he wanted to know, but now he was unprepared to tell the man what he wanted him to know. The guilt of allowing the man to escape tugged at Erif's soul. If he had done his duty and helped the guards capture this man days ago, his uncle would still be alive. So whom should he blame, the man or himself? The young Erif shook his head in despair as he turned and left, leaving what remained of his childhood locked up in that prison with his uncle's murderer.*

Since that day Erif had been a fanatic about these middle of the night wake-up calls. He was happy to see the Klan practice this technique and he was doubly happy to witness this first hand.

"Get her out of there," yelled Bennett.

Three men raced to the wooden structure with torches. They threw dry hay onto the porch and lit it with the torches. The hay captured the flame and fed it. The flame grew larger as it snaked into the house. The flame glowed red, orange and yellow as it ate the wooden structure. It moved, grew and consumed all that was in its way. For fifteen minutes the Klansmen watched, pointed and laughed as the flame embroiled the small cabin. Gray smoke billowed from the windows as the occupant smashed them for air.

Then out the door stumbled a tall thin black man holding a rifle. He coughed the dry smoke from his lungs, which alerted the Klansmen to his presence. Apparently blurred vision from the fire hampered the black man's sight as he raised his rifle, but before he could fire it, two Klansmen fired their rifles. One blast ripped into the black man's knee, the other tore into his stomach. The man fell backwards from the second blast. Then a stocky black woman ran out to gather the man. The Klansmen did not hesitate. Two more shots rang out, echoing over the crackling of the fire. The woman fell to her knees, then to her face. The two Klansmen rushed to the victims, beating back the fire on the porch as they did. Each grabbed a victim and dragged them toward the other Klansmen.

Bennett dismounted and walked to the man and woman. They were both dying from their wounds, but they were still alive, coughing and gasping for air. Bennett removed his revolver and pointed in the man's face. The man looked up and saw the gun. At first his eyes widened with terror, but then calm washed over him. He transformed from being scared to being defiant in a few short seconds. Bennett witnessed the change and became furious inside.

"Good-bye nigga," Bennett said as he pulled the trigger.

The man's head jerked as it split open from the force of the bullet. Blood oozed out along with gray brain matter. The man still contained the defiant look, which had enraged Bennett in the first place. Bennett kicked the body as if to persuade him to wipe the look off his face, but it was too late, the man was dead and the expression was etched into the body by sheer will and determination. Bennett realized he could do no more and turned toward the woman.

Surprising to Erif, the woman did not cry. This was strange, for he thought the woman would cry over this man's death and certainly over the fact she was about to die. However, she just coughed to clear her lungs as she looked at Bennett with the same defiance.

"What is with you niggas?" asked Bennett. "Where is Jeremiah?"

This confused Erif, because he thought the man Bennett just killed was Jeremiah. Oh well, guilt by association, he concluded.

Just then another shot rang out. It came from the burning porch. A young black boy, no more than eleven years old in Erif's estimation had picked up the black man's rifle and shot once in the air.

"Leave my momma alone," the boy said.

Bennett looked up and smiled, "Well there is Jeremiah."

Erif's stomach turned. The Klansmen came out in force to kill a boy. That was unacceptable. Even if the boy had done something to warrant death, using these many captors to do it was a sure sign of cowardice. Suddenly, Bennett's rhetoric meant nothing to Erif. The Klansmen were cowards hiding behind bed sheets, not heroes fighting for a cause.

The boy lowered his rifle and aimed it at Bennett. Erif thought the boy had a Kulusk spirit and grinned at the situation.

Without flinching, Bennett shot his revolver, expending a round into the woman's forehead. Fear and sorrow overcame the boy and he froze in his tracks as he witnessed his mother's murder. Two Klansmen walked up to the boy, as he stood frozen in time and spirit. Panic held Jeremiah in place. One Klansman smashed his rifle butt into the boy's head. Jeremiah crumbled under the force and fell onto his back. The other Klansman grabbed the boy by the wrist and dragged his lifeless body off the porch and into the dirt next to the dead couple.

One Klansman had readied the rope over a tree branch. They tied the noose around Jeremiah's neck. He moved a little and moaned as the white sheeted Klansmen worked to get the noose around his neck. Erif fingered his pagenay in his pocket. He contemplated if he should intervene or not, but the last time he aided someone to escape it ended in his uncle's death. He moved his hands away from his pagenay. He decided he was strictly a spectator, and would not get involved—no matter how repulsed he was by these cowards.

The cabin was engulfed in flames now. The night sky framed the fire like a picture. The smoke ascended to the heavens like a burnt offering to a god and the crackling of the flames vibrated like a symphony of one. Jeremiah lay on the ground with the noose woven around his neck. Erif closed his eyes in shame.

The Klansmen rough-handled Jeremiah onto a horse, and tied the rope to the other end of the tree. Jeremiah was still unconscious, but he appeared to be wakening. Erif opened his eyes and wished for the boy to never wake, but his wishes were ignored.

Jeremiah's eyes opened to the terror surrounding him. He cried for help, only to be drowned out by the laughter of the cowardly Klansmen. Erif again reached for his pagenay. He pulled it from his pocket and raised it. He aimed it at Bennett. His mind began to challenge his body. Deep inside of him his instincts told him to fire the weapon, but his training and his Kulusk beliefs told him to hold fast.

The boy was young, if he did wrong he should be severely punished, not killed. However, the boy was the enemy. Surely he was a descendant of a Chaktun; therefore, he was an enemy of his as well. He had vowed to kill all Chaktuns, whether woman or child, but that was in battle, this was not battle.

Yet they were still the enemy. Kulusks were trained to kill the enemy and wherever the enemy was, it was battle. However, this child was not pure Chaktun; he had no knowledge of Chaktun. Neither were the children he was sent to kill. It was a conundrum that began to make his head hurt.

Then it hit him. He came to do the same thing. He came to kill the children of the Osguard sisters—them and any children they may have. They knew nothing of Chaktun. They had no knowledge of their importance. Yet, when he finds them, he will kill them as just as the Klansmen will kill Jeremiah.

He lowered his weapon with a heavy heart. Then he heard the slap, the hand hitting the hindquarters of the horse. He dare not look, but his curiosity overcame his sense of honor. Jeremiah swung from the tree with his neck broken, evident by his head dangling backwards. At least his death was quick and painless, unlike his last moments of life, Erif thought. Then the body turned. Erif could see Jeremiah's eyes. They were bulging almost to the point of popping out. The blood from the head butt trickled down his forehead on the right side and dripped to the ground. Erif's stomach soured. He turned and released the meal he had so much enjoyed at the Gentry Farm from his gut. He tried to muffle the sound as he vomited behind the tree and close to the ground.

The Klansmen were too busy laughing and joking and recounting their deeds for the night to hear the muffled sounds of Erif vomiting twenty-five yards behind them. There was no honor in this kill. There was no show of strength or courage. It was a violation of Kulusk rule, but their mission was a violation of it as well. It was simple when the Kulusks did it, but seeing someone else violate the time-tested honor of Kulusk rule cheapened the meaning.

Erif wiped his mouth and looked back at the cowards. He was sure they did not notice him. He then pulled his timepiece and noticed he had twenty minutes before the next opening. He pocketed his pagenay, mounted his horse and slipped away into the night. He had some thinking to do. He understood the Klan, he even agreed with their methods in theory, but seeing their methods, put into practice against a young boy, was still sickening.

Yet, if that boy had lived, he could have done damage to Mr. Keith's daughter. There was no guessing at the future. He learned this long ago, when his uncle was murdered. He should not have let that man escape. He should have told the guards about him. He didn't and his uncle, his mentor, his only true family paid the ultimate price—with his life.

Therefore, what he witnessed tonight may have been tough, but it might have been needed. The boy must've been dangerous or Bennett would not have killed him. Besides, Bennett knew what he was doing...Right? Of course he knew what he was doing. He was the Ku Klux Klan Imperial Wizard. The leader of the closest thing to Kulusk this planet knew.

Finally, Erif's mind was at peace. Victory was the sole prize—victory at all cost. The Kulusks valued victory more than anything. Bennett valued victory more than anything. The Kulusks and the Ku Klux Klan had more in common than not. Erif was convinced what he witnessed was necessary and honor was a compromising currency, which had no value in times of war. And this was war.

# Chapter 12—Snake Bite

The fire in his leg subsided, but Efas was more surprised than hurt. The snake, something Jenny had warned him about, but he had never seen before, scared him. Yet the snake had bit him, and Jenny did say they were poisonous. It was still in the cellar with him. He glanced around, hunting for it. He saw nothing. His eyes continued to dart from side to side, he didn't want it to attack again.

As he watched the area, he pulled his pagenay from his pocket. He rested his wrist on his knee as he held the pagenay in front. He dare not get up, for he did not know where the snake went. Then it occurred to him, the snake could be behind him. As quick as his mind formed the thought his body reacted. He jumped up, whirled around, and scanned the spot he had just dug. His eyes darted back and forth as tiny beads of sweat began to form on his forehead.

Now he was scared, more scared than he ever was in his life. He knew he had been poisoned and he needed to get to the ship for medical attention. Yet, he was afraid to move because his predator was still with him, hiding in the shadows of the cellar. Efas felt the sweat gathering under his arms and the beads dripping down his face. He chastised himself for his fear. Then he heard it, the distinctive rattle of the snake. His mind processed the information causing his body to turn a quarter to his left and fire his weapon. A blue light zipped through the air, illuminating the cellar with heat and dark-colored light. The light flashed into its target. The snake's head ruptured from the intense heat. The rattle stopped and the threat was dead.

Efas blew a sigh of relief as he tried to calm his heart. He leaned against the dirt wall for support. The stinging in his leg began to burn again. During his search he had isolated the impulses from his leg and subdued the pain. However, now that the danger was over, the impulses flooded his brain like a tidal wave and he once again felt pain.

He tore a piece of cloth from his shirt and tied it around his leg, just above the bite. Then with shaky hands, he pulled his traveling med kit from his pocket and opened it. He felt for and found a square container in the middle of the kit that contained a nanobiotic injector. He slapped it on his thigh. Upon contact the injector pierced his skin through his pants and shot a stream of nanobots into his system. The job of these nanobots was to search out and destroy foreign objects in his blood stream. Efas didn't know if it would work against the snake venom, but it was the best he could do for himself at the moment. As he felt the cold stream of the nanobots enter his body, he took a deep relaxing breath and put his traveling med kit away. Then one single thought occupied his mind—'*get back to the ship.*'

He climbed the ladder. The pain reminded him not to put pressure on his right leg. The eight rungs of the ladder were hard to negotiate taking one step at a time with his left leg, but he managed to get to the living room. He placed the floor pieces back just as he found them. He looked around to make sure he had eliminated any evidence of his presence. When he was satisfied he exited the house and limped to the barn. He blew out the lantern and placed it back on its hook on the barn wall.

As he placed the lantern back he felt a little lightheaded. He placed his hand on the wall to steady his posture and catch his wits. He was afraid that the poison was taking effect and the nanobots were losing the battle in his body. He knew if this was true he did not have much time to get back to the ship. He pulled his T-Comm from his inside vest pocket and tried to contact Erif, but Erif's T-Comm was off. Whispering curses in Kulusk, he then activated the ELB on his T-Comm. He knew he was losing his strength and probably would not make it to the designated opening. He hoped his brother would make it back to the ship, read the ELB coordinates, and step him back to the ship.

Efas placed the T-Comm back in his vest pocket and hobbled to his horse. Dizziness overcame him, as he toppled head first onto the ground next to his horse. The horse did not budge. It stepped closer to his master as if he understood Efas needed help. Efas took a deep breath and lifted up from the ground. He grabbed the reins and pulled on them for leverage. He pushed to his feet, and then leaned on the horse for comfort as he attempted to gather his strength. His stomach ached, he was dizzy and he imagined he could feel the poison coursing through his veins fighting the nanobots. Death—was he dying? He imagined death—dark void of nothingness, no light, and no awareness—a dreamless slumber from which there was no wake. He imagined death to be a restful sleep with no conscious thought in which to tease the senses.

His eyes shot wide open chasing the last thoughts of death from the light of his mind. He did not want to die—not like this. If he were to die it should be in combat or after a long profitable life. Not on a prison planet by the whims of a legless creature—not by a snake, he would not allow it. The last thought gave him a surge of energy as he bolted onto the horse. The pain shot through his leg like a hot poker, but he fought it with all his might.

He nudged the horse with his heel. The horse understood the command and galloped through the barn doors, down the dirt drive and out the fenced area. The cool night air splashed against Efas' face, as the horse increased its gallop, invigorating Efas from his deathly slumber. The breeze stung open Efas' eyes, as he pushed for his conscious mind to stay alive, but the horse's hypnotic gait soothed Efas and washed over him a blanket of serenity. It wasn't just the nanobots fighting the venom. It was a battle of mind over body also. The body was weak and getting weaker from the battle between the venom and the nanobots raging in his body. The rhythmic massage of the horse's trot was hypnotic, lulling his mind into a daze. He now was scared that if his mind lost the battle, the never-ending darkness of death awaited him. These thoughts shot electrical stimuli to his body. He concentrated on parts of his body to keep his mind alive and working. He counted his toes, and identified the parts of the boot each toe touched. He concentrated on the pressure of his hands on the reigns. He concentrated on all his extremities, allowing his brain to work on worthless calculations of his senses. Yet dizziness soon invaded his brain and closed the connections with the rest of his body. It was an insidious take over. Efas never knew it happened. His conscious mind clouded from the peripheral toward the center. His vision closed in the same manner. Then without warning, without notice, his body shut down.

He hunched forward and then slid off the right side of the horse. His body hit the ground with a hard thud, but he neither felt it nor heard it. His brain was shut down as the nanobots in his body fought to save his life force. He laid face down in the dirt unaware if death was creeping up on him or not.

***

Leroy Johnson knew he was late. He had spent too much time at his girlfriend's house, and it was dark. It was a good five-mile walk and he began too close to sundown to make it home before the night had fallen, but Carmen was too beautiful a girl to leave so soon. However, the sixteen-year-old black teenager realized it was poor judgment. The Klan had been very active the last couple of months and if they caught him on the road this time of night, he knew he would not see the light of day.

Yet Carmen was so beautiful and she did beg him to stay and have supper with them. She had made the cherry pie herself. He could not refuse her, after all he thought he was in love and wanted to spend every waking moment in her presence. His mother told him it was typical for a boy of his age to think he was in love with the first beautiful girl who showed him any interest, but he knew she was wrong. This was love and someday he was going to marry Carmen, get some land for a farm and raise a family. He had his entire life planned and it centered on the thirteen year old Carmen.

Leroy had been walking for almost an hour. His day started early that morning at sunrise, when he received his father's permission to visit Carmen and her family for the day, but he promised he would be home before sundown. Now it was three hours after sundown and he was not even close to home. It usually did not take him this long to walk from Carmen's house, but it was late, and Leroy was being very careful.

Every noise he heard, he imagined it was the Klan coming after him. So he would hide in the bushes, watch and wait until he was sure it was not the Klan. Some people said it was Mr. Bennett, the county judge, who led the Klan. If that was so, there definitely was no justice for the Colored people of the county. Judge Bennett had sentenced his best friend, Jason Jefferson, to hang for stealing some chickens. Leroy told Jason not to steal Mrs. Perkins' chickens, but Jason didn't listen. And old Judge Bennett sentenced him to hang. No white man would have hung for it, but in this county any crime a colored man did he was hung. Leroy thought it was worse than slavery.

## Malcolm Dylan Petteway

Sometimes he heard his father profess he wanted the slave days back—at least in those days you were only whipped and not killed, because a dead slave was of no value to the master. However now, a dead Colored was more valuable than a live Colored. Leroy knew nothing about slavery and what he knew he learned from his father, who was a boy himself when slavery ended. Yet, Leroy knew there was a time after the Civil War when things were improving for the Colored, but that time had come and gone. The North had abandoned the Colored and allowed the Confederate whites to regain control of the South. Now things were worse than ever.

A Colored man had no way of making a living, and what living he could scrunch up was demeaning and paid next to nothing. Colored folks were poorer now than they were during slavery. They feared for their lives on a daily basis and could not speak as free men as the Constitution said they could. Jason had learned about the Constitution in school.

However, the more he learned about the Constitution, the more he considered it a lie. It was a piece of paper, which made the white man feel better. It had no value, it had no truth, and it was simply a piece of paper with writing. It had words he could not understand, but he knew it did not apply to him. The thing he knew for certain was someday he was going to die at the hands of the white man. The white man may not kill him directly, but he knew the white man would kill his spirit, his soul if not his physical being.

He had witnessed his parents bow to the white man's wishes—even putting him and his brother Jeremiah's needs on hold to answer to them. Something he vowed he would never do. However, he knew someday his manhood would be broken by the white man just like his father's manhood was. He dreaded that day, and he wanted to put it off as long as possible. However, he knew he had no control over his destiny and only God knew his future.

Leroy heard another noise. He stopped in his tracks and searched for the nearest brush to hide, but he was now out in the open. His thoughts had overtaken his sense of survival and he had followed the road with no brush for cover. His heart raced as he crept low to the ground. He heard it again. It sounded like a moan—a man moaning. He knew now someone was hurt.

Leroy moved to the side of the road and lay flat on his stomach. He strained his eyes to make out the scene. He could see a horse standing about fifty yards in front of him and he could make out a silhouette of a man lying on the ground. The man did not move, but he heard the moans again. They were coming from the figure lying in the road.

Leroy's first instinct was to turn and run, but he now was too frightened to move. This could be a trap, or it could be a Colored man who had the misfortune of running up against the Klan. Either way, Leroy was sure he did not want any part of it, but how to move on without being noticed was his next task. He did not know, so he lay in the dirt.

# Osguards: Revelations

The moans were getting weaker. He could hear the figure was dying. Soon his grandmother's words rang in his ear. His grandmother was deeply religious and attempted to quell Leroy's anger with talk from the Bible. It did not work all the time, but whenever Leroy had to make a decision, he would remember his grandmother. She was so sweet and forgiving. She was the only one he knew personally who spent most of their adult life in slavery. She had died when he was very young, prior to the Klansmen's uprising. There were stories he had heard from other states and other counties, but now they were here and this could be a trick of theirs.

His grandmother's voice still rang in his head. He heard her voice telling him the story of the Good Samaritan. Her angelic voice pushing the moral onto him echoed in his mind. He could not leave this person to die. Yet, was it a trap? He did not know. However, he had to help.

Leroy sprang to his feet and sprinted to the figure lying on the ground. His mind no longer controlled his actions; it was his grandmother's spirit controlling them. He was just along for the ride—ever so fearful it was still a trap. He reached Efas and turned him over. He gasped when he saw it was a white man. His instincts kicked in and told him to leave—to leave as fast as he could. However, his grandmother's spirit urged him to continue. The hesitation wavered in his spirit for several seconds as his instincts struggled with his grandmother's spirit.

Finally, his grandmother's spirit won the battle. Leroy searched the man for a wound until he came across the dripping blood from his leg. Leroy used his pocketknife to split Efas' pants leg open. He recognized the rattlesnake puncture wound; it was swollen and had turned purple. Leroy knew it was bad and probably too late, but he had to do something…anything and do it quickly.

He wiped his pocketknife with his shirt wishing he had fire or whisky to clean it with, but there was no time. He made an X-shape cut through the fang marks. Then he covered the wound with his mouth and sucked on the wound. Juices from the wound, including what Leroy hoped was some of the poison, flowed into his mouth. He spit it out and again sucked on the wound. He repeated this, several more times, hoping he was getting to the poison and it did not travel too far in the man's blood stream. Unbeknownst to Leroy, the nanobots running through Efas' body had overpowered the venom and broke it down into harmless waste products, which would be washed out through the liver later.

"Now what, grandmother?" he whispered to no one in particular. "You got me out here in the middle of the night caring for a white man who probably wants to kill me when he wakes."

"No I don't," Efas struggled to say.

The roughness in his voice and the suddenness of his speech startled Leroy. He fell back in shock. It took Leroy a split second to realize the voice

73

was that of his patient. He steadied his body and crouched back down next to Efas.

"Are you all right mister?" he whispered.

"I'm not sure," Efas admitted. "What happened?"

"You were bit by a snake. I sucked all the venom out, I hope."

"You did what?"

"I sucked the venom out," Leroy repeated. "You should be fine as soon as you get to a doctor."

"Thanks," Efas said as he propped up on his elbows. "It seems you did a great job."

"Thanks mister," Leroy smiled.

"What's your name," Efas asked.

"Leroy...Leroy Johnson."

"Well I owe you one, Leroy."

"No sir, it was my grandmother who told me to come help you. You don't owe me anything," Leroy said thinking he needed to get back home now. "Sir, I think you are fine enough to go to town and find the doctor, I have to get going now. My daddy and mommy must be plenty worried about me. I am late and it ain't good for me to be out so late. Besides, I don't want my little brother Jeremiah thinking he has the bed all to himself tonight."

Efas mind made the connection in an instant. "Jeremiah Johnson, the delivery boy."

"Yes sir, he is my brother."

"You say he is your younger brother?"

"Ah hum!"

"How old is he?"

"He's ten...a mighty fine worker for his age too."

"Jeremiah Johnson is ten?"

"Ah hum."

"Tell me son, do you know a Rebecca Keith?"

"Yes sir, Rebecca is Mr. Keith's daughter. Jeremiah works for Mr. Keith."

"And how old is Rebecca?"

"Shucks sir, I don't know. She must be about eighteen or so. She is pretty old."

"Are you sure?" asked Efas who now was becoming more than agitated.

Leroy recognized the agitation and became frightened. He inched backwards on his hands and knees and began to rise.

"Sir, I got to go now!"

However, before he could turn, a bright white light emerged from nowhere, like a curtain rising to let the sun in. Leroy froze as he watched a silhouette of a man step through the light. The man held something in his hand. Leroy thought he was looking at Jesus descending from heaven. He fell to his knees and bowed his head in reverence to the figure. Leroy was excited, for he thought God was rewarding him for being a 'Good Samaritan.' The figure continued to point at Leroy with something in his hand.

"No...don't!" screamed Efas. However, he was too late. A blue light flashed from the figures hand. The heat seared into Leroy's head and brought instantaneous death. Leroy fell backwards toward Efas. His eyes still closed in prayer and a smile of satisfaction etched on his face.

"I received your ELB. Thought you were in trouble. Come brother, get your horse and let's get back to the ship," Erif said holding his left hand in guidance.

Efas stood. The pain in his right leg was still there, but his mind was clear, although no longer peaceful. Leroy's death disturbed his spirit. The man who stopped to save his life was now dead because his trigger-happy brother did not stop to survey the situation before he acted. He grabbed his horse's reigns and hobbled over to Leroy. He looked down at Leroy in sadness, gazing upon the dead face of his hero in remorse. Leroy was dead and he was alive. He did not know how to take it.

"Come on Efas, we must go," Erif challenged.

Efas walked into the light with his horse in tow, the darkness slid down and swallowed the figures, leaving behind a teenage colored boy dead on the road, whose single failure was to stop and render aid like a *Good Samaritan*.

Efas would later learn from his brother, the Klansmen had killed Leroy's family earlier in the night. He did not understand, the killings were senseless and not necessary in his opinion, but his brother thought otherwise. His brother, although repulsed at first by Jeremiah's killing, now accepted it and relished his part in Leroy's murder. This hardened Efas' heart more toward the people of Ea rth and pushed the divide between his brother and him even wider.

# Chapter 13—The Search

The morning was cold. Efas awoke, feeling more vibrant than he had in the past week. His leg had healed and he was ready for the next step in his quest. He hopped from his bed and scurried to the ARIT panel on his desk. He opened his log and began checking his timetable. The accident with the snake put him several days behind schedule, but now he was ready for the next step in his plan. It was time to search for the next stop on the Underground Railroad.

Efas had spent his recovery time, scrutinizing the HVP. He thought it very fortuitous the Osguard sisters included the direction for the next stop on their HVP. Even though Efas thought it bogus information at first, after studying it awhile, he now thought it to be more factual.

According to the directions on the HVP, the slaves were to travel up the creek to find a red barn on the left bank. Directly across from the barn on the right bank would be a shed, covered by bushes. It would be hard to see from the road along the left bank, but should be easy to see from the creek.

Efas gathered his thoughts, dressed and met his brother in the gate portal room. Erif had brought the horses to the portal room and was waiting on his brother. The pale demeanor Erif wore told Efas he was in one of his moods.

"About time!" Erif nagged.

Efas looked at him with equanimity. He wanted to respond to his brother's unprovoked attack, but decided not to. Efas shrugged and moved to the panel, not changing his gaze from his brother. When he reached the panel he checked for the time intervals, periodically looking back at Erif without changing his composure. Luckily, Erif created multiple openings at various times, for the next couple of days. This way they would not miss their chance to get back. Once satisfied the time intervals for the multiple openings were correct, Efas waved his brother to the stepping platform.

Erif proceeded to the stepping platform with the horses in tow, making sure not to look at his brother any more than he had to, although he felt his gaze sting upon his presence like a mosquito—tiny and irritating. A minute later, the Ritchen brothers and their horses stepped from the white light of inner space into the cave.

Efas looked over his left shoulder and regarded the antiquated stepping box, created by his ancestors over ten thousand years ago, for several moments. He had anticipated they would be able to use the box to help them return to the ship, but his brother had informed him, he was unable to repair it. The multi-corder they had on the ship was incompatible, and Efas knew the multi-corder he left in Mr. Taylor's basement was of no use either. Efas knew the thing keeping either one of them from being stranded on Ea rth, was the random multiple openings from the ship's gate portal. This he did not like, but it was the best he had to work with. It just made him more nervous. He didn't like the idea of being stranded on a prison planet.

The brothers exited the cave without saying a word. Efas pointed north along the creek. Erif nodded and they mounted their horses. They followed the creek northward on horseback. Many barns cluttered the left bank. Some were new and some were in great disrepair, as if they weren't touched since the Civil War. They ran across shells of structures. They could not tell if they were barns or houses.

Efas wondered aloud several times, if they would find it—how did they know they did not pass it, or what if the barn was no longer red. Finally, they came upon an abandoned structure with all but one wall missing. The one wall was a burnt orange.

"You want to check this out. It looks like it could be a faded red color," Erif recommended.

Efas had grown tired of the search and did not argue with his brother. Besides, it was the correct height for a barn, and it lay in the middle of an old, unkempt and frayed farm. The brothers had spent the entire day traveling. They traveled twenty rings, equivalent to thirty-five miles, Efas learned later. He was hungry and upset that they were going to spend the night on the planet. It was too late in the day and they were too far away from their cave to make it back for the opening.

"You know, it only takes one person to search," Efas suggested. "One of us could remain onboard the ship. Then when the one searching the planet becomes tired or needs help; he could use the T-Comm to contact the other to use the gate portal to retrieve him."

At first Erif was leery of the suggestion. He did not trust his brother; but, he didn't know if he could trust himself. Since their arrival, Erif had either grown suspicious of his brother's motives, or he was having suspicions of his own motivation. Which, he did not know.

Deep inside, Erif resented his brother's stature and position. He always thought Efas was not fit to lead the Kulusk Empire, and that he was ultimately the right choice. Ever since they began this journey, Erif had fleeting thoughts of how he could discredit his brother and take his rightful place as the leader of the Kulusk Empire. However lately, these thoughts had turned into treasonous dreams. He thought of how he could leave his brother stranded on the planet and return to Kulusk, where he would report Efas' death to his father. Then he would step up and become the heir to the Kulusk Empire. He found himself relishing these thoughts more and more each day … to the point he was willing to formulate a plan to accomplish this goal.

Erif bit his lower lip as he regarded his brother's suggestion. A plan hatched in his mind on how he could leave his brother stranded, but he pushed the thought to the back of his mind. He realized he could not accomplish the mission at hand without his brother's help. First, they must find and destroy their enemy before he could obtain any satisfaction.

However, he knew his brother was well aware of this. He also suspected he was not as subtle with his brother as he should have been. Erif wondered if Efas knew he would betray him when the opportunity came. Erif looked into his brother's face. He saw he was tired, but he also saw Efas was weak. Efas offered a truce, an alliance out of weakness, not out of efficiency. This was why Erif could not see him as the next ruler of Kulusk. Efas bargained from a position of weakness, not strength. And Erif knew he would use that against his brother some day.

"Okay," Erif agreed.

It was the desired tactic in this situation. Erif understood that after he calculated the strength and the time it would take to keep returning to the beginning of their trek each day—even if they leapfrog their gate openings to the previous days advancement. It was just too much. Erif smiled, because he knew he agreed based on sound tactical judgment, not weakness as his brother did. However, the result was the same and he was agreeing with Efas. This worried him, but he decided he was the better strategist and would prevail in the end.

"Then it is settled," Efas declared, offering his hand. They grabbed each other's wrist and shook on the deal.

Once Efas received his brother's assurance he dismounted, took a deep breath and walked to the right bank. He noted if this was the spot, then the shed should be there. Erif watched his brother and was somewhat surprised at the boost of strength he demonstrated. Erif's mind raced. Was this a trap? Was he not tired? Then with a shake of his head, Erif dismissed the thoughts as fast as they were conceived. He did not believe his brother to be so cunning.

Efas grinned. Even though he was tired, he did not want his brother to confuse his momentary physical weakness with his ability to lead. Instead Efas summoned his remaining strength to showcase an imperturbable leader worthy of his younger siblings respect. Unfortunately, it was too late. His brother's opinion had been formed for years and there was nothing he could do to delimit the depiction Erif already had of him.

When Efas crossed the creek, his mind was deep in thought. Yet, the glint of wet wood sparkling in the sunlight caught his attention. He stopped to gage his bearings. The object flashed again from the water spots reflecting the sun's rays. Erif crept toward it.

The wood was broken, moldy and warped by time and water. However, it was the remnants of an old shack. The shack did not stand anymore, and its foundation was overrun with dirt and tall grass from years of neglect, but all the same, it was the shed. Efas knew it was the shed spoken of on the HVP. However, what was there to find here. Any clue to the next stop would have been long destroyed by nature years ago.

Efas' heart grew heavy as he closed his eyes. A useless search, he thought as rage replaced his frustration. He knelt down at the water's edge as he sifted with his hands the dirt and grass covering the old relic's foundation. He wiped the dirt away as slowly as his mind would allow, but his muscles tensed with the displeasure of the day. As his hands pushed the dirt away, they began to form a fist. Soon he was bulldozing away the dirt and overgrowing weeds of grass with his fist. His heart pumped with fury and his eyes swelled with enmity.

Erif touched Efas' shoulder with his hand. The touch soothed Efas' tension, for he did not want to demonstrate any emotions in front of his brother. He felt if he did, this would give Erif motivation to betray him at a later date. Efas understood his brother's diminutive loyalty was ready to abandon him. Although he never questioned this before, the words and actions of his little brother during this mission had gone beyond sibling rivalry, they now bordered on distrust and dishonesty. He knew he had to do something quickly to salvage the relationship or he would perish.

Efas took a deep breath, picked up the loose soil in his hands and let it slide through his fingers.

"A lost cause?" he questioned.

"No, not really," Erif answered. Now we have to go to town and find out who owned this land back then and maybe we can get some answers."

Efas looked up at his brother and recognized the brash smirk glowing in his face. He knew his brother's strategy was correct, but he despised admitting it.

"I taught you well, young brother," Efas snorted. "I am glad you are finally using your training."

Erif's grin evaporated as he watched his brother rise from the dirt. Their eyes never moved from each other's knife-like gaze. At that moment they both knew the gauntlet had been thrown, and they had crossed the imaginary line of defiance from which there was no return.

***

The brothers set up camp for the night in an abandoned barn they found near the banks of the creek. The next morning they rose and rode to the nearest town. They questioned all they could find, pretending to be prospective buyers of the land. After about three hours, they learned the property belonged to Mrs. Leslie Waters, the widow of a Confederate soldier. At first they thought they were following the wrong information. However, they had no other information to pursue.

Mrs. Waters was eighty-five years old and she lived at the end of town now with her daughter, Megan and Megan's husband, Todd Douglas. The upkeep of the land had been a drain on their finances for a long time. Megan was in the market to sale the land. It was good farmland at one time. She knew this from spending her youth on the farm, but she was not sure of that claim today. However, since her father's death, she and her mother could not make ends meet by farming. They no longer employed slaves for the manual labor and they both were too frail and ladylike to do the work themselves.

Her mother attempted to hire the labor, but she did not have the business sense her father had. The people she hired were lazy and abusive. They did not work one tenth as hard as the slaves had and the crop did not yield enough to pay them and sustain the standard of living they had grown accustomed. Then the Reconstruction period played more havoc on an already chaotic situation. The new Negro leadership drained them with taxes for the Negro schools and repair to the infrastructure.

Eventually, Megan met Todd and married him. Todd was a very respected and wealthy entrepreneur, whose wealthy status was not affected by the Civil War. Some said he made his money dealing in the weapons trade, and he had no scruples about selling and trading with the North during the Civil War. Yet, he also traded with the South, which allowed him to keep his respectability during the transition. Megan didn't know what her husband did for a living. He was always out of town on business. And she did not care, as long as Todd provided for her and her mother in the style and comfort they had grown accustomed to prior to the war, she was happy.

Todd had mentioned his irritation on keeping the farmland. At first they agreed to keep the land so they could build a house—a house that would rival some of the big plantation houses of the bygone era of slavery. However, time marched on, and other priorities seemed to arise. They never built the house and the land had become an albatross around her neck, threatening the harmony of their marriage. Megan saw selling the land as an opportunity to make amends with her husband and save her marriage. She did not want to leave the comforts of her modest home. She and her mother would be thrown out, with no money and no assets. She knew she was too old to start again, and her mother only had several more years of life left.

The Ritchen brothers appeared at her doorstep late in the afternoon. Efas tapped on the door. Megan, wearing a grayish hoop dress answered the door. A tight corset lifted her heavy bosom showing a healthy woman. Her green eyes danced with life, while her curly dangling brunette hair bounced as she spoke.

"Yes, may I help you," her voice wafted in the air.

"Hello madam, I am Efas Ritchen, and this is my brother Erif. We are new in your country and we are interested in the land by the creek. The people of your lovely town tell me the land belongs to you."

"Well, it really belongs to my mother," she smiled. She was excited someone was interested in the land after all these years.

"Well tell me…would she be interested in selling it?" Erif asked.

"She may be…she may well just be. Won't you come in?"

She showed them into her parlor and asked the maid, a burly black woman, to prepare some tea. Efas and Erif took seats on the imported French floral couch. They noticed the touch of eloquence they had expected at the Pathgo Plantation. Fine golden vases decorated the corners, plush rugs

80

covered the floor, and fresh paint highlighted the wood-paneled walls. Several portraits of Confederate soldiers adorned the walls. The furniture was neat, sturdy and comfortable. The interior was well kept, dusted and polished.

Erif knew Megan had fared much better than the Pathgo family since the war. Yet, the house was still small. Erif surmised it had four rooms downstairs, including the kitchen and maybe four rooms upstairs, unlike the Pathgo plantation, which boasted of fourteen or more rooms. Yet the gaudiness of the house far surpassed the Pathgo home. It was ironic to Erif, but sensible. The Pathgo family elected to demonstrate their worth in society by maintaining a large home; albeit, they could not maintain the upkeep to the proper standards for such a large home. The Douglas family elected to maintain a modest size home and demonstrate their worth in society by sustaining an eloquent but expensive interior, decorated with fine furniture and other imported eccentricities.

"So how did you come to hear about the land?" Megan asked as she sat in the chair across from the couch.

"To be honest, Mrs. Douglas—"Erif started.

"Megan…I must insist you call me Megan."

"Fine…Megan," he continued. "To be honest, we were just passing by and saw the land. My brother and I thought it could be profitable once we attend to it. So…we asked around town and well…here we are."

Megan regarded her guests with some skepticism. She knew the land was far from profitable. It had been almost thirty years since the land produced any type of crop. It would take much attending in order to revive the land. In her mind the land was dead…useless for farming. Yet these men were foreigners and seemed to want it. Her smile grew more pleasant as she pondered selling the land.

"But first, can you tell me some history of the land," Efas requested.

"Not much to tell, Mr. Ritchen."

"Please call me Efas."

"Okay…Efas it is," she smiled. "The land has been in my family since the turn of the century. My great-grandfather purchased it and started raising corn. We have raised corn ever since. Well…at least until the war." Her voice trailed to a lower sad tone and she looked at the painting of a Confederate soldier over the fireplace. "He was killed by the Yankees," she offered in a bitter voice. "My mother and I could not make much of the farm, so we abandoned it after the war. It has lain barren ever since."

"I didn't want to go, but she made me," shot a quiet voice from the doorway. Megan, Efas and Erif turned toward the parlor door. Mrs. Waters stepped into the room. Her gait was slow and riddled with pain, borne from her age. Erif rose and aided Mrs. Waters to the chair next to her daughter.

"Gentlemen…my mother, Mrs. Leslie Waters," she announced.

The Ritchen brothers passed on their greetings as Erif sat back down. Mrs. Waters smiled and nodded her head to the men. She wore her thinning gray hair, pulled back into a bun, like a crown. The stiffened back and rigid stance as she sat demonstrated a woman with strong resolve. Yet her wrinkled face and bloodshot eyes told her guests her time on Earth was long and not very pleasant at times.

After more inquires about the land, the brothers delved into the subject they wanted to know about—The Underground Railroad.

"Mrs. Waters," Erif addressed. "I hear that there was a shack on the creek behind your land that the abolitionists used to route runaway niggas to the North. Do you know anything about that?"

Mrs. Waters' eyes widened with disbelief as she stared at Efas. Efas imagined he could feel the sting of her stare burn through to the core of his brain. Yet, he did not avert his gaze from her. For several seconds that seemed like hours to Efas, the battle of the stares commenced. Then Mrs. Waters' lips parted.

"I assure you, no such thing occurred on or near my property," she proclaimed.

Megan averted her gaze toward the floor. Erif studied her. He recognized the body language. It was the language of someone with a secret. Megan squirmed in her seat moving from side to side as silence befell the room. Erif knew after several agonizing seconds Mrs. Waters may not know, but Megan knew something. It was getting dark and he had no more time for polite interrogations.

"Efas," he called. "Mrs. Waters is right. She knows nothing about the Underground Railroad." Efas turned to his brother with silent irritation. "No she knows nothing, but her daughter does, and we are running out of daylight."

Erif pulled his pagenay from his vest pocket and aimed it at the gold vase in the corner. He thumbed the pagenay and it shot a blue pencil beam light and vaporized the vase. Efas turned in horror, as did Mrs. Waters and Megan. Megan attempted to scream, but her throat tightened as it choked her yell back down into the pit of her stomach.

The corpulent black maid had caught a glimpse of blue light in her peripheral vision as she passed the corridor parlor entrance. She retraced her steps and entered the room to investigate the phenomena. When she entered the room, she saw her mistresses in apparent distress and approached the men, who sat with their back toward the door. Mrs. Waters' eyes gave the maid's presence away. Erif turned and fired.

The maid did not have a chance to react. The pagenay beam caught her in the chest. The pain of the burn was so immense, it stopped her heart instantly. The maid's eyes rolled to the back of her head and she plopped in the doorway without a sound. Upon seeing this, Mrs. Waters grabbed her left arm and bent to her left side.

She was experiencing complete and total cardiac arrest. She clutched her chest and formed words with her lips, but was unable to make a sound. Megan turned to her mother in utter horror. The scream, fused in Megan's stomach, now found life. Her voice screeched. Erif pointed the pagenay in her face. She interpreted the weapon and covered her mouth in a physical effort to muffle her own scream. Then she gained control of her vocal chords and took a deep breath. Her eyes watered with tears as she surveyed the dead in her parlor. Her mother had collapsed to the floor, curled up in a fetal position, grasping her chest. Her eyes were frozen open, devoid of life. The sight repulsed her and replaced the scream sequestered in her stomach with a sour acidic fluid on the verge of release. She felt the vile travel up her esophagus and she tried to force it back down from whence it began.

"Why?" Efas asked.

"She knows...and it's getting late. We can force it out of her now."

Efas pulled his pagenay from his vest and pointed toward the floor. Megan saw this and the panic she thought could not worsen, peaked to its highest level. She began to hyperventilate as her body fought to balance her oxygen intake and her carbon dioxide outtake. She still held her own mouth with her hands, to fight off the scream and the vomit.

Two hours later, Efas and Erif left the residence, armed with the information they needed to continue on their journey. Meagan had admitted she helped the runaway slaves to reach the North. She used the shack near the creek as a station to harbor the slaves, unbeknownst to her parents. The cornfields hid the shack from her parents who never ventured down to the creek. She also passed on the information she gave the slaves to go to the next station.

Efas' last sight of the house was ghostly. Inside laid the bodies of a Negro maid, whom he never knew the name of, Mrs. Waters, from an apparent heart attack, and Mrs. Megan Douglas, strangled with a curtain chord in an apparent suicide that Erif staged.

Erif figured they needed to make the cause of the deaths of the white women obvious for the coroner, but he knew no one would look too close at the Negro. He had plunged a kitchen knife with Mrs. Waters' fingerprints, into the wound left by the pagenay. If the Earth scientists were sophisticated enough, they would capture the fingerprints on the knife and assume Mrs. Waters killed the maid in a struggle prior to having her coronary. He figured, no one could figure it out, or even care—because she was a Negro.

Efas was upset, but he realized his brother was ruthless enough and determined enough to do what was necessary to complete the mission. Unfortunately, what his brother did in this otherwise quite house was exactly what needed to be done. Efas felt a tinge of shame as he wished he had the fortitude to be as ruthless as his brother demonstrated this day. He understood it to be a quality required of the next Kulusk Maxum.

The pair returned to the cave and stepped to their ship, where they spent a silent evening pondering the events of the past two days. Erif was proud of the accomplishments of the day. He had gained the information needed to continue the mission and he was sure his brother would not have achieved this feat if he were by himself. Therefore he knew he had to be the one to investigate the trail, and his brother would have to be the one to analyze the information using the ship's ARIT. Nevertheless, the question was – Could he trust his brother? For now, he had to. They needed each other to accomplish the mission. So he decided he would bury his animosity toward his brother for the good of the mission.

The next day, the brothers awoke and stepped to the surface to spend the day with Jenny and Ellen. The Pathgo sisters made a picnic basket and they traveled to the local pond to spend the day. In the presence of Jenny's sparkling blue eyes and mesmerizing smile, Efas forgot the horrors he and his brother performed the night before. He was oblivious of the mission and the ruthlessness he must bear in order to accomplish the mission. He was just happy to be in Jenny's presence.

He sat on the edge of a red and white-checkered tablecloth, chewing on a blade of grass and studying her face. He memorized every line, freckle and sparkle of her skin. She adored his attention. It was like she was the only person in the world and she drank it up with admiration.

On the other side of the pond, Ellen and Erif sat, enjoying their meal of fried chicken and cornbread. Erif too, was infatuated with his date. Her sparkling blue eyes also captivated him. Unlike his brother, Erif did not stay in one spot and study her face. He engaged in conversation about the South and its downfall at the hands of the North. He gave a sympathetic voice to the South's cause, which intrigued Ellen and made her more open to him. They spoke of the slave trade and the detriment Reconstruction did to the South. Then Erif opened up.

"I was with the men who hung Jeremiah," he informed Ellen,

Ellen seemed to be pleased by the information, which excited Erif more for this woman.

"You know Ellen, I was the one who killed Jeremiah's brother that same night," he confessed. "My brother was bitten by a snake that night, and Jeremiah's brother was trying to help him. I thought the nigga was trying to rob Efas or worse—kill him. So, I killed him."

Ellen smiled with delight. "Erif, don't you know the niggas think Leroy was killed by an evil spirit. They said he was burnt."

"Burnt?" asked Erif trying to feign innocence. He had forgotten he used his pagenay and now he had to explain. "Well I killed him with my bare hands then I tried to set him afire, but it was raining and I could not do it," he lied.

"Oh…that explains it," she responded. "Well for a moment, I thought the killer that murdered the slave catchers and my uncle had returned."

"Oh?"

"Yes, legend has it they were burnt as well." She fell silent as she gazed into his eyes. "But you know how legends are…ten percent truth and ninety percent fantasy."

"Oh! Then you don't believe they were burnt," Erif said as he moved closer to her.

"No…I don't," she whispered, as she took Erif's cue and tilted her face toward his.

Soon their noses touched as they tilted their heads and kissed. The kiss was long and passionate, signaling the start of feelings yet to come, but eager to explore. Her lips were full and luscious with the taste of love and roses. When the kiss was complete, they stared into each other's eyes, searching for meaning, truth or acknowledgement of what just happened. Her eyes glistened with understanding and longing as his did. They watched without thought, as their lips grew closer.

They kissed and embraced. Her lips were gentle but alive, sending encoded messages of want through his body. His passion stirred with conviction and soul as he held her tight. Her body felt heavenly against his. His heart pounded, as did hers. He felt her heart beating through her breast onto his chest. The pleasantly massaging beat was uniform to his heart beat. He did not want to stop the kiss. He closed his eyes and saw vivid colors of red and blue mingling and dancing in a liquid ballet…fluid in spots and solid in others. His mind tingled with feelings he had never experienced before … feeling he never wanted to end. Erif was falling in love.

# Chapter 14—The Cover-Up

Suicides left questions. And the apparent suicide of Megan Douglas was no exception. Todd Douglas had returned to his home to the gory scene left by Erif. He was mortified at what he found. The horror was too shocking to believe. Though he refrained from questioning it, he refused to accept the sheriff's official conclusion. He buried his wife and mother-in-law in a quiet ceremony and then began his own investigation.

His inquiries unmasked the presence of two foreigners, likely Germans, who were in town that Tuesday, asking about the old farmland. The local hotel owner had directed them to his house. Seemingly, no one had seen his wife, mother-in-law or even the maid after that day. More inquiries led Todd to a plantation outside of Danville, a town thirty miles southwest of South Boston. He convinced the sheriff to travel with him to continue his inquiries of the foreigners. It had been almost two weeks since that frightful Tuesday; he thought his wife died on. And he was convinced the strangers who routinely visit the Pathgo plantation were involved in the death of his family.

Todd and the sheriff of South Boston, Timothy Casey, arrived at the Pathgo plantation shortly before noon. It was just when Todd wanted to arrive. He counted on catching the family enjoying their lunch. People did not like to be interrupted during their meals, especially in the South. He knew this irritant would give him an advantage in interpreting their body language as he asked the questions. Somehow he thought he could determine if the Pathgo family would be telling him the truth, because their defenses would be down, drawn in by their hunger and thirst. It was a business technique he customarily employed. That is why he liked conducting business over lunch; it worked quite effectively on his clients. He saw no reason why it would not work just as well for him today.

A tall stout black man dressed in a dark coat answered the door. Beads of sweat from the afternoon heat, formed on his brow. His suit was pressed and his mannerisms were unflawed as he addressed the men.

"I am Todd Douglas from South Boston, and this is Sheriff Casey. I wonder if we might be able to see Mrs. Pathgo," Todd inquired.

The butler nodded, "This way please."

Todd and Sheriff Casey followed the butler to the parlor. He motioned for them to have a seat. Once they sat down the butler scrutinized the guests and then exited the room as if he was whisked away by some unseen wind.

A few moments later Jenny strode into the room. With a bubbly smile and a cheerful voice she greeted her guests.

"Hello, I am Jenny Pathgo." She reached out her hand mainly to see the breeding of her guests. Would they take it as gentlemen or would they shake it displaying the decorum of an uncivilized and therefore uncouth savage. To her delight, the well-dressed man stood and displayed the proper etiquette as he greeted his host.

"I am Todd Douglas from South Boston." He did a half twist toward the sheriff, remembering to never let his gaze leave his host's smile. "And this is Sheriff Timothy Casey."

"Please...sit gentlemen," she insisted as she sat. "My mother is still having lunch, so I thought I might see what I could do for you."

"Well...in that case..." Todd continued to stutter over his words. He did not estimate he would be ignored until lunch was over. However, he understood he was dealing with the plantation owner mentality. This was an aspect of the South he could not quite understand, although, he noticed the women of the South exhibited it more than the men. It was as if they were attempting to recapture the last bastion of plantation life through an air of protocol that no longer warranted his favor, but he decided to play along.

"Well then...can you tell us anything about two foreign gentlemen, believed to be German?" he continued.

"I assume you mean Efas and Erif Ritchen...Yes, I can speak about them. Why?"

Todd noticed the agitation and defiance peak in her voice. "Well dear lady, someone murdered my wife and mother-in-law two Tuesdays ago and your Efas and Erif Ritchen were in the area. I thought they might be able to help me."

Jenny caught the anger in Todd's voice. She knew it was more than questions Todd was after. She knew it was Efas and Erif he was after. She played with the ruffles of her dress as she feigned passive interest in the conversation.

"Well...Mr. Douglas is it?" Douglas nodded. "Well, Mr. Douglas, the Ritchen brothers are very dear friends of ours and they spoke of that trip to me just last week. It appears they spotted some land they thought about purchasing, but could not find the owners. They returned that night to have dinner with us. So, I don't see how they can help you."

"Oh, I understand," Todd lied. "Well, can you tell us where we can find them? I would like to ask them personally...no offense my dear lady."

"No...there is no offense taken," she lied. "If you want to talk to them, all you have to do is turn around."

The words stunned Todd. He did not understand what she meant. Then he replayed the words in his mind, his eyes shifting from side to side in confusion. Then he felt it, the presence of people standing in the doorway. He spun around in his seat. In the doorway, two men stood. They were both muscular, but the man to the right had an eerie quality about his features. Todd thought him evil and as soon as he set eyes on Erif, he knew he was the man who killed his family.

In a split second surprise, horror and rage baked in him in a smoldering emotional casserole. He wanted to lunge from the couch and kill both of them with his bare hands, but something drew his anger to the man on the right more. It was the aura of evil that seemed to hover over this man like a thunderstorm cloud.

Todd flinched, but he caught himself. He did not want to expose his inner thoughts this soon. After a few awkward moments of eye contact Todd surmised there was no soul in Erif's eyes. He turned to the sheriff and smiled.

The Ritchen brothers sauntered into the room with devilish grins, praising the lunch they just shared with the Pathgo ladies.

"I declare Jenny, if you keep feeding me like this, I might just have to marry you," Erif gleamed.

"I hope your brother would have something to say about that," she smiled. Efas smiled back in a boyish love struck manner. Then Jenny turned to the men on the couch. "Erif, Efas, this is Todd Douglas and Sheriff Casey from South Boston. It seems like Mr. Douglas' wife and mother-in-law were murdered two weeks ago…about the time you went to look for some land. I already told them, you were back here for supper that day."

Efas took the hint. He knew Jenny had just provided an alibi for them and she was now announcing that alibi to them so they would continue using it. However, Erif stood with his mouth opened, dumbfounded and ready to kill.

"Yes…that is right sheriff," Efas started. "We left that afternoon about two thirty…right after we stopped by their house. However, no one was home. So we left. We haven't been back since. You see, we want to buy something around here so we can be next to the Pathgo Plantation."

"You say around two thirty?" asked Sheriff Casey who had been quiet until now.

"Soli…I mean…yes sir," stammered Erif, who now realized Jenny, had given them a cover story.

"Well, Mr. Douglas that does it," sighed the sheriff. "I spoke to your wife about four o'clock that afternoon in town to tell her these gentlemen were looking for her. If they left at two thirty, then your wife was alive when they left town. And I questioned everyone in town. No one saw these men after two o'clock." The sheriff was agitated. He allowed Todd to include him on a wild goose chase and he did not like it at all. "I'm sorry to bother you good people, we must be going," said the sheriff, standing as a cue for Todd to join him.

Todd was mortified. He knew these people had killed his family, but the sheriff had ruled his mother-in-law died of a heart attack after killing the black maid, and his wife committed suicide when she came across the grotesque scene. It was unbelievable; especially, when he had the murderers standing in front of him. Yet, because of their lie, the sheriff was willing to close the case. He could not let that go. It was too hard, too unbelievable and definitely too unforgivable. Todd stood and walked in front of Erif Ritchen. He stood almost nose-to-nose, fueled by his grief. He stared into Erif's eyes, neither man blinking. The bravado quieted the room. Only faint heartbeats echoed in each person's ear as they watched the scene unfold.

Then without moving his lips, Todd whispered in a growling sound, "I know you are responsible for the death of my family and I will get you for it. You don't know whom you are dealing with. When I am finished with you, you are going to wish you had confessed today. Because hanging from the rope will be more merciful than what I plan on doing with you."

Erif smiled and took one step back. He fanned his hands in front of his face as to discard an unpleasant odor, "I know who you are, but you have no idea in jorum who I am. And I don't know the definition of mercy."

The air crackled with a burst of lightening. The weather outside had whipped into a thunderstorm, one of those unprovoked and unnoticed weather phenomena that abruptly appeared from nowhere. The sudden downpour danced on the roof like jungle drumbeats. The rapidity of the storm framed Erif's words and struck fear in Todd's heart. Yet, he did not show it, except for his eyes. And Erif saw that. The eyes echoed the soul and Erif read Todd's eyes like a book. He had won this little presentation of bravado, but he was not satisfied. He needed more.

"Gentlemen, I think you have worn out your welcome," Jenny argued. "I think it is time you left."

The sheriff eyed Jenny with caution. He knew they had outstayed their welcome. Besides, he did not want to be there anyway. It was Todd who insisted on this little excursion, and it took all of his patience to appease him on this trip. However, now a respectable Pathgo had spoken and even Todd, with all his success, could not fair against the power of the Pathgo family.

"Yes ma'am, you are correct. It is time for us to go," the sheriff remarked with an apologetic tone.

Todd shot a damning stare at the sheriff, but he remained undeterred. He had had enough and he was ready to return to South Boston. Todd sensed this and eased on his anger.

Jenny escorted Todd and the sheriff out of the room, through the foyer and to the front door. As they passed him, Efas patted his hand upon the sheriff's shoulder in a friendly gesture of forgiveness. The sheriff looked up and nodded in acceptance. However, unbeknownst to the sheriff, Efas slipped a black penny sized disk onto the sheriff's right shoulder. It blended with the dark material of his vest.

When Jenny reached the front door, she opened it and stared straight ahead into the storm. The rain shower was solid. The dirt road had turned into mud with standing puddles of water forming like small lakes. The raindrops hit the puddles, splashing the water like boulders falling into a lake. The mist of the heavy rain created a fog reducing visibility to a mere few feet as the clouds swallowed the sunlight adding darkness to the already blinding weather.

Both the sheriff and Todd raised the collars of their shirts to cover their necks as they stepped off the porch into the torrential downpour. The rain pelted the sheriff and his companion like hot pellets, stinging their skin, even under the clothing.

A stable hand rushed their horses to the front of the house and disappeared around the corner, running for cover from the merciless shower. The rain agitated the horses as they pranced back and forth, shaking and neighing; showing their fright of the storm. The sheriff and Todd raced to their horses and mounted them. They pointed the horses toward the gate and disappeared into the misty fog of rain.

Jenny huffed as she lost sight of her visitors riding off her property. Then she turned to Efas with a devilish growing smile and a sparkle in her eye. Efas understood the look. His heart dropped but he understood what he must do. And he understood Jenny knew what needed to be done. The door remained open as they read each other's eyes. Then he tapped his brother. His brother stared at Jenny and read the same expression in her face as his brother saw. Without any words, the brothers stepped out onto the porch.

The stable boy saw the two gentlemen and raced to get their horses. After several agonizing moments in the cool mist surrounding the porch, the stable boy brought their horses around. The brothers raced to their horses and mounted them with disregard to the rain or dimming weather. Efas tipped his hat to Jenny and then turned toward the gate.

When they too disappeared into the mist, Jenny closed the door and leaned up against it as if she was praying for strength. However, deep down inside her mind she was trying to decide her next move. When she decided, she straightened her stance and went back into the dining area to report the episode to her sister and mother.

After several miles, Efas caught a glimpse of their quarry in the light produced by the last lightening strike. They were on the path, which would lead them in front of the cave. Efas estimated they would be in front of the cave in a couple of minutes. Yet, it was hard to tell in the rain. He pressed his horse to pick up the pace. Erif matched his brother's pace, even though he was not sure how close they were to their objective.

The horses trudged in the mud, slipping on their once steady sure footing of the road. The horses were uneasy at the pace they were asked to deliver in this weather. Efas could feel the tension of the horse under his saddle, but he did not care. He needed the horse to pick up the pace, to catch up to his subjects and he needed to time it so it would be done outside the cave. Efas kept looking for references to tell him where he was, especially how close he was to the cave.

Erif remained confused, but he also remained silent. For once, his brother was taking charge and leading them. Several days earlier, he would have been suspicious, but since then, the Pathgo sisters had preoccupied both of them. And the time spent with them had been a welcome diversion and a source of healing between him and his brother. He no longer felt the animosity he did, or at least not at the level he felt it just days earlier. He now was more tolerant and this was a prime example of his goodwill.

Efas pulled out his portable ARIT, also known as a PARIT, and angled it in front of him. The PARIT was black and was form fitted for the human palm. The display window was approximately ten centimeters wide and five centimeters long situated at the top of the device. The portion that fit into his hand had a thumbwheel to the right and a trigger button on the left. He rotated the thumbwheel counter-clockwise, trying to get a fix on the tracking device he placed on the sheriff. The rain stung his hand as he tried to adjust the green display window. The water pooling on the display widow and the mist of the rain made it difficult to read. He wiped the excess water from his eyes with his free hand. He blinked several times trying to focus on the display. However, the rain splashed more water on his brow, which gripped the sweat from his forehead and then dripped into his eyes. The salt from his sweat stung his eyes, which made him squint even more than necessary to see the information from the display window in the rain.

He wiped the sweat and water from his eyes again, but this made the burning sensation of the sweat more painful. His vision blurred as he tried to steady his eyes. The uneven gallop of the horse made it even more difficult to concentrate. He did not want to stop his horse, because he would lose valuable time. However, the swaying of the horse interrupted his focus to the point he felt a headache starting. He looked up in frustration, as he came to the conclusion the PARIT was useless in this weather. He put the device back into his vest inner pocket and squinted to see if he could see the two men in the distance again.

He made out two figures about one hundred meters in front. They had stopped and dismounted. It appeared one of their horses was injured. The horse must have lost his footing in the mud and hurt his right front leg. The men appeared to be examining the horse. Then, maybe the horse just caught something in its shoe. That could be painful for the horse. Nonetheless, whatever the reason the men had stopped for, they were stopped. And as the Kulusk luck would have it, they were just a couple of meters from the cave. Efas chuckled at his fortune. He thought with all these technological devices, it was old-fashioned luck and determination that allowed them to catch up with their victims.

Then a cold chill ran through Efas like ice. This was the first time he thought of the two men as victims. He had ignored what he needed to do to the men, until now. It was like if he did not think about it, it would somehow make it magically okay, but it didn't. He knew he had to kill them, and it plagued his soul.

He looked at his brother who was already smiling at the prospect of what would come next. Efas knew he still had to demonstrate to his brother he was as ruthless as he, if not more. Because he knew this was a necessary trait for the next Kulusk Maxum to have, and he wanted to be the next Kulusk Maxum.

Efas retrieved his pagenay from his left vest pocket and held it in front of him as they galloped to the men. He had his thumb in the ready position. Erif looked on with amazement. He did not retrieve his pagenay.

Erif wanted his brother to do the dirty work for once. And if he did not, he would have all the justification he needed to impeach him in front of his father when they returned. Thus Erif smiled and allowed his horse to remain several lengths behind his brother.

Efas recognized this and knew he had to complete the task. There was no turning back. Surprisingly, the men did not hear Efas approach. They were so blinded by the rain and the task at hand Efas came within five meters of them before Todd looked up. Efas began his slow count to three, but before he reached three, something took over his body.

His thumb hit the firing button and a blue light sailed out and hit Todd in the chest. Todd's face recorded the pain and the surprise just at the instant of death. Efas recognized the look and knew his victim was dead, but something inside of him forced another volley of blue light to zero in on Todd's chest. Efas had no control. It was like watching someone else firing the pagenay.

He felt his conscious mind was no longer in the body. It was like he was floating above the scene looking down and becoming ill at what he was witnessing. A voice from his soul screamed for him to stop, but another, more foreboding voice from his Kulusk psyche said to continue. And his body listened to the years of Kulusk training embodied in the voice coming from his psyche.

When Todd fell to the ground, Efas turned to the sheriff, who was now reaching for his sidearm. Efas knew this was it. He had to fire or be killed. The silent angelic voice of his soul quieted and the voice of his psyche became louder. Shoot...shoot...shoot, the voice roared in his head. Then suddenly, he was no longer hovering over the scene watching the action, his point of reference was back in his own body and he realized he only had a split second before the sheriff had control of the situation. He swung the weapon toward the sheriff and fired.

The blue light sailed in a split instant and caught the sheriff in the shoulder. The sheriff dropped his sidearm and screamed in horrendous pain. His yell echoed in the lightening that flashed a split second afterwards. The yell penetrated Efas' soul and the beatific voice spoke—that's enough...let him live. However, the Kulusk sinister voice rang louder, drowning out the other voice. Efas jumped and fired again...and again, one catching the sheriff in the chest and the other in the forehead.

The smell of burnt flesh permeated the rain soaked air. Efas never could stomach the smell and began to gag. He forced the vile vomit back down his throat, adding the acidy burnt taste to the already putrid smell of burnt flesh. He turned his head to the side as he moved his horse to turn around. Now the rain that was previously annoying and sometimes painful had become a welcome relief on his skin. The wetness and the pain increased his senses and calmed his nerves at the same time. The smell soon dissipated in the weather and the vomit taste soon passed.

He looked up after several seconds to witness his brother's devilish grin of approval. For a split second he was relieved to know he'd finally done something that met with his brother's approval. Then the feeling turned into rage. He knew he should not have to seek his approval, but he also knew it was necessary to show to his brother his ruthless side to abate any ideas he may be harboring of confronting him for the throne.

Without talking, the brothers placed the bodies onto the horses and walked them to the cave. The silence between them was normal, but the reason for the silence was different. Erif now had admiration for his brother and was quietly celebrating his brother's warrior spirit, making him have second thoughts on his brother's rightful title as the heir to the Kulusk throne. He now favored it.

Erif mulled over if his actions had been too erratic and too rash while his brother's actions were more strategic and executed with meticulous precision. He watched him track the sheriff and Todd, and he did not know Efas had planted a tracking device on the sheriff. What also surprised Erif was his brother had the presence of mind to carry a PARIT as well. Erif stood in awe of him and did not know how to approach him yet to relay his newfound respect. Erif was not sure if he should even approach his brother at all.

Once in the cave the brothers waited for the next opening, stepped the four horses and two bodies into the chamber and onto the ship. Aboard the ship, Erif bedded the horses and met his brother on deck two, airlock five. Erif was confused. He was unsure why they brought the bodies to the ship, but he dare not challenge his brother—not after his performance on the planet's surface.

Efas placed the bodies in the airlock, closed the ship's door to it and then opened the airlock. The void of space sucked the bodies out and swallowed them in the black nothingness. Erif's eyes widened with angst at the horrific way his brother disposed of the bodies. He looked at his brother, eyes wide and mouth opened.

"Erif," Efas began. "You are too loose. You leave a trail of bodies that come back to us. I let you go, but now I must stop you. Your immature way of handling this mission has compromised us. I corrected the situation. No one will ever know they are dead and no one will ever link them to us." Efas took a deep breath and blew out hard. "No bodies...no murders...no crime," he lectured.

Erif lowered his head in shame, for he understood, his way had become too dangerous. He knew now he underestimated his brother.

"Now Erif," Efas said, putting a consoling hand on his brother's shoulder. "We do things my way."

"Soli," Erif responded.

Thirty minutes later the brothers were back in the ship's gate portal room. Erif set the timers on the portal to ensure their safe return. He still smarted somewhat from his brother's eloquent but cutting rebuke. He knew he had to work smarter, because he'd almost compromised the entire mission, and that would not aid him if he ever decided to challenge his brother.

Then Erif halted his thoughts. This morning he knew he was going to challenge him, but now he was unsure if he wanted to challenge him. What a difference a day made, he thought.

The brothers stepped onto the platform and several seconds later they stepped out of the light inside the cave. However, this time the lights were on in the cave. Efas and Erif reviewed their mental notes and thought the lights were off when they stepped to the ship. Then they heard it, the sound of a rifle bolt being pulled back. Instinctively, they raised their hands above their heads. Then they slowly turned in the direction of the sound.

"You know, Mrs. Gentry wrote about this cave as the last entry in her diary. We used to come here and play around this old equipment as kids, wondering if the spacemen would ever comeback," Ellen said as she walked out of the shadows holding a rifle on Efas and Erif.

"There is only one question I have to ask you," Jenny said coming out of the shadows from the other corner with her rifle at the ready position. "Are you Kulusk or Chaktun?"

# Chapter 15—The Wedding

Efas tossed the ARIT pad on his bed. He had stared at it for almost an hour contemplating his next entry. He was at a loss for words. He did not know how to annotate the events in the log. He had purposely not mentioned his relationship with Jenny for the past year in his logs, but now he had no choice but to annotate something. He knew his brother was dealing with the same dilemma. They both had only documented their journal about the time they spent searching the countryside, looking for information on the Underground Railroad. They had agreed to leave their relationship with the Pathgo sisters out of the logs. However, nature had taken an unexpected turn.

Efas stayed aboard the ship to operate the gate portal for his brother. His brother was amazing. With every step, he found the next station on the Underground Railroad to visit. Yet he was still using the Kulusk ruthless technique of torture and murder to do it. According to Efas' journals, he had murdered just over twenty-five people on his quest for information. It did not matter if they were men, women or children, nor did it matter if they were white or black. Erif killed indiscriminately and without remorse. Although he restrained from using his pagenay, he used his imagination quite well. He had learned from his first encounter with Megan he needed to be more discrete about his murders.

Suicides left questions. He learned suicides warranted investigations just like an outright murder. Erif had learned his lesson with the Douglas-Waters affair. He made them all look like accidents—horse riding accidents; falling off ladders or out of windows; hunting accidents. His brother's words guided him—"no murder...no crime." Regrettably, he conveniently forgot the first part of his brother's advice—"no bodies".

Yet Efas did not complain. His brother's newfound approach, though ruthless, did not leave a trail back to them. However, Efas thought it would be a matter of time before his brother's tactics would get him into trouble he could not handle. The one question Efas had was, was he going to help Erif when that day came. Efas didn't know. The fact he was teetering on the answer scared him a little, but more and more he realized his brother's actions were only a prelude to the final challenge—the fight for the throne.

The times were harsh and lonely following a thirty-five year old trail. The sole consolation they enjoyed was the time they spent at the Pathgo plantation.

The time spent there was pleasurable, pleasing and intoxicating. Jenny was delightful, soothing and beautiful. She had awakened urges in him he had worked his entire life to subdue. Her brilliant smile lit the recesses of his heart and her majestic blue eyes pierced deep within his soul. He found being away from her during his search for the Osguard offspring, became more and more unbearable. They both knew they were lucky to find such beautiful confidants as Jenny and Ellen. They were also glad being Kulusk saved their lives in the caves.

The Pathgo family knew about the Kulusk and the Chaktun Wars. The Osguard sisters explained everything to Mrs. Gentry that one night. And Mrs. Gentry wrote all she heard in her diary—a diary apparently the Osguard sisters knew nothing about. Efas read the diary and saw how Mrs. Gentry came to the conclusion she needed to help the girls get home. It was a long soul searching decision she recorded in her diary. Yet, it also gave insight to Mrs. Gentry they did not receive from watching the Chaktun holovidpics. It was disturbing to a Kulusk warrior to see the gentleness of Mrs. Gentry. It was surely a sign of weakness—a weakness that attributed to her death, Efas imagined.

Efas surmised Mrs. Gentry never had a chance to add anything to her diary after that initial night. He knew the Osguard sisters went into labor soon afterwards, and then Mrs. Gentry died of exhaustion brought on by her recurring battle with pneumonia. Thus, nothing about the babies was ever recorded. However, there were copious annotations about the Underground Railroad, and the brothers used that to their advantage.

His door announcer chirped, bringing him out of his consuming thoughts. Efas looked up and stared at the door as if it would open by sheer will. The door announcer chirped again. Efas wiped his face with his hand to get his personal bearings and stood from his chair.

"Enter," he commanded.

The door split along a "Z" like line and each side slid aside into the structure, parting and revealing Caroline. She sauntered into the room as she had several times over the last year.

"Mrs. Pathgo...I didn't know you were aboard," Efas said with surprise.

"It's a wonderful thing...these fancy T-Comms," she giggled as she held up the T-Comm he had given her to communicate with the ship. It was palm-sized and flipped open to reveal a small microphone and speaker with several keys. The keys had Kulusk lettering on them, but she soon learned to recognize their meaning. "I just push one of these buttons, speak into it and voila, I am talking to your brother. He sends the white light, and again...voila, I am here." She sat down at the table next to the door. "Now I have been on board your ship more than a dozen times, so why are you surprised I am here now?" she mused.

"Okay...I apologize. I was just not expecting you. That's all," Efas stated.

"Fine, but I brought you a little present."

"What?"

"A book," she smiled.

"A book?" Efas asked, irritated by Caroline's boldness.

"Yes, a book, but not any old book. I have brought you a book about the Underground Railroad." She threw a black bound book onto his bed. "It was written by a free nigga named William Still. He was one of those Northern niggas behind the entire thing. He has names and details of those who passed through Pennsylvania. Maybe you can use it to help you locate the niggas you're looking for. Then maybe you can take us with you to Kulusk."

Efas barely had time to react to the news about the book when her last statement struck him in the gut like a sucker punch. He had never thought about what would happen after the mission was complete, especially about what would happen to the Pathgo women. He just assumed they would leave and the Pathgo women would continue living on Earth. Yet, now the question smacked him hard. The Pathgo women knew too much, they saw too much, to be left alone on Earth. Kulusk protocol called for them to be eliminated. However, he had developed feelings for Jenny, as he was sure his brother had for Ellen. Death was not an option; at least for him it was not, but what about his brother…what did he think about it? Was he ruthless enough to eliminate the Pathgo women after all they have done for them?

"Well," Caroline asked, waiting for a response.

Efas looked into her eyes, searching for a sign. He studied the blue sparkle in them. She felt the extra attention he was paying her and smiled. He dare not smile. He thought of the fact he may have to eliminate this woman. His stomach knotted up and he felt it contract with nausea. His mind raced. He thought if he could forget about it for now, it would vanish. He soon realized that was a wish that could not come to fruition. The protocol pertained to everyone except members of the Maxum's family. Family—then it struck him like lightening from out of the blue. A smile grew on his face. He had the answer.

Caroline became frightened at the look Efas had given her. However, his smile soon eased her fright. She now was comfortable. She stared back into his blue eyes, broadening her gentle smile, dissolving her slight winkles of age and revealing signs of beauty she once boasted as a young woman. Efas thought her to be a beautiful woman who still could charge the hearts of men half her age. He understood where Jenny and Ellen acquired their beauty. He was staring at the source and she was staring back with a gentle peaceful smile. His love for Jenny just naturally extended to this woman for the mere fact Caroline was her mother and gave his love her life. He began to daydream of how Jenny would look at her age. Caroline's golden shoulder length hair with feathery tuffs of gray glowed ever so eloquently in the artificial luminance of his room.

"Well?" she asked again. "What do you have to say?" Her voice shook him from his daydream as he jiggled his mind to awareness. He realized several seconds had passed while he contemplated his situation, which slipped into total veneration for his guest.

Efas nodded and whispered, "Thank you."

***

Several weeks had passed and Efas could not believe he was standing in the Pathgo garden alongside his brother and in the midst of fifty of the area's most noted residents. Judge Bennett stood in front of them holding a black book he did not recognized. Behind him sat the others in white folding chairs, fanning the heat from their faces in a desperate attempt to cool themselves from the afternoon sun. To Efas, it was a cool day. On Kulusk it would be considered a cool day. Efas imagined the vain attempt to fan themselves was some extraordinary ritual confirming their pretentiousness.

The entire upper society, as Caroline designated them, came out to see the ritual. He was in awe of the formality and gaudiness of the entire event. He noted, on Kulusk the event would hardly merit a quarter of the attention it seemed to garner on Earth. Efas knew his discomfort displayed on his face for all to see. The more his agitation showed the more the episode seemed to be pleasing the honored guests.

The floral arrangements decorated the entire garden. Red roses with sprinkles of purple lilacs darted the white trellis he and Erif stood under. Several bees had visited the arrangement doing what nature had ordained them to perform with such delicate flowers. Yet the bees made Efas uncomfortable. No such creature inhabited Kulusk, at least not one with the ability to inflict such hot knifelike pain through a stinger. Efas was aware of each and every bee that decided to visit the floral arrangement.

Then at the end of the two formations of white wood folding chairs, lay a bouquet of flowers, each varied in color and species. Again Efas noticed the large bumblebees that were attracted to the arrangements. He was relieved, when he realized that the large stinging creatures were among the audience and not buzzing around his head.

Then he heard it. A violin playing what he had learned was the wedding march. After eying the musician in the background he wondered why these people insisted on having a marching song announce the woman's entrance. He also wondered why they called it a marching song. The beat was not useful in keeping time in any fashion consummate with the military. Yet, the rhythm was somewhat hypnotic and soothing. Then the song became stronger, pounding and overtaking. Somehow this must have been a signal to the crowd, for they turned to look behind them.

Efas followed their gaze and what he saw literally stopped his heart and made him gasp for air. Fifty feet in front of him stood Jenny and Ellen, both dressed in magnificent white flowing gowns with long white trains. He thought both the ladies to be the most beautiful creatures in the galaxy, but he knew Jenny was more than that. She was the most beautiful woman in the universe—without exception. She wore a white lace headband that anchored a frilly white veil over her face. Efas had to concentrate on breathing as Jenny and her sister effortlessly, eloquently and passionately glided down the aisle. Efas' breathing became labored, almost panting as he watched Jenny sail toward him.

Several sweet moments later, for what seemed like an eternity for Efas, Jenny stood beside him and Ellen stood beside Erif. His heart pounded in his chest and his palms began to perspire with anticipation. All he had to say was...*I do*. He kept reminding himself of that, tuning out the world and even Judge Bennett's words. He just kept thinking all he needed to say was *I do*. Then without conscious thought his mind wandered to the conversation he had with his brother about the entire affair.

It was the same day Efas had spoken to Caroline. Efas laid out the entire thought process in which the question of killing the Pathgo family was inevitable. Erif had not thought that far in advance. His blood thirst had focused on his original prey—the Osguard offspring. However, as Efas laid out the rules, Erif became painfully aware his brother was right. It had surprised Erif that Efas could be so cold and calculating. Again, Erif had underestimated his brother. This had happened too many times, and it made it glaringly obvious he could not afford to do that anymore.

However, he had fallen in love with Ellen, and even his coldhearted blood could not fathom the thought of killing the woman he had fallen in love with. So when Efas suggested marriage, Erif jumped at the suggestion. The clause that practically gave the Maxum's family total censorship of Kulusk law appeared to be the one loophole in the system. And marriage would enter the Pathgo family into the Maxum's family for life. Then only the Maxum had complete dominance over his family who were exempt from common Kulusk law. Yet, Erif was concerned about marrying an off world person. Then Efas reminded him the precedence had been set by their own great-grandfather, who married a woman named Reileia from Tilerist, a planet in the neighboring solar system. Since their great-grandmother was from Tilerist, they weren't pure Kulusk themselves. Therefore, they should be free to marry as they choose.

Their father, the ruling Maxum, had not given his blessing, which also was required by Kulusk law, making any wedding on Earth not a true marriage. They would have to return to Kulusk and get married under Kulusk law after they finish their mission. It was risky, but it was worth it. For the first time since their departure, Erif feared returning to his father. Now he wished his father dead and his brother to become Maxum, so no question of the marriage would prevail. He admitted this to Efas after several drinks of guild to celebrate their decision. He regretted the admission as soon as it departed his lips, but it appeared not to faze Efas. Erif slept that night more apprehensive than normal. He did not know if his brother had heard him or not. He feared the decision they made that night. Marrying women from Earth could possibly be interpreted as an act of defiance against their father and Kulusk law. Therefore, both Erif and Efas longed for their father's blessing.

"Efas…" Bennett's voice rang with urgency.

Efas woke from his deep thought to the perplexing eyes of the judge. He turned to Jenny and saw the worried look in her eyes as well. Confusion gripped his face, heart and mind.

"Well son, do you?" the Judge wailed.

"I do!" Efas voiced, realizing he had missed every word Bennett had spoken, and it was now probably his turn to say the only line he had in the entire ceremony. He looked over to Jenny just in time to see the worried expression wash away to be replaced by elation. Her smile confirmed he had said the correct words…late…but correct.

Efas' attention sharpened as he listened and witnessed the rest of the ceremony. He smiled when his brother and his now sister-in-law pledged their vows by the simple words—"I do."

At the end, Bennett declared them man and wife and the brothers held their new wives close and presented them with passionate kisses, which made the ladies of polite society in the audience blush.

It did not matter to Caroline. Let them blush she thought. No one but her knew the status Jenny and Ellen had married into. Her daughters were now the princesses to not just a nation, but also a galactic empire. The small peons fluttering around her yard could never fathom the significance of the event they just witnessed, and they never will. Caroline just smiled, collecting in her mind how she would act when she reached Kulusk.

# Chapter 16—Opium

The snow was heavy and the night air was bone-chilling cold. With every footstep, Erif heard the snow crunch under his feet. He never thought he would feel such frigidness, but the December night had chased any thought of warmth from his mind. His fingers and toes were numb and he thought he no longer had feeling in the tip of his narrow nose or small ears.

Erif wore the black pants, dual color shirt, knee high boots and thin overcoat of the Kulusk Guard, which afforded him no protection against the Philadelphia wind. He rubbed his hands together and blew on them, hoping to generate a split second of heat. His breath seemed to crystallize in the air as the white puffs of air floated around his closed hands. However, warmth did not prevail; only a cold breath onto a pair of already cold hands occurred.

Despair started to creep into his psyche. He had been walking in this neighborhood for three hours now, searching for the house used as the Philadelphia Vigilance Committee Headquarters, mentioned in William Still's book, *The Underground Rail Road*. However, he could not find it, and he did not want to admit he was lost either. So he kept walking and searching, to no avail. He would see houses that fit the description, but after inquiring about them, realize it was not the house owned by the white clergyman, James Miller McKim, who with Still, helped many slaves find freedom in the North.

William Still kept meticulous records on the slaves who passed through his station. He recorded names and stories in an effort to reunite families separated by slavery. Still had kept his journal hidden in a graveyard until 1872, when he then published the book.

Like many former slave owners bent on revenge, Caroline purchased a copy of the book, searching for the Gentry slaves, who she thought ran away using the Underground Railroad. However, she did not find anyone who fit the girls' description, name or background in the book. She never realized the girls had returned to their beloved Chaktun. She always thought they were still on Earth and posed a threat to the white people of America. Erif thought it fortuitous to find an ally in the Pathgo women, especially one as cunning and strategic thinking as Caroline.

Yet the fog of the cold slapped his subliminal thoughts back into reality, chasing away the reflection he had on his mother-in-law. He looked up and saw a two-story, Victorian style house, with a circular porch and three large windows on the first floor. The house, with smoke pouring from both of its chimneys, stood alone on what Erif perceived was a dead end street. He was at the edge of town, but it felt like he was at the edge of the universe. The house represented a lifeline, a chance of survival—it represented warmth. His bones ached with cold and his muscles were frozen stiff. Each movement of his body became exhausting labor. Each breath he took was like spikes piercing his lungs. He tried to cough, but his chest just convulsed in rebellion.

He knew he had to get out of the weather. His first thought was to call his brother on his T-Comm. However, he did not want to admit failure. In his previous four trips, he had not return to the ship without some type of information or evidence to continue the search. He was proud of his tactics and even more pleased of his results. It was sweet, unspoken revenge. The type of revenge he knew was chipping away at Efas' spirit and confidence. Yet, he knew if he returned to the ship without progress this time, all he had gained would be lost and Efas would once again find his spirit and confidence. Erif could not accept that. Thus he decided to press on. He decided to reach for the lifeline. He decided to go to the house at the end of a dead end road.

He marched to the garish looking house. He eyed it; knowing the smoke steaming from the chimneys indicated the house was inhabited. Erif didn't care. He just grinned, for he knew he was heading toward warmth. Somehow, this eased the pain and gave him the strength he thought had failed him.

He climbed the five-step flight of stairs onto the porch. He faced the double mahogany doors, took a deep breath and knocked, three short raps with his knuckles—not noticing he could have used the brass ring hanging in the middle of the door to knock. The coldness that gloved his hands kept him from feeling the wood of the door against his knuckles. After several seconds of silence, he knocked again, three short raps.

The door squeaked open. On the other side was a short Chinese man. His eyes were half closed and he swayed to an unheard melody, apparently only he could hear. He wore his hair in a ponytail that stopped at the base of his neck. His smock was silky bright blue. So bright, it hurt Erif's eyes to look straight at it.

"Yes, can I help you," the Chinese man said with a heavy accent.

Erif gawked at the man. He had never seen anyone who looked like him. His face, his eyes, his cheekbone and his skin color were all foreign to him.

"Can I help you," the Chinese man repeated.

"Excuse me sir," Erif stuttered. "It seems I lost my way, and it is cold. I wonder if I could warm up by your fireplace for a minute."

The man regarded Erif for a minute and saw he was shaking with chill. Feeling sympathy for the stranger, the man stepped back and motioned for Erif to come in. Erif moved as swiftly as he could inside the house.

The man led Erif to a sizeable room, housing a huge fireplace in the far corner. The wood in the fireplace sparkled with flame. The fire snapped and popped as it consumed the life from the wood. Along the walls, in several couches and chairs, seven people sat in a rainbow of colors. One man was a dark skinned Negro, similar to those Erif saw on Tir, a planet in the Chaktun Republic. On the couch next to the Negro was a tanned female. Erif thought her Indian or Mexican. He had no reference to judge, he only had Caroline's description of the race to base his assumption. Opposite the Negro and the Indian, two white men sat. They were well dressed and impeccably groomed. In the far corner, farthest away from the fireplace, an Indian male and two white women sat.

All stared at Erif with distrustful eyes. The Chinese man sauntered to the two white men and whispered something in the ear of one of the men. That gentleman stood and walked toward Erif. The gaze Erif endured from the forum put his senses into overdrive. His eyes darted from each person, looking for advantages, weaknesses; anything he could exploit if he had to. However, one thing became clear as he studied the room. Even though the people were staring at him, he doubted they saw him.

The glazed look in their eyes indicated their minds were adrift. They were disconnected from their senses. Their heads only turned in his direction as a reflex—a reflex to the noise he made when he entered. Yet, their minds did not register him, nor did their minds process the noise beyond the involuntary movement to turn in that direction. Then he turned to the approaching man.

The man appeared to be in his fifties, graying sideburns and he too, walked to an unheard melody. His gait was active, but sluggish. His eyes were glazed as well, as if he were walking without knowing he was walking.

"Good...eve—ning," the gentleman slurred. "I...I...I am Doctor Alexander Watkins. Wel—come to...welcome...to my home."

The doctor's slur was annoying to Erif. It was tough enough for Erif to understand English when it was spoken properly, but it was additionally trying to interpret the doctor's words after a long night in the Philadelphia cold.

"I am..." Erif thought for a moment. He had become accustomed to using aliases since the encounter with Todd Douglas, but he had not invented one for this trip. Then a thought struck him. He beamed as the words slid off his lips. "...Thomas Gentry. Doctor Thomas Gentry."

"Please, sit...sit...sit down, Doctor Gentry," Dr. Alexander beaconed.

Erif moved toward the chair situated in front of the fire and next to the couch Alexander had repositioned himself on. Erif turned toward the fireplace and placed his hands and feet out toward the fire for warmth. The fire felt good as feeling return to his fingers and toes. The chill evaporated from his body, replaced by the roasting tingle of heat. After several seconds of enjoying the fire, Erif turned to his host.

"Dr. Watkins, I want to thank you for letting me warm by your fire."

"That is quite alright," the gentleman next to the doctor interrupted. "My brother is...how should I say...a little inebriated." The gentleman offered his hand. "I am Alex's brother, Mitchell."

"Hello, I am Doctor Thomas Gentry."

"...Any relations to the Gentrys of Virginia?"

Bingo, thought Erif. He had made a connection.

"Yes, my great uncle and great aunt lived in Virginia, before the war. I was named after my uncle."

"Fine people!" offered Mitchell.

"Did you know them?"

"Only by reputation ... I knew Doctor McKim. I studied under him. You see I am a physician as well." Mitchell shifted to face Erif and to look into his eyes. "McKim was part of the Underground Railroad, which brought most of the Coloreds to the North. He used to speak of the operation to me on several occasions. He mentioned an Elizabeth Gentry in Virginia as one of his most trusted stations. Extraordinary!"

"How so," Erif coaxed.

"It appears two Colored girls were helping her."

"Interesting? Erif posed.

"Yeah, it was. It appeared some plantation owner killed the girls just before the war. What a shame."

"Yes, it was. My aunt died about that time as well. She died after delivering babies for those Colored girls." Erif leaned over as to whisper a secret. "Do you know what happened to those babies?"

"As McKim tells it, the last freight took the babies with them to New York."

"Are you sure?"

"I think so. But McKim told me many stories. But that one, kind of stayed with me. It was so tragic and all."

"Do you have a name of the last freight?"

"Nope, never did get a name. McKim was kind of secretive about names. He only told me that story. That's all I know. Why do you ask?"

"Well, I was hoping to catch up with the children, seeing that my aunt helped deliver them...sort of a bonding with my ancestors, if you understand."

"I guess I do, but it is pretty close to impossible. Those children must be close to forty by now. They are grown, probably married with children of their own. They probably changed their name when they got to New York, or they may have continued past New York. That entire experience is ancient history now. No one kept records...except for that Stills fellow. I hear he wrote a book. Maybe you can use that."

"Maybe!"

Mitchell pointed behind Erif. Erif observed Mitchell and then he turned to look over his left shoulder. When he turned, the Chinese man, who he assumed was the houseboy or butler, was leaning over him with a silver tray. Erif was startled. He did not sense anyone was that close to his personal space. However, the Chinese man was, and he had done it with the stealth of a Chaktun shredant.

The butler offered Erif a brass pipe with a wooden carved mouthpiece end, which lay on the tray. Erif remembered his first experience with a cigar—the burning sting that evaded his lungs, clobbering and consuming the oxygen his lungs fought to retrieve. It caused him to cough and he did not want to experience that again. He also did not want to insult his host. So he took the pipe and placed it to his mouth, nodding his appreciation to the butler.

The butler lit the pipe and smiled at Erif. Erif again nodded in appreciation in hopes the butler would leave, but he didn't. The butler watched and waited wide eyed for Erif to take his first drag. Erif regarded the butler for some time, the pipe still smoking on his lips. With his head, Erif gestured for the butler to leave. The butler nodded and continued to smile at Erif, but did not leave as Erif wanted.

"What?" Erif asked.

"You smoke," the butler urged.

"Yes, I will smoke," responded Erif.

"No, you smoke now," ordered the butler.

Erif squinted in angst at the butler's insistence. However, his apparent agitation went unnoticed. The butler nodded again.

"You smoke now," he demanded.

Erif understood the butler was not going to leave until he inhaled the putrid smoke from the pipe. He shook his head and lifted the pipe from his mouth.

Alexander coughed in a nonchalant manner. "Doctor, are—are you re…'fusing my hospitality?"

Erif turned to Alexander. He saw irritation in the doctor's smile. He then looked at Mitchell, who wore the same alarming smile. Why not, Erif thought. The night had become productive. He learned his next stop should be New York. Why not celebrate? He placed the wooden pipe tip back in his mouth and slowly inhaled the smoke from the burning end.

The smoke floated into his mouth. The taste was not sharp like the cigar smoke. In fact it was sweet and inviting. He mulled the smoke around in his mouth and then sucked it into his lungs. At first he felt the burn sting his lungs, but it was only for a split second. He gradually exhaled the smoke, reliving the sweet tang as the smoke passed his tongue once more. His taste buds chirped with life as the smoke washed them with the pleasing but biting flavor.

Erif inhaled once more, pulling the smoke into his lungs a little bit quicker this time. He held his breath for a second then exhaled, allowing his tongue to enjoy the pleasure of the smoke once more. He looked at the butler, then to Alexander and then to Mitchell, giving his nod of approval with each drag he took from the pipe.

"This is marvelous. What is it?" asked Erif.

"It is Virginia tobacco, mixed with some Turkish Opium for flavor," Mitchell responded.

"I like it!"

"I thought you might appreciate it. The Opium cuts the bitter taste of the tobacco and also allows for a sweet but pleasurable experience."

"I must agree. Usually I don't like tobacco, but this Opium makes the experience somewhat pleasurable."

"Finally, a colleague who agrees with me," Mitchell responded.

"What? What do you mean?"

"You know doctor. The medical profession is starting to look down on the use of Opium and those products made from Opium, like morphine as too addictive for medical use, let alone social use. I think those quacks are too serious. They need to enjoy life. And this mixture is a definite pleasure of life. Don't you agree?"

"It certainly seems so," Erif finished, as he took another puff from his pipe.

The opiate molecules now began to surge through his body, finding multiple nerve-receptor sites and producing an analgesic effect bringing on a foreign sensation of euphoria. Erif laid his head back and closed his eyes.

The smoke drifted from his pipe to his nose and found its way into his lungs as he took deep breaths.

A few moments later, Erif had forgotten the conversation or where he was. His mind sunk into a dark and peaceful swirl of blackness. He lost his balance and could not feel his body touching the chair or his feet touching the floor. He became oblivious to his surroundings. Then all of a sudden, his mind switched to another reality—a reality of dreams and memories—a reality of make believe.

*He was on the bridge of the Pride of Kulusk, with his Uncle Letel. The triangle-shaped bridge was smoke filled. He was leaning against the black railing encasing the communication station. The battle of Drow in the Drad system raged under him. In front of him, as evident in the view screen, laid five Chaktun cruisers. Internal systems indicated the Pride of Kulusk was severely damaged. Only one of the ship's five pagenay ports was operational.*

*Then the security sensors sounded its screeching high pitch whistled. Erif moved to the security station and pushed the display button. He read dozens of gate portal openings and dozens of Chaktun life signs. He turned to his uncle to report the situation.*

*Just then, a Chaktun soldier crossed his path. He withdrew his pagenay and fired. The Chaktun fell to the floor with a horrendous thump. Another Chaktun soldier, dressed in his warrior black battle armor, charged him from the left, again he fired. He fell dead onto the bridge floor. Then before he could collect his wits, another soldier attacked from the shadows, then another, and then another. Erif fired and fired and fired. He continued firing his pagenay, and the soldiers continued to drop dead, one upon the other, but each time a soldier fell; another soldier would materialize from the shadows of a blackened gate portal opening to replace him.*

*Erif continued firing his weapon. His heart pounded with anger. Adrenaline bolstered his blood, giving him inhuman like strength. His reflexes were crisp. His reaction time was instantaneous. And with every Chaktun he killed, he would find an inner peace for that split second. Each death brought him joy—happiness wrapped in euphoria, called invincibility.*

*Then he saw his uncle lying at the feet of a Chaktun soldier, who boldly occupied Letel's command chair. This wasn't supposed to happen. His uncle survived this battle. He won this battle. He received the Cross of Kulusk for this battle. His uncle saved a Kulusk battalion on the surface from five Chaktun cruisers. However, there he laid—dead at the feet of a Chaktun Rox ... blood flowing unimpeded from his mouth, eyes and ears. Rage consumed Erif as he aimed his pagenay at the Chaktun skulking over his dead uncle's body. He fired. The Chaktun was unfazed. He fired again. The Chaktun coughed, stood, smiled, and laughed—unhurt, unhampered, and undaunted. This further enraged Erif. He pushed the trigger longer, harder and with more anger. The blue light sailed into the Chaktun like a pole, but the black Chaktun soldier just continued to laugh.*

*Now Erif's fury emerged into fear—an emotion he never thought he would experience. His fear fueled his movement as he ran toward the Chaktun soldier standing over his dead uncle's body. Then he stopped. All of a sudden, he couldn't move. He felt a great weight pounce on him. His arms became heavy and dropped to his sides. His legs felt like cement and failed his command to move.*

*Then he saw it. The Chaktun soldier raised his pagenay rifle and pointed it straight at his head. Then the blue beam of death floated from its barrel. Time distorted its movement. The light punched through the air a fraction at a time—leisurely floating and gently sailing the blue hot beam of death toward his head. He felt the air propagate in his lungs. He wanted to force the air out in the most frightful yell, but even his lungs failed to obey his commands. He watched, unable to move, unable to scream. He unwillingly watched, knowing he was about to die, but not ready to accept it.*

*The beam came closer. He could feel the heat emanating off its blue light. Sweat beaded on his face. The hair on his arms tingled with heat. The air in his lungs tasted smoky. It tickled the back of his throat and he began to cough. His coughing caused him to gag on the smoky air. Now his lungs, which were so full of air just moments ago, were fighting for oxygen. He tried to suck in the air around him, but he only sucked in smoke. He continued to gasp for air, forgetting he could not maneuver from the blue ray of death magically but slowly piercing toward him.*

He screamed. He finally screamed. The yell pushed out like a sound quake from his lungs. The blue light faded, only to be replaced by darkness. Erif was confused. He was scared. He was dazed. He realized he was on his knees and his eyes were closed. He opened his eyes, still gasping for air to feed his oxygen starved lungs.

His vision was blurred—attacked by smoke. The room was on fire. Flames were consuming the woodwork around the doors, windows and fireplace. Dense black smoke carpeted the walls. Gray smoke floated in the air, smothering what was once an oxygen rich atmosphere. He continued to cough. Erif squinted, fighting for his vision to return. He surveyed the room. He was back in the great room of the house he had retreated to for warmth. In his hands he held his pagenay. It was warm to the touch. He knew he had fired it. He was confused. He didn't understand what had happened.

In the thick of the smoke, he recognized several forms. Inside the room, the occupants, all eight lay dead—killed by pagenay fire. The walls were scorched with pagenay burns. The curtains were ablaze and the floor also had pagenay burns. Flames danced in the room, jumping from furniture to wood and back again. The heat from the fire began to melt the iron around the walls.

Erif didn't know what happened, but he knew he had to get out of there. The doorway was blocked by flames. His mind was losing touch with reality due to lack of oxygen. He coughed black smoke from his lungs. He tried to cover his mouth and nose with his jacket sleeve, but he still could not filter out the smoke. He reached for his T-Comm and activated the ELB. Then he opened a channel to the *Sisen*.

"Efas," he coughed. "Efas, emergency gate portal opening…repeat emergency gate portal opening now!"

Almost as soon as he completed his last word, an invisible door lifted, revealing the white light of inner space. It gave the smoke in the room a halo, an almost godly, effect. Erif turned toward the light and crawled on his hands and knees across the threshold. The door slid closed. Erif took a deep breath, feeding his lungs with the pure oxygen contained in the chromerion field of the gate portal. He again coughed out black smoke, which was hampering his breathing.

As he coughed, the door slid open on the opposite side and a hand reached in and grabbed Erif by the arm. It was Efas. He tugged at his brother, pulling him out of the portal. He dragged Erif off the platform onto the gate portal room floor. Erif's pagenay and T-Comm dropped to the floor as he fell face down.

Efas ran a MARIT scan on his brother. The scan indicated smoke inhalation, third degree burns on his hands and feet and a foreign hallucinogenic substance in his blood. He retrieved a medical chair from the corner, hoisted his brother onto it and whisked him to med lab.

"You idiot…you damned fool!" Efas chastised.

# Chapter 17—New York

The Pathgo Plantation was no more. Caroline had sold it piece by piece, the land, the house and even the furniture, to interested buyers. Bennett had purchase the bulk of the property including the house. Caroline knew Bennett wanted to preserve the Pathgo Plantation as a status symbol of the old South. Most former plantations had disappeared over time, due to financial and physical neglect. A plantation was a high maintenance asset, the former owners could not sustain due to the cost of labor. This was another reason the South turned on its black population. The blacks were their inexpensive labor to offset the cost of maintenance of operating a plantation. Now that the black population wanted a day's wages for a day's work, the very foundation of Southern civility was rocked.

Nonetheless, people like Bennett continued to preach for the South's salvation through the subjugation of the black population. Now with the

Pathgo Plantation, Bennett had not only a bully pulpit to preach from, but he also had an example of how the South could *'rise again.'*

Caroline forewent the rhetoric for a richer lifestyle. Four months after the marriages of her daughters to the heirs of a galactic dynasty, she and her daughters moved onboard the Kulusk *TBC Sisen* and spent the past four months stepping to exotic places they only dreamt of before their enhanced fortune evolved. Caroline and her daughters had stepped to Paris, London, Berlin, San Francisco, Los Angeles, and New Orleans for various lunches, dinners, shopping and entertainment. Caroline was enjoying for the first time in her life, a sense of wealth, prestige and power. Her life was wonderful and she ensured her children's lives would be magnificent as well.

She calculated all the travel they had done as they stepped onto the gate portal platform one more time. Jenny and Ellen gathered behind her. This time they were bound for New York City. She wanted to catch a theatre show of Hamlet, which was playing at the Ambassador Theater. She was not a big Shakespeare fan, but she understood women of stature often frequented Shakespearian plays. And she thought of herself as a woman of stature. Furthermore, deep in the recesses of her psyche, she thought she was more important than any queen, king or president on Earth, but she could not say that aloud. Her distinction with the Kulusk Empire was furtive, for if released it would endanger more than she could comprehend, including her life and her children's lives.

She knew this would be the last step for a while. Ellen, her youngest daughter and Erif's wife was eight months pregnant, the fruit of a drunken honeymoon aboard a secluded ship. Travel for Ellen had become limited due to her size and stamina. However, she wanted to make this trip with her mother and sister. This would be the first time either of them had visited the North.

New York City had become the golden city of the New World. It bragged about being the first in the nation in population, industrial production, bank deposits and wholesale trade. Besides, Caroline wanted to see the new twenty one-story Flatiron skyscraper building that completed construction the previous year. Additionally, she always wanted to see the Brooklyn Bridge, a wondrous site, the world's longest suspension bridge, she was told, which connected Manhattan with Brooklyn and extended across the East River. She was more excited about this visit than any visit she had done prior—more than Paris, London, Berlin, Tokyo, or Vienna.

Erif worked the control panel as Efas stepped on the platform behind Ellen. This time, Erif and Efas would accompany the ladies. Their investigation had led them to New York as well. Therefore, they did not see why they could not mix a little pleasure with business.

Still's book coupled with Gentry's diary and the Mitchell Watkins statement aided the brothers in their search for the Osguard offspring.

However, New York City seemed to be where the road ended. A large pool of the black population appeared to be settling into a part of New York west of Harold and Time Squares known as Hell's Kitchen, the Tenderloin, and San Juan Hill. Therefore, the Ritchen brothers had concentrated their efforts in this area for the past two months, to no avail.

Erif, building on his Doctor Thomas Gentry persona, had a novel idea of setting up a free medical clinic in the Tenderloin area, on 42$^{nd}$ Street. The Tenderloin was said to be the best part of Manhattan. Therefore many theaters, saloons, dance halls, and famous restaurants and various hotels saw the potential in the area and began calling it home, plunging the already overcrowded population into a system of vice, which became the bedlam of corruption for unscrupulous police and political officials. Somehow, this made the trip more alluring to Caroline. For the brothers, this made an ideal base of operations. The free medical clinic blended with the scenery and offered no threat to the corrupt practices of the public administrators.

This also provided an excellent opportunity for the brothers to screen the inhabitants for Chaktun DNA. It was obvious the convergence of the black population in the area was playing havoc on their scanners. All the population contained a trace of Chaktun DNA. The trick was finding the right combination of Chaktun DNA, which his scanners could not discern from orbit. The scanners needed to be in close proximity to the subject in order to obtain an accurate reading. Additionally, Erif used this opportunity to introduce the black populace to Opium.

Erif learned from his experience, the drug terminated small fractions of the brain's cognitive reasoning ability. His cognitive brain function deteriorated by zero point thirty-five percent, after his encounter with opium. He realized normal use of this drug, or its more potent offspring, morphine, was more than addictive, it attacked and destroyed the higher learning ability of the brain … eventually turning its host into a bumbling idiot. Erif's plan was to introduce the drug into the populace and kill their ability to intelligently learn or judiciously formulate thought, but it also had another effect.

Erif discovered the drugs he created from opium also destructively bonded to Chaktun DNA. It destroyed the dormant genes he found in all blacks, which if properly stimulated, would activate their Chaktun acute intellect and physical prowess. The drugs neutered the quiescent properties and became a covert way of sterilizing the enemy.

For Efas, the situation presented a different opportunity. Efas surmised the Osguard offspring may have moved on and a scan of the population at close proximity would waste valuable time, effort and resources. Nonetheless, he was in no hurry to complete the mission and more than willing to entertain his new bride while they expounded on Erif's theory and execute his eradication plan. Besides, Erif had not eliminated anyone in the two months they set up in the Tenderloin area. This was a side benefit Efas was willing to accept as a compromise for what he considered was an ill-conceived strategy.

Also, Efas noticed the change in his brother as he watched Ellen's belly swell with his fruit. Becoming a father somehow calmed Erif's thirst for rash and unprovoked action. Efas watched with amazement as maturity grew inside of his brother. Where Erif was once foolish, he was now rational; where he once was unfeeling, he was now caring; where he once was rash, he was now prudent. The change was exhilarating to Efas. He now could concentrate his efforts on his wife and the mission and not on how to debunk any claim Erif would take to the throne.

Efas ran his fingers over the smoked glass console and a blinding white light illuminated from the floor to seven feet from the floor. Caroline, Ellen and Jenny shut their eyes and stepped into the light like old pros.

Erif watched, as the light seemed to bathe them from head to toe in an angelic aura. He had just started noticing the picturesque beauty of the gate portal, watching his wife and unborn child step in and out of the light shinning from inner space. He took a deep breath and jogged into the light and chromerion field protecting the portal's occupants from the cold oxygen less and radiation filled vacuity of inner space—the fourth dimension. After several seconds, the portal and the path behind them, leading to the ship, crept closed. As soon as it closed, an opening in front of them slid up revealing the back room of their makeshift free medical clinic in New York City.

The Ritchen family stepped out of the light and into the room without uttering a sound. Caroline, Jenny and Ellen had become old professionals at gate portal travel. Caroline had studied the physics behind the phenomena and grasped the concept quite well. Although she did not understand the existence of inner space and how it could connect different points of space, she knew how to operate and maintain the portal. Erif had attempted to explain the technical details of gate portal travel to her. Yet, all she understood was inner space was a fourth dimension, where upon space folds upon itself in many layers, which she could not see because she was a three dimensional being. Yet, these folds allowed different points in three-dimensional space to touch, overlap and in some cases co-exist with one another. The gate portal was man's way of manipulating the phenomena.

"Well, it looks like they are lined up for business," Efas observed pointing to the outer window and seeing a long line of black people congregate around the front door.

"Weren't you suppose to be closed today," Ellen queried showing her agitation. "I declare I don't know why you waste your time on these people. They don't deserve your attention. Can't you just throw the opium at them?"

Ellen never liked the idea of her husband working on niggas. She found it appalling and she had mentioned it on more than one occasion. In fact she always made Erif bathe twice before touching her after spending a day pretending to be a doctor for these people. The thought of him touching and prying all over the nigga caused her to become squeamish, if not nauseous. And she did not want Erif to touch her with those same hands until they were cleaned. Now they stood in the clinic with more of them waiting to be seen, when they should be home attending to their own problems.

"Promise me you will send them home, don't touch them, don't look at them...just send them away," she ordered.

Erif peered through the door that led to the outer office, and saw in the window the crowd Efas spoke about. He also saw the sign he had put in the window, stating they would be closed today. He didn't understand why the crowd had formed. "I don't understand...I put a sign in the window. Why are they here?"

Caroline shook her head in disbelief, "My dear Erif...niggas can't read." Then she looked through the door from behind Erif. "At least a majority of them can't read. And I bet that majority is at your front door right now."

Erif shook his head in despair, "I forgot."

"Now what?" Jenny asked with a slight giggle. She found the situation humorous and wanted to press the family more.

Ellen shot a stern look at her older sibling, but soon melted in the girlish smile. She thought it funny as well and soon began to giggle.

"You mean to tell me...you expected the nigga to read your sign and know the clinic would not be opened today." Ellen laughed.

"Well...yes I did," Erif acknowledged as he turned to his pregnant wife. However, something in her smile, which now was becoming contagious, melted his shame as he began to laugh.

Soon the entire family began to laugh as the thought trickled into their heads on how the incident constructed itself.

"Quick out the back door," Efas suggested after several failed attempts to contain his own laughter. "Whatever they need, it can keep until tomorrow. For tonight, we are taking you ladies to the show."

Erif moved to the door looking back at his pregnant wife, smiling and feeling the glee of the moment. He grabbed the doorknob, twisted and tugged at the door. Erif pulled the door open several inches and then the door pushed into him with such a force it knocked Erif to the floor.

Two men had pushed the door in when they saw it crack open the few inches. They both were white, the taller and heavyset balding man held a revolver in his hand. The other, younger and shorter man with a slight muscular build trained his rifle on Erif.

Efas lunged toward his brother, his mind not quite comprehending what was happening. His training had yet to kick in; only his instinct to aid his younger sibling pushed his reactions. Immediately when he felt the hot pinch punch his side, he realized they were under assault. The bullet's force turned him around and he twisted to the door and mentally recorded the scene in a split second, before the pain took hold and careened him into unconsciousness. He fell backwards into a shelf of glasses filled with different vibrant colored liquid mixtures. Then the shelf, the glasses and Efas bounced off the wall and crashed forward to the floor.

Ellen and Jenny screamed in horror, but were cut short by the assailants' ruthless disregard for life as the taller man fired his revolver two more times. The first round hit Ellen in the right shoulder. She spun to her right and stumbled backwards, tripping over her brother-in-law, Efas. She fell backwards and hit her head hard against part of the shelf, sharp broken glass pierced her skin as her body slammed to the floor.

The second round burned through the left side of Jenny's abdomen. She bent over in pain and fell to her knees. Her eyes tried to focus, but the pain made her gasp and lose her vision to the black world of unconsciousness. She fell forward toward Erif, silent and lifeless.

Erif gathered his senses in the few seconds it took for his brother, sister-in-law and his pregnant wife to be cut down, and moved with gazelle like quickness. Fueled by anger and guided by Kulusk training, Erif popped to a crouched level and started to charge the man with the revolver. The shorter man with the rifle lowered his rifle and fired a round, stopping Erif in mid stride. Erif collapsed at his intended victim's feet, blood oozing from his forehead, where the bullet grazed him before cutting through his left shoulder in a downward trajectory and lodging into his lung, barely missing his heart.

Caroline was decimated. She stood still shaking with fright. She saw the gun turn toward her. She covered her mouth with both her hands to contain her own scream of horror she felt gurgling in her stomach. Her mind focused on the gun as she replayed in her mind the damage it already had caused her family. The scream became harder to contain, and it grew stronger in her stomach. She realized her loved ones were either dead or dying on the floor, but her mind merely shrieked one thing—survive!

She knew she had to survive in order to render help to her daughters and their husbands. Every motherly instinct in her body wanted to dive onto the floor and attend to Ellen. She was pregnant and the most fragile of them all. However she witnessed Jenny take a bullet in her stomach. Caroline feared her already dead, but the mother in her refused to accept it.

Tears welled in her eyes as she focused on the gun, trying to use her peripheral vision to watch for a twitch or movement of some kind to let her know her daughter was still alive. She muffled her own breathing to sterilize the air so she could listen for a moan, their breathing—anything.

The man with the revolver lowered it toward the floor and stared into Caroline's eyes.

"Where's the opium?" he charged.

Caroline felt faint. The intruders wanted narcotics. They came in here and shot her family over narcotics. Then her uneasiness gave way to fear once more. She knew there were no narcotics in the room. Erif kept it on the ship. There wasn't any conventional medical equipment either. All they kept in the back room were bottles of harmless liquids in bottles, to give the place the ambiance of a medical laboratory. She swallowed hard, thinking of an answer to give the man. She lowered her hands from her mouth and stared back into the evilness of her captor.

His eyes were bloodshot and she now noticed a slight tremor wafted through his body. He was an addict. She'd never seen one before, but she had heard of the effects opium had on people. She turned to observe the shorter man with the rifle. He too had bloodshot eyes and his shake was more noticeable.

Now she was more than scared. Her heart pumped faster and she became light headed. Her vision became blurred again. She no longer felt the pressure of gravity's push and her mind could no longer grip her thoughts. Then without warning, she fell, losing her grip on the conscious world, sinking into the black void of nothingness. She didn't even feel her right arm as it fractured when it smashed into the floor.

Unbeknownst to the intruders, the brothers had attached monitors equipped with DNA scanners, called scanmons, throughout the setting. The one in the back room recorded the entire episode, but the scanmons placed on the outside front entrance also recorded something. They recorded the chaos resulting from the sounds of gunfire. The dozen or so clients waiting for the clinic to open for business scattered upon hearing the shots—all but two young girls.

One girl, who appeared to be the oldest, approximately eighteen years old and the other, who looked approximately sixteen years old, froze in their tracks and only stared in the direction of the gunfire. Then the girls ran toward the shots. They followed the echoes through the alley that separated the medical clinic from the next-door market, which was also closed. Their fleet footedness was angelic like. Their auburn hair waved behind them like a cape, highlighting their movements.

The girls turned the corner and reached the back door to the clinic just in time for their hazel eyes to record Caroline crashing to the floor. The intruders' backs were still turned to the door and they did not see the young black girls behind them. The girls stood in horror as they surveyed the scene—five people, two men and three women, one pregnant, lying on the floor, bleeding from apparent gunshot wounds. It took a split second for the young ladies to surmise what had happened.

They knew the white men, with their backs to them and holding the instruments of destruction, the guns, were the culprits of the massacre that lay in front of them. Without hesitation, the oldest girl grabbed a brick from the alley and threw it at the back of the head of the older intruder. The brick found its mark. The thud signaled the brick had broken skin and bone as it crashed into the man's head. The solid thump of the man's body hitting the floor confirmed it.

The younger man turned to see his fallen comrade, and then twisted around in time to see a two-by-four piece of lumber, the younger girl picked up, come crashing into his face. He could not react as the board crushed his nose, busting cartilage and blood vessels. The pain soon subsided into a cloud of blackness consuming his soul and extinguishing his thoughts as his body plopped on top of his partner.

It took a few seconds for the shock of the moment to wear off. However, the girls, feeling the surge of adrenaline pushing their bodies and souls, picked up the weapons, dragged the assailants out into the alley and locked the door behind them. They both leaned their backs toward the door, breathing heavily, trying to catch their composure as the danger of the moment played in their minds. The girls were unaware of the scanmons registering their Chaktun DNA.

Betty Nightman looked at her cousin Shirley Grace. Betty was the daughter of Kashara, aka Lilly Nightman, and Shirley was the daughter of Sharyla, aka Amanda Grace. They had been on their own for three years now, since they ran away from New Haven Connecticut. They moved to Tenderloin and had been working odd jobs, cooking and cleaning in the local restaurants. Many times they felt like returning home, but their pride restrained them from that course of action.

So they left in search of fame and fortune. They were singers and thought they were talented enough to start a career in New York City. However, their parents did not think so, and they forbade them from seeking their fortune, but the girls did not listen. They struck out on their own and came to New York, only to have the cold unfair facts of life slap them in the face.

Many nights, they were cold and hungry, fighting with the others for a place to keep warm and a bite to eat. Just recently, with their new jobs at a local hotel, they found solace in a place they came to hate, but could not give up—Tenderloin. They had made up their minds; they would return to New Haven and hopefully receive their parents' forgiveness and acceptance back into the fold.

The stare the cousins gave each other lasted a second. They knew what they had to do, and they knew they had to act fast. Betty moved toward Ellen first. She did not know why, she suspected she was drawn to her first because she was pregnant. She assessed Ellen's injuries, tore a piece of clothe from Ellen's dress and used it to put pressure on her shoulder wound. The bullet went straight through without hitting any vital arteries.

Shirley went to Caroline. She confirmed Caroline was not shot, but had fainted. Shirley went to the sink and pumped water into a glass. She splashed some water in Caroline's face. When Caroline stirred, Shirley raised Caroline's head and gave her the rest of the glass of water to sip.

Caroline drank the water, trying to clear her head. When she regained her senses, she turned in horror to see her family scattered around her lying in pools of their own blood. She was so distraught, she did not realize or care that her attendants were black. Something, if she were in full control of her faculties, she would have refused. Presently, fright controlled her senses, which allowed her to trust them. Shirley informed Caroline her arm was fractured, and splinted it using bandages from one of the tables against the wall and pieces of wood from the collapsed shelf.

Meanwhile, Betty saw Ellen's water had broken. This combined with the trauma that Ellen received, caused her unborn child to be in distress. She knew the baby was coming, whether she was ready or not. She called for her cousin to help her. After a few seconds of discussion, Shirley gathered a bowl of water from the pump at the sink and revived Ellen in the same fashion she revived Caroline. However, when Ellen awoke, the pain, which the unconscious state mercifully consumed, awoke with her. The pain in her shoulder made her feel like it was on fire. She screamed in agony. She had never felt such pain. The fire shot straight through her. She imagined she could feel every fiber in the wound cry out to her soul for relief. In the midst of her pain the fury of her prejudice broke through.

"Nigga...don't touch me," she shouted. The pain in her shoulder told her to submit, but she refused the pain's request. "I told you to let me go," she persisted. The cousins continued, ignoring Ellen's ignorant plea. However, the more Ellen protested the more the pain grew in her shoulder. She tried to break her injured shoulder free from Shirley's grip but soon felt the queasiness of unconsciousness stalking in her head. Her vision faded and she became weak. After several minutes of struggling with her attendants, the pain won out and she laid her head back down onto the broken glass.

Shirley worked to stop the bleeding from Ellen's shoulder and her head. Shirley thought it was good Ellen was obsessed with the pain in her shoulder for it took her mind off the danger her baby was in. Shirley and Betty aided Ellen to her feet. At this moment, Ellen realized she was in labor as contractions shot through her womb. She shrieked forgetting the pain in her shoulder, and grasped the cousins for more support. She had them in a death grip.

They moved to the bed on the far wall and placed Ellen onto it. After washing up at the sink, Betty returned to Ellen and prepared her for delivery by removing her restrictive clothing and covering her with a blanket.

Caroline sat next to her daughter, holding her hand with her maternal instinct to calm her daughter. However Caroline continued to peer at Jenny feeling she also needed her. Her instincts were torn and her feelings bombarded with guilt. Ellen was awake and her other daughter lay in a pool of her own blood. Caroline's stomach knotted with tension and apprehension.

Shirley saw the anguish in Caroline's face, "These ladies...are they related to you?"

"Yes, they are my babies," she said as tears rolled down her face.

"I'll see what I can do for her," Shirley said laying a comforting hand on Caroline's shoulder.

At first, Caroline jumped. Her upbringing detested any unsolicited touch of a black person. However, the compassion of Shirley's touch and the surreal situation melted the angst caused by her upbringing in accepting the situation. She tilted her head toward Shirley's hand, resting her cheek on it.

"Thank you," she whispered.

Charged with the unspoken request, Shirley moved like a nightingale to Jenny. She attended to her stomach wound, trying to stop the bleeding. However, Jenny was too deep in her unconscious state to wake, which Shirley was relieved about. If Jenny awoke now, she would be in unbearable pain. Once Shirley stopped the bleeding, she examined the wound and determined the bullet was lodged too deep in Jenny for her to attempt to retrieve it. All Shirley could do was to keep her alive until she received proper medical attention.

"Ma'am, she needs a doctor. I can go get one, but it will take a while. I have to go to the other side of the Tenderloin," Shirley said.

Caroline thought for a moment. She knew they needed real doctors to attend to the carnage in the room, but she was unsure if the doctors of Earth could do more for them than they could for themselves when they reached the ship. Maybe, she thought, the doctors could care for them until they reached the ship, but they could die without some attention now, especially Ellen.

"Do what you can for now...dear. Then you can go fetch the doctor." She thought again. "Wake one of them," she said pointing to Efas and Erif. "They are doctors."

Understanding, Shirley moved to Efas first. His wound was similar to Jenny's but not as serious. She worked to stop his bleeding. While she was working, Efas woke from his slumber. He stared into Shirley's hazel eyes and surveyed her auburn hair; he realized he was staring into the eyes of an Osguard. He knew the person hovering over him was a descendant of Nausona or Laurona. However, as fast as the thought formed in his head, the pain of his abdominal wound reminded him of the situation. The entire episode flashed in a split instant in his mind. His wife, his brother...what happened to them?

He lifted to his elbows and surveyed the carnage around him. He saw his wife bandaged but unconscious. His heart sank. Then he saw his brother, near the door, on his stomach with blood pooling under his shoulder. His mind screamed—No...it couldn't be! Then he saw his sister-in-law on the bed, in labor. Despair gripped him, but not for long.

His Kulusk training pushed the pain aside and he hobbled to his feet, aided by Shirley. He went to another cabinet and placed his hand against the middle plate without saying a word. Caroline watched, confused and disturbed. The cabinet slid open in the traditional Z-pattern of a Kulusk door. Inside was the medical equipment from the ship. He gathered several pieces of equipment and rushed to Jenny. He worked feverishly on Jenny, aided by an awestruck Shirley; until he was satisfied he had done all he could do. He had removed the bullet with a medical extraction device that Shirley never saw before, and was somewhat frightened of.

In the background, Ellen's screams of labor echoed in the room like a torture chamber. Betty and Caroline now diverted all their attention to Ellen and the delivery of her baby. Efas wanted to turn his attention to his sister-in-law, but he knew his brother needed his attention next.

He moved to his brother and stood above him. His mind was in debate. Should he save his brother or not? If he saved him, would Erif be grateful enough to stop challenging him or would he continue to challenge him at every turn. He knelt down next to him on one side and Shirley knelt down on the other side. Efas ran a scanner over Erif that read out his vital signs. He was alive, but his vitals were dropping. The bullet was lodged in too deep for the medical extraction device to work. All Efas could do was to stabilize him.

He signaled for Shirley to help him turn Erif over on his back. Once he was on his back, Efas attached a stabilizing MARIT to his neck as he did with Jenny. The MARIT injected the correct medicine to stimulate the body back into normal status. Efas knew if his brother was too far-gone, the MARIT would not work, but he had to try. It was all he could do until the ship's gate portal opened up.

Then Efas demonstrated how to use the medical extraction device on him to Shirley, before lying on the floor. Shirley placed the device, a cylindrical glass tube with wires and metal on one end leading to a digital readout that printed in Kulusk, over the wound. Efas showed Shirley what symbols she was looking for that would tell her the procedure was complete. Shirley did not understand, but she had witnessed its effectiveness when Efas applied it to Jenny.

Her hands were trembling with fear, but she complied with Efas' instructions. She placed the open end of the device over the entry part of the wound and pressed a blue button with her thumb. Several lights, blue, red, orange and white, merged together in an operatic blend of illumination. It was like peering at a rainbow through a prism. The entire tube glowed in a hypnotic blur. Shirley kept a watch on the readout at the top end of the tube for the specific symbols Efas wrote out on the paper. The symbols changed in rhythmic motion. She thought she was in a dream state. She did not understand the device she was working and was between delight and fear that she was operating it.

Efas explained the device searched the area of the wound for any inorganic material. She did not understand what he meant by inorganic, but she assumed he meant the bullet and nodded her head for him to continue. Then it uses electromagnetic forces to pull the material from the wound in the same path as it entered. However, the path must be straight, no angles— that way it will not cause more injury on the way out than it did when it entered. Shirley understood this to mean the machine sucked the bullet out of the wound. Efas nodded at the simplicity of her correct assessment and smiled. She understood this is why it could not be used on Erif. The entry wound was not straight and it was too close to other vital organs, including the heart, to use the simple device.

The readout kept moving as Efas gritted his teeth and fought the urge to scream. Shirley did not know how painful the procedure was, because she only witnessed its operation on Jenny, who was unconscious at the time. However, with every anguished, painful moan Efas let out, Shirley wanted to pull the device away, but she fought the urge for the simple reason Efas wanted her to continue. She kept asking Efas if he was okay, and he would urge her not to stop. Then after several painful minutes, the readout reached what she was looking for. She gleefully pushed the button, as Efas instructed, to stop the lights.

Perspiration soaked her face. She wiped her forehead with her forearm and said a silent prayer of relief as she handed the device to Efas. Efas felt weaker now and took the time to collect his senses. Then the faint cry of a baby shook him from his dizziness. He forced his body to turn toward the sound and saw Betty, whom he had not acknowledged before, holding what he presumed was his nephew or niece.

"It's a boy," Betty yelped, wiping the birth fluid from the baby with a clean cloth. Caroline's eyes watered with pride as she held her daughter's hand.

"Go, use this on her...quickly," Efas said recharging the MARIT and handing it to her. "Get the bullet out of her shoulder. Then put this device on her neck as I did to my wife and my brother."

Shirley moved to the bed and without hesitation put the device against the wound in her shoulder. She turned it on and watched the device hum to life. Ellen began screaming in pain as loud as she did when she gave birth to her son. Yet, something in Shirley gave her pleasure hearing this woman, who called her *'Nigga'* scream. It was sweet justice and she was happy to be the instrument of that pain. Shirley applied more pressure than necessary; stating it would make the extraction quicker, but she knew it only increased the pain.

Several minutes later, Ellen's afterbirth was removed and the bullet extracted from her shoulder. Shirley placed the device on her neck as Efas directed. Now, Efas had moved to scan the baby to ensure he was fine. The baby showed signs of distress and Efas placed a stabilizing MARIT on his neck as well. Then he wrapped the baby in a blanket and gave him to Ellen, who was now feeling no pain and filled with enough medicine to float her mind in an abyss of nothingness.

Efas checked his timepiece. It would be another four hours before the gate portal would open and give them an opportunity to return to the ship, but the object of their mission was there with him. What to do? The girls, who he had learned were Betty and Shirley, were now in his grasp. Yet, the girls helped save his family's life. He could not kill them for their reward. Or could he? The Kulusk training said he could, but his human side said he couldn't. Tears swelled in his eyes as he checked the scanmons for confirmation. It was his duty to kill them. He had to do it. It was his duty and he knew it. He grabbed his pagenay from his hidden holster under his black jacket. Shirley saw this and thought it another miracle medical device that Efas was about to deploy, but he pointed it at them like a weapon.

Shirley and Betty raised their hands over their heads, even though they did not recognize the device, the way Efas held it registered in their mind as a weapon. Plus seeing the other technological wizardry in the room, they did not have the courage to challenge the impulse.

"Efas, what are you doing?" asked Caroline, shocked at the appearance of a pagenay.

"I'm sorry Caroline," Efas admitted. "These are the Chaktun offspring we are looking for."

"No, they can't be. We are looking for older women...in their late thirties. These are kids...teenagers," she explained.

Efas thought for a moment and concluded Caroline was correct. "Then these are their kids," he offered. "Where are your parents, your mothers?" he asked raising the gun higher to deliver his threat with emphasis.

"They're dead," Betty murmured, hoping he would believe her. She did not glean much from the conversation, but she did understand her mother and her aunt were in serious danger from these people who they had just spent the last two hours saving. Betty was disheartened at the turn of events and her eyes swelled with anguish and hate. These people betrayed her and her cousin. Now revenge ate at her soul. She wished she had let the white men they threw in the alley completed their task. They would not be in this predicament if they had run like the others did. No, she thought, they had to follow their instincts, and intervene as nature had deemed necessary.

Fate…what an evil trick of life, she thought. Fate had determined they meet the people who were, for some reason, out to kill their mothers. Maybe…she thought…just maybe, fate intended her to protect her mother and her other brothers and sisters from death by sacrificing her and Shirley. Fate had decided their death was necessary in order to save the others. That is why they ran away three years ago and why they were drawn to this clinic today of all days. She cursed fate, but she also embraced her fate. She took a deep breath, shrugged off the thought of death, and considered it her fate … her way of protecting her family. "They are dead, killed by white people like you, for no reason," she yelled.

Efas believed her. Something about her tone and the anguish in her voice told him the query of their mission was truly dead, and the two young girls in front of him were all who were left of the Osguard bloodline on Earth. A nervous smile formed on his lips as he pointed to the door leading to the outer room. "In there," he ordered.

Betty and Shirley followed his directions and stepped into the other room. Efas followed, hoping his Kulusk instinct would continue, for he felt himself wavering in his determination.

The girls turned to him when they reached the glass door leading to the outside. Efas closed the door behind him and stood pointing the pagenay at them. Shirley's eyes welled with tears as fright took hold of her emotions. Betty wiped away her tears and now stood determined to be strong and not give this murderous monster the satisfaction of seeing her cry.

Somehow, Shirley picked up on this, wiped her tears away, and blinked several times, to control her eyes from welling anymore. She took a deep breath and exhaled hard as a defiant act to her new captor, who moments ago she had held in reverence.

"We saved your life," Shirley shouted. "And this is how you repay us. I guess I shouldn't have expected anything less from white people."

The words shook Efas a little, but not visibly. He knew there was a class difference between the whites and the blacks on the planet. He wondered if it was a carryover from the feud between Kulusk and Chaktun. Were the two natural enemies, no matter their situation, environment or timing? It was an interesting thought to see the grudge between the two races continued, even on this planet, by the descendants of two mighty cultures— and they didn't even know why.

Then he thought, he didn't know why either. The fight had started long ago, by different people in a different time and he didn't understand why. All he knew was his father raised him to hate these people, just like his father before him and his father before him. There was no tangible evidence or credence for their hatred. It was just there—hatred. It consumed them, it provided an industrial impetus to their economy, it provided a religious fervor to their lives and it provided a source of enjoyment to their being. Other than that—why? Why did it exist?

He lowered the pagenay, "Go!"

"What?" Shirley asked.

"Go, before I change my mind," he moaned. "Just go!"

The cousins scurried to the door, unlocked it and ran. As they ran, the Kulusk instinct in Efas kicked in and he raised his pagenay and fired. In the scanmons, the girls were no longer in view, but it captured Efas firing his pagenay at them. Efas had disabled the outside scanmons when he checked them. He figured the data was no longer required, since he had the object to their mission inside. Therefore, the girls' escape down the street was not recorded and automatically sent to the ship. Efas kept firing into the empty doorway and then to the floor as if he had hit his targets. The scanmons captured and recorded every shot, but not its target. Later Efas would use this recording as proof to his father he did indeed kill the girls after feigning he was allowing them to escape. He would say he wanted to torture them with the hope of escape only to take it away, painfully and succinctly. It was a natural part of the Kulusk training, and he knew he could convince his father he had done it. Plus he could manipulate the recordings so there would be no questions.

Then a loud crash caught his attention. It came from the back room where he left his family. Then Caroline's blood curdling scream pierced the silence and sent chills through his spine. He turned toward the back room but before he could take a step, he heard two shots. Now he ran to the door, kicked it opened and with his pagenay raised he rushed into the room.

His heart was pounding and the blood rushed to his head as he could feel the adrenaline feeding every fiber of his muscle. In his mind he thought he would find the girls had run toward the back and surprised his family in an effort to exact revenge. And if they did, he would not show any mercy. He would complete the job without remorse.

He raised the pagenay to eye level as he crouched in a firing position, ignoring the pain from his side that tried to grab his attention. He surveyed the room. Caroline stood by Ellen's bedside, with the revolver, he assumed the girls had confiscated from the original intruders. She pointed it toward the opened back door. Efas swung the pagenay toward the door. However, out of his peripheral vision he saw two figures lying on the floor. He rolled his pagenay toward the figures as he focused on them.

The figures were the original intruders, lying in a pool of blood; a mixture of theirs and members of his family, for the floor was starting to look like the floor of a slaughterhouse. Apparently, they regained consciousness and decided to raid the clinic, head injuries notwithstanding. However, they did not count on Caroline's maternal instincts turning against them. Caroline had had enough and when she saw the assailants returned, she had retrieved the gun from the table and fired two shots, hitting her mark with deadly precision. Efas imagined she must have moved with catlike reflexes in order to retrieve the gun and fire it so accurately.

Efas advanced over to the still figures and kicked them one by one. Then he fired pagenay shots into their faces, burning them beyond recognition. The air putrefied with the smell of burning flesh. It caused Caroline and Ellen to cough with sickness, but they did not complain. Efas then dragged the bodies into the next room and threw them to the floor.

A little more than three hours later, the Ritchen family was back on board the *TBC Sisen* and the Gentry Medical Clinic on 42$^{nd}$ Street in the Tenderloin district of New York City was aflame ... with two bodies, Efas hoped would be identified as he and his brother. Efas had entrapped his brother and wife in suspended animation to slow down the effects of their injuries until they reached Kulusk. He had decided it was time to go home.

# Chapter 18—The Escape

Caroline stood still, almost petrified, gazing upon the suspension tube that housed Jenny's lifeless body. She appeared dead and laid out for a memorial, perfectly still and not noticeably breathing. Tears streamed from both eyes as she played the episode, over and over, in her mind. With each replay, her anger grew, along with her guilt for not doing something earlier. She knew that if the black girls had not entered the scene, they would all be dead. She shook her head in disbelief, her family saved by niggas. The irony of the entire incident was more than her conscience could bear. She found herself questioning her values. The people she had come to hate so much, the people she blamed for the war that killed her husband, the people she blamed for her misfortune, now were responsible for the salvation of her entire family.

Efas interrupted her mental debate when he walked into the med lab. He came to check on his wife. He stood next to Caroline also mesmerized at the peaceful slumber Jenny appeared to be in.

"Did you kill them?" asked Caroline without diverting her gaze from her sleeping daughter.

The question caught Efas by surprise. He had not planned on speaking of the girls until he could alter the recordings from the scanmons, but here Caroline asked and he had to provide an answer. Or could he put it off? "What do you think?" he challenged.

Caroline was startled by the bravado in his voice. She cleared her throat with a soft grunt. "They saved our lives...no one asked them to...they didn't have to...but they saved our lives. So, I am asking you one last time, did you kill them?"

Efas turned his head toward his mother-in-law, his lips parted as he searched for the words. He wanted to tell her he had spared their lives, but he did not know where her heart was. He knew she despised blacks, and that she had a heart similar to his father's. Therefore, no matter the amount of compassion the girls showed in their efforts to save them, it was not enough to warrant their pardon from a death sentence decreed by the Maxum of Kulusk. He reminded himself, this secret he would have to take with him to the grave. Thus, Caroline had to believe, no matter how much it hurt, the girls were dead...executed by his hand.

He nodded, "Yes, they are gone." He rewarded himself for his choice of words. He did not lie; he just stated the truth in such a manner that allowed her to believe they were dead. He smiled with a wide grin, showing his teeth as he turned back to his sleeping wife.

Caroline, for the first time, mourned for blacks. The shock on her face at the coldness of his answer only aggravated her guilt. "You know Efas, I was once proud of your callous nature toward our common enemy. But now I am ashamed. I am ashamed of you and I am particularly ashamed of me."

The words pierced his heart like a dagger. He felt a sharp pain swallow his soul as his character screamed for redemption from the verbal assault. The words stuck in his throat as he tried to tell her, she was mistaken. His callous nature did not win over this time. He wanted to yell that he did allow the girls to live. His mind raced again and again, weighing the pros and cons of the situation.

Suddenly the ship's alarm buzzed. The loud cutting siren sound startled Caroline and she stepped back in fright. Efas, also startled, ran to the control keys next to the entry door.

"Report," he ordered.

The ship's ARIT voice, feminine, alluring but strong and commanding, rang over the intercom system. "Three Chaktun cruisers on long range scanners. Time to intercept...twenty galactic minutes."

"What...what is going on?" Caroline implored. However, as soon as the words left her mouth, she knew Efas did not hear her.

Efas' mind had already snatched him from the room and plunged him in a quagmire of reactions. Three enemy ships were sailing toward him. They must have already had him on their scanners. They must've known they were there. Should he stay and fight or should he run. He sized up his situation. He was practically alone on a Kulusk transport battle craft, large enough to house fifty warriors. It paled in comparison to a Chaktun star cruiser, fit for battle and housing a crew of approximately two hundred. Now there were three star cruisers bearing down on him.

"ARIT," he called. "Set a course back to Kulusk, use evasive maneuver Coronado-Three."

"Soli," the ARIT said.

However, Efas did not hear the voice report back. He was exiting the med lab, Kulusk training kicking into high gear, adrenaline flowing and fighting the fear that ached at his heart.

Caroline followed close behind, allowing her fear to grip her soul. Her breathing was labored and her eyes wide with anticipation—anticipation of the worse.

Only this morning she was so happy, stepping to New York in one of her last jaunts in her worldly travels. Just hours earlier, two opium addicts attacked her. In an effort to save her family, she ended up fatally shooting them. Now, her eldest daughter and son-in-law were unconscious in a glass tube, fighting for their lives. Her other daughter was laying in one of the rooms in shock. And she had a new grandchild struggling for its precious life after a stressful birth. Now there were Chaktun cruisers barreling down on them with guns blazing.

Several minutes later she was on a part of the ship she had never ventured. Efas called it the combat bridge. Until now, all she had witnessed were large corridors with brightly lit panels and viewports, which offered spectacular vistas of space and the planet Earth. Many times she stood breathless in front of one of those ports taking in the scene of the stars and the planet below imagining how God felt looking upon her planet. It made her ecstatic with euphoria to watch the deep blue oceans practically glow, washing onto the brown and grayish landscape of the earthly continents all covered with wispy puffs of clouds. Its beauty was utterly hypnotic; making her feel the most peaceful she had ever felt.

Now that peace was gone … erased by the inevitable danger of death, she stood behind her son-in-law, Efas, who was seated in a chair behind several consoles. To his left and right, the walls in the huge square room all contained monitors displaying symbols, lines, maps and charts. It was all so confusing to her. Yet the main view screen in front of her was not confusing, it was frightening.

Efas had asked for maximum magnification and the ARIT complied. In front of Caroline, displayed on the view screen were three enormous spacecrafts. The fronts of the crafts were shaped like arrowheads, slicing through the thick darkness of space. The arrowheads narrowed into a shaft, which widened again, revealing long barreled rods, she assumed were some type of weapon. Then the rest of the ship, behind the weapons grew in all directions in perfect symmetry. She knew one ship was several times larger than the *TBC Sisen*, and there were three of them. She gasped for air. However, fright had taken control of her autonomic systems and she began to hyperventilate.

Efas had no time to attend to her. He touched his control panels with each hand like a concert pianist and the ship lurched backward, spun around and sped off at maximum speed. Caroline stumbled as the artificial gravity tugged at her. She felt the sensation of the ship moving backward, spinning and then accelerating. The sensation lasted a split second as the artificial gravity compensated for the disturbance. In that split second, Caroline's hyperventilation ceased, but her panic continued to attack her body in other ways. She lost strength in her knees as they buckled under her. She grabbed onto the back of Efas' chair for support. However it only slowed her fall. She lowered herself to the floor. Again Efas ignored her. Now she felt alone, she closed her eyes and began praying. Yet in the back of her mind, she felt some relief that if she should die, at least it was in the stars she had admired all her life from Earth.

The ship was soon rocked by a pagenay blast as one of the three Chaktun ships pursued them. The other two ships slowed and entered orbit around Earth.

"Direct hit to stern starboard quarter engine plate. Chromerion field holding at ninety-five percent," the female voice of the ship's ARIT relayed as if ordering dinner.

"Reroute life support from unoccupied decks to increase field strength in aft quarters," Efas commanded.

Efas' display indicated the ARIT complied as he instructed. Efas again ran his nimble fingers along the smoky glass console, pressing and activating commands the ship instantly executed. A second blast rocked the ship again and another and another, in rapid succession.

"Direct hits on stern starboard quarter engine plate. Field is holding at sixty percent," the ARIT stated.

"They must have deciphered the Coronado-three maneuver," Efas thought aloud. "Change maneuver stratagem to Claymore four-three. Divert engineering power to the stern quarters," he ordered. His one strategy now was to outrun his pursuers, not outgun them. His ship was smaller and able to maneuver quicker than the Chaktun ship, so he thought. What he did not know was in the several years they have been away; the Chaktuns had replaced their ships calogenic engines with gravogenic engines, giving them speeds up to and exceeding thirty light years per hour. *TBC Sisen*'s calogenic engines maximum speed could only carry her at hyperlight speed, a third of what light could travel in a year per hour.

The Chaktun ship gained on the *TBC Sisen* to Efas' surprise. He checked his engines, their output, and their efficiency quota. All checked good, but he was still bewildered at how quickly the Chaktun ship was gaining. Efas ordered the ARIT to cease all maneuver stratagems and race straight ahead. He figured he was wasting precious time and space, losing his advantage by continuing the maneuver stratagem. His sole hope was to reach the outer rim of the solar system where his scanners recorded approximately a trillion comets, in what would later be discovered by Jan Oort in 1950 as the Oort Cloud.

Efas hoped he could use the cloud debris for cover to hide from the Chaktun star cruiser. He would cut his power and hug as much as possible to a comet in order to disguise his ships scanner signature. This was a risky venture, but he did not know of any other option.

He took the automatic pilot offline and steered manually from his console. He did not slow his approach to the cloud. He knew he had to keep top speed when he penetrated the cloud or the Chaktun ship would either catch him or track him throughout his maneuver. Sweat poured from his body as if he were in a sauna as he studied the display for the right angle and the right moment, but specifically the right comet to dive near and cut power. He had to do it precisely and accurately, in order to let his forward momentum carry him to the proper spot with no power and with minimum time. Then he planned on using grappling arms to catch the comet to slow and eventually stop his movement.

However, he did not see what he was looking for. His scanners went red as they became overwhelmed with the number of comets. He turned his scanners off because they no longer aided his manual navigation, and now became a hindrance. He kept cross checking between the main viewer and the monitor at his console. Doubts started nagging at him. The plan seemed so well thought out, but it seemed now he would not be able to execute it. Then doubt gave way to fright, which soon gave way to panic. He pounded the arm to his leather bound chair with his fist. Frustration clouded his mind as terror clutched his heart. He screamed with angst as he hit the chair again. His monitor calculated three seconds until penetration. His Kulusk training overpowered his fear as his fingers danced on the console once more.

First he ejected a nova flare, which spewed a blinding light equal to one tenth of the sun, hoping to blind and confuse the Chaktun's ship sensors, scanners and visual contacts. Then he pumped out several decoys to saturate the sensors and scanners, giving him precious seconds before they reacquired his signature. Next he deployed a full load of space mines, a complement of forty-five, ten-foot wide floating spheres packing two hundred megatons of nuclear explosive power, giving the Chaktun ship something else to worry about other than following him—their own survival. When the nova flares exploded, he put the ship into a thirty-five degree angle dive towards a path he saw at the last moment.

The ship turned sideways and down and cleared two comets, the size of small mountains. Then he veered right to miss smaller comets flying right at him. Tiny comets pelted the ship's hull as he concentrated on missing the bigger ones. The ship echoed with knocking sounds, reminding Caroline, who had now rolled into a fetal position on the floor behind Efas, of hail bombarding the roof of a house. The sounds became louder and louder, now putting in Caroline's mind, a large creature pounding the hull with its fists.

"Hull breach, sector eight, deck four," the ARIT voice relayed.

127

Efas took note of the information, but his entire concentration was on finding a suitable hiding place. However, he took a split second of his concentration to check on his pursuer. His eyes registered no contact with the Chaktun ship. He took a slight sigh of relief as he imagined the Chaktun ship ceased in the chase and didn't want to follow him through the cloud. *"Great!"* At least part of his plan was working. "Maybe I don't have to find a large comet to hide behind," he taunted himself. He was exhausted. He did not know how much longer he could fly at maximum speed in the cloud. He was maneuvering, jinking and jagging through a potential minefield of destruction.

Without thought, he pushed his hands forward and dropped his power. The ship jolted, then began the deceleration process. Efas still used his thrusters to maneuver around the comets, but the ship was sluggish. He knew the laws of physics would soon apply to him negatively and decided to apply *'All Stop'* procedures. The ship came to a rest, settled between a large egg shape comet to the right and a mushroom shape comet in front. Efas deployed the grappling hook, snagged the comet in front, and pulled the ship in tighter to the larger comet. Then he ordered the ARIT to cut all power except life support. Before the console shutdown, Efas recorded several explosions outside the cloud. Efas wondered if his space mines had found their mark. Then the bridge went dark.

The sudden loss of light caused Caroline to scream. Efas grabbed an ARIT hypodermic from the med kit in his chair's side pouch and without hesitation, turned and punched the machine into Caroline's arm. Sleep rendered her comatose in mid scream as she sank back to the floor. Efas sank next to her and took a cleansing breath as he prayed, to no deity in particular, for guidance.

***

Caroline woke up in med lab as the glass cover retracted from her animated suspension bed. She looked up and saw Efas' face smiling at her. She tried to talk, but the words cracked in her dry voice. Her head pounded with pain common to dehydration.

"Easy, there, Mrs. Pathgo," Efas warned. "You've been out for about three weeks now."

"What?" she moaned.

"Yeah, I put you in here so you wouldn't be scared. We stayed in that comet cloud until yesterday...in total darkness. I figured the Chaktuns would have given up on us by now, so I took a chance and we left the cloud. We are on our way to Kulusk."

"What about Ellen and the baby?" she asked with more strength.

"They are in animation. It was the best thing I could do," he said. "She was hysterical and with all she went through, I thought it was the best thing to do. Now we need to get the baby up, and eventually Ellen as well. We have a long trip ahead of us."

After several minutes, Caroline gained her bearings. Efas gave her a clear fluid she assumed was water. It was sweet, but it hit the spot as she felt her headache fade. She rose out of bed and walked over to the other beds. She shook her head in despair as she examined her entire family behind glass tubes laying in suspended animation. It looked so horrific, a tear formed in her eye. "What have I done? This is crazy," she chastised. "First of all, I'm too old for this. And second of all, I have put my family at risk. And for what?" she asked glowering at Efas.

Efas shrugged his shoulders and walked over to the baby's tube. He pushed some buttons on the console and the tube retracted as the glass split in the middle lengthwise and slid into the sides of the bed. Caroline helped Efas remove the baby from the animated suspension bed. He cried. The experience and the dehydration only aided to the baby's deteriorating condition. He needed nourishment and he needed it quickly. Caroline went to the food dispenser, gathered some formula in a bottle, and fed the baby. It was the first time she really held or fed him. Her maternal instincts flooded throughout her like a waterfall as she looked into her grandson's face while she fed him.

"It was worth it," she smiled. "It was worth all of it, just for this moment...Just for the opportunity to hold and feed my grandchild." She looked up at Efas, "Thank you Efas."

Efas simply nodded as he finally felt pride in his Kulusk training that had come through for him. He handled the situation like a warrior. For once his soul was at peace and his spirit was happy.

# Chapter 19—The Return Home

Fifteen galactic months later, Caroline, Ellen and Ellen's son, Erif II, stood on the combat bridge in awe of what they were seeing through the view screen. The *TBC Sisen* was starting its orbit around Kulusk. Efas was busy coordinating the medical retrieval of his wife and brother. In the main viewer, they saw the planet of Kulusk enter their view.

It was two thirds larger than Earth with several island continents scattered throughout its oceans. A red sun giving it a mystic fiery glow illuminated it. The largest continent was shaped like a 'Y' and occupied the northern hemisphere. The second largest continent was a large mass, almost rectangular in shape and it occupied the furthest southern portion of the planet, covering the southern pole. The most peculiar aspect of the planet was the skinny stretch of land that ran along the equator of the planet. It encircled the planet, from East to West like a belt. No one could travel between the south and the north portions of the planet without crossing this strip of land. It was jagged and not uniform, sometimes stretching over a thousand miles at its largest point, to fifty miles in width at its narrowest point. Caroline had never seen anything quite like it before. Like Earth, Kulusk was mainly water. However, the water did not reflect a sharp blue like Earth did from space. Kulusk's water reflected a brilliant aqua green, with pink clouds dotting the atmosphere.

*Breathtaking* was the only word Caroline could think of to describe it. It was more beautiful than Earth to her. Then it struck her. She would not ever see Earth again. She felt like the immigrants she had chastised on Earth for coming to America. Now she was the immigrant traveling to the New World. Again, the irony of her situation floored her sensibility and her conscience of right and wrong. *Isn't that what the European immigrants called the United States—the New World?*

Then the words rang out over the intercom. "The maxum is in a med lab in the capital...he is dying."

Fifteen minutes later the ship was buzzing with life. Caroline watched as the med staff released the chambers holding Jennifer and Erif from the bed frame in the med lab. A doctor, she presumed, was leading the six-man crew. Three members surrounded her daughter and three members surrounded Erif. They placed a cylindrical bar over the chamber and a ray of bluish light shone onto the chambers. Then the chambers lifted into mid air, suspended by the force within the bluish light. One of the members held a control pad that somehow manipulated the chamber bar combination. The chambers floated off the bed and into the corridor.

Several minutes later, the chambers had floated to the gate portal room, onto the platform and through the white light. Several seconds later, Efas tugged at her arm and tilted his head toward the platform. Ellen and her son were behind him. She knew it was their turn to travel the white light onto the planet, her new planet—Kulusk.

She had not experienced the white light of stepping since she left Earth, fifteen galactic months ago, which equated to almost two earth years. She remembered her first time; she was both scared and excited at the same time. Now she was just scared—no, more like apprehensive. She was tentative about the entire episode, but she also knew her place was next to her daughter. So with a deep breath she stepped onto the platform, closed her eyes and waited for the white light to envelope her. The event was unnerving. She had forgotten how lightheaded stepping made her.

When regular light dawned, she filed into it. She felt faint as she lost her sturdiness. Efas tugged on her arm, giving her support. She looked up at him, but she found it hard to focus. Efas grabbed her with both hands to steady her. Her weight started to sway Efas off balance as well. He swung her around and placed her onto a soft cushioned chair.

Efas looked around and saw a sentry in the corridor. "Get a med tech to look after her," he ordered. Then he swung to his left to see his sister-in-law and nephew looking over his shoulder in concern. "She will be alright, but we must go. I'll take you to Erif. I need to see my father."

Ellen nodded in agreement and they paraded down the corridor. After several turns and one quick coaster lift shooting them several hundred yards in one direction and several floors up, Ellen stood outside the room where a team of med professionals was feverishly working on her husband. She waited outside clutching her son and praying for the life of the man she loved. It was so much easier to see him in the suspension chamber, knowing he was asleep, but alive. Now he could die, and she had not prepared herself or her son for that possible eventuality. Tears streamed from her eyes like a faucet.

"What's wrong mommy?" asked little Erif.

His sweet little voice abruptly broke through the dark cloud she was painting in her mind. She careened her head back to look into his eyes. She saw his father in his face. She saw the father who little Erif never knew ... a father who little Erif only saw through HVPs and through the frost of a suspended animation chamber. She wondered if little Erif understood. Did he understand his father was fighting for his life all this time? Did he understand he was in the final throws of that fight right now in the other room?

Little Erif had one man in his life, his uncle. Could he adjust to his real father once he was well? That's right, she had to think positively, she had to think—no she had to believe her husband would get well. Erif did not come all this way just to die. He can't die before he sets his eyes on his beautiful namesake. No, she would not allow it. He had to live.

On another floor, Efas was in his father's room. Efas hardly recognized his father. Nom Ritchen, the Maxum of the Kulusk Empire, had several clear tubes feeding him intravenously through his right arm. He also had tubes running in his chest, mouth and nose. His eyes were drawn and his skin was chalky white. Efas had never seen the medical community do this to a patient. Usually they would put a patient in a life support chamber and use MARIT technology to provide oxygen and other stimuli. Somehow, this procedure seemed barbaric and archaic. He yelled for the doctor.

Doctor Iaoh Beldigih raced into the maxum's room. Efas could tell the doctor had something to say so he allowed him to speak first before he would question him on his unorthodox method of treatment.

"Your essence," Beldigih began.

Efas had not heard that term since he left Kulusk. It was a term of respect used to address the maxum's family. It felt wonderful to receive the respect he sorely lacked in the past years on Earth. The words cut away at his seething fury, but his anger was still present. Thus Efas nodded and tilted his head toward his father's med bed.

"I am so happy you are here. The empire thought you and your brother dead."

"Well as you can see I am not dead and as for my brother...you better hope he survives. However, if the treatment of my father is any indication of your competence..."

Beldigih lifted his hands gesturing he knew and understood Efas' worries. "The prime minister is responsible," he interrupted. "Prime Minister Relurah ordered no ARIT technology be used on your father."

"What...why?" bellowed Efas as he turned to his father.

"In you and your brother's absence, and with your father being incapacitated with a stroke, Prime Minister Relurah is the acting Maxum. My guess is he thought you dead as well and is hoping for your father's death by natural causes, so he can justify his assumption of the maxum throne."

"How long?" asked Efas, still in shock by what he heard.

"Two months," Beldigih replied. "I am surprised he lasted this long on this crude life support apparatus. I am sure Prime Minister Relurah is surprised as well." Beldigih took this opportunity to get into the emotional Efas' face. He stared him in the eye. "We don't have time for anymore questions. Your father lasted this long, but I don't know how much longer he can live without MARITs. All I need is a living, competent heir to say the word and—"

"Well I am not dead, and I am an heir to the Maxum throne. Therefore I order all technology, including MARIT technology to be used in saving my father's life."

Beldigih went to the control panel next to the door and pushed against the smoky plate controls several times. "I thought you would say that. That is why I took the liberty of cross matching and programming the MARIT attachments to use. Your father will be revived...oh let's say in about two galactic hours."

"Are you sure?" Efas asked, eying the doctor. Efas did not know if he should trust Beldigih, because he had just one side of the story. Although for whatever reason, his father was barely alive where he should be up and about. A simple stroke was controllable by MARIT stimuli. Of course the recuperation would be a long and agonizing process, but the hope of total recovery was almost assured at ninety-nine percent.

Beldigih did not have a chance to answer Efas, for the door slid open and a five-man team of med techs rushed in. They crowded around Nom like a swarm of bees and applied several devices, simultaneously removing the tubes from his body. They attached a helmet MARIT to stimulate Nom's brain, a chest MARIT to regulate his breathing and heart rate, and a MARIT to his forehead to facilitate communications when he awoke from his nightmare.

"Yes, I am sure," Beldigih said with a reassuring smile. "Oh by the way, the young lady you brought in with your brother."

"Yes." Efas was preparing for bad news. He wasn't a med professional, but he knew his wife's wounds were very serious. And he did not know if putting her in suspended animation helped or hindered her situation. "She's my wife," he added.

"Oh!" Beldigih was shocked. He lost his thought for a split second as he digested the words. The patient was royalty and required the best care. He turned to the control pad and entered several notations. One being the patient in operating room eighteen was a member of the Ritchen house.

"Well her injuries and your brother's injuries are very extensive. I just wanted to tell you that putting them both in suspension might have saved their lives. I hear from the ARIT that there is an eighty percent chance of survival for them both. I just thought you should know."

Beldigih moved to the med bed to check on the progress of the technicians. He smiled as he tested each MARIT. Then he looked back at Efas with a twinkle in his eye. "I think you returned just in time. Another day or so, these MARITs would have been useless. As it is, he will have a more difficult time in recovering. Plus his age complicates matters somewhat. However, he is strong and I think he will do just fine."

Efas nodded in appreciation. The words somehow made Efas trust Beldigih; although, Beldigih's actions alone merited his trust.

"Oh by the way, your essence, the planet's command center kept your arrival a secret, as instructed by your father. They only informed us, because of your father's condition."

"You mean no one knows we are back," Efas wondered aloud, contemplating his next move.

"No one, your essence...not even the Tonja. It was fortuitous that you arrived today. The Tonja, is in session right now, being lead by none other than Prime Minister Relurah."

Efas caught the hidden message in Beldigih's words. Relurah thought himself the acting Maxum. He was wrong. Efas was back, which made him the acting Maxum by default. This gave him absolute rule with impunity. Efas understood Beldigih's words to be a challenge. Beldigih was expecting a maxum type action to avenge his father's situation. And in that split second, Efas knew what he had to do. He nodded, acknowledging his acceptance of Beldigih's challenge.

On the ninth floor, the alert that Beldigih posted, flashed in Jenny's operating room. The attending physician, Doctor Jelin Tami, read the message. Upon reading the message she had renewed vigor, like her life depended on saving this woman, because her life did depend on it. Tami needed to ensure there were no side effects from the injury or her operation. She was operating on the future Maxim of Kulusk.

***

The Tonja, the advisory body to the Maxum, consisted of representatives from different continental islands on the planet. The capital city of Renard was on the main strip that stretched the entire planet's circumference. The two hundred and ten manned Tonja was in session in the Capitol building next to the Maxum's palace, Greenhaven.

The Tonja Hall contained several tiers of square tables. Three aisles separated the tables and at the top of the aisles were entry doors. At the bottom of the aisles and the center of the room stood a stage housing the Maxum's throne and the Prime Minister's Table. The room was old and modern combined. The chairs were of light colored wood with plush red, green, blue and gold cushions. The tables were of high-grade metal, made to look like wood to match the chairs. Upon the tables were ARIT consoles, monitors and communication devices. The flooring was a mixture of marble, wood and carpeting—again made of the same colors, red, green, blue and gold.

The gigantic hall was filled with the normal cacophony associated with lively debate, amplified by the towering domed ceiling hovering above the room. However, this session was beamed to all the inhabitants through video pictures—VP. The session was to formally announce the prime minister as Maxum, thus it needed the approval of all the Tonja and needed to be publicized for public record.

Relurah stood at the Prime Minister's table as he surveyed the hall. His commanding smile and grayish hair gave him the appearance of a strong leader, someone worthy of the throne. His chiseled chin and hapless dimples combined with his fiery green eyes also commanded respect. These are the qualities that allowed him to be elected out of the two hundred and ten body assembly to the position of Prime Minister, the maxum's right hand person in charge of domestic policy, but now he wanted it all. The maxum's unfortunate stroke, coupled with the five-year absence of his heirs, made this the most opportune time to grab for power. Plus, with the support of the Tonja, he was assured victory. Then he looked up and his smirk vanished from his face.

At the center doorway, Efas stood in his full general's attire and weaponry. Behind him was a complement of soldiers. He scanned the other exits, and saw that white shirted soldiers also blocked them. His heart pounded as he saw victory slip from his grasp. He shifted to the communications device and pressed the button. He called the assembly to order, several minutes ahead of schedule. Relurah recognized the confused expression on his fellow representatives' faces, but he had no time to address that now.

"Ladies and Gentlemen," he started. His voice was shaky and uncertain. "I present to you General Efas Ritchen, the heir to the throne of the Kulusk Empire."

Efas walked down the stairs of the aisle and stepped up to the platform. He looked Relurah in the eye. This look told Relurah, that Efas knew. Efas knew he had tried to kill his father and make it look like complications from the stroke—natural causes. Efas pushed Relurah aside taking control of the communications ARIT. He spoke in a low, soft but firm tone to the hall and to the public through the VP.

"People of the Empire...this is Prince Efas Ritchen...I am back. My brother is back. We have been away a long time, but it was important for the Empire. Unfortunately what we find upon our return is treason, treason by the Prime Minister and treason by the Tonja. The penalty is death for such a serious crime. And I am here to carry it out."

Without hesitation and in a blink of an eye, Efas withdrew his thigh-holstered pagenay and shot Relurah in the head. "As I said, the penalty is death. And I find the Tonja was a willing accomplice to the treason. Therefore, I order the Tonja members be put to death." He holstered his weapon as he watched his soldiers summarily execute the Tonja members. The executions were broadcast throughout the Empire and shocked many viewers. "I order their families meet the same fate. I want them arrested and executed by dawn."

Efas regretted he said those last words as soon as he said them. He was caught up by the moment. His anger had ruled his tongue and since his words were broadcasted on VP he had no route to rescind them. He would lose face if he did. He had to let his last command stand. He bit his lower lip as he tried to think of a way to countermand the last order without appearing weak. Maybe he could change the orders to just arrested, he thought. But inside, he knew even that would be a sign of weakness, and he could not afford to look weak. He had to be strong. He had to show his father he was worthy to be the heir. This last act would solidify his hold on the throne and disavow any words his brother would have on the matter.

Efas stopped biting his lip and sank into the throne as he watched the unbelievable carnage take place before him. Now the transformation was complete. He was as ruthless and conniving as any Maxum before him—even his father. His brother did not have a chance to steal the throne from him now.

# Chapter 20—Exile

It was their four-year anniversary. Jenny Ritchen and Caroline Pathgo were busy planning the celebration ball to be held later that night. The room was large and able to accommodate several hundred guests. It had a large floor, similar to marble for dancing, a large concert stage and several areas for dinning. Jenny was planning for political, military and social elite who she did not know, with food she was unfamiliar with and protocol she was unaware of. In the two years she had lived on Kulusk, she had not ventured outside Greenhaven walls. And now all of Kulusk seemed to be venturing inside to see her. However Jenny's mind was not into the planning. She was overcome with the doom of failure. She knew it and accepted it. She sat at the ballroom table staring into the floral crystal chandelier above her head … thinking.

Jenny had lost track of earthly accountability of time and concentrated on her adopted planet's way of accounting for time. The days were longer, making the months longer and eventually the years longer. However, her body as well as her sister's and her mother's adapted well to the new chronology, but it was still longer. Therefore since the years were longer on this planet she calculated she was closer to four and a half years of marriage.

Yet, she lost most of that time in animated suspension when they came to this planet. She spent close to twenty months in space travel, fifteen galactic months, which was almost equal to the Kulusk calendar. Then she spent several months in recovery while her husband did a world wind tour, solidifying his rightful claim as the next heir to the Maxum throne. Ellen and Erif II were touring the planet with Efas, giving the impression of a strong family and the continuation of the Maxum line.

She did not like it; she did not like it at all. She was suspicious of her sister's relationship with her husband. Both she and Erif were asleep during the travel time to Kulusk. And she wondered how close Ellen and her husband became during that time. Then while both she and Erif completed a long recovery period in the hospital, Ellen and Efas along with little Erif gallivanted around Kulusk. She watched the VP from her med bed, anguished by the knowledge she was not with him and jealous of the fact Ellen was.

It didn't help that Erif expressed his suspicions with her on a daily basis while they were in the hospital. Jenny denied the possibility, but she did not convince Erif or herself either. Their spouses acted like they did not exist during that time. Yes, they communicated on a daily basis. Yes, they visited twice a week, but the calls and the visits became less and less in duration. This only fueled her suspicions, and it amplified Erif's suspicions. Several times he was livid, but she knew it wasn't just about that. There was something else that infuriated him.

As if by mental telepathy, Erif strode in displaying his usual hardened face of despair. Jenny nodded, acknowledging his presence. He saw her across the long table and headed toward her with purpose.

"Jenny," he announced, changing his volume so his voice would not echo against the large stone walls of the hall. "My father has granted…you, Efas, Ellen and me, a night on his private sky palace as an anniversary present." He pulled up a chair to study her face to see how she accepted the news. He had worked for several weeks convincing his father of this special gift and wanted to see the surprise on her face.

"His sky palace?" she asked in confusion.

"The sky palace," he reiterated. "It is his private getaway. I haven't been on it since my mother died. It is a palace on gravitational stabilizers; it floats about thirty five thousand feet above the southern ocean. It is beautiful. It has a garden, a skywalk. It is romantic. I know we can capture the magic we had with our spouses once we get there. We leave right after the ball. I am telling you, this is great. It is exactly what we need for our marriages."

"Do you think?" she cautioned. She didn't want to build false hope, but she knew she and Efas needed something to rekindle their marriage. Maybe this is what it was. She needed to get Efas away from the public, away from the politics and away from his father, even if it was just for one night. It would be worth it.

"Yes, I do think it will work," Erif declared, adding a smile for emphasis.

It was the first time she had seen him smile since they left Earth. It warmed her heart and sprang hope in her soul. For the first time, she was looking forward to tonight. She was excited, reinvigorated and ready to take on the dreary details of planning the celebration. She smiled and nodded acceptance. She abruptly stood. "You take care of that, and I will take care of this. Please get your wife out of bed and get her to help me," she demanded with fire.

Erif nodded and scurried out of the room as instructed to get his wife to help plan the festivities. On his way up the stairs and toward his room he rang with a vulgar laugh. His heart was hardened with jealousy and he had other plans for tonight. Plans he had set into motion several months earlier. Before he left Earth, he thought he would make a better leader than his brother, and he would eventually become the undisputed heir to the Maxum throne. However since then, his brother had demonstrated impeccable leadership and a tenacious ability to be brutal.

Efas had won his father's favor by single-handedly destroying the offspring of the Osguards on Earth, as demonstrated in a HVP and evidenced by the scanmons recording. Then what finally won Nom's favor was Efas ruthless elimination of the Prime Minister, the Tonja and their families. Efas' newfound cold-blooded leadership ability had even surprised Erif. Erif did not know what he was more jealous of, his suspicions about Efas and his wife or the fact Efas was assured the throne. Erif thought he had lost it all, because he was shot and put into suspended animation. He had no chance to demonstrate his leadership to his father and that made him angry. He blamed Efas for his misfortune. Now tonight he wanted revenge and for the first time in ages, his soul was elated.

Erif topped the long spiral marble stairs with shiny organic metal framing the railing. He turned right toward his bedroom and sauntered through the corridor decorated with life-sized paintings of the former Maxums. He hoped his portrait would soon grace the walls. He had even picked a spot. It would take some decorative adjustment, but the spot would be well suited to bestow on him the patronage he felt was due.

The ostentatious thirty-pound door split in the usual Kulusk 'Z' down the middle and the halves slid into the doorframes with a loud whoosh. Ellen looked up from her vanity where she had just finished applying the last of her make-up. Her smile seemed to light the room, for a split second Erif's temper subsided and he felt the original pangs of love that drew him to her almost four years ago. He searched her eyes and found the warmth he once basked in so many years ago.

Ellen's expression changed from a welcome smile to bewilderment. "What? What is it?"

Erif continued to stare at his blushing wife. Her words melted in the air and touched him like a whisper, barely noticeable. His eyes saw, his ears heard, but his mind traveled back to Earth on the edges of a small lake in Virginia, enjoying his first picnic and kiss with Ellen.

"What?" she repeated. Her confusion began to melt to fright as her voice rose.

The sound of her question woke him from his daydreaming and he realized he was now scaring her.

"Nothing...nothing at all. I just wanted to let you know we will be spending our anniversary night in the sky palace. Well...we will be sharing it with my brother and Jenny. Plus, it is big enough for all of us and we won't see, hear or bother each other."

Ellen's smile grew wider as she fantasized about the evening. She rushed up and hugged him. Her warm body pressed firmly against his, awakening primordial urges he thought were long gone. Something about the moment brought back the magic he had not felt since Earth. All the arguments soon evaporated from his mind as he wrapped his arms around his wife. She had not felt this good to him for a while now and somehow it excited him. He gently kissed the nape of her neck

He pulled back, looked up at the ceiling and exhaled. "Your sister is waiting for you down in the ballroom. She needs your help."

Ellen reached up and pulled Erif's face closer to hers, touching lips. "Let her wait. I have an early present for you." Then she kissed him with the passion and intensity of an exotic woman on the prowl. And he kissed her back. The wrought emotion of lust filled his manhood as his heart fought against the resurging love he had once felt for her. Even though the two feelings were mutually compatible for a married man to have about his wife, Erif felt it a weakness.

Ellen felt the hesitation in his kiss, a hesitation she had feared for too many years, and a hesitation she vowed to eliminate today. She pressed her lips harder against his, slipping her tongue into his mouth and letting it dance with his. The exhilaration of the kiss excited her. And she could tell it excited Erif, as she felt his hips dig into her body with total abandon. She knew she had to feed the want…she needed to feed the want. Her body was as hungry for lust as she knew his was.

She stepped back from the kiss and shot him a smile full of seduction and mischief. She pulled the wrap holding her orange silk like robe on and let it unfurl, exposing her body to her husband like a prize. She shrugged at the shoulders allowing the robe to slip from her body to her feet. She stepped out of the robe and began to caress her breast and stomach.

Erif looked on like a child in a candy store. His brain had ceased to function and his body was taking orders from thousands of years of male instinct. His blood boiled and his body racked with sexual fever. His eyes focused on her hands as they rubbed her milky white skin. Her nipples were erect and beaconing him to attack. Suddenly he lunged at her, grabbed her, and for a split second he gazed into her deep blue eyes. Then he buried his head into her breast, suckling on her like a newborn.

Soon his passion overheated and he pushed her onto the bed. He quickly stripped, never taking his eyes off of her. Her body was so perfect. Ellen had maintained her warrior's physique and her femininity at the same time, making her the most sought after sexual creature in his mind. Her body was the object of his desire, but also the object of his jealousy.

He climbed on top of her and lay between her thighs. With a mighty push he entered her. The feeling drove him insane. It had been quite some time since he had touched Ellen. Every time he wanted to touch her…every time he wanted to make love to Ellen he would imagine her with his brother, making love in his bed…in the garden…or even on the throne. Jealousy consumed him and held him from showing any passion toward her.

However now, jealousy was nowhere to be found. The craze he had held in check for so long had found a release. He plunged his manhood deeper, faster and harder in her. With each movement he felt as if he was beating her, but her exclamations told a different story. She moaned with delight...she screamed with ecstasy. She had never responded to him like this...it was confusing, but it also was alluring. He liked it. In fact, he loved it. In the past, he made love to her as gently as the wind, but today he was as wild as a tornado, and Ellen loved it. And he loved it as well.

Sweat engulfed them as the animal instinct of mating raged in their souls. They moved in random unison, arching, clawing, squeezing, biting and kissing like young lovers. And when the feeling became too intense, too hot, too much to handle, they both gave in to the rapture and released their love onto one another with such explosive power they both roared with the ferocity of lions.

With the blood rush gone, Erif rolled over onto his back and stared at the ceiling, wondering what had just happened. He looked over at Ellen, who was glowing. He saw the woman he fell in love with. For a split second the pangs of that love rushed into his mind causing him to feel remorseful. However, as quick as the remorse rushed in, it had rushed out again. He sighed as he lifted up.

Ellen saw this and grabbed his shoulder and pulled him back down. Erif didn't resist. He didn't want to. She began to massage his chest as she moved closer to him; she draped her leg over his waist and rubbed her foot against his legs. Erif responded in kind. He began massaging her soft but firm breast. Her nipples were still erect and she had the same sensuous look on her face, coupled with the hungry smile of lust.

Then she moved her hand south and began massaging him to readiness. Her fingers felt like little spikes of electricity, pumping life to his spent manhood. With every stroke he gulped with elation—sucking in the air and blowing it out with a whimper. He felt the flood of lust energize his entire body. Before he knew it, Ellen was the aggressor. She straddled Erif and pointed him to her pleasure. She moved like a wildcat. Erif had lost control of the moment, but he did not mind. He grabbed Ellen's hips and guided the wildcat on her journey. Again, the two gave into their animal instincts and moved in pandemonium. For those few moments, their souls touched and became one...their hearts beat as one and their minds melded on one thought—each other. The universe was at peace, the world was right and heaven was that room, that bed, that moment...To Erif, heaven was Ellen...no, heaven was Ellen's body, and he was in heaven. Soon, his eyes rolled back and her head rolled back, only to be followed by the lions yell once again.

Then it was over...it was gone...no more universal peace, no more right world...and no more heaven. He looked up at the sweating flesh straddling him and he saw Ellen. Not Ellen of Earth...not Ellen from the pond...not even Ellen from his wedding. He just saw Ellen, the woman he had lost interest in, or whom he had thought lost interest in him. Or was that true anymore? Confusion again entered his once orderly mind. This time, he couldn't shake it.

He smiled at her, "That was great...more than great...it was wonderful. What got into you?"

Ellen shook her head, allowing her blonde hair to flow from side to side, and then she gazed into Erif's eyes for a long second. "I love you," she whispered.

Erif gulped at the words. He didn't know how to respond. He just looked at her, wondering if he was still in love with her. At the moment he didn't know. Confusion still clouded his mind. Then he saw the worried look capturing Ellen's face. "I love you too," he responded, more to appease the situation than to explore his true feelings. "I love you too," he repeated. Then they sealed their declaration of love with a kiss.

Ellen did not join her sister for another ninety minutes.

***

The ballroom was alive with music from instruments and songs Ellen had never heard before. It was a mixture of opera and classical music with a little bit of folk song beat thrown in. She imagined she was back in Virginia, attending a large southern gala, but it was hard. Her attire was different from what she was accustomed. Her blue gown was tight and hugged her body, leaving nothing to the imagination. It also hung from the shoulders and dared to venture down her cleavage lower than any Southern lady would allow. However, she was on a different planet, with different customs. Besides, the dress somehow freed her soul and let loose a wildcat in her she never knew existed. She was now uninhibited and she liked it. She also liked the attention she was receiving from the elite gentlemen attending the ceremony.

She had a vivacious shape and she knew it. Now she could exhibit the shape in the boundaries of the blue dress and it was all perfectly tasteful. The clothing she wore on Earth always hid her body, disfigured it to the point that no one, not even she, knew the true shape of her body. However, on Kulusk, she had become enamored with the different clothing choices. They were very progressive, almost sinful, but intoxicating and with the opportunity of self-expression.

However, the night belonged to her and her husband. She would not dishonor the moment by flirting or self-absorption. The past four years were not as perfect as she would have liked. She understood she had some culpability in the disorder of the marriage. She knew her husband was jealous of Efas, and her initial travels with him did not ease that disturbance. However, she was caught up in the moment, a new planet, an adoring public—all the things a woman wanted to validate her self-worth. Efas gave it to her and she drank it up like the nectar of the gods. She had paid for it for the last two years...painfully paid for it. Only today was she able to break

141

through to Erif and act as a married couple once more. She felt she was on the road to recovery. She broadcasted her newfound happiness through her dazzling smile that she beamed at all who came, especially her husband, Erif in his white formal uniform.

He had attained the rank of general, just like Efas. Now Efas only had time over his brother, but they were both equal in rank and responsibility. Erif controlled sectors E through H of the Empire, some twenty worlds. Efas controlled sectors A through D, approximately twenty-five worlds. Both halves were equal in importance, economics and political strength. Both answered to the Maxum. Yet, this did not satisfy Erif's jealousy. Ellen did not know what could, but for tonight, she did not care. All she knew was she had her husband back. She was content with that.

She strutted toward him and latched onto his arm like a vise. She peered into his eyes, blanking out her surroundings, both sight and sound. She reached up to his face to draw him closer and planted a sweet, but passionate kiss on his right cheek, a reminder of the love they shared earlier in the day.

Erif smiled as a tingle tickled his heart reminding him once more of the woman he fell in love with on Earth a few short years ago. He turned toward her and hugged her, holding her deep within his bosom.

On the other side of the ballroom, through a sea of brightly dressed people who seemed to engulf the floor, Ellen saw her sister Jenny and her husband Efas. They as well looked like they were enjoying the night. Jenny wore a red dress with the same daring cut, but different in design. The dress revealed Jenny's entire back and it draped from under the arms. It flared at the ankle and had a nice black wrap that hung loosely around her waist.

She also was beside her husband like a shadow. Several members of the Eslar, the political body representing the worlds under Kulusk rule, surrounded them. Obviously, the members of the Eslar were courting the next Maxum and Maxim, but that did not bother Ellen. She was acutely aware of her position as Erif's wife, and she was satisfied to play that role.

The present Maxum, Nom, was seated at the front of the banquet hall, in a big metal and stone chair, covered with plush red and violet fabric. It was the throne, used for special ceremonies such as this. He also wore the white garb of his military, embellished with ribbons and metals capturing his once youthful military career. He held the highest honor ever bestowed onto a Kulusk soldier, the Golden Circle of Kulusk. It signified an act of heroism, patriotism and selflessness in the service of the Maxum.

Nom had received it from his father, when he was the mere age of twenty-six. He earned the honor while commanding a regiment during the hostile occupation of Senarith, a planet in a binary solar system thirty-four light years from Kulusk. During his time on Senarith, he was captured, tortured and sentenced to death by the rebel forces on the planet. Somehow, he managed to escape, and rescue two-dozen other Kulusk prisoners at the same time. During his daring escape, Nom single-handedly killed half a dozen guards. When he returned to his unit, he quietly took charge of the unit and quelled the rebellion of the indigenous people by ruthlessly executing their leaders, who had unwittingly revealed their identities to Nom while he was a prisoner.

His actions that day fueled many folklore legends that seemed to increase his reputation with the Kulusk people. Therefore, his ascension to the throne was solidified with respect and never questioned. He was the first Kulusk in recent history to experience the taste of combat. Now it was expected that all Kulusk Maxums prove their worth in combat.

Nom rose from his seat, which caught the eye of the entire assembly. The music stopped on cue and a hush fell upon the crowd. All turned toward the throne, awaiting the message that Nom was about to speak.

Nom raised his glass of guild in the air as a toast, "Good people of the Kulusk Empire. It has been my distinct honor to lead you as the Maxum for these so many years … years of victory and growth. And during my time as your leader I have lost a wife to the treacherous Chaktun Republic, a wife who bore me two glorious sons … two sons who I am so very proud of. Two sons who traveled to a strange world to avenge their mother's death and returned to punish the deceitful Tonja who planned to rid me of the throne. And while they did this, they returned with three beautiful women from this strange world. Two of the women are my daughter-in-laws and one…"

He turned to Caroline who was seated several feet in front of him. He smiled with a gleam in his eye that no one had witnessed in a long time. He stopped to clear his throat. The crowd remained silent as he searched the crowd for expressions, but found none. Then he reached his left hand out toward Caroline. "…And one who has consented to wed me, Caroline Pathgo."

The silence in the crowd turned into a clamor of whispers that buzzed like hornets. Caroline stepped up to the throne and clasped Nom's hand as he kissed her on the cheek.

Erif's mouth dropped as he replayed the words in his head to ensure he heard his father correctly. It took a split second for the words to echo in his head several times, before he turned to Ellen and saw the same quizzical look on her face. Erif allowed the drink in his hand to spill over, as his mind no longer controlled his body. He was in shock, and his brain disregarded all other functions for that moment. Neither he nor Ellen had imagined this. Ellen corrected Erif's hand so the liquid would stop pouring out of his glass. Then she snuggled close to him as to celebrate the news of the impending marriage. Erif hugged his wife, but his mind did not register it.

## Malcolm Dylan Petteway

Caroline stood next to Nom, blushing at the attention she was now receiving. Nom turned back to the crowd, which was now clapping in approval of his announcement. Nom waited for the applause to die down.

"My sons are married and I have a handsome grandson who will someday be in line for the throne of Kulusk," Nom continued.

Erif knew his father was about to announce the heir to the throne during this speech. He had hoped his father would not do this tonight, but simply congratulate them on their anniversary. Erif knew if his father announced the heir this evening, it would most likely not be him, and it would be an insult on his anniversary as well. Erif closed his eyes in shame as he listened to his father's voice resonate throughout the hall.

"We are here to celebrate the common anniversary of my sons to their beautiful brides, Jennifer and Ellen. They could not have done better. And I thank them for bringing their mother along to warm my heart in my remaining years." The crowd applauded again, and Nom waited for it to die down. "Because my sons did an outstanding job, led by my eldest Efas, I am hereby announcing this day to be a Kulusk holiday from now on." Again the applause broke the toast. "Because of their heroism and patriotism during adversity and the accomplishment of their mission of the destruction of the Osguard family line, I hereby call my sons, Efas and Erif Ritchen to the throne to accept the Golden Circle of Kulusk."

Erif's heart swelled as he heard his father call his name for the most honored praise the Empire had to offer. Ellen nudged him forward, awakening him from his thoughts. He walked toward the throne, catching up with his brother, several steps in front of the throne. They both faced their father and knelt on one knee.

Nom reached behind him and retrieved a golden necklace with a golden circle containing a golden replica of Kulusk in the center from a proffer who appeared from behind the throne. He placed this around Erif's neck. "For your gallant efforts and for being wounded in the service of the Empire, I hereby award you our Empire's highest award...Congratulations son."

Then Nom repeated the process with Efas. "For gallant efforts and for exemplary leadership in the face of hardship in the service of the Empire, I hereby award you our Empire's highest award...Congratulations son." However before either son could stand, Nom reached for the proffer's plate and pulled a pin from it. "Also, I hereby announce the heir to the throne to be my eldest son, Efas Ritchen." He placed the pin to the right side of Efas collar. "From now on, you will be granted the rights and privileges of Maxum and upon my demise assume the title and duty of Maxum."

All applauded, even Erif, who did not want to appear jealous in front of his father or the assembly, but deep inside he was seething with anger and hatred. His fears had come to fruition. Efas was now the named heir to the throne, and only death would stop him from accepting the throne upon their father's demise. Erif shrugged. He knew this day would come, but he'd hoped he could prevent the official announcement, but it did not matter. The official announcement did not interfere with his plans. By morning he would be the official heir to the throne, and all would have forgotten about this night.

Four galactic hours later, Erif, Ellen, Efas and Jenny were in the Greenhaven's portal room. They had changed into traveling clothes, and carried overnight bags in preparation to spend a romantic evening in the sky palace. They were giggly and somewhat intoxicated from the guild and the evening's events. All appeared to be in high spirits. Erif moved to the control ARIT and set in some coordinates.

On the platform, the normal white light of inner space appeared as an invisible door slid up. Efas moved toward his wife. He had an urge to grab her, but fought the urge.

"I forgot something, you guys go on ahead, I will be with you directly," Erif said.

"Do you want me to wait for you," Ellen questioned, disappointed that Erif forgot something, and wanted her to leave without him.

Erif stood silent for a second. He wondered if what he was about to do was necessary. If he should have her stay with him or let her go. Could he rebuild their relationship? Could he rekindle the love he once had for Ellen? Or was it lost that fateful day on Earth when he was shot? He wanted to, but he knew in his heart she had given herself to Efas. He had no evidence, just an intuition. And he could not forgive that.

He shook his head. He stared into her eyes searching for something; something to tell him he was wrong. He saw nothing. He felt nothing but contempt "No!" he squealed. Then realizing he had let his anger surface, he lowered his tone. "No honey, warm up our room and I will be with you in a moment." Erif hugged her and gave her a passionate kiss making her a little dizzy with anticipation. He stepped back to the control panels as he motioned for her to go.

Efas looked at Ellen and tipped his head toward the light. "Come on Ellen, he'll only be a minute."

Ellen nodded in agreement and stepped onto the platform. The images of the room slid down, extinguishing the white light and swallowing the three occupants. Erif looked on in horror as the light disappeared. Then he pulled out a small transmitter device from his cloak. He held it for several seconds, pondering if he should go through with his plan. His conscience fought his greed for a split second, but eventually succumbed. Erif pushed the button.

In the skies over one of the Southern Oceans, a cascade of explosions rocked the sky palace. The rock and metal soon crumbled as the fiery balls consumed the area like an avalanche. Soon the destabilization of the palace weakened the thrusters that kept it aloft and the palace began losing altitude. The explosions became stronger and more frequent until finally, one big explosion incinerated the palace into bright red-hot sprinkles of ash and silt floating toward the ocean.

Erif double-checked the coordinates he had set in the ARIT control. They were set to the continent of Taiole, a sub-zero wasteland of frozen tundra. He had sent his brother, sister-in-law and wife to this area instead of to the sky palace. He had supplied them with food and shelter to last for quite some time. In his heart he could not kill them in the explosion of the sky palace, but he wondered if the fate he had set for them was any better.

When the investigation was complete, Efas, Jenny and Ellen would be listed as killed in the explosion, set by rebel forces sympathetic to the Chaktun Republic and Erif would be labeled lucky to have escaped, all because he left his slippers in his room and had to go back to retrieve them.

# Chapter 21—Confrontation

The stage area went dark as the last image of Erif faded through the doorway of the portal chamber on that fateful night. Kie sat, strapped in the black chair, refuting in his mind, what he had spent the last four galactic hours watching. Yet it fit. It all made sense to him. It answered some of the questions that over time had nagged him.

"Oh! I see you recognize the truth," Opel deadpanned. He had watched Kie during the retelling of the history and took note of the different times Kie's face registered enlightenment. He knew he was opening new views while dismissing long held views Kie had seized for so many years.

Kie turned to his captor and summarily dismissed his comment with a shrug of indifference, while inwardly he challenged his history. If this was true, it explained why the HVP he held so dearly was created ten years after his ancestors' returned to Kulusk. Erif must have forged it to give himself more credit for the destruction of the Osguard line. In his rendition of the events, Erif was never injured and the offspring were hung by his hand as Efas stood and watched. Efas was portrayed in history as a weak, pacifist whose only service to the Kulusk Empire was to die in the sky palace explosion. Yet, that characterization never left the confines of Greenhaven, for if it were to get to the public, it would demean the entire Ritchen lineage. At least so he thought.

"Erif changed history after that," Opel said with no emotion. "Over the next ten years, he altered the HVPs to make himself more appealing to the people. He was preparing the people for his eventual ascension to the throne...an ascension that never happened." Opel rose and walked over to Kie. He bent over resting his hands on Kie's armrest and placing his face three inches away from Kie's face. "As you recall, dear cousin, Erif and Nom were assassinated on the twelve year anniversary of the sky palace disaster. Erif II, your father, ascended to the throne at the tender age of fifteen. He and Caroline Pathgo...I mean Caroline Ritchen...well anyway... they decided the fate of our people for years, at least until her death some five years later. However, you know all this." He stated with a devious smile.

The words rolled in Kie's head like a boulder as he fought the reality of the story. It shattered his history. He couldn't allow this. He remained poker faced, smelling the fishlike breath of his captor. Then he realized it didn't matter. He was the Maxum and history is whatever he decided it would be. And this version of history will never see the light of day. He collected the saliva in his mouth and spit it out with force, into Opel's face.

Opel winced back by surprise and then disgust as he wiped the spit from his face. What he did not feel or realize during that split second was that Kie pulled Opel's pagenay from his belt. When Opel opened his eyes again he saw Kie holding the pagenay on him. "You must be joking," he remarked.

"No, but I would love for you to test that theory."

Opel, knowing Kie's hands were still bound to the chair, thought if he could move to the side, he would no longer be in the line of fire. He slid his right foot to the side, only to be met with pagenay fire that stopped short of hitting his foot.

"No...no...no, I wouldn't do that if I were you."

Opel stopped. He read in Kie's eyes a callousness he never saw before in any man, a shared evilness reserved for the most despicable. He was staring into the eyes of the devil. There was something else fueling the evil, something more than the pagenay he held in his hand.

"What?" Opel questioned. "There is something else. What is it?"

"Just unhinge these shackles," Kie hollered. When he saw Opel not move, Kie released another blast from the pagenay. The blue light sailed within a quarter inch of Opel's right ear.

The shot disturbed Opel. In reality, it made him afraid. He realized Kie had more control of his aim than he had accounted for. Or was it a lucky shot? Either way, Opel did not want to test his luck. "Release," he commanded. The gray metal clasps opened and slid back into the black chair, releasing his feet and hands.

Kie stretched out his arms, disregarding Opel. In that instant, Opel moved like the wind and laid a power front kick into Kie's chest, knocking both Kie and the chair backwards. Then Opel pounced on top of him, grabbing his wrist in an effort to gain control of the pagenay. The weapon fired upwards toward the ceiling, nearly grazing Opel's left cheek.

# Malcolm Dylan Petteway

Opel felt the searing heat from the weapon as the air charged with energy when it blew past his face. The sensation drew excited energy and activated his adrenaline to the point he felt his strength increase. Opel then stretched his right hand across his body and unleashed a powerful backhand across Kie's face. The hit shocked and weakened Kie, but he kept a tight grasp on the pagenay. Opel realizing another blast was forthcoming began slamming Kie's wrist against the ground. With each slam of Kie's wrist, Opel let out a ferocious and primal yell, summoning his inner strength and focusing it onto the weapon.

Kie felt his grasp of the pagenay loosening and arched his body, curled his right knee into Opel's crotch and pushed him up and over. Opel slammed onto his back, knocking the air from his lungs. The pain rattled his entire body. His world clouded as his vision grew narrow. His head felt woozy, but he knew he had to react quickly. So he arched his back, pushed with his shoulder blades and sprung to his feet. He turned poised to move to his left or right, just in case Kie had the pagenay in a firing position, or charge if he did not. But he saw nothing.

Kie was gone. He scanned the room. Still he did not see him. His heart pumped harder as he strained his senses to see, hear or feel Kie's presence somewhere in the cave. He turned around and saw no one. He heard nothing and he felt...alone. Kie was gone. Did he lose consciousness? He didn't know. He had felt he was awake when he hit the ground, but now he wasn't sure. In that brief span of time between the conscious world and the unconscious world, Kie must have escaped.

Opel ran toward the ARIT control and activated a sensor sweep. The ARIT registered a PGP opening outside the room on a lower level. Opel knew it was Kie. Somehow he had a backup PGP and now he had stepped back to Greenhaven. He knew this post was now in jeopardy and he had to leave. Kie would be back with his army and it all would be over before it started.

Then the communications ARIT center chirped, signaling an incoming message. Opel activated the controls and read the message. His eyes widened with horror as he deciphered the encoded message. It was from one of his operatives deep within the Maxum's laboratory ... an operative whose grandparents were exiled to Taiole almost fifty years ago. With forged papers and a solid education in chemical derivatives, this operative became a highly placed trusted agent within the Maxum Laboratory.

The message read, 'MAXUM RELEASED TERINOLICE VIRUS ON USSTAP MORGUE SHIPS.'

Opel pounded his fist on the control panel and screamed a blood-soaked howl. The echo vibrated through several levels and walls of the icy cave like thunder clap. The pain was evident. His failure was apparent. Opel had lost the element of surprise. Kie knew about his revolution. Opel thought the time was right. Kie's army was defeated, weakened and on the verge of nonexistence after the battle with USSTAP. Opel was going to elicit USSTAP's help in his revolution, but now Kie had inadvertently stopped that. The Terinolice virus was virtually undetectable and one hundred percent fatal without the antidote. Kie had released it to an unsuspecting USSTAP Capitol Station. His one hope was to get the antidote to Capitol Station. But how…how could he get the antidote to them? Then he remembered an old Earth saying passed on through generations, probably originated by Jenny or Ellen. *"If Mohammed can't come to the mountain, the mountain must go to Mohammed."*

Several minutes later, the caves of Taiole exploded in a spectacular series of blasts, destroying all equipment, evidence and any traces of its former inhabitants.

# Chapter 22—Return To Earth

Startram 01–5654 went pitch black as the slitanium skin energized to absorb, bounce and deflect any energy aimed at it. The tiny ship floated through the Oort Cloud, surrounding the outer region of Earth's solar system, better known to USSTAP as the Gentry Star System. Startram 01–5654 slowed to hypersonic speed and descended to negative two hundred on the galactic plane, putting it below the Gentry System and starting the Oort approach to Earth.

The Oort approach was a straight-in approach taking Startram 01–5654 below Earth's orbit, directly in line with its southern polar cap where Earth's surveillance and tracking satellites were lacking. Then the startram rolled inverted, relative to Earth's position in the heavens. For in space the definition of upright, sideways or inverted was a relative term. Most ships sailed the heavens using planetary northern hemispheres as reference to upright, but some galaxies use the southern hemisphere as their reference to upright lending themselves to sail one hundred and eighty degrees opposite of the USSTAP norm. In those galaxies, the USSTAP instrumentation was altered to compensate and the ships rolled to match the norm of the galaxies. Those galaxies, using the southern reference, were southpaw galaxies, and those using the northern hemispheric references were north-paw galaxies. Galaxy One, the Millmum Galaxy was north-paw.

Startram 01–5654 entered Earth's atmosphere, descended to five hundred feet off the surface of Antarctica, and pushed on a course bringing it out over the Atlantic Ocean. Moving at half hypersonic speed, puncturing the sound barrier and lifting heavy waves from the ocean under it, the startram sailed the dark skies of the night. This ride, barely five hundred feet above the ocean floor, frightened Sarah. She did her best not to show her fright, but she was scared. Juanita and Stelana were in the cockpit, oblivious to her, attending to the ship's flight, and she did not want to distract them from that duty. Yet, she had to fight the impulse to call out, to tap the communication console. She also had to fight the onset of airsickness. From her port window she saw how close and fast to the surface they were flying. This was a life for a younger person, not her. Sarah was surprised she did not have a heart attack.

The low level flying was specifically designed to evade radar, thus avoiding detection from Earth's governments. The ships scanner and sensor sweep reached out several hundred kilometers to detect ships and other manmade objects that may be in the startram's path. When detected, the ship automatically altered course and altitude to avoid contact. This part of the approach was very stressful for the pilots, but monotonous for the occupants. Any deviation in error while traveling over ten times the speed of sound could slam the ship into the ocean, killing its occupants and spreading wreckage over several square miles. Thankfully, minutes later, the startram slowed to a halt and hovered over the ocean surface.

The ocean surface broke, revealing a platform pushing its way up. The startram settled onto the platform. A chromerion field enveloped the platform and its content in a bubble of scientific shielding. The platform descended, swallowed by the ocean as the sea returned to its natural state, leaving no indication of manmade disturbance.

The elevator ride through the depths of the ocean made Sarah claustrophobic. She had to keep repeating in her mind this was no different than traveling in space, yet she had a difficult time believing it. Space itself was nothingness, a picturesque void. One forgot the dangers of the environment, because to her it was like watching a summer's night's sky. It was a solid blanket of blackness, with the stars illuminating the darkness, shedding tiny sparkles of light. The ocean was different. It showed its dangers, with bold tenacity—water. One did not think of drowning in space, but one feared drowning in water. Yet, both did kill. Lack of oxygen was lack of oxygen, whether it was from drowning or suffocating.

The platform descended deeper into the ocean, pushing volumes of water out of its way as the waves hugged the chromerion field shielding the ship from flood and pressure. The platform descended one thousand two hundred and fifty fathoms, sinking into the bowls of USSTAP Planetary Headquarters, Lilly Station, named after the Pathgo slave who demonstrated so much compassion to the Osguard sisters, ages ago.

Lilly Station was a conglomerate of spherical sectors connected in the shape of an octagon. The central portion was the original Kulusk station Laurona and Nausona visited when they first stepped to Earth. Over the years, USSTAP added several other portions to make the half-acre facility the nerve center of USSTAP's command, communication, control and intelligence on Earth.

General Wang Lo watched the capture of the startram from his perch in the command center, the original Kulusk chamber. The platform settled into the entry chamber of Alpha bay, pushing the ocean water from the chamber. The dome doors hovered close above them and the pressurization automatically oxygenated. Then the ship glided through a set of vertical doors into Alpha bay.

Juanita, Sarah and Stelana stepped through the startram's opened hatch. Sarah's eyes showed a mixture of complex emotions. They were red from crying, due to her sister's loss and they were also wide with fright because of the exciting trip she just witnessed during the startram's execution of the Oort Cloud Approach.

She had become accustomed to the space travel over the eighteen hours it took the startram to reach Earth. The passenger cabin was comfortable with plush black leather-like chairs. The double columns of two chairs were situated almost like an airliner, with a communication console set in front of each one. The monitor at the front and over the door of the passenger hatch could be adjusted to monitor the scanners, sensors or to display a selected HVP. The galley in the back contained almost every delicacy she could think of and some she never heard of. She particularly enjoyed the Ysae, a type of roasted bird from Chaktun. It exuded a taste similar to a mixture of chicken, turkey and steak. She also enjoyed the green and yellow vegetables that enhanced the meal's taste. Yet, eighteen hours was still nerve wracking on her. She thought she would not make it in time to comfort her sister or her niece in their time of need.

She cried during the trip, unable to find comfort in her new world— no, her new universe, or at least her new acquired understanding of her universe. Until two weeks ago, her universe was a universe, she had no notion of. Now she knew her universe was made up of a highly intelligent technologically advanced collective of sixty galaxies, in which her daughter was a master. However, with all this knowledge and comfort, she had witnessed a universal war and the deaths of countless lives, more than she could fathom. And now she was returning to Earth to attend her great nephew's funeral...Her nephew who was killed in a drive-by shooting dealing with drugs, the scourge of the African American community.

Drugs had always been someone else's problem, until the death of her beloved nineteen-year-old son, Conrad. Conrad had died so young. It was almost fourteen years ago, a mere nine months after she buried her husband, Frank. She had suspected...no she had known, but chose to ignore it. The mood swings, the disheveled appearance, the rudeness and the telltale sign, money and jewelry disappearing. All were classic signs of chemical dependency...drugs

# Malcolm Dylan Petteway

It didn't matter if it was crack, cocaine, heroin, ice or any of the faddish names the kids gave to the drugs. It was addictive and deadly. Conrad had been on the stuff for years, but she looked the other way, praying for God's deliverance. However, God didn't deliver. Conrad fell deeper and deeper into the culture. She tried to show her love, but it was hard. Soon Conrad began cursing her and though she never told Juanita, even hitting her, begging for money to feed his thousand-dollar a day habit. Then there were days she would go without seeing or hearing from him. She enjoyed those days of peace, but she also was consumed by fear that Conrad was in a crack house slowly dying. Her biggest fear was he would return, which he seemed to do each time.

She had lost her furniture, jewelry and an assortment of other valuables. Soon Conrad started stealing her insurance and her pension to feed his drug habit. Sarah got behind on the house and car payments. She did not have enough money to buy groceries and several times her electricity and heat were disconnected. Conrad was spiraling into death and Sarah unwittingly paid for it, taking her closer and closer to her own death as she did. It took all her power to shield Juanita from the truth. Until that fateful Tuesday, when she learned Conrad died in a crack house. At first she felt relief, it was finally over. The nightmare had ended. Then she felt guilt for feeling relief. It took a week after the funeral, when she was going through his things, to actually feel grief. The notion she had lost her first-born had finally settled into her consciousness. She cried for weeks and fell into a deep depression.

Since then, Sarah had witnessed the systematic destruction of her community, her friends and her family. She could not conceive what the attraction was to drugs. She did not understand how drugs became so popular—taking it and selling it. She condemned those who took drugs as suicidal fools and she condemned those who sold them as murderers in the pursuit of self-annihilation, getting rich off the death of others. It was tough enough being black in America, but to propagate the very essence of something that could potentially eradicate your race was unconscionable. She hated them. She hated them all. She prayed for God to eliminate her pain and her hate, but again, God had not answered her prayers. She saw too much death. She had endured too much pain. Now she had to endure more pain.

She followed her daughter and Stelana through the doors and down the corridor. She was in a daze, soaking in her own grief, so much to take in, and her brain was about to explode.

A man, she later learned to be General Lo, met them at the end of the corridor and escorted them further. Juanita and Lo spoke in low whispers. She could not hear them, and she did not care to hear them. Her single thought was getting to her sister. The only comfort she had now was that her daughter was with her and her daughter seemed at ease with their travel accommodations. She took a cleansing breath and blew hard. This awoke her mind as she fought the daze she allowed herself to creep into. The sudden exhalation reverberated in the corridor, making Juanita turn in concern.

She surveyed her mother from head to toe and for the first time recognized the worried look shadowed by fright in her mother's face. She took her mother's arm into hers and snuggled to her mother's side. She knew she had been in her own little world during the trip and she had neglected her mother's apprehensions. She realized this was new to her mother, and she was accepting all without a guide or explanation. Juanita looked into her mother's eyes and said, "I'm sorry mother."

Sarah patted her daughter's arm and nodded in acceptance, while fighting back the tears she had thought she had long lost some five hours ago. The moment of sympathy opened a floodgate of emotions her frail body could no longer hide. The jolt of realization had pierced her mind like a spear. She started to tremble from wrought emotion. Juanita held on tight. Lo summoned medical attention to tend to Sarah. Sarah heard Lo's voice, but it was distant. She tried to focus, but her vision narrowed. Soon the sounds faded and her mind clouded. She felt limp as her legs buckled. Her world went dark.

***

The call was too early in the morning for him, but it was what FBI Special Agent Anthony Musoto was waiting for. He jumped out of bed, excited at the new prospect that lay ahead. He slipped his pants on, trying to be as quiet as he could.

"Where are you going?" Mona Richards asked in her most sexy voice.

"Got to go, honey…duty calls," he whispered.

Mona reached for the night lamp next to the bed and turned on the light. The light illuminated the smile she was flashing at Musoto. Then she removed the sheet from around her, revealing her tanned nude body. Musoto's jaw dropped as he stared at Mona. He gazed upon her as if she were a goddess. Her toned muscular build and firm perky breasts evaporated any sense of duty he had from his mind. Soon his thoughts were consumed with desire—desire for her. She was a drug and he was an addict. He could not fight the lust burning in his heart. Soon his body ached with want. To him, Mona's body was like a fine tuned engine, built for one thing and one thing only—sex.

Without thought or word, Musoto undressed and slipped into bed next to her. Her body heat ignited his passion as he caressed the curvature of her hips. His hands moved around her back as he drew her closer to him. Mona continued to smile as their lips met. Soon their tongues explored each other in passion as their bodies pressed hard against one another. He could feel her chest move with each breath, and he could feel the pounding of her heart against his chest.

Soon, as if in a rhythmic dance, Mona rolled on top of Musoto and used her feminine sensuality like a homing beacon to mount Musoto. When she did, the childlike smile that formed on Musoto's face let her know she had released a deep dark and satisfying rapture. For the next fifteen minutes, the two engaged themselves in a carefree although torrid dance of sexual ecstasy. At first, Musoto prayed he was giving as much pleasure as he was receiving, but soon, those thoughts faded. He lost his mind; he was content on what he was feeling. Then with his energy spent, a cloud of darkness overcame him, called sleep.

Mona nudged his side. Satisfied he was asleep; she rolled out of bed and reached into her nightstand. She pulled out a circular red device, no bigger than a silver dollar. She rolled back into bed, reached over and with a solid click snapped the device onto Musoto's head. He was in a deep enjoyable sleep, too exhausted from his tryst with Mona to guard his thoughts and too happy in his slumber to try.

She then leaned over, fingering a small five-inch long gray cylinder that fit between her trigger-finger and thumb. A green light flashed between the cylinder in her hand and the device on Musoto's forehead. She held the cylinder approximately six inches from his head for three minutes. When she was done, she unsnapped the device from Musoto's head, and placed it and the cylinder back into the nightstand. Satisfied the job was complete, she rolled back toward Musoto.

She peered at him and kissed his chest. He stirred, aroused from her kiss. She moved closer, pressing her bare body against his and wrapped her arms around his waist. Within moments, Musoto was in the thralls of ecstasy, dancing again in sexual pleasure, lost inside her, losing his mind, his soul and his very being. He was too far to even notice the slight itching on his forehead. His mind was consumed with the tingling racing up and down his spine and the explosive pleasure he was fighting to contain. However, her body felt too good, her rapture too complete for him to succeed. With a twist of her back and a squeeze of her thighs around his waist, Musoto exploded, draining him of all feeling, including the tingling in his spine, into her.

With sweat rolling down his back, face and chest, Musoto collapsed next to Mona, out of breath, depleted of all energy and still crazed from the episode. He closed his eyes, panting and searching for words to say, trying to say the words he felt, but only wheezing in delight. Mona understood and smiled. She didn't know what pleased her more, putting Musoto in this feeble state or the actual act of making love to him. All she knew was she had done it before and she had done it once again…in more ways than one.

***

Stelana did not waste any time reaching the gate portal room. She was under explicit orders from Juanita and she knew she had to carry them out. When Sarah collapsed in the corridor, Juanita gave Stelana the gesture to continue on. So she did.

Now she was standing outside the Hoover building, the Headquarters for the Federal Bureau of Investigation, waiting. She had lost all track of time, but she knew it was still early in the morning. She surmised by the lack of activity on the street it was about six thirty. Dawn had just broken. It was still dark when they had reached Lilly Station and Juanita ordered her to call him on his CC. It took him some time to answer the call. She guessed it was because he was not familiar with how to operate the CC yet. However, he eventually answered and informed her he would be there, but he wasn't there yet.

Stelana wanted a cigarette. She had never smoked the foul things, but she always saw in movies people in her situation, waiting for someone, always found some perverse pleasure in smoking a cigarette. She wondered if it calmed the nerves, because right about now she needed something to calm her nerves. She was uncomfortable. She did not like it. Why couldn't she just step to him, and be done with it? Why, all of sudden did he want to play cloak and dagger? It felt like a setup.

She would give him ten more minutes, and then she would leave. If she left, how was she to explain it to the Osguard? She would tell the truth, that's how. The simple truth would be she left because she felt strange. How much did intuition play in logic? None, she answered. Therefore, she decided she would have to wait as long as it took. She stomped her foot at the thought. She still did not like it.

"Hello, Rican," a voice bellowed from the shadows of the doorway.

Stelana spun around in time to see a man appear from the doorway. "How long have you been there?" she queried.

"Not long," Musoto answered, stepping up to her. He looked different from the last time they met. His dark hair was combed, his face was clean-shaven and he sported a smile, taking up the entire lower half of his narrow face and displaying slight dimples. "In fact, I just got here, came through the underground garage."

Stelana was irritated, but she decided to hold her irritation in check. She smiled back, reached out and grabbed his arm. Then like a parent ushering her child, she turned him away from the building, half pushing and half pulling Musoto along as she began to march down the lonely street. Realizing the agitation in her manner, he did not resist.

"Musoto," she began. "I have something for you…"

*\*\**

Sarah awoke in Lilly Station's med lab. A USSTAP doctor was fidgeting around her. She arose, half sitting and half laying on the med bed. She observed her daughter sitting in the corner staring with a glazed look. "How long?" she asked with a foggy throat.

"Not long," the young male doctor answered. "You'll be fine. You had a little jet lag." The doctor entered something in an ARIT pad and continued examining Sarah's eyes, hands and arms. "I gave you a mild sedative. That should do the trick for now." Then he turned to Juanita. "Osguard, your mother will be fine. I think you can take her now if you would like."

"Thank you doctor," Juanita whispered. She moved toward her mother, smiling.

However, her mother could tell she had been crying moments earlier. "Is everything okay, Juanita?" she asked.

"Yes, everything is fine. You just gave me a scare mother."

"Sorry!"

"Nothing to be sorry about," she said, giving her mother a tight hug. "We need to go. We will step to Shreveport and meet someone from the Dallas precinct. He has our room ready and he has our transportation."

"Our room?" she shot back. "What do you mean our room? Aren't we staying with Jessica?"

Juanita started to say no, but thought better of it. She continued to hug her mother; feeling the life in her body and thanking God she was not seriously ill. "As you wish mother," she said. "We can change the arrangements later, but for now Aunt Jessica is expecting us. We need to step soon. That is, if you are up to it?"

"Yeah baby…even if I weren't up to it, I would go."

"I know mother…I know"

# Chapter 23—Terinolice Virus

On the security sub-station at Capitol Station, it started with Ensign Leo T. Sentry's throat. It was sore to the point he could barely speak. It felt like he swallowed a hot piece of gravel that scraped all the lining from his throat, leaving bare muscle exposed to the air he tried to breathe. With each breath he took in, the pain burned deeper and deeper. He tried not to breathe. He tried to hold his breath, but that made things worse. He gasped and gulped for air hoping the passage of air would not irritate him as much, but it did. He soon found himself hyperventilating.

He moved from his bed to the mirror over his sink. He looked in the mirror and saw his once fair white skin had turned a gruesome red, with blotches. His blue eyes were blood shot and he could tell he was running a fever. This was no ordinary virus, he thought. He needed medical attention. "ARIT, contact the med lab," he mumbled. His throat hurt with every word he spoke.

The familiar tones of the communication protocol hummed in the background. However, Sentry was oblivious to the sounds. His mind was losing all contact with reality as the room began to swim around him as if he was fighting off a hangover. He soon could not tell up from down, left from right. The labyrinth in his inner ear faltered as he lost his balance. His mind gave one command—fall. His body obeyed the command as he thumped to the floor, hitting his chin on the sink as he fell. He was unconscious before he hit the floor.

"Med lab," crackled the voice over the ARIT communications net. However, Sentry was in no condition to answer. "Med lab!" the voice came with more urgency. Still there was no answer. The voice tried to establish contact several more times, with the same result—no answer.

A few moments later a white PGP light illuminated the room and a four-man medical squad pushed through. They saw Sentry lying on the floor, blood oozing from his mouth. The first med tech pulled out his PARIT and scanned the ensign's body. High temperature, muscular anomalies and various other items registered on the PARIT. However, the main thing was his heart and lungs were bigger than usual. They were swollen to a very dangerous proportion.

The med tech leader knew the med lab on the security station was inadequate to render the proper medical attention. The med labs on each of the seventy stations, comprising Capitol Station, were designed to attend to minor accidents and illnesses. However, the med tech realized this was not one of those occasions. He knew the ensign needed transport to the medical station. In the med tech's estimation, it was better equipped to handle this sort of emergency. The med tech tapped his CC and announced his team's intentions of delivering Sentry to the medical station emergency ward. The med team placed Sentry, also known as Alpha-One, onto a hover cart and rushed through the light.

On the other end, Doctor Susan Tillman, the emergency room physician on duty, received the med team. The med team leader barked out Sentry's vitals. Dr. Tillman pointed to the medical alcove to her right, "Put him over there." Then to no one in particular she commanded, "MARIT stabilizer field on."

A blue sparkling light engulfed the alcove as a MARIT descended from the ceiling and covered Sentry's chest. Another MARIT descended from the ceiling and covered his forehead. The readouts flashed on both MARITs in Chaktun. Then the MARITs suggested medication and the dosage. Dr. Tillman studied the suggestion. She would amend them accordingly, but for the most part she concurred with the MARIT and placed her thumbprint on the scanner to register her approval. The MARIT recognized the approval and introduced the appropriate medication. Nonetheless, Sentry's vitals were still failing. Dr. Tillman was perplexed. The medication suggested was the normal medication for such an illness. In Sentry's case it was not working. Now she began looking for other answers.

She had to stabilize the patient, as she started thinking of him. If she thought of him too personally, she would get emotionally involved, and she could not afford to have emotions cloud her judgment. She had deep concern this patient was dying and she could not stop it. Therefore, it was better for her to start thinking of Sentry as another patient.

Then the ARIT communications speaker sprang to life...Another emergency call, then another, then another came over the intercom. Dr. Tillman's technicians answered the calls as expeditiously as they could. The calls were many and her emergency lab only had so many technicians to retrieve the ill. Then the first of the many calls slipped through the PGP. The lead technician barked the vitals, and they were ominously similar to Sentry's vitals. She directed the new patient to the med alcove next to Sentry.

The same MARITs descended and covered the new patient. The same order of medicine flashed over the MARIT. This time Dr. Tillman rejected all suggestions and prescribed heavier dosages and stronger substitutes. It was to no avail. The patient's vitals were still deteriorating. Then out of the corner of her mind, she heard the crash horn sound from Sentry's alcove.

Sentry's heart had stopped. He was experiencing a massive coronary. Dr. Tillman ran to him and began MARIT resuscitation procedures. The MARITs stimulated Sentry's heart and sprayed medication into it. Another MARIT covered his mouth, tilted his head, and shot oxygen into his lungs. His lungs inflated then deflated, but would his autonomic functions fail? The MARITs worked on Sentry and would have continued working on Sentry, but Dr. Tillman, with a sigh of disheartenment, pushed the stop button and pronounced him dead.

She did not sign on for this. She always accepted the fact she would lose patients. She even had lost patients before, but never this quickly. When Michael recruited her after college, she was full of ambition and optimism. When Michael told her he could guarantee her an exciting and rewarding career as a doctor in his organization, she hardly believed him. Then he did the unthinkable. He stepped her onto his ship. He must have known she would accept his offer after seeing the extent of USSTAP's medical technology. She always regretted her inability to share the knowledge with her compatriots on Earth. The secrets she held, the cure for cancer, AIDS, and other medical problems that plagued Earth like a locust. The USSTAP charter stated 'no interference with Earth.'

*No interference*. She never accepted that pledge, but she has to live by it. She didn't understand how sharing medical technology would hamper her home planet's growth. She saw the greed in the medical profession when she, with USSTAP permission, cured her mother of breast cancer. At least USSTAP had a heart in allowing family members the benefit of their medical expertise, even if they did not realize it. However, her mother's attending physician became curious. He ran a battery of test and discovered an anomaly in her mother's blood. Of course the anomaly was the residuals from the medication she had given her mother. This doctor isolated and was on the verge of reproducing it. At first, Michael allowed this mistake to continue. He figured if the doctor was smart enough to isolate and reproduce a complicated synthetic compound like T-seven–ninety-U, the cure for this particular cancer, then so be it.

However, the doctor made a deal with a pharmaceutical company. The deal was in the millions, but then business got in the way and the company had planned to substitute the key but costly ingredients with inferior elements, which would do more to harm than help the patients. USSTAP pulled some strings in the business, the company went under for false advertisement, and the doctor barely escaped the fallout with his license intact. Dr. Tillman learned a very important lesson that day—Earth was not ready to join humanity. However her conscience was not completely cleared, knowing thousands of people died on Earth every day with diseases she had the cure for in USSTAP.

Michael had once told her, he was drafting a plan to set up Unlimited Associates Incorporation on Earth as a pharmaceutical company and dispense the advanced drugs to doctors. Yet, it would be tricky, because in most cases it took the precision of MARITs to introduce the medicine into the human body. In many cases it takes MARIT nanobiotics to cure the diseases. And if Earth's military industrial complex discovered the secret behind MARIT nanobiotic technology, there would be no telling how they would use it for chemical biological warfare.

*Biological warfare...nanobiotic technology*. Could this be? She activated three buttons on the MARIT control panel, and scripted several notes into the MARIT journal recording the Sentry's death. She then blew out a heavy breath, looked into Sentry's face. "Good-bye Ensign Leo T. Sentry."

Then she raced back to her second patient, retracing her steps to make sure she did not make the same mistake with this patient as she did with Sentry. She read the flashes on the MARITs and disagreed with their findings, because they were the same as Sentry's. She thought she was dealing with nanobiotic technology and she knew she had to do something fast or she would lose this one as well. If it were an injury, she could operate. If it were a pagenay hit, she could operate. If it were a mation wound, she could operate, but this was a virus, most likely man-made; or so she thought, and viruses, whether man-made or not, ran their own course. However, this virus was resistant to all the antibodies she had tried. She started going down the list of the most powerful antibodies to combat this fast acting virus. None worked. She introduced nanobiotics, but she was purely guessing now. Nonetheless, a guess was better than doing nothing.

Then the crash alarm sounded. The MARITs went right into resuscitation procedures. Dr. Tillman knew it was fruitless, but she watched as the automatic systems fought to bring life back into the second patient. She watched, drained of ideas of what to do next. She felt so helpless. She knew she had the best medical knowledge in the universe, the best facility in the universe and the best cure rate in the universe. She successfully fought all forms of cancer and Aids from Earth, Genome disorder and Percy's disease from Litheria. She had seen and cured all infectious diseases from every galaxy in the known universe. She dared to think she had even fought off death, but her confidence was shaken. She did not know what to do next. After several agonizing minutes, she stopped the procedure and pronounced patient two, Ensign Carline Patchet ... dead.

The med team came through the PGP with other patients. By now several doctors had joined the fray and were directing the placement of the patients. Soon the circular facility with sixteen alcoves was filled with patients, all with the same symptoms. One by one, many of their hearts failed.

Soon, Dr. Tillman began placing the patients who had not succumbed, in cryogenic suspension, hoping with time she could get a handle on the situation. Other emergency rooms in the medical station soon filled up, twenty-three in all. In three hours the entire medical station was full. In four hours the overflow pushed Dr. Tillman to order med labs on other stations to take patients. In Six hours, half of Capitol Station was in cryogenic suspense. She felt hopeless. There was one thing left to do. She ordered autopsies on the dead to investigate the virus further. She needed confirmation she was dealing with a man-made virus.

*** 

Michael sat in his office on Capitol Station with his head in his hands. The line of contamination was clear. Those who fell first came from the security station. The forty teams who inspected the morgue ships contracted the unknown virus first with a mortality rate of eighty percent. His security station was decimated, one thousand two hundred and eighty dead, eighty-one percent more casualties than he suffered in battle against the Kulusks. Now the virus had spread to other parts of Capitol Station. The economic station, the five supply stations, the sixteen engineering stations and the four civilian travel stations had all been contaminated. Half the population, those still living, were in suspension, waiting in a silent slumber for them...no him, to save them.

Michael thought the saving grace was that the political establishment, along with the parents and most other dependents were still on Chaktun, and therefore, not confronted with this catastrophe. All the Osguards and their crews were at risk, since they were at Capitol Station during the outbreak of the virus. Seven of them, including his dear sister were in suspended animation.

*Why*, he thought. Why did he succumb to his humanity and send the dead back to Kulusk. He should have buried them in space. But no, he had to be the stronger one. He had to give solace to the families of his enemy. Now he was paying the ultimate price. A few short hours ago, he thought the worse was over. Never in his wildest dreams did he imagine the battle was just the prelude to a biological attack. He slammed his fist upon the desk, shaking his woodcarving statues of the *USSTAP Galaxy Cruiser Justice*, and the *USSTAP Galaxy Protector Neraka*. The *Justice* was the first starship he ever sired.

The sudden violent pounding of the oblong shaped oak desk rattled Centurion Gloria Katrengin from the planet Toilomy, Capitol Station's security chief; Commodore Tion Leitl, from the planet Derf, Commander of Millmum Security Corps; Admiral Solan Toneilk from the planet Sailgon, Capitol Station's sire; and Colonel Motga Funm from the planet Rilgato, Capitol Station's medical chief. They had been sitting in front of Michael's desk as Osguard One digested the initial report. However, when Michael was through reading the report on the ARIT docboard, he placed his head into his hands in despair. An emotion never witnessed by any of the foursome before. That simple motion spoke volumes to the four. It said, 'all appeared lost.'

Michael looked up at them with eyes red with rage. He appeared demon-like to his guests. Admiral Toneilk wanted to speak, but his voice died in his throat as he gazed upon his Osguard. He had never seen this reaction from him, no matter how dire the situation seemed. Yet today, he saw, and he did not know how to respond. He searched with his peripheral vision—first to his left at Centurion Katrengin and Commodore Leitl, and then to his right at Colonel Funm. All three sat with their hands gripping their chair arms. He didn't know if they were more afraid of the situation or the Osguard. Either way, he could not tolerate fear, and he had to let the Osguard know that fear in this situation, or anger, which ever present, would hamper more than help.

"Osguard..." he managed to stammer out.

"What?" Michael shot back, spinning his gaze toward Toneilk. Michael's look felt like it bored through to his soul. Toneilk diverted his glare to the top of the desk. Michael realized he was on an emotional edge and it was dangerous. If he showed his fury or his fright, he did not know at the time which emotion was in command, it would cloud his judgment and stymie creativity—and creativity is what he needed right now. "Sorry Solan. This is quite a lot to take in at once. There is no way—" Then he stopped. He did not want to put a negative spin on an already bad situation. He needed solutions, not doubts.

"Osguard," Funm interjected, breaking the awkward moment. "Dr Tillman has isolated the virus…somewhat, from preliminary autopsy reports. She thinks…" Then he corrected himself. "She thought it to be human engineered and it has some of the characteristics of the AIDS virus on Earth."

Michael stopped his penetrating glare as his emotions softened. He read in the report, his college friend and confidant, Dr. Tillman was also in suspension. Apparently, she had contracted the disease while attending the first patients. Nonetheless, her notes and sharp instincts allowed them to get some sort of handle on this thing. He just hoped he could tell her someday what a blessing it was to have her on his team. He didn't get that chance with Sanchez.

"That's good…isn't it," Michael said with hope. "I mean, we have a cure on the shelf for AIDS…right?"

"Yes, but the virus we are dealing with has an accelerant component that negates the effect of T-two—one-T-three, our nanobiotics for the AIDS virus." This new virus has an incubation period of hours, sometimes minutes, compared to HIV, which is measured in years. It tears down the immune system and literally eats the vital organs…the lungs, the liver, the brain, and eventually the heart. We have no medicine to counteract the effects."

"It says in your report it is an airborne virus. Correct?" Michael questioned, standing to stretch his legs. When he was finished he came around to the front of his desk and sat on the edge, giving personal emphasis on the question by physical proximity.

Funm shifted in his chair to address Michael with eye contact. "Yes, this is airborne. We breathe it in as others breathe it out. It is transmitted that way, not by contact"

"Why didn't the air filtering units catch it?"

"They did sire, but they did not recognize it as a threat. The system was not equipped to fight this virus."

"Can we adjust the filter to do so?" Michael rubbed his forehead to clear his thoughts.

"Yes sire, we have. Nevertheless, the damage is already done," interjected Toneilk. "Commander Terilela tells me that the virus has infected everyone in Capitol Station."

"Everyone?"

"Yes sire," Katrengin confirmed. "Including us…including you," she added.

Michael shook his head in disbelief. "You mean we are all—"

"Yes sire, in twenty four hours we either should be in suspension or we will be dead," Leitl added.

Michael's eyes glowed with understanding. His next step was clear to him. However, he was not sure how long. "How about the ships?"

"All of them are infected as well," Katrengin reported. "We have informed their sires to quarantine their crews until further notice."

"I took the liberty of quarantining the station sending out an all USSTAP message for all traffic to steer clear of the facilities until further notice as well," responded Leitl.

Toneilk glared at Leitl. Michael saw he was not informed of such a broadcast.

"Problems?" asked Michael to no one in particular but pointed in tone to Toneilk.

"No sire, I guess that was the most prudent thing to do. I just didn't..."

"I agree," Michael stated firmly to squash the moment. "Solan, order the nearest cruiser to rendezvous and pick up my cousin, Osguard Fifty-Five. Besides being the surviving Osguard, she may..." then he stopped. "Just do it," he said after several seconds of contemplation.

"Osguard," Funm interceded. "Suspension doesn't stop the process, it just slows it down. In suspension we have a week at most before the virus completes its job."

"Thank you doctor," Michael said. "Order all personnel into suspension. I want this place locked down in three universal hours. Also, set the automatic defenses, only to be deactivated by Osguard level command. Understood?"

Then the familiar beep of the comm center rang in the air. Michael circled his desk and activated the switch.

"Osguard," Terilela called, "Incoming hail from Kulusk for you only."

"I guess Kie wants to gloat."

"No sire, it is from Opel Ritchen. He says he is the leader of the resistance and he knows about the virus. He is offering to help, but he will only speak to you."

"Resistance? What Resistance? And who the hell is Opel Ritchen?" Michael sat down and motioned for his guests to leave.

The foursome stood and left through the side door, wondering if their business was complete. They stepped to their stations to carry out the Osguards request.

"Put him through," Michael ordered.

Several seconds later, Opel's face appeared on Michael's ARIT screen.

"Hello cousin, I am Opel Ritchen."

"Cousin?"

"Yes, it is a long story. I am attaching an HVP to the carrier of this hail to explain. However, for now … I must help you. I have the antidote for the virus you are experiencing that my cousin, Kie, set upon your people. It is called *'TERINOLICE VIRUS*.'

# Chapter 24—The Resistance

The red sun faded behind the mountains, leaving a ring of fiery light that illuminated the sky covering the Dijanai Continent in the Northern Hemisphere of Kulusk. Opel sat in the basement of his home in the city of Langoni, contemplating his errant posturing with Kie Ritchen that caused him to destroy his fortress in Taiole.

Things did not go as he planned. He wanted to embarrass, imprison and make Kie watch the destruction of the Ritchen Empire by his resistance fighters. However, now Kie was loose and knowledgeable about the resistance. He had lost the element of surprise, and it was a very important piece to his strategy. Now, he had sent the stand down message to all the cells, until he could figure out the next move. He knew Kie would fortify his strategic position with more guards. This was something he was unprepared for.

Opel regarded his basement for a moment. It had taken him years to construct the basement. It was more like a bunker, sunk several feet under his house with a hidden entrance from his living quarters in the house. It was complete with state of the art communications, command and intelligence ARITs—more sophisticated than the Empire's … because his people, the exiles and their descendants, built the technology during years of isolation and secrecy. The technology only shared its conception with Kulusk technology. That is where the similarity stopped. In Opel's eyes, his technology branched off in a completely different arena than that of Kulusk, Chaktun, or even USSTAP. His ARIT used taonic circuitry powered by jorelli plugs. Jorelli plugs were ten times more powerful than Asher power cells the Kulusk and USSTAP were still using after almost a century. It would seem the two most powerful entities in the galaxy would have discovered a new form of power for their ARITs by now. However, they were both set in their ways.

Then a noise broke Opel's concentration. He turned and saw his sister, Tirana staring at him. He was so deep in self-admiration he did not notice her enter his bunker. He chastised himself for failing to notice her earlier.

"Opel, I have been thinking," she stated with a condemning tone.

Opel recognized her tone and was frankly in no mood to get in a philosophical debate with her, but he knew he had to placate her sense of duty with his attention.

"What is it now?"

"Brother, you said Kie ran off?"

"Yes..."

"And you said you must have blacked out for a second, because you did not see him run off?"

"Yes..."

"And you said he had the pagenay when he left?"

"Yes...yes...yes...so what of it?"

"Then, why did he not kill you?"

"What?" Opel was surprised at the question. "I guess he just wanted to leave."

"This is Kie Ritchen...ruthless Kie Ritchen. A man who has killed hundreds of people personally, do you think he was so frightened of you that he simply ran away?"

Opel regarded the question for a moment. He had thought the shock of the truth and the struggle between them had caused Kie to run. However, running would involve fear and there was no sign of fear in Kie's eyes during the fight. Kie's eyes were the eyes of a soldier—a soldier doing what he was trained to do—kill or be killed.

"What are you saying?"

"ARIT," Tirana commanded. "Sweep for tracers."

Opel's face turned flush. *Tracers?* Little ARIT probes that sent a homing signal to an outside source. He had never suspected nor did he imagine Kie had any tracers with him. However, now the seed of doubt, spoken aloud, had spun him for a loop.

"Sweep in progress," the male ARIT voice boomed from the communications console. A yellow light flashed in the bunker as the ARIT did as it was commanded. The yellow light was a scanner searching for power pulses associated with tracers.

"Tracer found," the ARIT announced after several mind agonizing moments.

"Where?" Tirana shouted.

"Commander Opel's belt, just inside the right quarter."

# Chapter 25 - Shreveport

The hotel room view overlooked the winding Red River separating Shreveport from Bossier City. Over the years, several casino riverboats littered both sides of the river's banks, introducing gambling and other assorted vices associated with gaming. The hotel belonged to the newest of the gambling ventures to weigh anchor on the Shreveport side. The building was shinny, cut with reflective black glass to rival the red glass and golden glass structures of its competition. It appeared the more gaudy a hotel was built the more appealing it was to tourist as a place to spend their money. It was quite psychological. The more expensive the hotel appeared the more it took on the liberal mystique of rewarding gamblers with large payouts. Unbeknownst to the tourist, it was quite the opposite.

This hotel with its black reflective glass stood thirty floors tall, dwarfing its competitors' establishments. The triangular shape added to its ostentatious flavor, leading the people in like a moth to a flame. Furthermore, like a moth to a flame, the people usually *'got burnt.'* However, in this twenty-eighth floor room, the man did not come to partake in the gambling venue.

A tall black man, built like a linebacker, Thomas Reed had driven in from Dallas as soon as his supervisor gave him the word. He did not know if he should be thrilled or scared. At the moment he felt both. He had never dreamed of what he was about to do. He was surprised at his apprehension. He quietly, but diligently checked the room as he was trained.

The room was a two-bedroom suite with a living room area separating the two, and a kitchenette to the right of the entry. Reed, dressed in a white crew neck T-shirt and tan Khaki pants, stood in the middle of the living room eying the surroundings. He went first into the kitchen and searched every drawer and cabinet. His broad muscular build made it awkward for him to search the cabinets below the sink and table top, so he reached in with his hand and swept the space. When he was satisfied, he moved back into the living room. He searched the chairs, couch and table. Then he searched the bedroom on the right. Then he moved to the bedroom on the left to complete his search.

He felt a little better, but not completely. He just didn't trust his PARIT, but he trusted it more than he trusted himself. He pulled out his PARIT. It was silver, resembling a cell phone. He flipped it open, revealing a fifteen key keypad on the bottom half, a LCD window and a speaker to the left of it on the upper half. He stroked the mute button with his strong nimble finger then held it out in front of him, reading the digital LCD as he swept it around the suite. It was his third time doing it, but he still had a sinking feeling in the pit of his stomach. He flipped it closed after it reported the room had no electronic devices or weapons.

He placed the PARIT back in his thigh pants pocket and brushed his short skintight haircut with his hand, wondering what else he could do? He didn't want to mess up this assignment. It was probably the most important assignment he would ever receive. He wanted it to be perfect. *Search it again.* He moved toward the kitchen once more. Then the familiar hum, like static, slight and undetectable to the novice, but to a trained USSTAP operative, it was unmistakably the hum of a gate portal about to open. He turned toward the direction of the hum.

An invisible door slid open, revealing the white light of inner space. Two figures stood, shrouded within the light … the halo effect making them look like angels sent from heaven. The figures stepped out from the light into the room. The figure on the right was a beautiful young woman. She stood about five feet—six inches tall, slightly bow legged with skin of high polished light bronze, deep set hazel eyes and wavy shoulder length auburn hair. She wore a crew neck sleeveless black dress, cropped short off her kneecaps and clinging to her hourglass figure, revealing her slim but toned arms and legs and illuminating her muscular but sexy build.

The other lady was about the same height, but some years older and of a darker mahogany skin color. She had gray streaks in her short cut, curly jet-black hair and was more heavy set with a barrel body frame. Her eyes were dark brown, almost black, and not quite as alluring as the younger woman's. However, her chin and cheek structure were identical to the younger woman's. She wore a conventional black dress, with a V-neck collar and short sleeves. The dress was rustic and flowed down to her ankles. She wore a black shinny belt around her waist, which made the dress more flared above the hips.

"Major Reed?" The voice coming from the younger one sounded almost angelic, but authoritative to Reed.

A few seconds passed as the invisible door slid closed, taking with it the pure white light of inner-space. The younger woman stared at Reed waiting for a response. He stood agape with excitement, trying to steady his breathing. The woman moved toward him and placed her hand on his arm to help calm him.

"Please tell me you are Major Reed," she said with concern.

The touch coupled with the angelic, authoritative voice quelled Reed's anxiety. He turned and looked at the older lady and moved his head back to the younger woman who was comforting him.

"Forgive me Osguard," he pleaded. "It is such an honor to meet you that I forgot my manners." *...And my training,* he wanted to add.

"That's quite alright. It happens a lot to me," she joked. "Are we all set? The funeral is in three hours I think."

167

"Yes, I have your vehicle ready in the parking garage and your bags are in your rooms," Reed announced with composure.

"I am staying with my sister," Sarah conveyed, almost childlike.

"Yes, mother, I know…but first I think you should call and tell Aunt Jessica we are in town and make sure she has room for us both."

Sarah stared at her daughter showing confusion on her face, as did Major Reed.

"Now I know you didn't think I was going to let you stay by yourself at Aunt Jessica's. For Christ sake, mother…they just had a double murder at their house. There is no way I would let you stay there without protection…meaning me."

Major Reed's confusion turned into concern as his mind raced for solutions for this unforeseen event. "Osguard, I will have to change security protocols to—"

"I know…but let's talk about that later. I have a baby cousin to bury." Juanita turned to Sarah and let go of Reed's arm. She guided her mother to the phone next to the couch. "Call, Aunt Jessica must be worried."

Sarah sat on the couch and called her sister. After several painful emotional moments talking with her sister she hung up. "It's settled. We stay with Jessica," she announced wiping tears from her eyes.

Then the familiar faint static whine of a portal gate hummed in the room. By now, even Sarah had begun to recognize the sound. She peered up, blinking the tears from her eyes to the spot she estimated the portal gate would open. The door slid open and Stelana stepped out followed by a young, well-dressed Anthony Musoto. Stelana turned toward the light and pushed the deactivate key on her PGP. The door slid closed.

"Osguard, this is FBI Agent Anthony Musoto. Tony, I present to you, Osguard Fifty-Five, protector of the Bletherien Galaxy and Sire of the USSTAP Galaxy Protector Sharyla, Osguard Juanita Genesis-Clark and her mother, the lovely Sarah Genesis."

Musoto stood dumbfounded. He never thought he would ever be at a loss for words, especially with a beautiful young woman. Yet, something about Juanita put him into a trance. He stared at Juanita, never blinking. He tried to command his hand to reach out to shake hers, but the hand disobeyed. He tried to eke out a word but his lips failed to part and all he managed was a low moan.

Juanita turned to Reed, "See I told you…I get that a lot."

Stelana nudged Musoto with her elbow. The nudge popped Musoto back into reality.

"Forgive me. It is just that this is an honor for me to meet you."

Reed sighed, realizing just moments ago he had made the same fool of himself as Musoto was doing now.

Juanita took Musoto's hand inside both of hers to reassure him she was simply human and no one to be frightened of or enamored by. She squeezed his hand, "Nice to meet you Agent Musoto."

"Osguard," Stelana interrupted. "I have briefed Tony in on what happened to your family here, and he has agreed to help in the investigation."

"Thank you Agent Musoto," Juanita said.

"No sweat...and please call me Tony. I mean, if that is okay with you."

"Tony it is," she said giving his hand a final shake then releasing it. The warm feeling ran through Musoto like love on a spring day. He felt welcomed and comfortable around her now.

"Well, Tony here has given his oral report to the president and..."

Musoto interrupted Stelana, "—and I am now the official liaison between the U.S. and USSTAP. The president wanted me to set up some type of unofficial diplomatic relations with USSTAP. He thought since you have precincts in every major city in the world that the other countries, including Russia, would also have a person acting as a point of contact with USSTAP."

Juanita turned from him for a split second to contemplate the offer, and then she spun around. "Tony, let us take one step at a time. I am not sure we are ready for such an agreement, and right now my mind is not on anything but my cousin's funeral."

"I understand and I totally agree. However, let me offer this one bit of advice. Say no."

"What?" she said in stark surprise.

"I'd advise against it. This world is not ready for you. There is no such thing as unofficial diplomatic relations. It is bad enough they know of your existence, but to continue communications with every country would be tantamount to disaster."

"How so?"

"I will explain later. Just say for now, Earth is still in its infancy. It is not mature enough for USSTAP. USSTAP is like sex, if it is exposed too soon in a child's development, it will be detrimental to the child. The child will grow up not respecting the sanctity or the responsibility of sex."

Stelana rolled her eyes at the analogy, knowing Musoto was one of those who did not respect the sanctity of sex, made her furious he was using those words to make a point.

"Sex is needed because of procreation not necessarily growth," Musoto continued. "This planet is still growing, still maturing, we do not need the knowledge of USSTAP yet, and we aren't ready for procreation. But I digress. For now you have a family that needs you. This can wait. But let me tell you. Whatever you decide, I will honor the decision. I believe in you and your organization."

"More than you do your country?"

"Not more, just differently."

"I know what you mean. I am a U.S. citizen as well. It is a different loyalty, isn't it?"

Musoto just nodded his head.

With that Juanita asked Reed to have the baggage moved to the car. Stelana and Musoto helped Reed transfer the baggage to the car. Juanita then suggested Musoto and Reed keep the room and Stelana stay with them at the house to satisfy the security aspect of the trip. Reed reluctantly agreed.

***

Juanita, Sarah, Stelana and Musoto drove out of the parking garage in a white SUV with gold trim and red lettering. It was a special order vehicle for Unlimited Associations Incorporated. This particular SUV was from the Dallas precinct. Reed had driven it up from Dallas the night prior. Naturally, USSTAP made modifications on it, like they did all the UAI fleet. It had ARIT attachments, scanners and sensors. It contained a small pagenay port under the headlights capable of all three levels of fire, and it contained a coronet gun above its front and rear license plate holders. The controls for all the devices were hidden in the steering wheel's center console, which flipped open to reveal a myriad of lights and switches. The rearview mirror and the lower portion of the driver's side windshield doubled for an ARIT monitor. Not surprisingly, the car contained a chromerion field generator, reinforced metal and bulletproof windows.

Juanita drove north up Market Street, through the heart of the city. She saw a pick-up truck sporting a bumper sticker of the Confederate Bars and Stars. She read aloud, "Heritage not hate," then she added with angst, "You mean a heritage of hate."

"What?" Musoto said surprised at the Osguards quiet outburst.

Juanita realized she may have opened up a discussion she did not wish to finish, "Nothing!"

"Osguard, I agree with you, but I was just interested in why you said it. I mean, coming from someone who has seen as much as you have, could shed some enlightenment on the subject for me. I was raised entirely in the North, in fact this is my first real visit to the Deep South and…"

"Okay…okay," Juanita said somewhat agitated. She adjusted her body in the seat, squirming from the conversation. Then she let out a deep sigh. "Mr. Musoto, do you know there were several different Confederate flags flown during the Civil War. What is considered the Confederate flag today was the battle flag used by the Confederate army, not the Confederate flag." She stopped to check Musoto in her rearview mirror, wondering if she had successfully deflected the conversation. She saw Musoto was listening with earnest interest. She continued, "The first Confederate flag was adopted in 1861 and looked much like the United States flag at that time. It had a star for each of the seven seceding states in a circle in the top left corner on a field of blue, with two red bars separated by a white bar. The confusion in the battlefield caused many casualties for the South. So then the South adopted the Tennessee battle flag to lead their troops into battle. Then in 1863 the South changed the flag once more. This time, the battle flag's stars and bars were placed in the upper left corner on a white flag. This time the stars represented the eleven seceding states and the territories of Kentucky and Missouri. Again, this caused confusion because it resembled a flag of truce. So in 1865, the South added a vertical red bar on the far right side. To tell the truth, it was pretty ugly."

Juanita checked the rearview mirror again, and saw the sought after surprised look in Musoto's face. She flashed her beauty pageant smile. "So you see Mr. Musoto, if the people really wanted to show pride in their Confederate heritage, they would use one of the adopted Confederate flags. Instead, they cling to the battle flag. In my mind that means confrontation, but most likely it means they truly don't know their own heritage."

She checked the rearview mirror once more. She saw the look of satisfaction on Musoto's face and she knew she had successfully deflected the conversation to an appropriate history lesson.

She did not want him to know her true feelings about the flag. At least she respected the Kulusks. They didn't try to hide their contempt for her people. Not like these people. She likened the Confederate flag in her face with a NAZI flag flown in front of a Jewish person. It was a reminder of the hatred, deaths and torture her people had to endure to achieve their freedom. She called it a Pavlov Dog syndrome, but it was more real than that. She thought blacks were conditioned for over a hundred years to be afraid of the Confederate battle flag. Whites flew the flag as a symbol of pain, torture and death to blacks for years. They flew it at lynchings, they flew it at Ku Klux Klan rallies and they flew it in a war to keep blacks enslaved. These people may not have understood it. She knew some whites today flew the Confederate battle flag out of some benign sense of misplaced loyalty to their ancestry, but she would bet the worth of the entire Bletherien Galaxy, most of them flew it as defiance to black independence. They lost the war—a war about slavery, not states' rights...or better yet, the states right to keep slavery. *Whatever happened to 'the victors go the spoils of war?'*

She had traveled to the deepest corners of the universe. She'd battled militarily, politically and diplomatically with different races from different planets, in a different galaxy, humans as treacherous as the Kulusks, with a history of killing and torture. The difference was those races didn't lie; they didn't hide under a banner of heritage. They were artfully truthful; they were brutally honorable in their convictions ... no matter how ruthless or immoral those convictions were. Therefore, she understood them, she could avoid them, or she could fight them. This was good, but here, she couldn't fight, she couldn't talk and she couldn't avoid them. They flaunted their hatred in her face and called it a proud heritage. They weren't fooling anybody, but themselves. There was no pride in hate.

*Was hate for your enemy really such a bad thing? Look at the Kulusks.* USSTAP learned to tolerate them and look what happened...a war. Tolerance needed to be tempered with vigilance. Vigilance was either fueled by a sense of duty or hate. With the Confederate movement, she had no sense of duty; just hate. The same hate she was developing for the Kulusks about now.

The car grew quiet once more. Musoto noticed the slight tension, which Juanita was exuding. He realized only peaceful contemplation would defuse it. What did she mean by '*in my mind that means confrontation?' Confrontation? Between whom? Between Earth and USSTAP?* He was interested in her view, but knew Juanita was on an emotional roller coaster, fighting her pain from the war and now the pain associated with the death of a family member. He surmised her thoughts were not clear and her judgment might be somewhat clouded. He would have to satisfy his curiosity later. For now he was willing to wait.

Juanita turned left onto Martin Luther King Boulevard and then took a series of turns prior to driving in front of her aunt's house. The funeral limousine was in front of the house. Juanita found a parking spot several houses beyond her aunt's house. They exited the vehicle as Juanita placed the security alarm on. Sarah moved the quickest toward the house. There was a small crowd of well-dressed mourners gathering on the porch.

Sarah entered the gate and stopped. The chalk outline of Tyree's body was marked on the path in front of her. She stared at the outline for a moment, imagining her great nephew lying in a pool of his own blood. Tears streamed from her eyes as mourners from the porch looked on. Juanita, Stelana and Musoto caught up with Sarah and escorted her to the house. The crowd fell silent as they parted to make room for the foursome to enter the house. Inside the doorway was another chalk outline. This one was of Nelson's body, the blood stains still visible.

Again, Stelana and Juanita had to physically help Sarah pass the scene. They entered the living room where Jessica and Yolanda were sitting on the couch with what they later learned was the pastor to officiate over Tyree's burial. Jessica looked up and saw her sister. She hopped to her feet and rushed to hug Sarah. The two embraced...wailing in tears...lost in each other's arms, comforting each other and receiving comfort simultaneously.

After several tearful moments, Sarah hugged Yolanda, never releasing her sister's hand. Jessica hugged her niece, Juanita. Her squeeze was tight and strong, like a mother grasping her child after an accident. Juanita allowed the embrace without saying a word. Then afterwards she introduced Stelana and Tony as friends.

Yolanda did not speak or acknowledge Juanita's presence. Juanita felt the snub, but did not let it bother her. She was here for her aunt. She knew Yolanda would not allow even the death of her son to be a catalyst to better their relationship. Yolanda looked through the window in an apparent act of indifference to her cousin.

The indifference lasted through the entire funeral and burial. Juanita offered her condolences several times, only to be met with a sigh and a glare of contempt. After the fifth time, Juanita resigned to the fact Yolanda would never accept her presence and decided to forgo any other sign of family affection.

During the funeral the pastor stated Tyree was with God, he was in a better place—a place where he was safe from drugs, a place he was safe from guns. The pastor also took the time to make his commentary on black on black crime. He bellowed with the emphatic and emotional character of a Southern Baptist minister, he was tired of young black men dying over nothing. He preached drugs were nothing, clothes were nothing, brand named shoes were nothing, sleeping around with everyone was nothing compared to the love of Jesus Christ. And until we found Jesus Christ we were nothing.

Juanita thought the sermon, and she thought of it as a sermon, was on target, but the pastor delivered it in the wrong forum. Tyree was a child, devoid of drugs, mindless of the trapping of name brand clothes and shoes, and oblivious to sex. His death was an accident brought on by the adults in search of these things, but it was not of Tyree's doing. Juanita looked around and saw, what she perceived, were young gang bangers…friends of Nelson, who attended Nelson's son's funeral, sitting in the audience as the pastor preached. She understood the pastor was using this opportunity to speak to these young people, while he had them captive in the church.

However, she knew the pastor was wasting his breadth. There was nothing he could say or do to turn these gang bangers from the life they now choose to live. It was a shame, she thought. It was a terrible shame. She looked again at the young gang bangers in the audience. Both men and women, teenagers and young adults, a perfect sample of the small spectrum of the youth of black America, a cornucopia of faces, graced the church. She wondered if they knew what a proud culture, what a dynamic people, and what a majestic lineage they derived from; would they continue on the self-destructive path they were presently on.

She had had this talk several times with Yolanda, especially, when she began dating Nelson. She told her of the dangers surrounding Nelson and his way of life. Yolanda would hear none of it. She closed her eyes and mind to Juanita's so called rhetoric. She was jealous of Juanita's success, and felt she was demeaning to her and her situation in Shreveport. Then, when Yolanda became hooked on drugs, and then a prostitute, Juanita went off to college and became a successful entrepreneur with UAI.

Fortunately, Yolanda did not know UAI was a front organization for USSTAP. Even though Juanita did not endeavor in drugs, or embrace the legally protected free sex life, she often wondered where she would be if Ortho and Michael had not recruited her to join USSTAP as a mighty Osguard heir apparent. Would she have fallen into the gangster life? Would she have fallen into the drug culture like her brother did so many years earlier? She did not know how difficult it was to resist the temptation of street life.

What if she was uneducated and had a child, a single mother? Would she have turned to prostitution for money, or dancing in strip clubs? She knew education was the cure for a black woman to be successful. They also needed someone to provide them with the opportunity. That was the formula for luck. Luck was when preparation, which in her case was education, met opportunity, which was USSTAP. But what did Yolanda have? She had neither preparation nor opportunity. Yolanda looked for Juanita to provide her the opportunity with UAI, but she refused, seeing Yolanda as a liability—a risk—to her. Or was Yolanda just an embarrassment? A tear rolled down Juanita's cheek as she weighed her true feeling for her cousin. Was she the one at fault?

She shook her head no. However, she could not run from the fact she was not any help either. Her cousin had asked for help and she refused. Now Yolanda had paid the ultimate price, the death of her son. Should she pay anymore? Technically, Juanita could not introduce her to USSTAP. Yolanda had subjected her body to harsh drugs, causing permanent damage to synaptic nerves required for USSTAP integration. Yet, she could work for UAI at a level oblivious to the real function of the organization. She decided she would find a position in the UAI Dallas office as soon as she could. She would also ask her mother to take Aunt Jessica back with her to Osguard Gardens to live with her.

The rest of the funeral was very emotional. A female soloist sang R. Kelly's *'I believe I Can Fly.'* The lady did not leave a dry eye in the house. Juanita began sobbing as well. The song reached into her spirit and tugged at her heart in a way she had not felt since her father and brother passed on. She had seen death many times since then. She had witnessed many funerals as well, but something about witnessing a relative's funeral cut deep inside the soul and this one was no exception. So she cried.

The burial was just as emotional. Juanita's eyes were red from crying. She did not know if she had any more tears left. Her head ached from the sobbing, and her body wrenched with raw emotion. When they lowered the small silver casket into the grave, the wrought scream that emanated from Yolanda's lungs set off a chain reaction of emotion, which shook the graveyard like an earthquake. People, who were composed, now screamed in anguish as well. The air echoed with wails of sorrow, pushing out the veil of comfort that had started to descend on the crowd after the pastor's last words.

"Ashes to ashes. Dust to dust. I consecrate thy body back to the Earth from whence it came—In the name of the Father, the Son and the Holy Ghost."

When they arrived back at Jessica's house, Reed was waiting for them on the porch. He snuck Juanita an ARIT tablet, which she slipped under her arm. She introduced Reed as an associate from her Dallas office and excused herself into the back bedroom.

She returned to the living room after fifteen minutes and asked Sarah, Reed, Stelana and Musoto to the back bedroom. They all moved to the tiny bedroom, finding a place on the bed or against the wall to sit or stand against. Juanita huffed as she tried to gather her thoughts. She paced the few steps in front of the bed back and forth for several seconds, gathering her thoughts and planning her words. Then she decided she would start with her mother and work her way to the bad news.

"First mother, I want you to ask Aunt Jessica to live with you at Osguard Gardens," Juanita blurted out. Her mother started to interject, but Juanita raised her hand for her not to interrupt. "Reed, I want to place my cousin in a job with the UAI, a code four or lower position will suffice." Reed looked surprised, but realized it was not his place to argue the decision. "Now that that is over, I have some bad news." She stopped and took a deep breath once more. This had been a horrendous day and the message on the ARIT tablet did nothing but add to an already dire situation.

"Kulusks have attacked Capitol Station with a biological agent." She paused to let the words sink in. "The agent was on the morgue ships when they returned." She swallowed hard. "Everyone is contaminated and about a quarter of the station is dead. The rest..." she paused to check her watch..."the rest are in suspension." The horrific look on their faces told the story. "I am the last Osguard. The others were on the station when the agent was delivered. Michael has sent the *Galaxy Cruiser Destiny* to pick me up. It shall rendezvous here in about three hours. Michael asked me to go to Kulusk, meet an operative, and get the antidote. Of course, this will be a covert mission and Osguard One has reminded me that I am not obligated to accept it." She paused and allowed herself to smile for the first time today. "That idiot...like I would turn my back on the Osguards or USSTAP. So I must go." She turned to Musoto. The smile vanished to be replaced by a stern 'all business" like look. "You find my cousin's murderers. If your laws don't apply...mine will."

# Chapter 26—Politicians

He peered down the empty shaft that once held the mighty Minuteman III missile. He could not make out the bottom of the long one hundred-foot deep shaft. It seemed eerie, almost unreal to see the space without its charge sitting in it. This was a sight Captain Daniel Tomkins thought he would never see, for if it was empty, it had been fired. Furthermore, if it had been fired, nuclear destruction would have taken his life prior to him being able to witness this scene. However, it had happened and he was here. Almost two weeks to the day, he with his partner, Lieutenant Wanda Coles, had turned the keys to rain destruction halfway across the world. Yet, nuclear destruction did not occur—why?

"Captain, do I need to repeat myself?" asked the firm but polite female voice.

Tomkins turned to face Representative Joyce T. Eldridge, the Speaker of the House, from Texas. She stood almost as tall as he did, about six feet. She wore her customary black business suit with a white blouse. Her eyes burned with emotion, which Tomkins assumed was irritation. Behind her was Senator Thomas C. Payne, the Senate Minority Leader and his facial expression was not any lighter.

"No Congresswoman, you don't have to repeat the question," Tomkins said, showing his own irritation. "As you can see the missile is gone. We fired it like I said, like I reported and like you can obviously see," he continued pointing to the empty silo.

"Captain Tomkins, I am sure your superiors will be more than interested in your rudeness in answering our questions," Eldridge warned.

Tomkins looked away and gave a heavy sigh. Then he turned toward his political inquisitors, as he began to think of them. He could feel his blood burning inside as he fought for composure.

Eldridge narrowed her stare to emphasize the seriousness of her threat. This agitated Tomkins more.

"Congresswoman, I am cooperating, and any perceived rudeness is only because I have just come through the most frightening experience of my life. I turned the key to blow up the world and you...and you come here, see the missile is gone, you read the report, you questioned me and Lieutenant Coles for four hours like we are some sort of criminals—and you expect me to act civilized. I'm not sure I don't need a lawyer."

"Now calm down Captain," Payne urged.

"No sir, I will not calm down," Tomkins yelled. "Think about it. Put yourself in my shoes. I took a pledge...an oath to do my job and I did it." He turned around flustered. "More than I can say for you," he murmured.

"What?" Eldridge demanded.

Tomkins turned to face Eldridge, squinting in anger and feeling his stomach turn. He took a deep breath to calm himself.

This gesture surprised Eldridge somewhat as she stepped back. She now knew she had crossed the line, but she could not back down. She continued to stare into Tomkins' eyes, but this seemed to fuel Tomkins' anger more. Before he realized it, his voice rang out in the silo. "I said I did my job and it is more than I can say about you."

"Tomkins, I warn..."

"You warn me...you warn me!" Tomkins repeated in shock. "Look lady, I stared down death. I made my peace with my God and I turned that key, expecting the end of the human race, as we know it. Then you...then you...come down here and challenge me for what you train me to do. No. No." He shrugged his shoulders. "If my memory serves me right, you voted against every military bonus, build-up and improvement that came to the Congress. Lady, I don't think you like the military. You know something," he continued with a smirk. "If it weren't for people like me, you would be a smoldering wisp of smoke right about now. So don't give me any shit about what I did or how I did it. If you don't like it, see my superiors, or better yet, tell it to my lawyer."

Payne, who was enjoying the rebuke Eldridge was receiving, now stepped between them with his hands chest high motioning for Tomkins to calm down. "Listen son, we both know we can't introduce outside parties to this incident. It is a matter of national security."

"No sir, I don't believe that anymore," Tomkins said. "I think you are on a witch hunt. You are looking for someone to fry, but you don't know who to fry or how to fry them. The entire military shot their nuclear wad and you don't like it. You don't like it at all and you are looking for someone to blame. And I ain't going to be that person and I ain't going to help you fry anyone in my chain." Tomkins then looked back at Eldridge and pushed his way past Payne toward the door.

"Captain Tomkins, you come back—"

"No, let him go," Payne urged as he grabbed Eldridge by the elbow.

"What! Why? Eldridge demanded.

"Look Joyce, we have what we came after. We have been to fifteen fields, we've seen over fifty silos. All of them empty. I suspect we will find all of them that way. And even if we don't, there are enough missiles missing to justify supporting the president."

"I know, but there is more here. I can feel it. I know it."

"You know what, Joyce?" Payne huffed. "Whatever fishing expedition you are on, it will have to wait. We have more pressing matters." Then Payne wiped his lips with the back of his hand. "I'm not sure the captain didn't hit the nail on the head." He stared into her eyes, looking for a reaction in her brown pupils. "You hate the military—don't you?"

"What do you mean? No, I don't hate the military," she protested.

Nevertheless, the split second of hesitation convinced Payne. He had enough. "Let's go," he ordered, half pushing and half guiding her toward the exit.

Eldridge started to protest, but she recognized Payne's determination. However she was just as determined. She knew she had overplayed her hand and needed to retreat and collect her wits before pursuing her hunch again. She smiled and followed his direction.

\*\*\*

President Frederick Walter Peters gazed upon his computer screen, reading the email over and over again. He was surprised at the message. It came on his private e-mail, reserved for his top aides and now Musoto.

Peters had just finished reading the report on how the committee's inspection of the empty silos was going. Representative Joyce T. Eldridge, the Speaker of the House, and Senator John W. Bass, Senate Majority leader, both Republicans and sworn enemies to him and his Democratic Party, were still skeptical, but neither one could refute the empty silos. He knew it would be a matter of time before they conceded to his wishes. Yet, time was running out. He had two more weeks before his treaty would come to a vote in Congress. He had to move quicker, but now he was mesmerized by the e-mail from Musoto.

It had been forty-eight hours since he spoke to Musoto in his office, in which Musoto reported he had made contact with the elusive USSTAP, the Osguards' organization. He could not believe what he heard but he had to. Musoto knew the details of the HVP detailing Nausona and Laurona Osguard's visit to Earth over one hundred years ago. And he knew the details of the averted nuclear crises, in which saboteurs in both the United States and Russia infiltrated and shot their nuclear arsenal to have them inexplicably destroyed by what he later found out was USSTAP. He could only have gained that information from the source, the Osguards, or the next best thing—USSTAP.

Musoto did not disclose any further information on their whereabouts or how to contact them. Musoto defied the president and took it upon himself that it was in the best interest of the nation this information remained secret. Then Musoto offered his resignation to the president.

The president was shocked. He knew he could not force the information from Musoto. He knew he could not arrest him for treason. That was the problem with secrets; one could not enforce punishment for defiance without revealing the secret to more people. Thus, Peters had no option other than to refuse the resignation and sweeten the pot for Musoto to stay as his confidant.

Peters had read Musoto's file and knew if he appeased his ego, he could not refuse. And it worked. The president gave Musoto a special title, *'Special Assistant to Presidential Affairs.'* Musoto kept his FBI status and garnered a large office on the second floor of the Hoover Building, along with a small staff. His one duty was to be the liaison between him and USSTAP.

Now Peters was reading an e-mail from Musoto:

*"Mr. President,*

*I am in the company of a USSTAP agent. We are in Shreveport LA. There's a murder case down here that is of particular interest to the Osguards. They are requesting my assistance in the investigation. The victim is a young five-year old black child, named Tyree Smart. Request your office clear the way for our investigation.*

*V/r*

*Anthony Musoto.'*

*'Our investigation.'* Those words seemed odd to the president. However, he knew he needed to comply. The murder of a young black child receiving the interest of the most powerful organization in the universe meant he needed to devote more than a perfunctory concern to it.

*'Particular interest to the Osguards.'* That could mean anything from anger to curiosity. Was this Tyree Smart an up and coming Osguard? Was he related to the Osguards? Shit, was he an Osguard? Could this murder add tension to an already edgy situation? Peters wanted to… Then he stopped. He didn't know what he wanted.

Did he want to make the Osguards an ally? Did he want to keep the Osguards a secret? Peters shook his head in frustration. He was unsure what his next step should be—an olive branch or a closed door. He knew if he did nothing, nothing would change. Was that so bad? However, if he did something, maybe—just maybe—he could use the Osguards.

Peters laughed. Use the Osguards, he questioned. That won't happen, he realized. It is best to stay on their good side. That is the best he could ever hope for. He read the e-mail one more time—almost chewing on each word, tasting it, dissecting it—searching for hidden meaning. Yet, there was none, so he decided after several seconds.

He shook his head and hit the intercom switch, "Mrs. Charles, get me the governor of Louisiana."

# Chapter 27—Surrounded

Opel's face flushed with anguish. His eyes widened with fright. How stupid, he thought. He had let his own ambition blind him. He had been unwittingly tagged with a tracer, snuck on him during a battle with Kie. He should have known better and by the look of dissatisfaction on Tirana's face, she knew he should have known better.

"ARIT, scan for soldiers," Tirana ordered.

Opel turned to the ARIT control panel as if he could mentally reach in and witness the machine scanning the area. His pulse raced with anticipation, for he already knew the answer. Sweat formed under his armpits as he thought of his next move.

"Five air cruisers and twelve land cruisers moving toward Langoni, estimated time of arrival—five minutes," the male ARIT voice grunted.

"ARIT," Opel yelled. "Copy and repeat tracer signature on outskirts of city—position X-two–J-four."

"Complete," the ARIT notified Opel.

Then Opel reached into his belt, grabbed the tracer, threw it on the floor, and smashed it with his boot. "There," he said with a hint of satisfaction. "ARIT close all ports to the basement, echo indigenous soil and dirt signatures when scanned until further notice," he ordered.

The ARIT flooded the room with green light, blinding Tirana and Opel. The siblings reached under the control panel and retrieved large black goggles with gold lenses. They put the goggles over their eyes, which filtered the green light and restored almost normal lighting to their eyes.

"I should be up top. It will look strange for no one to be home," Tirana suggested.

"No, I think it best you come with me. It's safer."

"Are you sure, brother?"

"No, but I feel better having you with me," he admitted. "We are in the final stages of the beginning of this revolution. Hiding is no longer a valuable tactic. Kie won't stop until he tears this town apart. The new echo technique will only work for so long. It will buy us some time before our next move." He hugged his sister. "It's time for you to take your place next to me in the revolution—it is time for us to start our revolution."

"Air cruisers over X-two–J-four," the ARIT announced as it displayed targets onto a chart.

Opel read the signal. He tasted the salt of sweat on his lips. He looked at his sister for support. She stared at him for several agonizing seconds, and then she closed her eyes as if in prayer and slowly nodded.

Opel pressed several sensors under the brown glass control panel. As he did, part of a rock formation slid open in area X-two–J-four on the northern outskirts of Langoni, exposing a blue crystal like multifaceted, eighteen-barreled weapon … ten feet long, four inches thick and three feet wide. It also was constructed of taonic circuitry and powered by jorelli plugs. It shot invisible beams of energy more destructive than coronet pellets or melenai pulses. Opel called his weapon a *'Kwainique.'* He was unable to create a man-portable version of the weapon, but he had mass-produced the weapon in sufficient quantity to equip every one of his land cruisers, air cruisers and his small array of star fighters with the weapon.

About two rings from X-two–J-four, five single seat Kulusk Air Cruisers, KAC for short, flew just below Mach speed toward the false signal. The KAC was shaped like a spade, with two of its four cigar shaped engines neatly tucked under the fuselage and the other two engines molded on top of the fuselage. Its underbelly was mauve to camouflage it against the Kulusk sky, which was painted by its red sun. Its upper coat was brownish gold to match the indigenous surface of the planet. The pilot sat at the tip of the spade in a diamond shaped clear canopy. The pilot's rear view was slightly obstructed by the top engines, but his rear view Imcam, located in his cockpit, made up for the lack of vision. Inside the cockpit, the pilot had an array of search, surveillance, defensive and offensive equipment, including a chromerion field generator, a newly fitted twin barreled shockdel gun that targeted and aimed in a two hundred and seventy-degree forward arc, and a rear shooting pagenay.

Behind the KACs were twelve Kulusk Land Cruisers, KLCs. They were tan to camouflage them against the planet's rugged terrain. Each KLC contained a crew of three, sheltered in a boxlike clear covered cockpit. One member piloted, one member navigated and one member operated the pagenay turrets—one turret situated in front of the cockpit and the other in back of the cockpit. The KLC also contained a chromerion field generator. Its rectangular body with smooth rounded edges, hovered four feet over the ground, using magnetic coil suspension for stability. They were traveling at their maximum speed of one hundred rings per galactic hour—almost one hundred and twenty miles per hour.

Opel observed the KACs and KLCs approach the area through his ARIT monitor. He aimed on the lead KAC as it orbited above the false signal, directing the KLCs to the spot. He paused with his finger over the firing sensor, waiting for the KLCs to get within range. When the ARIT displayed the KLCs within his firing range he closed his eyes in a moment of meditation and then pushed the sensor.

A whining, ear-busting sound rang through the air just a split second prior to the first ship exploding into dime size pieces. Metal, blood and fuel rained on the ground like colorful balls of hail, dissipating in light as they cooled from the fall to earth. Then the second ship, the third, the fourth, and finally the fifth ship exploded in the same fashion, lighting the twilight sky with a tremendous fireworks display—making colorful, but morbid, circular designs in the air.

The three man teams in the KLCs were caught off guard. They hesitated as the explosion of the five KACs happened in less than ten universal seconds. Then the explosions happened on the ground. The KLCs exploded before the men could take a breath. They did not have time to be afraid. It was quick, painless and very destructive, leaving little if any evidence of what they once were—soldiers—men and machines.

Opel breathed a slight sigh of relief as he activated the rock façade to hide the weapon once more. Then he activated the micro-portal and transported the Kwainique out of its hiding spot.

"Let's go," he commanded. "The resulting confusion of what just happened will keep Kie guessing for a while. Hopefully, it will be long enough for us to regroup."

"Won't he take it out on the people of Langoni?" Tirana asked.

"I don't know. I hope he is smarter than that. I am counting on him being smarter than that."

"This is Kie, I never knew him to use his brain over doling out pain and suffering."

"Okay, Tirana—what do you suggest?"

"We start here…we start the revolution here."

"Tirana, we just did," Opel asserted.

"No," she insisted. "We go on the offensive. We attack Kie…we attack the Capitol. We attack Renard…Tonight!"

***

"Osguard on the bridge," the security officer bellowed.

Juanita stepped onto the bridge of the *Galaxy Cruiser Destiny*, followed by the ship's sire, Centurion Deon Jackil, from the planet Thirion. Juanita stepped down toward the two command chairs in the center of the bridge. The flashback rushed into her consciousness of when she commanded her own galaxy cruiser—*USSTAP Galaxy Cruiser Hope*. She moved to the navigator pilot station in the front of the bridge similar to her own bridge on the *Galaxy Protector Sharyla*. The front wall contained two screens. The right screen displayed the ARIT-projected layout for the navigator and the left screen displayed the star field for the pilot. Additionally, situated throughout the bridge floor were several stations, engineering and communications to the right, life-support and the science stations were on the left, tactical next to the pilot station, and the defense next to the navigator station. Yet, because of the smaller stature of the ship compared to its galactic protector cousin, it did not have a battle bridge, for it did not carry defenders.

Jackil motioned for Juanita to take the command chair. She looked at the seat tempted by the gesture but shook her head. "No, this is your ship. I am only a passenger until we reach Kulusk and then I am simply the mission commander. You are still and will continue to be the sire of this vessel."

"As you wish," Jackil responded. Then he turned to his navigator, "Set course for Kulusk—most expeditious route."

"Course set," the navigator responded.

"Execute—MOP sixty," he commanded.

The pilot pushed three sensors, "Tiah, sire."

The lights on the engines flashed to blue as the ship disappeared, seemingly defying the laws of physics, but adhering to the laws of light as it traveled through space, sixty light years per hour.

"I'll be in my quarters," Juanita said. "Please let me know when we reach Kulusk."

"Tiah, Osguard," Jackil responded in surprise. He had thought the Osguard would brief him on what they were doing. He was in the dark. He just received a coded black encrypted message to pick up Juanita from Earth and transport her to Kulusk. The message came from Millmum Station and was signed and coded by Michael. Jackil knew USSTAP was in disarray after the battle a few weeks ago and he was weary of this mission. However, he had full trust in his Osguard and by association he had trust in Juanita…although, he could not help but feel a little uneasy about the mission—especially since he knew nothing about it. He turned to watch the Osguard retreat from the bridge, now he was more curious than ever.

# Chapter 28—Clout

It was just one more thing Police Chief Daniel Delecroix did not have time to deal with this morning. He slammed the file onto the desk as the buzzer from the outer office buzzed. Didn't he tell his secretary he was not to be disturbed this morning? Then why was she buzzing him? He pushed a glaring glance at his door as if he could reach out and grab his secretary by the throat using nothing but his mind.

He tapped the comm center on his desk. "What?" he screamed.

"Sorry to bother you sir," the secretary, Mrs. Jillian James said. "It is the governor on line two for you."

"The governor?" Delecroix's voice softened as his mind raced through the current cases to see why the governor would be calling him. He could not think of any at the moment. "Thank you, Mrs. James," he said.

Delecroix switched the comm center and pushed line two on his speakerphone. "Mr. Governor."

"Yes, Chief Delecroix, this is Governor Williams."

"To what do I owe the pleasure?"

"I'm sorry, this is not pleasure. It is business," Governor William Williams stated. "You have a murder case up there. I believe it is of a five year old boy named Tyree…Tyree Smart."

"Yes sir," Delecroix said somewhat perplexed. "A drive-by shooting. We think the intended target was the boy's father...a Nelson Ford. We think it was some type of retaliation from a bad drug deal the night before. Why?"

"Well it looks like this Tyree Smart has some big time clout. I received a call from the president of the United States...about thirty minutes ago. He says an FBI agent by the name of Tony Musoto will be nosing around in the case. We are to give him full access...him and whoever is with him. It seems Tyree is special to someone important...national security important...if you get my meaning," Williams emphasized.

"Are you sure?" asked Delecroix. "From what we can tell...Tyree Smart's mother is a drug addict and an ex-prostitute. His father, who was killed in the shooting, was a two-time loser as well. We put this case in the blue file."

"The blue file?" Williams asked. "What the devil is the blue file?"

"Cases that we probably won't solve are put into the blue file. You know...the ones that are almost cold from the beginning. No witnesses—no evidence—no suspects."

"Well you better put this file on the top of your priority list...ASAP! The president was mighty particular about this one." Then the governor paused to let his words sink in. "Delecroix?"

"Yes sir."

"Delecroix, I hope for both our sakes you did not put this case in your blue file because the victim was black. Because if you did—"

"No sir," Delecroix tried to plead. "It is like most of the drug related killings. We don't have much to go on. Our resources are limited, so I put my strength in those cases that have leads."

"Delecroix, you need to put your strength on all the cases. And I suggest you get rid of that blue file before Musoto gets there. Understand?"

"Understood sir?"

"I don't like this. I don't like this one bit," Williams said after a moment of reflection. "Look, I am going to send you some help from the Louisiana Bureau of Investigations. This is something I am sure they can sink their teeth into. I know they don't have jurisdiction, but neither does that FBI agent. However, the federal government is going to be up our ass on this one and I'm not sure I want you to be the only person they see."

"Sir, we can handle—"

"Shut up Delecroix!" Williams interrupted. "I'm trying to help you."

"Yes sir," Delecroix relented.

"Expect agents from the LBI to be there within the hour. Make available everything you have."

Then the phone went dead. Delecroix listened to the dial tone for several seconds as he imagined his twenty-seven year career crushing down around him. He nudged the speakerphone off and sat in his chair. He swung the chair around to look out his window and onto I-20 that passed by in the distance. He blew a hard breath and closed his eyes.

The buzzer from the comm center on his desk sounded. Delecroix covered his face with his hands as he wondered what now. The buzzer sounded again. Delecroix swung his chair around and answered the buzz.

"What now?" he barked.

"Sir, there is a Special Agent Musoto and his partner here to see you. He said you should be expecting him," Mrs. James added.

"Send them in," Delecroix said without thinking.

Several seconds later, Musoto and Stephanie Rikes, also known as Sentinel Stelana Rican of USSTAP, stepped into the office.

"Chief Delecroix, I am Special Agent Musoto," Musoto said revealing his badge for identification. "And this is my associate, Stephanie Rikes," he said nodding to Stelana.

"Yes, I just received a call from Governor Williams, telling me to expect you…something to do with Nelson Ford?" he responded as he pointed to the chairs for them to sit down.

"Not quite," Stelana interrupted as she and Musoto sat in the two chairs in front of Delecroix's desk. She knew Delecroix was fishing for some answers—anyone would in this situation. So, she was ready to feed him some—half-truths anyway. "We are here unofficially to lend a hand in the investigation. You see, young Tyree Smart is a relative of some very influential people, and we want to be able to tell them all is being done in finding young Tyree's killers."

Musoto looked over at Stelana, half amazed and half shocked at her openness. He was ready to stonewall Delecroix and let him hang on a tether, but Stelana didn't. She just smiled, revealing her white teeth and allowing her natural Chaktun beauty to quell the tension somewhat. Her light brown eyes danced with gleam as she batted the conversation back to Delecroix.

"Influential? I say! It seems the president of the United States is very interested as well. I tell you, I didn't know Nelson had influential relatives." Delecroix handed the conversation back to Stelana.

Stelana squinted her eyes as if she were struggling with a thought. Then she let out a small giggle. "No, it isn't Nelson, it is Yolanda," she offered. "Even unbeknownst to Yolanda, she has relatives who care about her that have…well…they have clout. So please do not let Yolanda Smart or her mother know we are involved. It is somewhat a…well…it is a secret."

"National security?" asked Delecroix.

"It's kind of a global concern," Musoto said.

"Global?" Delecroix was now getting scared. Before he was just nervous about his career, but now he felt he was involved in something larger than he or his department could handle. "How is the death of the five year old son of a drug addict and an ex-prostitute a global issue?"

"You would be surprised," Stelana added. "Many international incidents started with small seemingly innocuous happenings."

"I suppose, but I can't see this one being so critical," Delecroix added.

"I bet you that is what the cops who stopped Rodney King said as well," Stelana charged.

"Well, we ourselves have had a couple of problems that caused this country an international black eye," Musoto interjected trying to gain control of the conversation. "Hanssen, Ruby Ridge and Waco just to name some. We all have things we wished we handled better. Right now we don't want Tyree Smart to be one of those."

"Okay, point taken," Delecroix pushed to change the subject. "What can I do for you?"

"Well, can we see your file, and talk to the officers in charge of the investigation?" Stelana pushed.

"Sure. If you give me about two hours, I will have the officers and the file at your disposal...let's say about nine-thirty," Delecroix requested.

Stelana did not like the wait, but she knew there was nothing she could do about it. She turned to Musoto. He shrugged.

"Fine," Musoto said with authority. "We shall return at nine-thirty."

They exchanged pleasantry as Musoto and Stelana left the office.

***

Two hours later, Musoto and Stelana returned. Delecroix had delivered on his promise. He set them up in a room with two copies of the file. The pictures were gory, but telling. The murders were somewhat amateurish, but planned. The file linked Nelson to the slaying that happened the night prior. Something left out of the paper and they did not know before. Musoto read, two men from the Dallas area were shot and killed, by a John Carter, alias J.C. J.C., who was killed in the altercation, was also a known associate of Nelson Ford. The police believed Nelson was involved and his murder was in retaliation. Thus, the Shreveport police were waiting on information on the two dead Dallas men, from the Dallas police.

"It sounds right," Musoto commented.

"Yeah, it sounds right," repeated Stelana. "Although, it sounds like the local yokels punted the ball to Dallas, and I bet Dallas fumbled it."

"Yeah, I bet you are right," Musoto relented. "Look at this fax they sent the Dallas police. They requested the known associates of the two men." Then Musoto paused.

"What?" Stelana asked.

"They name Yolanda as a witness who can identify the men," he noted. "Did she ever tell you she saw the men, or she could identify them?"

"No, she has not spoken to me at all. I bet there is much she has not told anyone."

"Listen, if those idiot cops in Dallas let on there is an eye witness—"

"...Yolanda may be in danger!" Stelana declared.

"I tell you what...you go back to the house and keep an eye on Yolanda and the family. I will interview the detectives—okay?" Musoto offered.

"Yeah, I best do that. I'll catch up with you later." Then she thought awhile. "We better call Major Reed. He may be able to get the Dallas office moving on this."

"Okay, let me make a copy of this fax," Musoto said, standing and pushing his way toward the door. He walked to the copier in the main office next to the water fountain on the far wall. As he copied the file, he pulled out his cell phone and pushed speed dial number four.

"Hey Mona, this is Tony...

...Yeah, I know I missed our date last night. But duty called....

...Now calm down...I'm sorry...but I had to leave town...

...That's right...Yeah...you would never guess where I am...

...Shreveport...Shreveport LA.

***

Outside the chief's office, Mrs. James was enjoying her third cup of coffee. She liked it hot, black and sweetened with aspartame. She emptied the contents from a third blue package into her personalized ten ounce coffee cup that read *'World's Greatest Secretary.'* The cup was a gift from members of the department, who came to know her as *'Mother.'* The bifocals she wore and the flower print dresses she was infamous for enhanced her motherly demeanor.

She gently stirred her coffee, diluting the aspartame so she could taste its sweet presence in each sip, when she saw them. The first one, a white man, was impeccably dressed in a double-breasted suit and tie. His red hair was cropped close and he did not show any signs of battling the sweltering heat and humidity—not a drop of perspiration noted. The other was a beautiful mahogany skinned black woman—about twenty eight with shoulder length hair tucked toward her neck at the end. Mrs. James commented she would kill to get her hair permed to look half as good as this woman. The woman wore a smart business suit with pants. Under the suit, she wore a white pullover, long neck cotton blend blouse. She also looked cool and not bothered by the heat.

The pair approached her desk, not smiling, but business like. The man spoke first. "I'm Lieutenant Elvis Tornado and this is my partner, Lieutenant Sally Coleman. We are with the Louisiana Bureau of Investigations. I believe Chief Daniel Delecroix is expecting us."

187

# Malcolm Dylan Petteway

"Yes, that's correct," she answered, trying to sound as professional as Tornado. "Let me announce you." She tapped the intercom and announced the two LBI agents.

Delecroix accepted the announcement and instructed Mrs. James to let them in. The two LBI agents followed Mrs. James into the inner office without saying a word. This was particularly rude, Mrs. James thought. She prided herself on being friendly, as did most of the people she knew in Shreveport. She made a mental note she would bathe them in Shreveport hospitality before they left. If they still were unfriendly then so be it.

"Close the door behind you," Delecroix barked.

\*\*\*

The white Lear Jet cut through the air like a dart, pushing through the sky and sailing into a beautiful sunrise. Senate Majority Leader, John W. Bass from the State of Washington; Senate Minority Leader Thomas C. Payne from New York; Speaker of the House, Joyce T. Eldridge from Texas; and House Minority Leader, Warren S. Leaks from North Dakota sat in the passenger compartment reviewing their notes.

"I am ready to concede the fact we shot our wad. But did Russia?" Eldridge blurted out, ruining the silence in the cabin. "And has anyone seen this weapon that's supposed to have shot down Russia's missiles?"

"No, I suppose not," Leaks conceded after several seconds of silence.

"When I see this weapon, then I will be convinced," she said, "but until then, I feel we may be part of an elaborate hoax. I am not comfortable with this at all."

"You know I hate to agree with you," Leaks submitted. "Most of those missiles are from my state and agreeing to this pact will inevitably hurt North Dakota. So, I think we need more evidence. I need to see the weapon system that allegedly destroyed all of Russia's missiles. Plus I need to see records, tapes, video or something to confirm Russia's missiles are destroyed."

"Think about it," interjected Bass. "Obviously we shot our weapons, they shot theirs and we are still standing here. Something had to stop them. No video, tape or written report is better evidence than us walking and breathing right now."

"No, I am not convinced," Leaks continued. "I need proof. I at least want to see this awesome weapon."

"To tell the truth, I am curious about it as well," Payne added. "I mean our report and cooperation will not be complete unless we see everything and we know the entire truth," he added smiling at Eldridge.

Eldridge smiled back. "Where do you imagine this awesome weapon to be? Is it one weapon or several linked together? How does it work? There are so many unanswered questions."

188

"I tell you something," Bass stated. "I think you are all wasting time, but I do agree. If the president wants the backing of his own party as well as my backing, he has to be more forthright than this."

"What do you suggest?" Leaks asked.

"I suggest we report to the president that we…as a group…are not convinced about his story," Bass suggested. "We tell him, we know the weapons are gone, but we are not sure of Russia's involvement. As far as we know, the weapons were never there and Russia has its full arsenal."

Payne, Leaks and Eldridge all nodded in deliberate contemplation. None of the three had ventured to say it aloud, but all had thought it at one time or another. Group thinking was now dominating the politicians' minds. The weight of the responsibility thrust upon them by the situation had made them overly cautious and afraid to voice acceptance of the president's suggestion. However, acceptance now was far away. It was pure defiance, which clung to the heart of the four politicians. Defiance in the face of what they conceived to be deception on the president's part or at least disloyalty. Either one, was not acceptable to the group now. They had to answer to their constituents and not their president or party. This was too important to draw on the partisan views.

"I agree," Payne bellowed. "I at least need more time and more evidence."

"So what is it going to be," Bass asked, looking at Leaks.

Leaks looked around as if he could find some comfort from an invisible source on the plane, but he knew he couldn't. Eldridge had voiced her opinion from the start, Bass was now coming alive and Payne just crossed the line. There was no turning back now. Leaks had edged the conversation and now he had to put up or shut up. He turned back to his companions and nodded.

"Then that's it," Bass said with gleam. We confront the president today. We let him know, it isn't over yet. We let him know we still have the clout to make this happen, whether he acknowledges it or not."

***

"Detective Russell," Musoto addressed.

Detective Robin Russell and Detective Peter Allensen had joined him in the room where he was pouring over the several papers in the Smart file. Russell was a thirteen-year veteran on the force; she had several commendations for bravery. She stood merely five-feet tall, with curly black shoulder length hair. She dressed in a striped shirt and blue jeans. Allensen was a black man and stood about five-feet, nine inches tall. He was a ten-year veteran and the junior partner of this investigative team.

"Yes, Agent Musoto," Russell answered.

"I gather, the Dallas police have not answered your fax yet."

189

"That's right…they haven't."

"How long ago did you send it?" Musoto asked.

"The day of the murder," she snapped back.

"Nice work, piecing the two together," Musoto commented. "Have you followed up on your fax?"

"No…I can't say that we have. We've been following some other leads," she lied.

"Like what?"

"Like J.C.'s cousin," Allensen interrupted.

Russell looked at her partner in disbelief. Then she turned to Musoto, "Yeah … Carter's cousin!"

"What about his cousin?" Musoto inquired.

Russell gave a blank stare. Musoto knew she knew nothing about this line of inquiry. He then turned to Allensen. "What about his cousin?" he repeated.

Allensen regarded his partner for a moment, and then he turned to Musoto. Musoto knew Allensen didn't want to speak freely around his partner. He thought a minute on how to handle this one.

"Russell," he said. "Can you check on the Dallas police? See if they have an update for us."

Russell observed Allensen and realized he had information, she did not have. "If you don't mind, I'd rather stay," she requested. "I will be truthful with you Musoto…I followed established procedure and put this in the blue file—a holding place for cold cases. If the Dallas police gave us something, we would have pursued it. Since they haven't we've dropped it. Allensen and I have had some…well…some heated discussion on how to handle this case. He is new to homicide, you know—"

"And that means what?" Musoto sassed.

"That means I don't know how to handle the drug related murders. They don't get our full attention, even when they involve a five-year old kid," Allensen chastised.

"No, Pete…that's not what it means," she yelled back. "Look, we get fifty or so homicides a year. Fifty percent of them are drug related. We solve about half of them, including half the drug related ones. However, if we reach a dead end, we put it in the blue file and concentrate our resources on those we have leads on. This one had no leads other than Dallas."

"No leads you were willing to follow up on," Allensen commented.

"What leads are you talking about?" continued Musoto.

"I grew up with J.C. and Nelson," Allensen admitted.

"You what?" shouted Russell. "You never told me that."

"I tried to tell you," Allensen shouted back. "I told you I knew them. You saw me with Carter's mother. Or did you think that was an act, or did you even care?"

"Never mind that," Musoto pushed. "Tell me more about these leads."

"Lead…Agent Musoto…a lead," Allensen corrected. "Carter had a cousin from Dallas…a Jean Carter. I thought there was a connection, so I asked around. I found out there was a connection. Jean was a known associate of our victims, along with a Tommy Turner."

"Was?" echoed Musoto.

"She's dead…killed the same day as Nelson," Allensen responded. "She was stabbed…throat slit…a snitches execution." He adjusted his seat. Then he looked into Musoto's eyes, trying to decide if he should continue. He saw something in Musoto's eyes—compassion—concern—curiosity. Whatever it was, he decided to continue anyway. "A Detective Dave Charles is heading the case. I told Detective Charles of Dallas, we might be looking for the same guy—Tommy Turner."

"You got a description?" asked Russell.

"Better," he smiled. "I have a photo. I want to take it to Yolanda Smart this morning to see if she can identify Tommy Turner as one of the people who shot her son."

"I thought she didn't see the people who shot Nelson or her son," Russell shot back in defense.

"Maybe…maybe not," he insisted. "I think it is worth a try." Allensen looked at his partner and threw the mug shot on the table in front of her. "I don't think I wasted resources on getting this picture. Do you?"

# Chapter 29—Posturing

"Soli, I want your people on the east side in two galactic hours. And no one moves until they receive the signal from me. I have everything like a fine tuned timepiece. Everything…and I mean everything depends on precise timing." The orders flowed from Opel's mouth into ARIT comm like a drill sergeant. He was speaking to his air component commander, Mota Silliw. He had just finished barking instructions to his land component commander, Tsrif Slod. The plan was coming alive and Opel was the architect of the entire episode.

Once satisfied Mota understood his instructions, Opel terminated the conversation over the secure communication link. Then he turned and smiled at the layout he had constructed on the ARIT monitor. He had coordinated the air and ground attack on Renard, positioning forces he had planned for over twenty universal years. His forces, as he now thought of them…would be in place in two universal hours. He never thought this day would come, but after explaining the situation, especially the situation with USSTAP, the revolutionary council vote was almost unanimous to start the inevitable.

Tirana stood behind her brother, watching and reviewing his plan. She had listened for years to how he planned on attacking Renard and taking control of the government. However today, that plan was just a mere few hours from fruition. She could not believe it. Additionally, she could not believe she was the one who suggested they give his idea life.

The plan seemed bold but flawless. It had everything needed for a short but decisive military victory. It had surprise, deception, mass concentration of forces, and if all went on time—tempo. For years the revolutionary council amassed superior air cruisers, land cruisers and soldiers. They trained in the remote countryside, away from the prying eyes of the Kulusk military.

Ten squadrons of air cruisers and air bombers, ten battalions of land cruisers and land bombers, two surface action groups of sea cruisers and destroyers, practiced almost on a weekly basis on the furthest reaches of the Dijanai and the Taiole land masses and shores—flying, rolling and sailing in the cold night skies, harsh deserted lands and isolated oceans, unhampered from Kulusk surveillance satellites. This was a weakness of the Kulusk Empire—holes in their planetary surveillance coupled with the false believe that a ruthless dictatorship assured internal security. The Maxum also believed no one could muster the resources necessary to execute a genuine revolt against his regime. Thus, he concentrated his resources in building the largest and strongest space force known to Kulusk, leaving a weak budget and inferior personnel to build and train the Kulusk Planetary Guard.

This was a concept Opel and Tirana built their entire plan on—better training and better resources, coupled with true leaders. Their leaders were borne from exile, raised in hate and fed with revenge on a daily basis. More than ideology … more than money fueled their motivation. Their motivation was fueled by the never-ending knowledge that if they failed, there was no tomorrow for them.

Tirana's heart pumped heavier with glee as she imagined every step of the plan in its execution. In her mind she saw the air, land and the sea battle. She saw casualties for the Kulusk Empire, not for the revolutionaries. She knew this was idealistic and most unlikely, but she wanted to hope, she wanted to dream. For she thought if she hoped enough, if she dreamed enough, it somehow would come true.

The enemy was at its weakest point. Its space borne fleet was destroyed. The true Kulusk soldiers were either dead or captured by USSTAP. What was left was an inferior group of five hundred air ships, a small amount of land soldiers with a torrid disarray of land cruisers and a non-existent sea fleet. The thing that stopped them from proceeding with this plan earlier was the enormous space fleet. Just one battleship and its fighters could have destroyed the revolution before it got started. But now…but now, she thought, the time was right. And apparently, so did the Revolutionary Council.

The sea fleet will attack from both sides of Renard. The air cruisers will come from the east with the sun at their back and over the mountains. The land cruisers, which traveled through the micro-portal system, will advance from the west. A pure squeeze play, the action will leave no flank uncovered. Plus the additional deceptive play from their man inside will add to the distraction.

"It can't fail," Tirana wondered aloud.

"What?" Opel responded.

"Nothing, my brother," she dismissed. "I was just reviewing the plan once more. I can't find a flaw in it!" She added, trying to control her excitement. "Efas would be proud of us today. We finally avenge him and take what is rightfully ours."

"Yes, my sister," Opel joined in. "We will be on the throne by sundown."

\*\*\*

"Mr. President," Leaks whined. "I am afraid we can't support your plan unless we have more evidence."

The president was silent for a moment, sitting back in his chair in the oval office contemplating why a member of his own party was siding with the opposition and challenging him. He expected it from Bass, and had a plan ready to combat any rhetoric Bass intended to offer, but he was surprised by Leaks.

He observed the four politicians sitting around his desk, ominously in the same arrangement they sat a few short weeks ago. However, this time they looked like they were in control. They were in control? No, he had to gain control. He couldn't allow the situation to slip through his grasp.

"Is this the feeling of the group as a whole?" asked Peters.

"Yes, Mr. President. It is," Payne replied. "I am afraid it is," he added.

"Did you not see the empty silos?" Peters asked, showing his agitation.

"Yes, we did," retorted Eldridge.

Peters noticed Bass smug in the corner—and why not? Somehow Bass had convinced the others to do his dirty work for him. Peters stared at Bass, letting him know he knew he was behind the sudden revolt. Bass shrugged in response, which made Peters angrier about the circumstances.

"What else do you need?" Peters petitioned.

"We need more information on what destroyed the missiles," interjected Eldridge. "We need to see reports, pictures—touch, taste the damned thing."

Peters sat back in his chair with his eyes on his desk. He did not know what to say or do next. He knew he couldn't tell the truth, or could he. For a moment, he batted around the idea of telling the truth, but a little voice inside of him said not to. However, he was not sworn to secrecy, it was just inferred by the message. Yet, he knew the information would cause panic, but for a fleeting moment, he was willing to take the chance.

"Well," he moaned. "No," he then roared. "I can't do that."

"What?" Bass yelled. "What do you mean?"

"I can't do that," Peters repeated in a more civil tone.

"Why not? We've seen all the numbers," Leaks questioned.

"I can't tell you that either," Peters responded.

"With all due respect sir...that's bull," Payne charged.

"I must remind all of you, of where you are," the president started, pursuing a tone of command. "I am the President of the United States, and this is the Oval Office. Spirited debate is always welcome, disagreement is inevitable...but I will demand respect and a common air of civility throughout. Is that understood?"

Bass looked around in disbelief. This was the same president who a few short weeks ago used the position of his office to threaten him with treason, and now he is asking for respect. Bass shook his head several times, wanting to speak, but opted to let the president's words linger in the air.

"Fine, Mr. President," Leaks offered. "We have spirited debate and we have disagreement. You don't get our support until we get yours."

The president looked into Leaks' eyes and realized any further discussion would be futile. Leaks' mind was made up. And if his was made up, there was no chance of changing the others' point of view. "I'll think about it," he said. "I'll give you my answer in a couple of days. Until then, I request nothing be said to anyone about this."

Bass looked at his companions. They all shrugged indifference.

"Okay, Mr. President," Bass said. "We will give you twenty-four hours...no more...just twenty-four hours. If we don't see anything by then, then our support is withdrawn."

"You know, you are hurting your country," the president began to plead. "We need this treaty or we will be fighting every warlord in every third world country, while we scrape the bottom of the budget to rebuild a useless nuclear inventory."

"I don't see it that way, Mr. President," Leaks offered. "No one has to know we don't have our inventory anymore. The threat can stay alive, whether it's real or not." Leaks smiled. "Plus, if the Russians are truly in the same position, I doubt they will say anything."

The president stared at Leaks. There was much merit in what he said. However, running such a deep level deception would take resources and people he did not have faith would last long. Yet, the deception had lasted this long without repercussions. He pondered the thought for several seconds. Either way, it was deception. Leaks just offered him a way out. Or did he offer him an early grave?

"Fine, Mr. Leaks. In twenty-four hours we will meet again." Peters stood and motioned toward the door. "Until then?"

"Until then," Bass replied.

The group then departed the oval office, confused but happy—they'd stood their ground and the president had blinked. It was a small reward, but it was a reward just the same.

***

Musoto and Allensen walked up the bloody pathway. Tyree's blood still stained the pavement and parts of the grass. A small white chalk outline still marked the spot in which Tyree lost his battle with death. Allensen paused at the spot; water filled his eyes as he shook his head in disbelief. Musoto let him have his moment of silence.

After a few seconds in quiet memory, Musoto tapped Allensen's arm. They moved up the walkway onto the porch, where Yolanda and Stelana sat. Yolanda was glassy eyed and in deep contemplation. Musoto could tell her mind was somewhere else, perhaps remembering a happier time with Tyree.

Stelana was in a lawn chair fanning herself from the heat. She wore a sleeveless shirt and blue jean shorts. Around her waist she wore a Charlie belt. It was the Delta belt combination, minus the coronet pistol. To a casual onlooker, it would appear Stelana had wrapped a black belt around her waist with black charms attached to it, but on closer examination, one could see the charms were a Mation II, pagenay and a PGP.

Stelana was on guard duty, protecting Yolanda from any possible harm. Musoto recognized this and nodded to Stelana as he approached. Then he turned to Yolanda, who appeared not to notice their approach.

"Yolanda?" Musoto called.

She looked up, staring past the men.

"Yolanda, do you remember Detective Allensen? He has some photos for you to look at."

Allensen nodded and passed a page with eight photos to Yolanda. Yolanda, still in a fog, took the photos and laid them in her lap. She looked down at them. She reviewed eight mug shots—black men in their twenties, all with short hair and long sideburns. Three of the photos had men with mustaches and the other five had men who were clean-shaven.

"Do you recognize any of those men?" Allensen asked.

Yolanda stared at the page for several more seconds, yet it seemed like minutes to the investigators. She studied each picture, closing her eyes every so often and then opening them again. Tears rolled down her cheek as she reviewed the pictures. Then she handed the page back to Allensen.

"No, I don't know any of these men," she wept.

"Are you sure?" Allensen pursued. "Take another look. We think the person responsible for your son's death is among these men."

"You tell me which one and I will point him out," Yolanda screeched. "Lord knows I wish I saw the coward that shot my baby...but I didn't. If you tell me which one of these bastards did it, I will testify to Almighty God Himself he did it."

Allensen looked at Musoto as he folded the page back in his pocket. "No Ms. Smart. I wish I could, but I can't do it that way." He looked at her with sorrow in his eyes. "Again, my condolence on your loss. And rest assured, I am doing everything I can to catch this bastard.

She looked into Allensen's eyes and found some solace in his spirit. She nodded and then allowed her mind to drift back to her special place. Musoto and Allensen took their cue and left Yolanda to her thoughts.

All Stelana could do was watch. She knew Yolanda was at a fragile point right now, and any interference, especially from a stranger like her, could prove detrimental, so she watched and said a silent prayer to Jus, to give Yolanda the strength to get past her grief and move on. There was nothing else she could do.

After her silent prayer, Stelana watched the two men walk down the little concrete path leading back to the main sidewalk and the street. Allensen and Musoto walked back past the death scene toward the sidewalk. This time neither one stopped. When they reached the sidewalk, Allensen turned and looked down the street.

"There are some stores and a gas station down that way," Allensen shrugged. "I think I will go flash these pictures around there. Who knows? I may come up with something."

"Right, you do that," Musoto conceded.

With that, Allensen disappeared down the street. Leaving Musoto to his thoughts, which were interrupted by a small chirp coming from his inside suit jacket pocket. It was the secure cell phone the president had given him. He had almost forgotten about it. The president had given it to him as part of his assignment – liaison between the United States and USSTAP. It was secure, using state of the art technology, including special satellite bouncing and frequency shifting in synchronicity to the president's phone in the oval office.

Musoto retrieved the phone from his pocket and pushed the answer key, "Agent Musoto."

"Musoto, this is the president. I have a situation. I need to speak to one of the Osguards."

"Sir, you must be joking," Musoto responded. "I just can't grab an Osguard because you say so, even though you are the president. They are kind of busy…you know…running the universe."

"Listen Musoto, I need to speak to someone…and I need to speak to them soon."

"About what, sir?"

Peters took the next five minutes explaining his plan and treaty deception he conceived with the Russian president. He explained the deal he had with the four politicians and how those same politicians were changing the proposal. Then he ended by saying he needed to confer with the Osguards on what he was expected to do.

Musoto took in all the information, sighing in spots in which he recognized the tremendous complexity and mentally laughing in spots in which he recognized the pure politics of the situation.

When Peters was through, Musoto moved back into the yard and stood next to the bloody spot where Tyree died. He studied the blood as silence bathed the airwave between Peters and him. Musoto imagined he saw the boy lying in the spot, bloody and lifeless. His heart wrenched at the thought. Then his mind jumped to last night, hearing Juanita describe the horrid details of the Kulusks' last attack. Until now the words had not sunk in. He was pursuing Tyree's killer and nothing else matter—until now.

"Mr. President," Musoto said. "I think you need to sit down for this."

Musoto then described what he knew about the latest biological attack on USSTAP. How Millmum Station was literally deactivated and how the Osguards were incapacitated—all except for Juanita. He told Peters that Juanita was on her way to the Kulusk home world to retrieve the antidote. This was more information than Peters had ever known before. Until now, he did not know the name of a single Osguard, and he did not know how many there were or their situation.

Again, silence dominated the conversation. Then after several minutes of contemplation Peters spoke. "Do you think they're dead?"

"No sir. But I don't know how long they will be alive."

"It sounds like USSTAP is destroyed and the Kulusks are about to claim their territory, including us," Peters surmised.

"No sir. I doubt that seriously," Musoto proclaimed. "The Kulusks took a beating. USSTAP is bigger and stronger. They rule sixty galaxies, while Kulusk only rule thirty light years of space."

"Thirty light years is still too big for me to fathom," Peters commented. "Even one ship can command our surrender."

"Sir, I think you are spinning too much doom into the situation. I know it is dire, but it is not uncontrollable," Musoto said to convince himself more than Peters. "Plus, there appears to be a revolutionary factor on Kulusk. I think they have their hands full dealing with internal issues without bothering us." Then Musoto switched ears with his cell phone. "Look Mr. President...thanks for paving the way for us down here. I think we are making great progress. And if we clear this up, it will go a long way toward making points with the Osguards."

"Yeah, if there are any left," Peters commented. "Look you gave me much to think about here. I need to be alone for a while. Call me as soon as you hear anything. And I do mean—anything."

"Yes sir," responded Musoto. He closed his phone and replaced it back in his jacket pocket. He looked up at the porch and waived at Stelana. He noticed Stelana did not seemed worried about the situation in the slightest. He knew she had more to lose than he did if Juanita was unsuccessful, but she wasn't worried.

He moved toward the porch and sat next to Stelana. "Aren't you worried about Juanita and the others?" he blurted.

Stelana looked at him in surprise. When she saw he was serious she changed her demeanor to reflect the professional officer she knew she was. "No," she whispered. "They are Osguards."

# Chapter 30—Revolution

Maxum Kie Ritchen was in his office in the military complex in the capital city of Renard. He was practicing his Misuip, the Kulusk version of golf. Kie picked up the silver ball and placed it in a long metal rod. He set himself about four feet from the makeshift hole, pushed the button on the handle of the rod and swung toward the makeshift hole. The inertia made the ball sail past the hole. Kie stomped his foot in disgust, because he had not made the shot in the last five attempts. His mind was preoccupied with other thoughts. He was angry, hurt and ill tempered.

Kie reflected on the HVP Opel forced him to watch. He couldn't believe it was true. His grandfather banished his grandmother, great-uncle and great aunt to Taiole, after faking their deaths. Why? Why not just kill them, if they were that much of a threat? Why allow them to live? Maybe his grandfather thought it a more horrific death to live in Taiole. However, it was not a horrific death. It was a new beginning—the beginning of a secret revolution.

This revolution had been growing and thriving in secret, not just on Taiole with the multitude of exiles, but in other parts of Kulusk. He had never figured the exiles would survive the harsh conditions of the continent. He could not believe the exiles had created the superior technology that destroyed his air and land cruisers so readily outside Langoni. He didn't know how they did this underneath his nose.

Granted, he did not waste resources for surveillance in the region, because he thought there was no need. However, the exiles not only bore their revolutionary ideas on Taiole but they were on the northern continent of Dijanai … another piece of Kulusk where the Maxum thought the small population too backwards to worry about. Although Dijanai contained the biggest land mass on the planet, engulfing the last part of the northern hemisphere like a hat, leaving an oceanic region at the polar cap with its unique 'Y' configuration, he never thought it a breeding ground for advanced thought. Society, science, technology and the heart of Kulusk civilization came from Renard continent—or so he'd thought until now.

Kie knew his Kulusk guard units were too small to seek out these people on both continents. So he had to wait. Kie knew it would be just a matter of time before Opel would become bold and attack. Thus he'd spent the last hours fortifying his defense strategy—a strategy that lacked support from a space fleet for the first time in Kulusk history.

This thought started to choke Kie. He felt invisible hands clutch his neck. How could he allow his entire space fleet to be demolished—his entire elite force to be destroyed? Why didn't he keep a strong force in reserve? Now he was threatened on two fronts—USSTAP and Opel. It was a matter of time before one of them decided to attack. He hoped he had eliminated the Osguard threat with the Terinolice Virus, but he wasn't sure. Doubts attacked him. A few short weeks ago, he was in a jubilant mood. He saw victory within his reach. He saw the destruction of the Osguards. He saw the end of USSTAP. And he saw the Kulusk Empire take its rightful place as the leader of the known universe.

It seemed so surreal for a leader who had not ventured beyond his territory. He had never traveled more than thirty light years from Kulusk, but his actions reached out and touched sixty galaxies. He gambled…and he lost. And now, he was alone. His son, Xer, was killed during his vengeful quest for dominance, and now, he faced an enemy he never knew existed, Opel. He was on the cusp of another battle, ill-equipped, ill-trained and ill-manned.

Kie threw the Misuip rod across the room. It crashed against the stoned wall and shattered into several pieces. He stared at the wall where his rod had hit, but he did not see the wall. He saw fear instead—red, ugly and blinding fear. Kie, for the second time in two days, saw and tasted the sourness of fear—beating his taste buds as he tried to lick his lips. He had never felt the emotion before. He had felt anxious. He had felt unsure. However, he'd never felt fear—until he met Opel.

The door chime broke his concentration as it rang several times. Kie turned toward the door, not realizing how long he had been in his office. He shook his head, cracked his neck and shrugged his shoulder to chase fear from his body. It didn't work. It was still there, like a tick. Kie's voice cracked as he spoke, "Enter!"

The door split in the middle as it opened. One of his guards marched in. "Maxum," he yelled. "The ARIT is predicting Mt. Renard to erupt within the next three hours."

Kie turned to the soldier, "What?" He was stunned. Mt. Renard, the volcano a mere thirty-five rings from the city had not erupted in over two thousand years. The ARIT had labeled it inactive. Kie wondered how an inactive volcano could come to life and threaten eruption with little warning.

"Scientist confirmed it sir," the soldier continued. "Mt. Renard will erupt soon."

"Just perfect!" Kie complained. "A little too perfect." Kie walked to the window where he had a view of Mt. Renard. He retrieved ARIT binoculars from the dresser next to the window and peered through them at Mt. Renard. "Funny, it doesn't look active," he said aloud. "Also, I haven't felt any tremors associated with active volcanoes. Have you?"

The guard shook his head, "No Maxum, I haven't"

Kie cranked his neck to the side, trying to remember his studies in geology. He was always fascinated by geology and he had visited Mt. Renard several times as a kid. His studies of the volcano confirmed it was dead—no lava flowed in or around the volcano. Then he snapped his finger.

"You may go," he told the soldier. Then he sat at his desk, keying in coded commands to his Kulusk guards. Several minutes later, five hundred air cruisers lifted from the military complex and headed west away from the volcano. The land cruisers and evacuation ships soon followed them. It appeared Kie was evacuating Renard.

***

Two Hundred rings, east of Renard, Opel scanned his ARIT monitors in disbelief. Opel was leading the air assault on Renard in his one-man air cruiser. The Revolutionary Air Cruiser, RAC, was thirty feet long, 'X' shaped with the cockpit strategically placed in the middle. One multi-axis jorelli powered engine was placed on each end—four in all. This configuration gave it more speed and agility in a fight. It was equipped with a chromerion field generator and one Kwainique gun on the belly of the ship.

He activated several sensors and scanners trying to catch a glimpse of something. What, he did not know, but his mind raced for answers. It seemed unlikely Kie would accept the false readings he fed the Empire's ARIT about Mt. Renard without checking it.

The volcano decoy was meant for a distraction to place Kie off balance prior to the attack. However, the decoy seemed to produce another effect—totally unexpected. Kie evacuated the capital city. Opel watched his monitors record the entire episode. *If it was a ploy, it was a good one,* Opel thought.

"Taiole lead to all squadrons," Opel announced over the secure interlink. He was speaking to the other nineteen squadron leaders, commanding ten ship formations. "It appears our friends are leaving the house...repeat...it appears our friends are leaving the house. I don't like it. Proceed with caution. We are a go. Birddog...Birddog. Taiole lead out."

Birddog was the password to pursue the attack. The password filtered to all land, sea and air forces within several seconds, and all of Opel's revolutionary forces pressed forward with the attack.

On the northern and southern shores of Renard, just on the tip of the ocean's horizon, the revolutionary surface action groups sailed toward the city. Both fleets contained eight Jorelli Missile Carriers, JMC's, a Command JMC, and twelve support ships. The JMC's were 609 meters (2,000 ft) long and 91 meters (300 ft), weighing 93,000 metric tons and carried a crew of 1,000 personnel each. Each ship carried a complement of fifty Jorelli Missiles, and two missile launchers. Three above water jorelli engines, stationed on the stern upper brackets, powered the ships at the top speed of one hundred and fifty knots, pushing them in a seamless glide across the top of the green sparkling water.

Five minutes later Kie's command post surveillance bunker's ARIT announced the engaging forces. Multiple contacts by sea, land and air filled the screen, surrounding the middle, representing Renard, like swarms of bees.

Kie smiled. For the first time in hours the taste of fear had left him as adrenaline fueled his training. "Opel, if I knew you were this predictable, I would not have worried so," he said aloud. Then he pushed on sensors at his command chair.

The RACs continued to advance, unhampered by any defenses. Opel was getting worried. He knew Renard had ground defenses in place and expected to have engaged them by now, but they had not. Opel checked his monitor again. All that registered was enemy scans and sensor sweeps. Opel understood Kie knew they were coming...But why no action? An uneasiness bathed Opel's consciousness. *Something's amiss here.* The air cruisers will be over the city in five minutes and the sea forces will be in range about the same time. The land forces will be in range to complete a constant barrage of weapons fire soon afterwards ... *yet Kie has done nothing to defend the city.*

\*\*\*

"Opel's DNA match found," Kie's ARIT announced, waking Kie from his thoughts.

"About time," Kie announced, silently praising himself for extricating DNA from Opel's blood on his cloak and programming the ARIT to detect Opel from it. "Where?"

"Lead air cruiser," the ARIT proclaimed, putting a circle around the dot in the monitor.

"Is it within range?" Kie asked.

"Soli," the ARIT replied.

"Acquire and fire grappling beam!" he ordered.

***

Opel saw a red light flash from the ground, like a beacon, for a split second. Then his air cruiser came to a complete stop and was yanked from the sky in a downward trajectory. The sudden stop, threw Opel against his restraints with such force he blacked out. His engines whistled, coughed and chugged as the thrust attempted to push forward, as the plane descended, dropping toward the ground. The stress factor tore at the fuselage, ripping fuel and other ARIT lines and rupturing the structural integrity of the ship. The ARIT, detecting imminent implosion, activated the ejection sequence for the pilot.

Ten seconds after the grappling beam snatched Opel's air cruiser from the sky, Opel's cockpit separated from the air cruiser in an upward force. The cockpit parachute opened and floated Opel fifteen thousand feet above the ground, before it started its slow descent toward the surface. As it descended, Opel's RAC imploded above him. The revolutionary air force could only watch. As the new Taiole leader, Mota Silliw, Opel's wingman, marked the spot where his leader went down, he rang orders for the attack to proceed.

Kie watched, working with his ARIT to project the landing spot. He sent the coordinates to his land troops, who had pretended to evacuate the area earlier. Actually, the land cruisers left using remote control, and maneuvered to an underground system that led them back to the compound. Now he gave orders to release the ground forces to retrieve Opel and engage the revolutionary forces.

He sent another signal as soon as he saw the revolutionary air forces pass by Mt. Renard. This time the signal went to his air force that had doubled back, flying below ground radar coverage and rooting itself at the foot of Mt. Renard. When they ascended, they were behind the revolutionary air cruiser, poised in a prime location to attack.

The first shot was unexpected. As the Air Component Commander, Mota did not expect a rear attack and unwisely chose to drop rear surveillance from the ARIT routine. Eight RACs exploded instantaneously from shockdel fire. Mota began rearview surveillance and learned the entire Empire Guard air cruiser fleet was now behind him. This was not where he wanted to engage the fleet. Then another barrage of melenai pulses sprang from the KACs. Fifteen more pilots were blown to oblivion. Mota made a mental note that the pulses ripped through their chromerion fields like butter—almost like their Kwainique guns.

"Evasive maneuver Opel two-B, multiple KACs, three to nine…repeat…multiple KACs, three to nine."

Upon hearing Mota, the last half of the RACs began maneuvering, banking to the right, diving then pulling back through a one hundred and eighty-degree turn. During the turn, the two hundred and seventy-degree arc of the KACs shockdel guns tracked and fired upon the RACs. Fifty more ships exploded. Then the KACs trained their weapons on the receding ships. Eight more blasts and Mota found he had lost half his fleet without firing a shot.

Mota had one hundred ships left out of two hundred that started the attack. He was the target and not the aggressor. It was not the position he relished. He had expected to lose men and women today, but not like this— not without killing the enemy as well—not without a fight.

"Evasive maneuver Mota 1," he yelled into his interlink. "Base this is Taiole one, we have been ambushed. I am breaking off the attack. I've lost half the fleet and we have not fired a single shot. I am breaking off the attack."

Decoys shot from the RACs as they descended toward the surface. The decoys confused the ARIT targeting systems on the KACs, displaying multiple targets. It took a split second for the KACs' ARITs to disavow them as targets, but it was long enough for the RACs to get out of their field of fire. The KACs descended in pursuit. Yet, something was different.

Mota's fleet had turned and descended backwards with their guns pointing skyward. When the KACs followed, they maneuvered directly into the RACs targeting solution. Mota ordered full spread fire. The Kwainique guns whined and hummed as they charged then released their destructive beam onto the KACs. Thirty seconds after execution of the Mota 1 Maneuver, the sky rained with red, blue, orange and purple hot embers from the annihilation of seventy-five KACs. The resulting explosions caused several of the remaining KACs to terminate their pursuit. As they pulled up from the descent, the resulting discord caused several ships to plunge into each other, causing further explosion to rain in the skies over Renard.

Mota raised his fist in victory as he counted the kills on his monitor. He tallied one hundred. The score was even now. He felt he had avenged his brethrens' deaths. Now he ordered the fleet to level off five hundred feet above the ground and press westward toward the capital—time to intercept one minute and twenty-five seconds.

***

Meanwhile on the ground, General Tsrif Slod felt he had control of the situation, until he heard his air cover retreating. Slod wanted the air cover so his ground troops could achieve their objective. Yet he felt confident he could achieve the objective without it, since Kie had evacuated Renard.

Then it hit ... the first volley from the KLCs, fifteen explosions from pagenay fire. Slod scanned his ARIT monitor. There were twice as many KLCs than he expected and somehow they appeared behind and in front of him. Slod did not understand how they got behind him. He pushed full scan and sensor sweep. Then he saw it. Something that never made it to the intelligence report, Kie had underground tunnels stretching the entire sector. The ARIT never scanned under the surface until he asked it to. They must have used the underground tunnels to get behind them.

Slod ordered his rear echelon to engage the Kulusks to the rear, while he handled the Kulusks in the front. Slod ordered his teams to return fire. However, they weren't in the clearing yet. The RLCs were in the midst of the trees and their Kwainique beam's power dissipated as it obliterated debris, trees and leaves standing in the way between them and the Kulusks. The beam accomplished little more than a knock on the door when it hit its target. However the destruction it laid prior unnerved the Kulusks for a second—they failed to return fire.

Slod understood and ordered a second barrage. The second barrage found its mark, destroying fifteen KLCs in front and back. The Kulusks adapted and fired melenai pulses in retreat. The pulses found ten revolutionary land cruisers. The destruction of the RLCs gave them a sense of false bravado. They terminated the retreat and began advancing as they continued firing.

Chromerion fields hampered neither weapon, thus every shot found its mark as the KLCs and the RLCs sprayed each other with destruction and bloodshed. The forest was afire and the sounds were deafening. Red, blue, purple embers flew in all directions, setting small fires throughout the battlefield. Slod knew it would become a battle of attrition. Which army could destroy the most in the shortest amount of time?

Slod also knew he had a disadvantage; he had less to start with and more to destroy. He pushed his sensors to send all data, including the charts of the underground tunnels to base headquarters over a secure net. He had a premonition he would not survive the day and he wanted this information to get to base as soon as possible.

Then his ARIT recorded RACs coming in low, strong and fast. They had not abandoned their mission. It must have been a ploy. He was about to hit the capital from the east and they were still fighting from the west. It was not pretty, but it was a small victory. Then he received a coded message, requesting position of enemy land cruisers.

\*\*\*

Admiral Arual Xam, the Sea Force Commander, heard everything. She knew the plan was falling apart for the land and air forces, so she decided to deviate, a little to lend them support. She requested the position of enemy land cruisers so she could coordinate weapons onto them. She received the coordinates from Slod and she pushed them to the fleet she entrusted with the deed.

She had thirty-six Jorelli Missiles from both the south and north trained on the capital and timed to fire a few seconds after the KACs made their first pass. Two of her Jorelli Missiles now gave much needed support to Slod and his forces, which were pinned down west of the city. Two twenty-five-foot missiles launched in a freewheeling arch, streaked above the aqua green waters, trailing a green plume of smoke behind them. Five seconds after launch they were over land and bearing down on the KLCs.

The men in the KLCs registered the impending doom and tried to escape their vehicles, but the Jorelli Missiles were too fast. The Kulusks hardly got their doors open before the missiles hit and exploded sending a minute shockwave, strong enough to bend and topple trees within two hundred and fifty feet of the explosion.

The windblast from the missiles' explosions rocked the RLCs, from the front and rear, almost knocking them over on their sides as the men grabbed on to anything to steady themselves. Slod fell to the floor and bumped his head, causing a small gash to spit blood from his forehead. Other men fell as well, bruising and breaking arms, legs and ribs.

Xam witnessed her missiles' destruction on her ARIT monitor and turned her attention to the capital. When she adjusted her monitor, she saw the Kulusk seaboard missile defense targeting her fleet. She ordered readjustment of Jorelli Missiles to target the defense system on the docks and piers of Renard. She diverted eight missiles (four from the north and four from the south) of her remaining thirty-four missiles toward the shore, but it was too late. Rays of pagenay blast ripped through the sky toward her ship. The chromerion fields took the blunt of the hits. Five JMC's were damaged, but operable. She still had thirteen JMC's in battlefield condition. Xam closed her green eyes and breathed a sigh of relief. For a moment she thought the seaboard defenses had the new weapons as well. She did not know what it was, but she knew the chromerion field had no effect on the new weapon.

Then she watched her monitor as the seaboard defenses on the north and south shore exploded from the force of the Jorelli Missiles. The destruction was total and complete. Piers collapsed, docks disappeared and ships sank as the aqua green water swallowed the wood, metal and stone that once housed Renard's wealthy and vibrant seashore.

"Attacking force, this is Kie Ritchen, Maxum of the Kulusk Empire," the Maxum's voice rang over the secure interlink frequency. This shocked

Mota, Slod and Xam. "Stop all actions, I have my cousin Opel with me and I will kill him if there is one more weapon fired upon this city, the Capitol, or Greenhaven." Kie had Opel strapped to a chair, with his hands and feet bound by ARIT shackles.

Tirana at base headquarters heard Kie. "You have twenty-five seconds to prove that," she hollered over the interlink.

"If I must?" Kie replied. Then he smacked Opel across the face with his open hand. "Say something dear cousin."

Opel shook his head.

"Pity dear cousin," Kie said as he reached for a mation. He then cut deep into Opel's left cheek.

Opel refused to scream as he sucked in the pain from the cut.

"Say something you fool, or they will blow you to pieces," Kie demanded.

Opel just smiled, letting Kie know he was willing to die for his cause.

Kie panicked for a moment. Then he opened a visual frequency. "I am broadcasting on Dark one-beta three. I am sure you have access...see for yourself."

Tirana switched to visual and saw her brother strapped to a chair and bleeding. She had ten seconds to choose. She had to choose between her brother dying thereby ending the revolution, or her brother living as a prisoner of the revolution. The fight was about restoring him as Maxum of Kulusk. If he were dead, the fight would be for naught. She watched the time tick off the clock. In five seconds Mota, Slod and Xam were going to decimate the Capitol. The plan was to take it without destroying it. However, the plan changed during the battle to the backup plan—now the plan was to kill Kie Ritchen! Sweat beaded on her forehead. She looked at the people in the room and she saw they all diverted their eyes toward the ground.

This was not fair. They were so close, but now they are so far. The pressure built in her head. There is no greater sacrifice she thought as she made up her mind to let them destroy the Capitol. Then it came...the message announcing Juanita was approaching Kulusk space, in the *USSTAP Galaxy Cruiser Destiny*. The extra leverage she needed—a galaxy cruiser. *And it must be providence the galaxy cruiser was called 'Destiny,'* she wondered.

"All forces, this is Tirana," she screamed. "Terminate attack, return to recovery base. Kill any Kulusk Guard attempting to follow. Use covert recovery." She repeated the message three more times. When she finished, she told all forces to go to backup interlink frequency. She stayed on the main frequency for a few minutes to relay a message to Kie. "Maxum, this is your other cousin Tirana, Opel's sister. You may have won this battle, but the war is mine. And if I have to win by sacrificing my brother...I will do that. So your leverage is only temporary. I believe we did significant enough damage to your forces that if I choose to; I can walk in and slap you off the throne. Tirana Out!"

# Chapter 31—Retaliation

The day was fading into night in Shreveport Louisiana. The street lamps flickered on, glowing with a dim orange light. The neighborhood children disappeared into their homes. Yet, Yolanda remained on her porch step staring at the chalk outline on the narrow walkway. Other than the conversation she had with Musoto and Allensen earlier that afternoon, she had not said a word.

Stelana remained on the porch with Yolanda most of the day. Her awareness was waning from the day's activity. She had watched every person, car and animal that moved in front of the house for the last six hours. She studied them, memorized them and categorized them using a PARIT that looked oddly enough like a cell phone. Therefore it did not bring undo attention. However, she was getting tired and wanted to go inside now.

"Ms. Smart, don't you want to go inside now," she pleaded. "It's been a long hot day."

Yolanda turned to Stelana and acted like she just noticed her for the first time. "Who the hell are you anyway? Why are you staying at my house?"

Stelana raised her right eyebrow. She didn't know if she was more surprised at the question or the rudeness in which it was asked. After a brief second to calm her anger, she replied, "I am an associate of your cousin—."

"—I know that bitch," Yolanda interrupted. "I want to know why you are here. My cousin left last night. The bitch couldn't even stick around for one day to help me through this. The high mighty yellow bitch had to run off to some business meeting. That shows where her priorities are…she'd rather be in a business meeting than here with family."

"That's not true, Ms. Smart," Stelana replied. "Mrs. Clark would have liked nothing better than to stay here during your time of grief. However, a life and death matter came up that needed her immediate attention."

"Life and death? Who does the bitch think she is…Foxy Brown?"

"Who?" Stelana asked in surprise.

"Nothing…never mind." Yolanda then looked Stelana up and down. "I don't know why you wannabe white girls came any way."

"Excuse me!"

"You heard me bitch," Yolanda replied rotating her neck for emphasis. "You and my cousin come down here talking all proper and acting all white. You two are sellouts. You forgot where you came from, driving your white folks' cars and wearing your white folks' clothes. Money changed her, and I bet it changed you. If it was me with the money, I would still be black. You don't know what it is to be really black. It's bad enough we have to take shit from the white man, but to have our own kind come down here and give us shit. That is just too much. The white man owns everything. A nigger can't get a break around here. Now I guess he owns my cousin too. Does he own you as well?"

Stelana stared at Yolanda, amazed at her words and feeling combative at her accusations. Her eyes were ablaze with censure. "Look, I understand you're grieving, and you don't know what you are saying."

"Oh, I know what I'm saying. And you hear me good," Yolanda hollered pointing her finger in Stelana's face. "...This is my house, my hood and you better damn well show me some respect, or I'll kick your ass from here back to wherever you came from."

Stelana was stunned. Her jaw dropped. She tried to speak, but she did not know what to say. No, she knew what to say; she just didn't know how to say it. Then her surprise dissipated and changed into pain. She closed her eyes and took a deep but shuttering breath. She was insulted and she did not understand why. She fought back the urge to cry. As she fought the urge, the more she thought about it, the more she became angry.

Yolanda witnessed the emotional transformation in Stelana's face. She received a small glee from inflicting the insults. She grinned and then, out of habit, Yolanda patted her jean pants pockets. "Damn'it, I'm out of smokes." She looked up at Stelana. "Hey you got keys to that ride," she barked, pointing to the gold SUV.

Stelana nodded.

"Then make yourself useful and drive me to the store so I can cop me some smokes."

Stelana stared into Yolanda's eyes and realized there was no sense in arguing. But at the same time she wondered what part of the UAI Major Reed could find to place Yolanda in the Dallas Precinct.

Then before Stelana realized it, Yolanda had jumped up and started to the SUV. Stelana regarded her with contempt at that moment. Up until now, she had sympathy for her, but the few seconds of conversation had turned it all around. She wondered why she should even care about the safety of this woman. Then she shook her head, *because the Osguard asked her to*.

Then her training caused her to turn her head to the right. Something was out of place...but what? She stared down the street for a moment, and then she noticed it. A slow moving SUV was gliding down the street. It was not moving at a normal pace. That was not the odd thing. It seemed to be slowing and speeding, slowing and speeding, like it was calculating a timing point, a reference point. Then she noticed the Texas plates.

She turned to Yolanda who had made it to the SUV. Stelana's heart pounded, her adrenaline kicked in. She retrieved her pagenay from her Charlie belt and stood.

"Yolanda get down," she yelled.

Yolanda looked perplexed until she saw the direction Stelana was looking. She dove to the ground upon seeing the car speed up toward her.

Stelana took one step, jumped the wooden four-foot banister, and landed on the grass in a crouched position. She held the pagenay out and aimed it at the car. "ARIT," she yelled. "Chromerion field extend—Rican three–eight–nine."

A white glow sparkled for a second around the SUV and encompassed Yolanda on the sidewalk next to it. Then the car passed laying down a spray of bullets from automatic weapons. The Chromerion field stopped the bullets as they fell to the ground—six, twelve, twenty...twenty-five quick shots rattled off, simultaneously from two automatic weapons.

Stelana ran to the SUV and jumped over the top in one leap. Yolanda turned just in time to see Stelana fly over her and the car. Stelana landed in the street, turned and fired her pagenay at the speeding car. A blue beam flowed out and discharged onto the car. The back hatch blew off and the back window shattered as the car turned left onto another street.

"Door open, Rican three–eight–nine," Stelana ordered. The ARIT recognized the command. The door flew open on the driver's side and Stelana jumped into the car. Stelana pushed several sensors and the vehicle started up. She put the car into gear, when Yolanda jumped in the passenger side.

Stelana looked at her for a split second and decided it was too late to change course now. "Buckle up," she ordered as she spun the car around. "ARIT full scan." The windshield glowed with numbers and a local map. Stelana gave the description of the SUV and told it to scan for metal distorted by pagenay blast. She also ordered space surveillance Imcams to assist in the search. It took the ARIT system several seconds, but it honed in on the vehicle. The ARIT displayed the vehicle inside a yellow blip on the windscreen traveling on I-220 heading north to intercept I-20 to Dallas. "These idiots aren't very smart are they? They are missing the back hatch and they don't think the state troopers won't stop them?"

Yolanda just looked over at Stelana, half scared and fully confused. "Who the hell are you?"

"I'm someone your cousin sent to protect your spoiled brat ass," Stelana scolded. "Now sit back and keep your mouth shut," she admonished. *Bitch*, she wanted to add, but decided against it.

Stelana found the on ramp to I-220 and sped onto the highway. She pushed a sensor and a police siren wailed from the car and red and blue lights flashed from the grill. Although she was not a legitimate law enforcement agent, she carried several fake credentials, including the FBI, just for emergencies like this. Besides, she had the backing of a real FBI agent just in case local authorities ever pinched her. The traffic was light, and she was able to manipulate around the traffic. She pushed her vehicle to ninety-five miles an hour.

She tapped her CC and called for Musoto. After a second of hums and beeps, Musoto answered. She rattled off what happened and their situation. Musoto acknowledged and told her she will have back-up shortly.

"Boy do I love this cop talk. It's the only thing – ." Then she looked at Yolanda, who was still staring at her with her mouth wide open. "Don't worry, we'll stop for your smokes on the way back home," Stelana joked.

"Shut up, bitch," Yolanda demanded.

"Listen you little—"Stelana stopped as she concentrated on swerving to the left of a car in front of her. "Tell me…you are so busy trying to be black, you are missing the point. You are rude. You're crass. You purposely butcher the English language. You go out of your way to insult people. You wear your lack of education like a badge. You take drugs. You were a whore. You have no respect for others, let alone yourself. And you wonder why…the world turned around and shit on you?"

Stelana paused to collect her thoughts. "You blame the white man for everything. Well let's look at it a little more closely. The white man brings the drugs you shoot into your arm, but a black man sold it to you. The white man buys your body, but it was a black man who pimped you. You are too busy, listening to others telling you what it takes to be cool…what it takes to be black. You listen to the music telling you that you're a whore, a bitch…a woman with no self-esteem. And you believe it. You drool over two hundred dollar sweatshirts, two hundred dollar sneakers and gold chains because some advertisement agency tells you it is the black thing to do. Well let me let you in on a little secret. Blacks do not financially back those record companies, selling those records and those name brand sweatshirts, sneakers and gold chains you buy. People who want to see you destroy yourself and make money in the process finance them. And what better way to make it happen than to get a black face to peddle it as a black thing. Just like the drugs, the whores and the cheap beer. Honey, there is no black thing. There is no black culture. It was taken away years ago and everything since has been a lie that stupid people like you swallow hook-line-and-sinker.

Stelana looked at Yolanda. Yolanda still wore a stoic look of defiance, with her lips out and her forehead furled. "You live in a world where sex is the only entertainment, drugs are the only recreation and killing each other over sex and drugs is the only sport. Where did that get you? I'll tell you. It got you to be a single mother. Now it got you to be a grieving mother. So you can drop the attitude, because I have no time for it. Understand?"

"Bitch, let me out of this car...now!" Yolanda screamed.

"No can do," Stelana mused.

In front of her, several car lengths, was the SUV she was tracking. Stelana gunned the accelerator and closed with her siren still blaring and her lights still flashing. The SUV made a sudden turn, cut from the far left lane to the right lane, and jumped a median to an off-ramp. Stelana swerved right to follow. She took the off-ramp and continued to close in.

The SUV moved up the small incline of the off-ramp and barreled through a red light and turned right onto the main street, causing a station wagon on the main street to veer left and hit the overpass bridge embankment.

"ARIT check for injuries," Stelana commanded as she passed the car.

"Two people. Driver, male, approximately fifty years old, unconscious but stable. Passenger is conscious with broken left femur. Automobile condition—"

"—That's enough," Stelana interrupted. "Contact emergency services...give location and status of accident and the victims." Stelana turned right onto the road, keeping the damaged SUV in sight.

"Tiah!" the ARIT responded.

"What the hell is that?" Yolanda screamed, showing signs of fear.

"It's my OnStar!" Stelana lied. It seemed to satisfy Yolanda for the moment.

Stelana gained on the SUV. She was now one car length behind them as they sped on the dark, wooded and winding road. Stelana grew weary of the chase and wanted to end it now.

Stelana pulled a flap from her steering wheel, exposing several blue, red and white lights behind a smoky class panel. She tapped the right white light, labeled coronet. The sensors displayed on her part of the windshield, invisible to Yolanda. A small coronet gun barrel popped from the front bumper just above the license plate. Stelana chose the coronet gun because the coronet pellet was invisible and would appear to the casual observer, namely Yolanda, that the SUV had simply blown a tire. Yolanda used her free hand to manipulate the sensor to target the left rear tire. It took several attempts, because the road was winding and the SUV made erratic turns. Stelana recognized the turns as evasive maneuvers. Yet, she managed to target the left rear tire for an instant. An instant was all she needed.

She then pushed the second right button. A low whine rang inside the car. At the same time the SUV's right tire disintegrated in pieces as the back end lifted up and over. The rear axle flew off and to the right, as sparks ignited the undercarriage like fireflies. The car slid upright; on its front grill several yards before it tumbled. It tumbled back over the front, four times, crumbling and shedding parts of metal like dry skin onto the road. It tumbled into a culvert in a bend in the road, miraculously landing on its wheels. Smoke filled the air, like a fog.

Stelana skidded to a stop about thirty yards from the SUV. She knew the car was about to explode. She had miscalculated the strength of the coronet pellet on Earth metal. She admonished herself, but soon realized she needed to act. She got out of her vehicle and ran toward the damaged SUV. She grabbed the door handle of the driver's door and ripped it from its hinges. She scanned the inside. There were three men, two in the front and one in the back. Ordinarily she would not move them, but the car appeared it was about to explode. She grabbed the driver, a young black man weighing about two hundred pounds, by his arm and yanked him up and over her shoulder. She sprinted about twenty yards and laid him down.

She rushed back to the car to see one of the other men emerge from the driver's side, bleeding from a cut right above his left eye. He saw Stelana and raised a nine millimeter handgun in her direction. She rolled to her left as the first round rang out. She felt the dirt kick up to her right from where the bullet hit. She popped up on one knee and fired her pagenay. A yellow light sailed through the air in a flash. It found its mark as the young man fell to the ground. Stelana rushed to him, retrieved his gun and picked him up over her shoulder. She sprinted back twenty yards and laid him down next to his partner. She turned with her pagenay in hand and raced back to the SUV.

Flames were now visible, crawling under the belly of the SUV, next to the gasoline tank. Stelana did not falter in her run. She reached the SUV and looked in the back seat. The third man was gone. The opposite door was opened. She looked out into the woods in front of the SUV. She saw nothing. She began coughing as the smoke became thicker. She could hear the crackling of the flames. She then dropped down to look under the vehicle. He wasn't there either. However, she did see the flames roasting the gasoline tank. She knew she had mere seconds before the car exploded.

She sprang to her feet and started running back to her vehicle. She reached about ten yards when the car exploded. The windblast picked her up about five feet and flew her another three feet. She landed hard on her stomach; her pagenay flew from her grasp as she hit the ground. For a split second, everything went black. She rolled over and tried to suck in air, but all she sucked into her lungs was smoke. She coughed the smoke out as she got up from the ground. She walked over to the two men on the ground and grabbed with each hand the back of their collars. She then dragged them the extra ten yards behind her vehicle.

Yolanda, still strapped in the passenger side, just stared at her. Disbelief framed her face. Then she shook her head several times. "Bitch, who the hell are you?"

# Chapter 32—More Revelations

"I simply don't believe it," Vice President George Willis laughed. "According to this, we are all descendants of prisoners, political exiles and other assorted societal misfits." The vice president's voice resonated with bitterness. "You're telling me that there is an entire universe more advanced than us and they have been living, breathing and walking on our planet and in our country without us knowing it. Impossible, I tell you. I just don't believe it."

Peters exhaled. "I've been reviewing this for several days, and I'm not sure I believe it either," he said from the security of his desk in the Oval Office. "But this does explain a lot of things—for instance the UFO sightings in Phoenix sometime back in June of 1997. That entire event had the Air Force jumpy for days. According to Musoto, that was a galaxy cruiser that misjudged its coordinates when it transitioned from hyperlight to hypersonic speed. Think of the devastation it could have caused if it crashed."

Peters regarded his guests for sometime after his statement. George Willis; National Security Advisor, James Hall; Secretary of Defense Paul Thompson; and Chairman of the Joint Chief of Staff, Army General William Oliver sat across from him in an eerie reminder of the day after the averted nuclear destruction of Earth.

This time the president shared with his guest all the information he had garnered in the last couple of days, including Musoto's sketchy report on his encounter with USSTAP. The report was something straight from a science fiction movie. It highlighted the advanced technology of humans outside of Earth. The ability to travel to different worlds, solar systems, and even different galaxies with their gate-portal technology just astonished Peters. The report stated USSTAP had the ability to travel faster than light. Not only that, but the report described the ability of USSTAP starships traveling light-years like automobiles traveling on highways. This was disconcerting to Peters. He did not understand the concept of Mass Object Projection. All he gleaned from the report was it used invisible gravitational particles he suspected even the greatest scientific minds in the country didn't know existed in space. All he knew was it was exciting and frightening at the same time.

Then Musoto reported on their weaponry. Particle generator arrays, pagenays the report called them, plus cornet guns and Asher torpedoes ... all made the United States nuclear arsenal look like cap guns. The pagenay at full power had the radiant heat of one thousand times the sun. Coronet guns shot energy pellets at the speed of light and the Asher torpedoes were bordering on being the tenth generation to his nuclear arsenal. Just one hit from an Asher torpedo had the potential of sending half the planet into a nuclear winter that scientist could never imagine.

Then the gigantic ships—space ships, also troubled Peters. Magnificent and enormous floating cities in space that housed awesome weaponry, utilized the entire speed spectrum from thrusters to MOP, and the gate portals that carried humans throughout sixty galaxies.

Peters picked up his glass of water and took a sip. His mind was frantic as he tried to visualize the things Musoto reported. He knew he had to see them for himself. The report was so fantastic only personal experience would lend it the credence it deserved. Then he laughed. In all his wildest dreams, he would never have imagined what was in this report. And now he is asking his most trusted and able advisors to believe it.

The saving grace in this, Peters thought, was neither the Kulusks nor USSTAP had invented time travel. He had asked Musoto about this. Musoto had assured him USSTAP scientists had dismissed time travel long ago. They believed time was a universal constant consumable good that could not be recouped once used. An instant in time, a human experienced on Earth, was the same instant in time experienced on a planet in another galaxy. It was distance that separated time. If one could travel instantaneous from one spot to another, they would discover time was the same. However, USSTAP could visit the past through time-light studies.

Basically, as Musoto put it, time-light study involved parking a ship in space at a certain light year distance from an event, and then manipulating the light waves containing that instance onto an HVP ARIT. Thus one could see, not hear, but see history unfold in front of their eyes. The principle was the same as radio and television waves. The waves travel through space; long after the event had terminated. Although, to someone with the proper reception equipment, it would appear to the naked eye like the event was happening right then. Of course with time-light studies, the event had to occur outside, so the reflected light waves would carry it through space.

Peters shook his head as he fought to understand the report in more detail. He could not understand how Musoto grasped the intricacies of USSTAP technology so quickly. Then again, he was there. He saw it, touched it and metaphorically tasted it ... whereas; Peters only had a report, destroyed nuclear weapons and an HVP, to educate him.

The foursome had watched the HVP, mostly in disbelief and read Musoto's report, which still left questions in Peters' mind. After several hours of indoctrination he had given the foursome two hours to prepare responses, proposals and comments. Now they were back, confused and just as befuddled as Peters was.

"I don't like it," murmured General Oliver. "I don't understand the threat. I don't know the enemy. I have no way of preparing for any type of encounter. If all you say is true, they are powerful, numerous and very technologically advanced. Shit, they knocked our entire ICBM arsenal out of the sky."

"Not just ours. They knocked the Russian's ICBM arsenal out of the sky as well," added Thompson.

"They aren't the enemy gentlemen. It is the Kulusks," Peters reminded them.

"How do you know that?" Hall asked. "The Kulusks could have saved us. This USSTAP could have started the entire episode. There is no way of knowing who is telling us the truth."

"Musoto is in constant contact. He met an Osguard for heaven sake," Peters preached. "He saw their technology. He saw their headquarters...well at least the one on Earth. If they wanted to start military action, I am sure they would have by now." Peters then looked up at the ceiling with a slight smirk. "The Osguards are Americans. That has to count for something."

"They are also black," countered Willis.

"So, what does that have to do with anything," asked Peters.

"Well, the last polling numbers suggest the black community is not very happy with—"

"—Irrelevant!" Peters interrupted. "These people are so far removed from what is happening here on Earth. Shit man, they are fighting for sixty galaxies, and they seem to be losing. Do you think how the vote went in the last election matters to them? Get your head out of your ass. You have to think bigger than that," he scolded.

"Nevertheless, Mr. President," Thompson offered. "We are in trouble. If this USSTAP are the good guys, and they are losing like you said...then the bad guys are coming. And they seem to be pretty pissed off at us."

"Maybe...maybe not," Peters countered. "The Kulusk military is wiped out. They reverted to biological warfare as a last resort. They don't have any ships, men or equipment to transverse space to get to us. We have time, but we need to divert our attention from conventional weapons to weapons of mass destruction on a universal scale. I want to be able to fight them when they get here. I just don't know how long that will be. I mean I don't know how long it will take them to generate forces and equipment. It could be days, years or even decades," Peters commented.

"They may not need forces," Oliver surmised. "They could strike us using these gate portals, deliver their biological weapon or some chemical weapon to wipe out all life on Earth, sit back, and wait until it is safe for them to collect their spoils." I mean my own Vice Chairman was a Kulusk. We don't know who else is or how many are already on the planet. For all I know you could be one, Mr. President. Mr. Thompson or Mr. Hall could be one as well. We are just in the dark here. We need more information before we go off half cocked."

"I know, general," Thompson agreed. "But time is running out and we don't know how much we have."

Oliver shifted in his chair. "Then I suggest we use it wisely," he commented to no one in particular.

"And how do you suppose we do that?" asked Thompson, showing his irritation.

"I don't know," Oliver admitted. "But we have a man in place. I suggest we let him do his job."

"And what is his job, pray tell?" asked Thompson.

"Reconnaissance and Intelligence," Oliver answered, "Reconnaissance and Intelligence."

***

"Osguard Fifty-Five, I am Tirana, Opel's sister."

Tirana's face filled the screen on the bridge of the *USSTAP Galaxy Cruiser Destiny*. Juanita stood in front of the command chair facing the screen. She regarded Tirana. Jackil stood next to her and one step behind her to clearly show she was the person in charge of the situation.

"Nice to meet you, Tirana or should I say cousin?" asked Juanita, letting her know she had seen the HVP or at least testing her on the HVP. However, the bridge crew was shocked by the words, yet their professionalism allowed them to keep their same foreboding outward appearance.

"Tirana will do just fine," she said flashing a disarming smile. "I am terribly glad to see you, Osguard. It seems we are in a bit of a mess here."

"Well, I am truly sorry to hear that..." Juanita revealed. "But I am here for only one thing—the antidote."

Tirana's smile disappeared as the words washed over the comm link. Her hesitation made the hair on the back of Juanita's neck rise. She felt the entire affair a trap, but it was a risk she had to take. Now she was feeling uneasy, "Well Tirana? Do you have the antidote or not?"

Tirana's smile perked to life, she batted her eyes several times and water formed in them. "No, Osguard I don't," she admitted. "My brother does and he has been captured by Kie Ritchen. I am afraid the maxum will execute my brother very soon."

The words sunk into Juanita's heart like a dagger. She stepped back, barely feeling her own weight as she groped behind her for the command chair. She sat back into the chair staring at Tirana's face on the view screen but not registering her form. Her mind went blank for an instant. Then her mind flooded with images of the dead bodies at Capitol Station—hundreds, then thousands of men and women wearing the USSTAP uniform laying—no crumbled on the floors of the station. Then her mind imagined thousands of people in suspension chambers, clinging onto life with nothing but a prayer. She saw Michael in a suspension chamber, waiting—hoping—and counting on her help to save him and the others. The doom of failure swallowed her face. She lowered her head in despair.

"What happened?" she whispered.

"We attacked Renard and—"

"You did what?" Juanita's voice thundered. She was now up and racing to the view screen.

"The time was right...so we thought," Tirana attempted to explain. "Kie's forces were in disarray and he knew of us. It was either him or us."

"You idiot!" screamed Juanita. "All of USSTAP was depending on you, staying safe until I got here. And you decide to start your little revolution anyway. What the hell were you thinking? You thought Kie wouldn't be prepared for you. You thought Kie was that weak?" Juanita shook her head and threw her hands up in the air. "Let me guess," she began, pointing at the Tirana. "You went in with a full assault from the east, west, south and north. You used a diversion of some type to throw Kie's remaining forces off balance. Then you came in with guns blazing. Do I have it right so far?"

Tirana nodded. "You have the main points correct."

"Then Kie faked you out somehow. He probably made it look like his forces were in retreat, and then he circumvented your main forces, got behind you and voila. You were faced with his automatic defenses in front of you and his not so weak forces behind you. Oh yeah, let me see. He used a DNA scan to find your brother in the mix and captured him somehow." Juanita's voice was terse and lecturing. "Am I right?"

Tirana's only reaction was a ghastly stare. Her blue eyes watered with shame, guilt or remorse. Whichever it was, Juanita didn't care at the moment.

"Well, am I right or not?"

"You are correct," Tirana answered after a painful pause. "But how—"

"How did I know?" Juanita finished.

Tirana nodded.

"Because, we have been fighting the Kulusk for over a hundred years—what I described to you is the most basic tactic in the Kulusk book. It is most effective with small forces like you described Kie had. If you had studied him just a bit, you may have known it." Juanita took a deep breath and blew out hard lowering her eyes to the floor. "Well Kie should know we are here by now. I had hoped to get the antidote and get the hell out of here before he knew we were here." Juanita looked back up at the view screen. "You don't have any idea about the antidote? I mean, according to your HVP, you have the greatest minds working for you. Someone, besides your , brother must have the antidote?"

"The Terinolice virus was created by Kie's people. Only my brother had contact with the man who fathered the virus. Only my brother and this man know how to make the antidote. And I am afraid, only my brother knows the man's name."

"Shit!" Juanita said to no one in particular, "Now what?"

"You have a ship; use it!" Tirana urged.

"Kie would rather die than give up the antidote under force. Shit, he just sent his son to die for his shameless cause."

"Then come and lead our rescue party to save my brother."

"What?"

"We are gathering a rescue mission to get my brother out."

"You must be crazy."

"Look, I am sure Kie does not know we are talking. He can't imagine we would join forces. So, let your ship threaten him from the heavens, while we hit him from hell."

"What are you talking about?"

"One of the ways he circumvented our forces is a series of underground tunnels, we had no knowledge of. Now we do. We may be able to use them to our advantage. However, we would need someone trained and knowledgeable in Kulusk tactics to lead us. Obviously we have not done a good job of it so far."

Juanita turned her head in serious contemplation. The images of her fallen comrades and the others on Capitol Station started to flood her mind again. She knew she had to do something and she had to do something quick. The situation did not have the luxury of time, so neither did she. "Hold that thought, cousin. I will get back to you in twenty universal minutes. Change frequency to backup on my return."

"Your return?"

"Yes, we need to put a couple of more light years between us and this planet. Kie has defenses and he will use them. Let us do some planning ourselves. I need you to upload the schematics of the underground tunnels."

"Better yet," Tirana interjected. "I can bring them to you."

"You can do that?" Juanita asked.

"Yes," laughed Tirana. "Neither Kie nor my brother signed the USSTAP ban on interplanetary gate portals that Nausona and Laurona asked for at the conception of USSTAP."

Laurona and Nausona had ensured peace under USSTAP by banning interplanetary gate portal technology in the USSTAP charter. In this manner, no planet would have the portal system capability to secretly advance an invading force onto another planet. Thus conventional travel was necessary to move a force forward; hence, giving notice to USSTAP of impending hostilities. For a while, it was a point of contention for all involved. However, after much spirited debate and diplomatic discussion all parties agreed upon the ban, which guaranteed peace throughout USSTAP's domain and ultimately became the linchpin to the Osguards' success as the stewards of the universe.

"Kie still has planet-to-planet gate portals and so do we," she continued. "I can reconfigure ours to reach you, even though you are outside our space."

"Thirty-five light years?" Juanita questioned feigning surprise.

USSTAP had known for quite some time of Kulusk's interplanetary gate portals. She knew this is what the Kulusks used to attack Osguard Gardens. However, USSTAP had discovered most of the return portals, especially the ones on Earth. That is why USSTAP suspected Larson, Prepovnov and Patterson, the Kulusk infiltrators who started the nuclear attack on Earth, had to use a shuttle to escape. Still, those portals remained a threat to USSTAP, and if she had a chance to destroy them she would.

"Yes…even thirty five light years," Tirana boasted. "Transmit your coordinates."

"Indeed, let's talk," Juanita smiled. "I am sending you the coordinates now." She motioned to Jackil, who barked orders to an officer posted at tactical.

The screen went blank and soon was replaced by the star field. Juanita sat down in the command chair for a moment, obviously in deep reflection. She turned to Jackil, who stood at her right side. "Please assemble your senior staff and meet me in your briefing room. Also, have someone meet my cousin and bring her to the meeting. In the meantime, let's put some distance between this sector of space and us. Your choice, but let's do it fast and let's go to stealth ten when we get there."

"Tiah, Osguard," Jackil responded. Then he stopped for a moment, "Osguard, may I suggest a time-light shuttle be sent to capture the battle and verify Tirana's story."

Juanita looked bewildered for an instant, and then she nodded. "Very well; however, let it be an unmanned shuttle. It will be in harm's way. The battle was not that long ago and the capture coordinates for the light wave will probably be within Kie's defenses."

"Tiah, I will send an automated time-light shuttle in stealth ten to the capture coordinates. We shall see if Tirana is telling the truth."

When Tirana was aboard Jackil gave orders to his crew and the *USSTAP Galaxy Cruiser Destiny* maneuvered deeper into space and disappeared from view as its engines shot from hypersonic, through hyperlight to MOP sixty. All that was left was a trace of yellow, red and blue light identifying where the galaxy cruiser was once located.

A lone unmanned time-light shuttle, launched from The *Destiny*. The shuttle traversed the light-speed spectrum until it reached Kulusk. Then it maneuvered at hypersonic speed at stealth ten on an intercept course to preset capture coordinates. Several minutes later, the time-light shuttle sent an encrypted HVP signal to the *Destiny*, confirming Tirana's story. To Jackil's dismay, two minutes later, Kulusk's planetary defense grid destroyed the shuttle. Kie knew they were there.

***

Jackil studied his senior staff. They displayed the same stoic look he had become accustomed to, but deep down inside he knew they were horrified. The Osguard had just informed them of Capitol Station's fate, and that they were the last hope for its survival. The news was bitter, but it explained the irrational attitude Juanita displayed throughout the trip. Now no one questioned her. They understood the strain she was under and empathized with her. No one wanted to trade places with her either. This was a stress only an Osguard could handle. Furthermore, from what they witnessed, she was handling it just fine.

Colonel Alicia Springs, from Toledo Ohio, was the second in command and sat next to Jackil at the round table. To her left sat Commander Kinl Sast from the planet Lortnoc, the Offensive Weapons Officer. To his left sat Major Treylo Gnig, from the planet Ybo, the Defensive Weapons Officer. Captain Rudolph Hulpman, the lead pilot from Berlin, Germany, sat next to him. Then lead navigator, Captain Laura Toms, from London, England sat next to him. Tirana sat between Toms and Juanita. The ship's engineer, Commander Yaw, the ship's economic counselor, Major True and the ship's doctor, Colonel Tsu attended through video from their stations.

"I have plotted all the automatic defenses," Gnig commented. "I believe our chromerion field, and decoys will buy us time if need be. But I am worried about that shockdel gun. I'm sure Kie has a couple of satellites in the defense perimeter that harbor that monster. We will be sitting ducks, if we run up against it!"

"I have a little something for that," Yaw interrupted. "I have reinforced the chromerion field with slitanium particles. It may not be as effective as the energized slitanium hull, but it will afford us some protection from the shockdel gun."

"Wonderful news, commander," Juanita smiled, "How much protection?"

"It will deflect fifty percent of the melenai pulse," he countered. "But if we have to, we can go strictly stealth ten and redirect the field strength to weapons for more accuracy."

"That will be Jackil's call," Juanita suggested. "Remember, I won't be here."

"It's too bad we don't have enough time for you to use the schematics on our Kwainique gun," Tirana offered. "It may even the odds a bit."

"I'm sure we have enough firepower to handle anything Kie has to throw at us," Sast insisted, rebuffing the suggestion that their weapons were inadequate for the task at hand.

Juanita recognized Sast took the comment as an insult. She beamed her most autocratic look at Sast, who interpreted it correctly as an order to shut up. Once satisfied her wishes were being complied with, Juanita turned her attention to the holographic chart of Kulusk the ARIT projected in the center of the table.

"These tunnels … are you sure Kie doesn't know they've been compromised?" Juanita asked Tirana.

"Osguard, I'm not sure of what Kie knows anymore. If you asked me yesterday, I would have said Kie was a fool. But after today, I realize he is a cunning and ruthless tactician."

"Yes, it is the ruthless part that gets him in trouble," Juanita responded. "But we must take the risk that he doesn't know."

Juanita's guts were turning. She'd never felt so unsure about a mission as she did this one. She wasn't sure if it was because it was on Kulusk, or if it was because she was putting her life in the hands of Kulusks. Even though they say they were fighting Kie's regime, they were still Kulusk. And Tirana was still Ritchen blood. What made it worse was Tirana was also of Pathgo blood. That was just too much evil for any soul to handle. Kie was living proof of this.

Juanita turned to Hulpman and Toms "Are we ready?"

"Course in and ready for execution," Toms responded.

Hulpman recognized the lingering glances in his direction. "Look, I can fly rings around any Kulusk fighter, drone or satellite. I'm ready!"

Hulpman had been a cruiser pilot for six years, ever since he was recruited from the Berlin Station. When he was a boy he flew crop dusters throughout Europe, doing a bit of old fashion barnstorming as he flew. He loved showing his talents. One day he showed his talents to a USSTAP agent in Berlin. The agent contacted him and ran him through the recruiting process—a secretive, cloak and dagger process, which would be the envy of the KGB or CIA. He was amazed and thrilled. He never counted on something as magnificent as USSTAP. He spent two years in the recruiting process, then another three years at the USSTAP Academy on Chaktun. He graduated in the top ten percent of his class and was assigned as a cruiser pilot—his number one choice.

Now he was the lead pilot out of sixteen aboard The *Destiny*. He understood her controls. He felt as one with the ship when he piloted her. He felt every turn, every bump and every speed change. It was a total mental rush and he knew he could maneuver her in a plasma erupted field if necessary. He was cocky and arrogant, but he was good. He knew it and more importantly, so did Jackil. In the heat of battle, he knew he was needed. And he wasn't about to let the Osguard down.

"Osguard, I respectfully insist you take a standard exploration team with you," Jackil noted.

"Centurion, it is a violation of all protocol for me to go. You think I will drag an E-Team with me?"

"Osguard, I don't think it could be considered dragging," Springs commented. "We all know what is at stake here. And protocol…be damned. You may be the last of the Osguards. I don't want to be party to your demise. I must insist as well you take an E-Team with you."

"I thank you for your concern, but my mind is made up. I will go to the surface ... alone, get Opel out, retrieve the antidote and return in time for dinner. Of course you will play your part as well. I am counting on the talents of Captain Hulpman that you bragged so much about. Besides, I have the entire Kulusks Revolutionary Army at my disposal."

"I still don't like it," Jackil commented.

"I know, Centurion. I don't like it either, but I must do what I must do." Juanita stood. The rest of the table stood as well. "Please set course back to Kulusk. We have a mission to do."

"Tiah," Jackil replied.

# Chapter 33—Interrogation

Sirens blasted and the hallway filled with howls of pain in Shreveport's LSU Medical Hospital Emergency Room. Two gunshot victims from a minor dispute that escalated had become the primary concern of the emergency room staff. The first victim had a thirty-eight caliber slug lodged in his neck and another lodged in his chest. The second victim was luckier. He had a nine millimeter round go through his thigh. The ambulance had rushed both victims to LSU Medical for urgent care, followed by two police cruisers. The incident was classified as a crime until the officers were informed otherwise. Standard procedure dictated they stay close to both men, to retrieve evidence and statements if possible.

The emergency room swinging doors clamored open, and Stelana and Musoto stepped through. They passed the outer waiting room where approximately a dozen people who considered their minor ailments, scrapes, bruises and sprains such an emergency it required immediate attention. However moments earlier, in the brief time it took the emergency technicians to wheel the gunshot victims in, the people forgot their aches and pains and became social investigators, stretching their necks and scurrying to the main hall to catch a glimpse of the blood and gore of the two gunshot victims. Some patients pointed at the blood soaked gurneys, others whispered, while some just turned their heads away for they saw more than they wanted. Once the moment passed, they settled back into their ritual of complaining and crying over their inconvenience.

Stelana and Musoto pressed their way pass the patients toward the reception desk. They waited a moment as the nurse finished with a telephone call. When she finished the call, she shuffled some paperwork crowding her workspace, evidently in an attempt to ignore them. Stelana cleared her throat to let their presence be known to the nurse. The nurse kept her head down, still shuffling the paperwork.

"Excuse me?" Stelana said.

"Wait a minute, I'm busy," the nurse retorted.

"FBI," Musoto responded, displaying his badge. "I don't have a moment, but soon as I do, I will be happy to see your supervisor and let him or her know what a courteous nurse they have in you."

The nurse looked up at the badge, and then she rolled her eyes in definite disapproval. "What do you want?"

"Two men were brought in by police escort earlier this evening…about a half hour ago. Where are they?" Stelana questioned.

"Two black men?" the nurse asked, letting her southern accent round her words.

"Yes, two black men."

"They are in Treatment Room C, awaiting transport upstairs…down the hall to the right. You can't miss it. Two cops are outside standing guard." Then the nurse leaned in closer to Musoto and whispered, "What did they do anyway?"

Musoto just looked at the nurse. His eyes told her he wasn't going to answer the question. She leaned back, rolled her eyes with a slight huff and went back to shuffling her paperwork. Musoto turned to Stelana and shrugged. Stelana shook her head, closing her eyes in disbelief.

The two followed the nurse's directions to Treatment Room C. Like the nurse indicated, two uniformed police officers stood outside. Musoto flashed his badge. The officer on the right, who had more stripes on his sleeve nodded and allowed Musoto and Stelana into the room.

The two men she had saved lay in beds in front of them. Each had an IV attached to one arm and handcuffs attached to their wrists, binding them to the bed railing. The first man she dragged out of the wreck was still unconscious. He had several monitors hooked to him and was under an oxygen mask. The second man was awake, but groggy. Stelana did not know if it was from the medicine or the aftereffects of the pagenay blast. Either way, the man was in a weakened condition.

"Normally we would not interrogate or question suspects in this condition without a lawyer present," Musoto warned.

"I don't plan on doing that…well not in the sense you mean."

Stelana pulled a brainwave MARIT from her denim cloth bag she had draped around her left shoulder. She clamped the half-dollar sized metal piece on the second suspect's forehead. Then she pulled out what appeared to be a cell phone, but was actually a portable ARIT, commonly called a PARIT. She opened it, pushed a couple of buttons and then put a wireless earpiece into her right ear.

"Who are you calling?" Musoto inquired.

She shook her head and motioned for Musoto to be quiet.

Tony Musoto watched in awe. "You know we can't use anything you get using your equipment in court."

"Don't plan to," Stelana explained.

She pushed several more keys on the PARIT. "Track and record," she whispered. Two short beeps sounded in her earpiece. Then she walked over to the second suspect.

"Do you know Tommy Turner?" she asked the suspect.

He opened his eyes and tried to focus on Stelana. The drug, induced haze crowded his mind and the cool, stale, antiseptic filled air hurt his throat, but he understood even through his fog he was in a hospital, handcuffed to a bedrail. He also understood the lady, no matter how pretty she looked; speaking to him was a cop of some type. He continued to steady his eyes, fighting to focus on the person speaking to him. Then after several seconds his eyes calmed and his vision cleared. He recognized the woman speaking to him as the lady who busted up the kill.

It was to be his first kill, his indoctrination into the gang, but this bitch got in the way. Anger swelled in his mind and rage filled his heart. Soon the fog lifted and he was fully aware. He pulled at the handcuff. It rattled, but held firm.

The PARIT registered his thoughts. He wanted to kill Stelana.

"I say again, do you know Tommy Turner," Stelana repeated.

He just stared at her, not. Stelana received her answer. He knew Tommy Turner.

"Okay, let's move on then," Stelana said trying to lower his defenses. "Where can we find Tommy Turner?"

Again, the suspect just stared at Stelana, trying to show resolve in his stubbornness. However, his mind registered the answer, which was recorded by the PARIT. Stelana smiled.

Her smile disoriented him a little. He wanted to ask her what she was smiling about, but he decided otherwise. He was told, if he ever was caught, to keep quiet and wait for a lawyer. *Keep quiet*, he kept reminding himself. He had to keep quiet about the drugs, the attacks and the women, he thought. Nevertheless, unbeknownst to him, these thoughts also registered on the PARIT.

However, this was chaff—information Stelana did not need. She wanted to keep him focused on the subject. The drug the hospital administered to him was making it easier for the MARIT on his forehead to pick up on his thoughts, but it also made it easier for his thoughts to wander. She needed to stay in control. She needed to direct his thoughts. Then she picked up two blips on the PARIT. It was chaff she could use…his name and his gang.

"So Bulldog, you are a member of a gang—the Blue Street Gang?" she asked.

Bulldog, shook his head in disbelief. *How does this bitch know me? How did she know about Blue Street? Big Mac must have talked. That punk!*

"No, Big Mac didn't talk, Bulldog," Stelana continued, trying to execute the shock factor. "We have had your gang in Dallas under surveillance for some time now. We know about your crib on Beacon Street. We know about the drugs, the guns and all of it. You know you boys have violated several federal laws. You know—you are looking at some big time in federal prison—Bulldog."

Bulldog shifted in his bed. The word federal made him believe she was FBI. Then he turned to Musoto. It was the first time he noticed him, but he did recognize the bell shaped badge hanging from his belt. He was definitely FBI. The stubborn, fierce look in his face vanished. His mind raced, filling with thoughts of all he knew about the Blue Street Gang. The more he remembered the more the PARIT recorded. As it recorded, Stelana rattled off the information.

"Little T's murder…the white woman from the mall…cop killing in March…the fire on Franklin Street…the one hundred and fifty thousand dollar drug deal with the Cuban…carjacking last Saturday…Jean Carter…J.C. Carter…and little Tyree Smart. You were part of it all…weren't you?"

Sweat beaded on Bulldog's face as fear gripped him. He squinted his left eye as if it would help him get insight on his interrogator.

Musoto watched Bulldog squirm in the bed. It was almost comical to him, if it weren't for the victims. The laundry list included the deaths of a cop as well as young Tyree Smart. And he couldn't use this information against Bulldog, but there had to be a way. Musoto shuddered. He wanted to put this guy away, but everything he just learned was inadmissible in court. He wondered what probative value this information had. Why were they here? His hand wiped the brow of his forehead, swiping at imaginary sweat but actually massaging an invisible tension that started to grip him.

"Look Bulldog, I suggest you cooperate with the locals," Stelana preached. "It's better you go down for attempted murder than what the FBI has on you. Your people are going down. And when they find out you have been captured, they are going to think you squealed on them anyway. If you don't cooperate with the locals, you go down with your gang. We put you in the same prison and I bet you won't last a day!"

Stelana paused to let what she said sink in. She watched the mental gymnastics play out on her monitor as the PARIT flashed every thought and every feeling.

"Yeah, you won't last a day," she continued. "Unless you come clean with the locals, you will be in their system not ours."

Musoto shook his head in disbelief. Stelana's interrogation technique appeared flawless. She had scared, bullied and maneuvered Bulldog in five short minutes, better than any investigator he had ever known. She had the use of some technology he didn't know of, but all of a sudden wish he had.

"It's your call," Stelana whispered, patting Bulldog on the chest. "Live or die, it makes no difference to me. I'm after Tommy Turner, not you." She reached for the MARIT and ripped it off his forehead.

The sting shocked Bulldog. His eyes widened and his mouth opened to yell, but all he managed to do was cough…three hacking dry coughs.

Stelana motioned for Musoto to follow her out the door. Musoto complied. The two started toward the door, but a sound caught them off guard.

"Wait," was the sound. The only word Bulldog had spoken since the accident.

Stelana stopped in her tracks, as did Musoto. Musoto looked at Stelana, but both still had their backs to Bulldog. Musoto could tell Stelana was thinking about turning back. Her eyes sparkled with interest, but she continued to stare straight at the door.

Stelana took a deep breath and blew it out hard.

"Wait," the voice said again. It was whispered, full of pain, spiced with fear and definitely hoarse.

Stelana rolled her eyes toward the ceiling, and then pushed forward, opened the door and both her and Musoto stepped out, never looking back at the pleading Bulldog.

"What now?" Musoto asked outside the room.

"Simple," Stelana replied. "We get Tommy Turner."

***

Opel Ritchen blinked several times. He even closed his eyes and counted to ten, but he was still there. Kie Ritchen stared with a gloating smile over his foe inside the security cell in the Greenhaven's basement.

"Oh yes, my dear cousin. It's me, Kie Ritchen. I bet you never thought you would see me again."

Opel opened his eyes and regarded Kie with incredulity.

"How?"

"How did you get here?" Kie continued.

Opel nodded.

"Your blood," Kie laughed. "I got your DNA from your blood. You bled on me during our struggle—a fortunate happenstance for me. Then I programmed my defense scanners to search you out. You know the rest. We shot you down."

Kie moved away from Opel and found a seat on the opposite side of the cell. Opel sat up and swung his feet to the floor.

"Your people lost," Kie laughed again. Then he stopped and glared into Opel's eyes. "What were you thinking? You thought you could challenge the Maxum of the Kulusk Empire and win. You may be my cousin, but you don't think like a Ritchen."

"So you admit I am a Ritchen?"

"Yes, I suppose. Your DNA confirmed it. I must admit my grandfather was more cunning than the archives give him credit. I guess that in itself is evident, I mean…you exist. Therefore everything you said must be true. You attacked me. That also gives credibility to your story. Frankly Opel, I am amazed."

Opel bowed in acceptance.

"But my forces repelled your modest army and now I have you." Kie smiled with eyes of evil. "All in all, it was a good day. Well…until that pesky USSTAP galaxy cruiser appeared. However, it is gone now. I guess they saw I wasn't as weak as you thought." Kie raised his finger as if in an afterthought. "Say Opel, do you know anything about a USSTAP ship showing up in my space? Were they part of your plan?"

"No, I didn't know anything about that." Opel lied. "Don't you think if I had a USSTAP galaxy cruiser at my disposal, I would have used it?"

"So your petty forces do not have space born ships? That is good to know."

Opel rebuked his absentmindedness in information security. He had to remember, he was not in control of the situation—Kie was. Also, the situation was an interrogation ... informal, but still an interrogation. "What do you want with me Kie?"

Kie smiled as the words lingered in the air for a few moments. Kie knew he was getting to Opel. Opel had lost the first round. He gave out information and he was frustrated. "Cooperation," Kie stated.

"You must be crazy," Opel blurted. "The only cooperation you will get from me is in your death. I failed earlier, I won't fail again."

"Oh, so it is my death you want. That is another nice tidbit of information to know. Thank you."

"You're welcome. However, you need not have captured me to find that out. I would have gladly told you that from afar."

"Like where?"

Opel stopped. He realized the more he talked the more information he would compromise. He observed Kie and noticed he was frequently checking his wrist timepiece. This is an interrogation he thought. Why would Kie be interested in time? Unless... Then he knew. He had a brainwave MARIT in the room somewhere, probably preprogrammed to his brainwave.

Opel reverted to his mental anti-interrogation training. He released his mind to a flower field of Tainville. He and his people had trained on beating the brainwave MARIT, by concentrating on obscure and unrelated information—information having no tangent connection to information relevant to the revolution. Opel picked the flower fields of Tainville, on the Renard continent.

The fields of Tainville contained one hundred varieties of flowers, indigenous to all three continents and some roses, tulips and other assorted flowers from Earth, which Caroline Pathgo-Ritchen planted long ago. Opel had visited the fields several times during his youth and always loved it. He could escape from his destiny and his fate when he walked the fields. He lavished in the yellow, white, red and blue flowers. He knew every breed, every variety, every hybrid and every form of flower. His mind was at peace in the fields. So this is where he went to blank out. His eyelids widened and his eyeballs rolled to the back of his head as he fell backwards onto the bed with a thump so hard his legs flopped up from the force and then his feet slammed back onto the floor.

Kie looked up from his ARIT monitor disguised as a timepiece. The last item registered on his monitor was *'brainwave MARIT.'* He knew Opel was aware the cell was reading his mind. Kie knew he did not do a skillful job of camouflaging the interrogation.

Kie stood and moved toward him. He knew what had happened, but he still had to examine Opel. He knew Opel initiated a self-induced trance—a counter interrogation technique he had heard of and tried to master. However he had never seen it, especially as perfect as Opel appeared to be performing it. He reached for Opel's wrist. He checked for a pulse. His pulse was low, barely noticeable, beating below thirty beats per minute—a comatose state. Kie pushed several buttons on his timepiece.

"Medical scan," he ordered.

The timepiece monitor face flashed blue and then red. Then Opel's vital signs raced across the screen. He read the monitor with dejection. Each number, blood pressure, heart rate, respiratory rate confirmed Opel was in suspended animation without the aid of an ARIT. Kie shook his head.

With each shake of his head, Kie became more enraged. His hand went up and he threw it down in a fist, connecting to Opel's jaw. He checked the monitor on his wrist again—no change. He punched Opel again—no change. He then picked him up and slammed him to the floor—no change. He kicked Opel across the face, in the side and in the groin—no change. Kie kept punching and kicking Opel in a vain effort to wake him. He executed such wretched torture onto him that he cracked two of Opel's ribs, broke his left wrist and left Opel's face so bruised and battered he no longer resembled himself anymore. After fifteen minutes, Kie realized Opel was for all intents and purposes—gone.

During the beating Opel's mind escaped to Tainville, where he stood on the outer edge of the southern boundary of the flower fields. He stepped up to the white flower, known as Sisle. He leaned over to the flower, studied its angular shape, with its large four-petal configuration. Then he leaned in closer and smelled its sweet but biting fragrance. Then he reached out and touched it, feeling its soft silky, almost comforting texture. His mind, heart and soul concentrated on that flower and nothing else. When he was through, he moved to the next Sisle and began the ritual again.

With the hundreds of breeds of flowers, making up thousands of flowers, Opel could play this ritual for an entire lifetime. That is why he chose this subject for his trance. He was able to lose his mental awareness in here as long as it took, waiting for the code word that would penetrate his subconscious mind and wake him to the real world.

Yet, he was not completely in the trance. He felt some stinging and some pain when Kie Ritchen administered the brutal beating. It was a great strain on his mental capacity to keep the pain out and keep the picturesque setting in his mind. After several minutes and several adjustments to his technique the sting of the beating evaporated and his life was pleasant, he was once again enjoying the beauty of Sisle flowers.

Back in the cell, Kie Ritchen grew tired of the beating he was dispensing on his cousin. He tapped his communicator at the base of his throat. "Med lab, this is Maxum Ritchen," he bellowed. He waited for the proper connection and when satisfied he continued, "Come to Greenhaven detention, cell alpha and pick up the prisoner. Administer proper medical attention and see if you can wake this bastard up."

# Chapter 34—Fight's On

The heaven's shine was exceptionally bright. The stars twinkled with a little more brilliance in this sector of space. The ten planets surrounded a red sun called Zor. The third planet, like most solar systems, contained life, it contained human life. The sun had nurtured this life, since the beginning of the third generation of mankind. Now in the midst of the fourth age of the third generation, this planet, called Kulusk, was in turmoil—a turning point—a revolution.

The *USSTAP Galaxy Cruiser Destiny* traversed this part of the radiant sky on an intercept course to Kulusk. The *Destiny* descended to two hundred and fifty below the galactic plane in an effort to approach Kulusk's blind spot—this was new information Tirana provided. Until now, USSTAP had assumed Kulusk had no blind spot in their scanner surveillance. The *Destiny* traveled at full hyperlight speed around the solar system at a distance of eight light years and sailed under the Kulusk solar system from the opposite direction. Juanita hoped this small deception would gain them several valuable minutes of surprise. She anticipated Kie would be scanning the stars in the direction of Capitol Station or of Earth.

The *Destiny* slowed to full hypersonic speed as it approached the imaginary extension of Kulusk's southern polar cap. Then the ship ascended toward the planet. Commander Kinl Sast, the ship's Chief Offensive Weapons Officer, targeted key satellites in the Kulusk defensive perimeter during the ascent—twenty-five satellites in all. Sast ignored the scanning and sensor satellites, he only targeted the weapons satellites that specifically protected Renard.

"Five seconds until contact with sensor and scanners," Major Treylo Gnig announced. "Four…Three…Two…One…Now."

Sast stroked his console, hitting several pressure sensors. The top forward pagenay ports fired, slicing through the planet's atmosphere on a tangent and coming out in space over Renard. The penetration and the exit of the pagenay blast through the Kulusk atmosphere caused the pagenay beam to bend and refract somewhat, but the ARIT firing mechanism compensated for it brilliantly. The blue beams rained through the pinkish clouds like reverse spotlights. The beams entered the atmosphere, bent toward the surface at a eight degree angle, six less than the curvature of the planet, sailed toward the sky once more as it traversed the atmosphere and exited at an eight degree upward trajectory.

Six weapons satellites exploded with the first barrage. Sast strummed his console again. The majestic flow of six more pagenay beams sliced the atmosphere on a slightly steeper tangent, heating the air molecules into frenzy as they passed through. Six more weapons satellites expanded, burned and then disintegrated into fireball cinders. The coldness and vacuum of space stamped the fire out, leaving billions of small penny-size embers floating toward the planet's surface.

Three more times Sast adjusted his computations and let loose with a barrage of pagenay fire, reacquiring satellites he was not sure he destroyed and acquiring new satellites for destruction. When he was satisfied he had destroyed all the targets, he sent a signal to Captain Hulpman, the lead pilot.

Hulpman acknowledged the signal, swung the ship out and continued the ascent to coordinates putting them in a synchronized orbit above Renard. Captain Laura Toms pushed the coordinates into the ARIT, setting the distance above the city to standard defensive orbit height.

Jackil remained in his seat as he observed his crew executing Juanita's plan without instructions or interruptions from him. He was proud of his crew and inwardly smiling at their seamless completion of each task. However, time was drawing near to the execution of his part in this game.

"Standard defensive orbit over Renard," Toms announced.

"Have they energized their planet's shield grid yet?" Jackil asked.

"No sir," Gnig's voice rang.

Jackil tapped his CC, "Osguard...you are a go."

"Tiah," shot Juanita's voice from his CC subdural receiver.

***

Kie had just washed Opel's blood off his hands and change his cloak when the alarm sounded. He tapped his communications device located on his ear, "What is it?"

"Sir, twenty-five weapons satellites went off line in the defensive perimeter above Renard," a chilling voice responded.

"Scanners and sensor readings?" Kie asked.

"Coming up now," the voice said more calmly. After several agonizing seconds the voice announced with the same earlier chill, "Surveillance reports a USSTAP galaxy cruiser in synchronized orbit above Renard."

Kie pounded his fist down on his clothes dresser. "Shield grid up," he ordered.

"Soli," the voice replied.

Kie knew he had a lack in space security while he was dealing with the revolutionary assault, but he had fortified his space surveillance since then. There was no way a USSTAP galaxy cruiser could have sneaked into his space, especially close enough to destroy his weapons satellites, without the alarm sounding. "How did they get through?" he requested.

"They appeared from the southern sky sir."

"What?"

231

"The southern sky sir, they just appeared from the southern sky," the frightened voice repeated.

"Opel!" Kie yelled. "He must be in league with USSTAP...I knew it...damn it...I knew it." Kie paused for a second to let his mind grasp the situation. "Well those Rox will not get away with it," He admonished.

Kie tapped his communications device to terminate the communication and then moved toward his desk in the other room. He pressed two bottoms on his ARIT panel, and a three-D holograph of his planet with the defensive grid came up. He took a moment to study the holograph. He deleted the twenty-five satellites representing his weapons satellites above Renard. Then he pressed his ARIT keys and watched as several satellites in the grid maneuvered to cover the vacant area.

"Time for adjustment?" he asked his ARIT.

"One universal hour," the male ARIT voice responded.

"Do it," Kie commanded.

Several minutes later, Kie used his PGP to step into his military command center on the other side of Renard. The recently promoted General Tovi Lixlen snapped to attention when he recognized the maxum. Until a few short days ago, Lixlen was a commander of the maxum's planetary guard. However, since the devastation of the Kulusk military and most of its strategic leaders, including Xer, the previous General, Lixlen was removed from guard duty and placed as the head of what was left of the military, which now consisted of the planetary guard, new recruits and the original command center staff. He did not have an armada of star ships, nor the millions of conscripts at his disposal like his predecessor, Xer did. Nor did he possess the military training, experience or skill. He felt good about repelling the revolutionary assault, but now he had a strange feeling about confronting a USSTAP galaxy cruiser.

When the USSTAP shuttle appeared he did not know what to make of it. His mind was consumed by the revolutionary assault he had just thwarted. Moreover, he had no assets to deal with it, other than the automatic defense grid. Unfortunately, he had not activated the defense grid until ten minutes after the assault when Kie ordered it. A rookie mistake he did not acknowledge to Kie. He had altered his report to say the grid engaged the shuttle once it was in range. And he had debris to prove it. Although the debris turned out to be an unmanned USSTAP time-light shuttle, another fact he omitted from his report, it was enough to quell Kie's curiosity. However, now a USSTAP galaxy cruiser had arrived, and Kie's curiosity must be on a rise about the earlier incident. Lixlen was scared. He was scared he would be executed for his mistake and his deception.

"Welcome Maxum Ritchen," Lixlen greeted.

"Have you made contact with the cruiser yet?"

"No sir. We have not attempted contact."

"Why?" Kie asked. Then he raised his hands signifying he did not want Lixlen to respond. "This is better...I will make the initial contact."

"As I figure you wanted," Lixlen lied. Actually, Lixlen had rejected the idea of making contact because he was afraid—afraid he couldn't handle the situation and would escalate it.

Kie walked toward the communication suite with Lixlen in trail. Kie's black cape waved behind him like an airplane's contrails, marking his presence and authority. The clang of his boots against the metal grated floor rang out like an announcement of his coming. Everyone on that deck knew Kie was there, and he was not in a good mood.

Kie nudged the communication officer from her seat, without a word and sat at the console. He pressed some keys on the board and waited for the ARIT to signal his channel was open. A dark skinned muscular black man appeared on the screen. He was bald with no eyebrows and sharp piercing purple eyes. It was Jackil.

"I am Centurion Deon Jackil of the Universal Science, Security and Trade Association of Planets' *Galaxy Cruiser Destiny*."

"This is Maxum Kie Ritchen, Emperor of the Kulusk Republic of Planets. You have engaged in an unprovoked attack against my security defenses...explain yourself."

Jackil shook his head and gave a childish smile, "Unprovoked?" Then he sat down at his command chair. Now it was time for him to play his part and buy some time for the Osguard. "You send an armada to destroy Capitol Station...you engage in a universal uprising against us and in the face of a truce...you send a virus to Capitol Station and kill everyone on board. And you call my actions unprovoked?"

Kie grinned. Those were the words he wanted to hear. "My virus killed everyone onboard...all are dead? I hope that includes your Rox Osguards?"

Jackil received the confession he needed. Kie Ritchen admitted his duplicity in the virus attack on Capitol Station. That gave him the ammunition he needed and also gave him sanction for firing upon Kie's defense perimeters. Juanita was correct. Kie was a vain son of a bitch. He could not go long without taking credit for his deeds, even if it meant admitting his guilt and setting his world on a path of destruction not seen by any man. However, Jackil's part was not over. There was more he needed to do.

"Unfortunately it does," Jackil lied. "Our congress and parliament were on Chaktun, so they are safe. And they have issued orders...the first galaxy cruiser sire to bring you back, dead or alive, will assume the title of First Osguard and begin the rebuilding of USSTAP. And guess what? I am first of about two hundred galaxy cruiser sires headed this way to collect on that promise."

Kie swallowed hard. He had not expected the governmental body of USSTAP to react so swiftly and so decisively. The astonishment of the news resonated in his face as he contemplated his next move. He could not imagine two hundred USSTAP galaxy cruisers barreling down on his planet. He had not counted on this. USSTAP always prided themselves on their humility...on their humanity. Such an order was uncharacteristic of USSTAP.

"You are bluffing," Kie responded. "USSTAP would never place a bounty on anyone...not even me."

"You're wrong," Jackil said focusing his purple eyes on Kie. "It was the Osguards who enforced those sorts of policies. However, now that you have removed the Osguards, there is no one around to enforce them. You have untied our hands and now we can act and react as we see fit to accomplish the mission." Jackil paused to let his words find root in Kie's heart. "You pushed a little too far. Now it is our turn. You can come with me peacefully, or you can come with me dead. It is your choice."

Kie lowered his head in contemplation. He wondered if what Jackil said was true. Did he release the devil? He hit a sensor and the communication terminated. He sat back in the chair and looked up at the ceiling. For the first time in his life, he pondered what death would be like.

He imagined it as a long and endless sleep, filled with dreams and comforted with...with...with. *With what?* Nothing can comfort death. It was the final realization of nothing. Nonexistence! Not to be alive is not to exist...and not to exist was unfathomable. Dreams cannot exist if you don't exist. The pleasure of feeling life, tasting exquisite food, savoring magnificent drink, the thrill of an exhilarating dance or the sensuous touch of a beautiful woman would not exist either. The thought shuttered through his body like a quake. Now he felt alone. Again, he felt scared.

He shot up as the alarm rang out.

"*Destiny* is firing!" Lixlen announced. "Shield grid holding at ninety-nine percent"

Kie hoped the shield grid would hold long enough for the other satellites to reach a stable orbit and attack *Destiny*. Then the satellites would probably be destroyed, and *Destiny* would finish the job. Well they can't finish the job if they can't find him. Kulusk was a big planet. It would take a more discrete search to find him on the planet. Kie knew he had to escape. He had to escape now!

"Maxum!" Lixlen yelled. "The revolutionary assault is beginning again."

Kie turned to see the big holograph of the area display in the middle of the circular room. He saw the ships approaching both the northern and southern ports; the RACs in the air coming from the west this time, and the land cruisers approaching from the east in a reverse replay of the morning's attack. Then the monitor flashed on. A young slender curly haired blonde with blue eyes emerged on the screen. It was Tirana, and she wore a slight smile with a devilish sparkle in her eye.

"Kie, your temporary leverage is over," she reported. "The revolutionary council has elected me heir to the Maxum throne in place of my brother. So get ready, I am coming to slap you off the throne. Tirana...out."

Kie turned to Lixlen, "What are you standing there for? Get your men out there. Fight them off...fight them off now!" he yelled.

# Chapter 35—Pieces Fall Together

The sun rose bringing with it the heat and humidity, which was so well known in the south. It was only seven thirty and the temperature was climbing to eighty-five degrees. The humidity was already at ninety percent, which made the morning muggier than one wanted. Over the Shreveport landscape, the towering red, orange, brown and gold casino hotels bordering the Red River welcomed the day with the same activity that closed the day out prior—gambling.

People drove from Mississippi, Texas, Arkansas and Oklahoma to take a chance on the tables or the one-arm bandit called a slot machine. The gambling industry had brought prosperity and new jobs to the area, albeit replacing some of the high tech and manufacturing jobs that once adorned the surroundings. However, the casinos also brought something else, a drop in the crime rate.

Prior to the casinos operating in the area, Shreveport-Bossier City contained some of the vilest, unwanted gang activity. Fortunately, the prospect of prosperity and the encouragement of the casino owners had quelled the gang activity to a mere shadow. Shreveport Police Chief Daniel Delecroix took additional pride in that. Some years back, Shreveport had won the distinction of being named one of the country's *All American Cities.'* This was another point of pride fueling Delecroix.

He never had pressure bare down on him from any political office or commercial organization prior to Tyree Smart's murder. The phone call from Governor Williams played special havoc on his pride. Then to add insult to injury, the governor insisted agents from his new LBI would be included on the case. Delecroix soon realized the two agents from the LBI were more of a nuisance than Musoto or Rikes, at least Musoto and Rikes stayed out of his way. The two agents from the LBI insisted on questioning every police officer involved, going over every note written and second guessing every decision made. They were the true thorns in his side, and it had just been one day.

Chief Delecroix met the day with renewed vigor. He had something. Oh yeah...he had something that would stop all the second-guessing and behind-the-back whispers. He had evidence.

He walked into the briefing room where he summoned the two LBI agents, Tornado and Coleman; Musoto and Rikes; and his detectives, Russell and Allensen. They all sat around the briefing table in squeaky wooden chairs. The room was cigarette drenched and the table was coffee stained in several places. Just what one would expect from a twenty-year-old police station.

Delecroix took his place at the head of the table and threw three folders out onto the table. One set slid toward Tornado and Coleman, another set slid to Musoto and Stelana, and the last set flew to Russell and Allensen.

"Agent Rikes chased down three suspects who shot at Ms. Smart last night," he began. "She was able to apprehend two suspects after they crashed their vehicle into a ditch. They are in stable condition at LSU. Unfortunately, a third suspect remains on the loose. We retrieved several weapons from the scene—two nine millimeter handguns, a thirty-eight caliber and a semi-automatic rifle. These guns were miraculously thrown from the car during the crash and did not burn. So we were able to lift prints from them. We have three good prints."

Delecroix stopped to let the people review the files. He looked up, inwardly smiling at his findings but outwardly keeping a professional front.

"James the Bulldog Cameron, Leroy Kitchums, a.k.a. Big Mac and Tommy Turner, a.k.a. T-Square; one of the guns was a positive match to the slug we took out of Tyree Smart. People, we have our killers."

Stelana looked at the others in the room. She felt somewhat out of place. She was not a cop, even though everyone in the room, except for Musoto, thought she was. And she was amazed Musoto did not say otherwise, he just played along with the charade. She pushed the thought aside and reviewed the file. She was surprised Delecroix's information was almost as good as hers. The same conclusion reached by two different methods—hers was by superior technology and his was by inferior technology—fingerprints and ballistics reports. Well, she now garnered newfound respect for the archaic method of investigation.

She turned to Musoto and whispered, "Score one for you guys. Now let's see if you can follow through. Remember, if justice does not prevail by your method, it will prevail by mine."

***

The smell from the kitchen was hauntingly delicious. The aroma of scrambled eggs, bacon, grits and rice, the staple of a southern breakfast, wafted in the Smart home, trying to chase away the despair and heartache that had plagued the house for the last week.

Sarah stood at the stove, preparing the breakfast while contemplating how to broach the subject of moving to her sister. Juanita had requested she move Jessica to the gardens so she could leave the memories behind. Although, she wasn't sure it was the proper thing to do. She and Jessica had grown up in Shreveport. They had memories, family and countless friends in Shreveport ... people who by the pure virtue of being from Shreveport, would not abandon her sister in her deepest time of need. Jessica had lived all her life in Shreveport. She married and buried her beloved husband here. Now she has buried her only grandchild. Sarah knew she would not move—at least not right now.

However, the attack on Yolanda was a different matter. It suggested her daughter was not safe here, even though Stelana stopped it and promised there would be no other attack on Yolanda. The question now was did she believe it? Did she believe Stelana had eradicated the people who threatened her niece's life? The thought frightened her so, but she needed to think about her daughter as well.

She had not heard anything from Juanita since she left. She knew by her limited exposure to space travel Juanita should be dealing with the Kulusks about now. This made her nervous. Sarah had been in a daze since she found out USSTAP was in trouble. And to think, just last month she knew nothing of the Kulusks or USSTAP. Now she wished she had never heard of either. It was so true ... ignorance was bliss. Yet she had more than her share to worry about. She had neither control to change the outcome, nor the patience to accept the situation. Nor did she have the wisdom to understand the complete danger. All she knew was her daughter was mankind's last hope at peace. As dramatic as that sounded, she comprehended the importance her daughter's life held. This knowledge sent a chill through her body as she giggled in despair.

"What are you doing?"

Her sister's voice startled her a little. She turned to see Jessica standing in the doorway, showing the wear and tear of mourning for her grandchild and the concern for her daughter's safety on her face. Jessica's eyes were red, with bags outlining the upper half of her cheeks. Her hair was a mess and she was still in her nightgown. She stumbled like she was intoxicated toward the four-seated round metal kitchen table. She eased down in one chair and lowered her head into her hands.

"I'm fixing us some breakfast," Sarah answered. "A good hot meal will do both of us some good."

"I suppose..." Jessica's voice trailed off.

"How's Yolanda doing?" Sarah asked moving toward the opposite seat.

"Yolanda is crazy," Jessica spurted. "Damn fool girl is spouting off something about Stephanie acting like some bionic woman last night."

"You don't say," Sarah commented, shuffling in her chair. "Well I guess Stephanie did take out three guys...that in itself, sounds pretty amazing. Maybe it did look like she was a machine."

"Who the hell is Stephanie anyway?" asked Jessica raising her head to look into Sarah's eyes.

"I really don't know," Sarah said averting her eyes from her sister. "She works for my daughter's company. I just met her coming to the funeral. My daughter knows more about her than I do. All I know is Juanita wanted Stephanie to stay here and do whatever she could for us, including providing protection. Stephanie is some sort of security specialist. And last night was a prime example of her abilities. Don't you think?"

"Speaking of Juanita...where the hell is she anyway?" Jessica's voice turned from questioning to demanding. "I mean this is when we need family the most and she sneaks out in the middle of the night...doesn't say good-bye to anyone. Shit, she didn't even say kiss my ass dog."

"She had to leave...something came up." Sarah was now getting a little defensive. "It was very important and it couldn't wait."

"Nothing is more important than family."

"Well I'm here," Sarah maintained.

"I know that...and I thank God for you. However, Yolanda needs someone too, besides us two old hags to talk to. Shit, she lost her son. Juanita could have stayed around for that. What can be more important than family? What can be more important than Yolanda right now?"

*The universe,* Sarah wanted to say, but refrained. Until now, she would have agreed with her sister about Juanita's priorities. Now she was recounting the numerous times she spoke to her sister about Juanita and how she blew off spending the holidays with her. Juanita was her living child, her only immediate living family besides her sister; and on more than several holidays in the past twelve years, Juanita skipped coming home and insisted Sarah go visit Jessica. Juanita would pay for the plane fare and arrange everything. Well, someone in UAI did, she concluded.

On those holidays, Sarah sat with Jessica in her living room and accused Juanita of being an ungrateful, selfish and spoiled daughter, who was too self absorbed and too materialistic for her own good. Now those conversations were coming back to haunt her. Little did she know at the time, her daughter was trouncing around the universe, light years away protecting life and serving others in a way no one could imagine—risking her life over and over and over again; while she comfortably sat in Osguard Gardens or Shreveport, sulking because her child did not want to spend time with her. It wasn't because she didn't want to, she now realizes. It was because she couldn't.

A touch of guilt stabbed Sarah in the heart. The pain was accompanied by fear. Sarah was terrified for her daughter and she could not talk about it. At least the other parents on Chaktun had each other to cope with their fears. Conversely, Sarah had no one, and she was supposed to be the support for Jessica and her spoiled brat kid, Yolanda. It was weighing on her soul and the pain was getting harder to bear. She didn't know if she could do it anymore. She didn't know if she could pretend her life was okay and she was strong enough to take on Jessica's problems. She just didn't know.

"Frankly Jessica ..." Sarah paused to think over her words. She took a sip of coffee and laid the cup down. She looked into her sister's eyes. For the first time she saw the pain hovering in her soul through those eyes. She didn't know what to say or how to say it, but she knew it had to be said. She stood to turn the stove off and let the grits cool down. She returned to her seat. As she did, she noticed her sister's gaze never left her.

"Frankly what?" asked Jessica

"Frankly this...Yolanda doesn't like Juanita and it wouldn't matter if she stayed or not. In fact if Juanita stayed, they would have only gotten into a fight—like they always do."

Jessica stiffened up and huffed. She began shaking her head. Sarah was preparing for a verbal assault. If it came, Sarah knew she couldn't defend herself. Her sister was in a weakened state and didn't need to fight with her. Sarah condemned her comment as she saw the emotions execute on her sister's face.

Jessica remained stiff shaking her head. Then she burst out laughing. Sarah stared in amazement. She didn't know if Jessica snapped. Was her sister having a nervous breakdown? She dared not move. If she were having a nervous breakdown, a sudden movement may cause her to become violent. Then she thought, *this was her sister, she didn't have a violent bone in her body.*

"What are you laughing at?" Sarah questioned.

"You...I am laughing at what you said," she responded between chuckles. "Yolanda never did like Juanita...you're right about that. She always thought Juanita too...too...too...stuck up ... too...too...too much like a little spoiled white girl."

"And what's that suppose to mean?"

"Plenty!" Jessica said controlling her laughter. "—and nothing! Juanita was always the perfect angel. She never gave you a moment's worry. She never did drugs. She did well in school; she grew up, got married. She did everything perfect. I guess Yolanda was and still is a little bit jealous. I know I am."

"What?"

"Look, I love my daughter with all my heart and I wouldn't trade her for the world, but she was a handful. And I wish she was a little more like

239

Juanita...a little more responsible...a little more self-confident...a little more self-reliant. I mean..." her voice trailed off. "She's everything I wanted Yolanda to be...everything I pushed Yolanda to be. I guess Yolanda saw that and resented Juanita for it. Hell, she might've resented me in some deep psychological way."

Sarah took a sip of coffee and stared out the window.

"I mean the drugs, Nelson, the prostitution, the early pregnancy, the talking back...it was all because I pushed too hard...I guess," Jessica continued to confess.

"No, Jessica. You did everything you were supposed to do. You were a perfect role model ... a perfect wife...a perfect mother. You showed her what to do, you taught her right from wrong, and most importantly, you loved her through all her trials and tribulations. That's all a mother can do. That's all I ever did. And believe me, Juanita isn't the perfect angel I made her out to be. She got into some stuff too," she confessed. "Sometimes it is the luck of the genes ... the DNA if you will. There is nothing we can do about it, but trust in God. And right now, your daughter needs you and you need her. That's what is important. You've got to be strong. You got to be her mother and her friend. Juanita can't do anymore than you can. She needs you...no one else...just you."

Sarah moved over to hug her sister as she noticed Jessica's eyes swell up with tears. As she wrapped her arms around her, the tears flowed and Jessica began to sob into Sarah's bosom. It was time to start the healing and Jessica began her first steps from mourning to recovery. She now realized Jessica needed to stop being a grieving grandmother and start being a supportive mother again. Yolanda needed her mother.

Sarah held on tight to Jessica. She now knew her instincts were correct. This was not the time to separate the two. They must stay together. They must stay together here, in Shreveport. So they can recover from this tragedy.

***

It was 10:00 AM in Washington D.C. and 6:00 PM in Moscow. The weather in Washington was a warm eighty-four degrees with no sign of rain. In Moscow, the temperature was quite a bit cooler, but comfortable for a summer night. U.S. President Frederick Walter Peters sat in his oval office with Russian President Sergay Vladimir Repustinov on the speakerphone. Leaks, Eldridge, Payne and Bass flanked Peters' desk.

"Hello Sergay, I have you on speakerphone," Peters informed the Russian president. "I have my congressional leadership in the office with me. I have Senator Majority Leader, John W. Bass; Senator Minority Leader, Thomas C. Payne; the Speaker of the House, Joyce T. Eldridge; and the House Minority Leader, Warren S. Leaks. I have just informed them of what really happened that Friday and I have allowed them to see the HVP and all the official reports. I'm afraid you were correct Sergay. We can't keep this a secret any longer. However, my esteemed colleagues are still somewhat dubious of things. So I figure you should enlighten them from your perspective."

"I understand Walter," Repustinov commented. "I wish it could be different, but I guess it was not meant to be so. I had to let my staff and certain leaders from the Duma know as well."

"Oh!" Peters exclaimed. "That is interesting." Peters wondered how many other people knew the total truth. The charade was getting out of hand, too big to control and could backfire on them. He took a deep breath and blew it out hard. He saw his career dying in front of him, but most importantly, he saw the chaos, he so fervently tried to avoid, explode. It was a matter of time before the leak would seep into the media. "Well go ahead," he urged.

Repustinov rattled his version of events over the secure line. His voice rang throughout the oval office with fear, confusion and pain as he recounted the series of events leading up to the nuclear launch that fateful Friday and the event after the nuclear launch that revealed the existence of USSTAP, but most of all his voice rang with the truth.

The four politicians listened with the excitement of a child being told a bedtime story. A few times they jotted down something on the yellow legal pads Peters provided to them, but the rest of the time they remained quiet and attentive. Surprise and dismay blanketed their faces during the thirty minutes Repustinov spoke. When Repustinov finished, the foursome stared into space. Peters wondered what they were thinking. He could not tell one way or the other by the blank looks on their faces.

Peters thanked Repustinov, and then terminated the phone call. He continued to study their faces. They remained blank and drawn. Peters expected Payne to lead the attack and was poised for him to charge, but he didn't. He remained speechless like his partners. Peters waived his hands in front of Payne's face. Payne shook his head as if he had just been revived from a coma.

"I figured you would have something to say," Peters commented.

"I have plenty to say, Mr. President. But none of it is important right now," Payne commented. "However, I will say this. I am not sure I approve of the way you handled the situation, but I understand."

Peters regarded Payne and his statement for a few seconds. He didn't know what he meant or what he was leading to. It was the sort of off the cuff remark he was not prepared for.

Peters took a deep breath and exhaled hard. "What would you have done?" he asked Payne.

"Don't know. I'm not sure I would have handled it any differently than you…except for stringing us along, albeit, the Russian president brings up an interesting point."

"What's that?" inquired Peters, trying not to let his anger show at the slight comment Payne made about stringing them along.

"This is too big to hide," Leaks interrupted.

"Obviously it has been under wraps for over fifty years already," the president responded.

"Yes, that was before World War III broke out," Bass interjected. "We are missing nukes…the Russians are missing nukes, and the entire U.S. Air Force knows about it. Frankly, I am surprised no one has leaked it to the press yet. And Lord knows how long the Russian military will keep it a secret. They've been having trouble for years just keeping accountability of their nukes. Now this!"

Peters raised his eyebrow at the last statement. Peters knew he could squash the story in America, but Bass had a point. He had no control over the Russian military. And there were times he wasn't sure Repustinov had control over the Russian military. "So what do you propose?"

"Full disclosure," Leaks informed. "Maybe to the United Nations, a joint disclosure between you and the Russian president could do the trick."

"Are you crazy?" screamed Eldridge. "That is exactly what we don't need. It will bring the chaos we all fear."

"I agree with Joyce," Payne added.

"There is no other way," Leaks barked. "This is bound to get out!"

"Yes, and it will have the conspiracy theorist busy for a century," Peters informed. "We just have to stick to our guns. What I need from you is your support to swing the votes for the treaty. Let me do the rest."

"I'm not sure about that either," replied Payne. "We are dealing with two countries' military. I am not sure we can keep our people from talking, and I damn well doubt Repustinov can keep his people quiet."

"We are talking about Russia," Peters laughed. "If anyone can keep secrets, it is the Russians."

"Maybe the Soviet Union did," Bass pointed out, "but I am not so sure about the new Russia."

"I tell you what," Peters bantered. "If we see it is a bust, I will go to the United Nations with Repustinov and make a full disclosure. But until then, I need time to build up our conventional strength again."

"As does Russia?" questioned Leaks.

"I imagine so," Peters replied, "but I don't think Russia has the funds to do it as quickly as us."

"Then what?" Leaks asked. "Then we have two armies staring each other down without fear of total annihilation. It is the beginning of another

Cold War ... I tell you ... that is bound to break out into a hot war of global proportions."

"Look Leaks, they are going to rebuild anyway, even if we don't. Didn't you hear Sergay, he told his people…he told his leadership and he did not say he had any disbelievers. He is trying to talk us out of it so he can build his army. Then what? I tell you what…we will be on the wrong end of a rifle…that's what." Peters' demeanor turned sour as he punctuated his fears.

Leaks twisted his head to the side and thought about the situation for a few seconds. "I will support what you ask, but…but we need full disclosure in the near future. This is too important to keep deceiving the public with."

"Grow up Leaks," Eldridge countered. "The government has been deceiving the public on a regular basis since the framing of the constitution. I am sure there are larger secrets than this locked away in the history of this office. What's one more? Besides, we need the time to court this USSTAP. Maybe we can win favors from them. They are Americans after all. Whose side do you think they would take if the shit hit the fan? Don't you think Sergay is aware of this as well? The president is right. Sergay is trying to stall so he can build his army up. He probably sees USSTAP as an extension of the American military and he is running scared."

"No shit!" Payne observed. "I didn't think of it in those terms. Eldridge is right. We need to build up, both nuclear and conventional in preparation of a pre-emptive strike from Russia. And while we do it, we need to find a way to establish diplomatic lines with USSTAP." Payne looked into the president's eyes. "Do the Russians know about Musoto?"

"No." Peters responded with glee. "And they won't know. They don't even know about the First Universal War, or the biological incident on Capitol Station. In fact, we have the latest and greatest intelligence on this. And we have something better—a man on the inside."

"Great!" Leaks conceded. "As long as we have the upper hand, I will agree to continue on this course of action. However, if things worsen, or USSTAP loses this battle with the Kulusks, I want full disclosure to the public. They have to know what we are up against. Who knows? Maybe we can unite Earth under one banner, led by the United States, and defeat the Kulusks if they attack."

"However, we must build our nuclear forces up first," Payne insisted. "They will come in handy in staving off the Russians and might come in handy when and if we have to deal with the Kulusks."

Peters thought for a moment and realized these politicians were thinking like his staff. "No. We must build our conventional capability first. Then we will build our nuclear force up. And if I suspect a Kulusk attack as Leaks suggests, you will have your full disclosure and both Russia and us, will begin building our nukes; because, we will need all the armies, nukes and people in the world to help us defeat the threat. Yet, I am telling you, USSTAP will prevail. We must go that route. We must establish diplomatic ties to USSTAP. That is the first order of business. And in order to do that, we must keep their existence a secret a while longer. Because if we don't, someone will purposely damage any relations we could have had with them in the name of some insane cause."

The foursome looked at each other. Eldridge vigorously nodded while Payne and Bass meekly nodded. Leaks looked defiant but realized he'd lost his support. He looked around the room one last time as if he were beginning to lobby for a recount, but as he looked at his colleagues he saw it would have been a futile effort; so he also consented. It was a compromise they could live with for now.

"Then it is settled. You support the agreement and I will push for diplomatic ties with USSTAP," Peters said in summary.

# Chapter 36—Second Strike

The air was stale and salty. The red mist hovering above her was somewhat disconcerting, and the humidity was physically taxing, but she was here. She was the first Osguard ever to touch this planet in recorded history. Juanita Genesis-Clark, the sire of *Galaxy Protector Sharyla*, the protector of Galaxy Fifty-Five, the Bletherien Galaxy, was standing on Kulusk soil. More specifically, she was standing in the western underground tunnels leading to Renard.

The tunnel system walls were the natural rock and dirt of Kulusk, only the floors were paved. The tunnel system appeared to Juanita to contain large pockets of storage areas where the KLCs parked. Around these pockets, were large garages and several honeycombed passageways that contained rooms and sleeping quarters. A tunnel road connected each one of the systems. On the schematic, Tirana provided, this was the furthest system. She was five systems away from Renard, a distance of forty miles, she estimated, and was inside the protective barrier of the shield grid now. Something she couldn't have done prior to the second strike.

The one flaw to gate portal technology was it would not penetrate another chromerion field. Thus, she had to step prior to the attack. She also had to step somewhere she estimated no sensor or scanner device would detect her. The tunnels were the most logical place.

She had stepped into the tunnels several minutes prior to the beginning of the second strike, loaded in full combat gear, including a delta belt, a black body vest, black helmet and black barreled coronet rifle.

She stepped using coordinates Tirana supplied. She remained hidden in the shadows of a small corridor, watching the Kulusk soldiers scurry to their KLCs in response to the attack. This is what she was counting on. This was another reason why the RLCs attacked from the east this time. She suspected the Kulusks assumed the RLCs could not maneuver to another point for another attack, so they fortified this area against another attack.

However, Tirana used her micro-portals to transport the RLCs into position. This was a massive undertaking by any measure. Yet, transferring her entire fleet of RLCs, in the few short hours they had, was more than impressive, it was astounding. Juanita surmised Tirana and Opel would be assets as allies, or formidable foes. She would rather it be the former.

Juanita heard the pounding Mota and his RACs were delivering onto the shield grid surrounding Renard. With each hit, the ground shook and loose dirt and gravel floated from the ceilings. She commanded her body not to cough from the debris littering the air and finding root in her lungs.

She regarded the Kulusks as they passed her position, running toward their KLCs, unaware of her presence in the shadow of a side doorway. She waited until the last one passed her and then she stepped from the shadows and ran up behind him. She caught up to him in the garage area as he stepped on the rail of his cruiser. Luckily, it was the closest ship to the entrance and the last cruiser in the garage. She estimated twenty-five KLCs were parked in the garage. She took her rifle butt and jabbed it hard into the small of the green suited man's back. He crumbled backwards, slipping off the rail. She then grabbed him by the collar and pulled him toward the floor. He fell with his arms outstretched and his eyes wide with surprise, but before he could scream, Juanita's rifle butt crashed into his face, cracking his jawbone.

Juanita stared at the unconscious soldier with eyes of pity. A touch of remorse tugged at her soul. She did not enjoy taking a life, even in combat, but she especially didn't enjoy taking a life in a covert manner. It was almost like murder. She dare not use her pagenay. The blast may set off a weapons alarm. All of her actions had to be done with no weapons fire, that's why she had the ship's doctor make her some knockout MARITS.

She reached into her thigh pocket, retrieved a little black circular MARIT and slapped it on his cheek. She knew the MARIT would keep him unconscious for at least four hours. *That should be enough time.*

Then she jumped onto the hatch of the cruiser. She knew three people usually manned the vehicle. Thus, she had two more Kulusks to worry about. The KLCs engines rang to life under her. The soft, low hum echoed more in the tunnel like a high pitched ringing in her ears. The fumes of dialairtic gas pierced her nose as the cavern filled with exhaust from the twenty-five KLCs starting their engines. She coughed for she never could get use to the smell. It was the energy used to fuel most engines, even USSTAP land, sea, air, and space vehicle engines. It burned clean without any pollution in its pure form, but if degraded or not used correctly the initial smell irritated the olfactory senses in human noses. This is how they could detect fuel leaks in the system, but for some reason the Kulusk version of the gas didn't burn clean. She hoped it was due to it not being of premium grade gas or it being an inferior substitute; because, if it were a fuel leak, the entire tunnel system would evaporate with an ignition source.

She pulled her PARIT and scanned the fumes. The PARIT reported the fumes as the byproduct of an inferior substitute, pialairtic gas, highly toxic, but low on combustibility. Satisfied with the report, Juanita knew she had to move fast. She pulled on the hatch door and jumped into the cockpit, behind two soldiers. The two occupants did not turn around for they were expecting their partner.

"You're late," the one on the right yelled over the hum of the engines. His voice echoed in the tight chamber of the KLC. "The regiment is starting to pull out and we still haven't run our checklist!"

The absence of a response made the man look over his left shoulder. He couldn't make out the figure but he knew it wasn't his partner. When he realized this he reached for his pagenay. This alerted the soldier to his left, who responded in kind.

"I wouldn't do that if I were you," Juanita said, pressing her coronet rifle into the base of the soldier's neck on the right.

He terminated his reach and stiffened. The soldier on the left, seeing the coronet rifle, froze as well.

"What do you want?" the soldier being held barked.

"Just keep doing what you were doing. I am just here for the ride."

The two men looked at each other with puzzled looks.

"First, hand me your weapons," Juanita commanded.

The men reached for their weapons once more.

"No...no...no," Juanita warned. "Not so fast and with your opposite hands," she commanded, nudging the rifle deeper into the soldier's neck for emphasis.

The men again stopped. After a second to compose themselves, they glided their opposite hands toward their weapons, retrieved their pagenays...upside down...and raised them in the air next to their heads. Juanita snatched them with her free hand as she pushed the rifle into the soldier's neck for balance. She threw the pagenays toward the back of the cockpit. Then she stepped back and smacked the soldier she had trained her rifle on, with the rifle butt. He crumbled into his seat.

"What you do that for?" the other soldier screamed, showing fear in his voice.

Juanita liked this. She knew the one she knocked out was senior brass and would have been hard to control. He had no fear, just professional hate. However, this one…this one was new, a babe in the woods, still full of fear, uncertainty and a healthy respect for self-preservation. She trained the rifle onto him, which confirmed her assumptions. The younger soldier's eyes widened with panic as he took a deep breath to steady his nerves.

"He talked too much," Juanita said raising the rifle to his head, "How about you? Do you talk too much?"

With beads of sweat forming on his forehead, the youngster shook his head—no.

"Good," Juanita smiled. "Then we will get along just fine. Now, I suppose you know how to drive this thing—right?"

The soldier nodded several times.

"Good! Then drive."

The soldier moved his hands over the controls and the KLC lurched forward. Two minutes later, the KLC caught up to its regiment and fell into line, heading east and hopefully close enough to the command bunker for Juanita to use her PGP without alerting any security devices.

***

On the surface, the Kulusk shield grid surrounded a twenty-five-ring radius around Renard. Mota led one hundred RACs, for the second time today, in an air assault of Renard. This time, they traveled low, at tree top level. The blast from their wash toppled trees and set the wildlife in the area running. They pounded the shield grid with their Kwainique guns from the west, Slod was advancing from the east, Xam had her northern and southern navies pounding the grid with Jorelli missiles and Jackil was pounding the grid from the heavens with pagenay fire. Jackil dare not use his Asher missiles or coronet guns, because the dissipating energy would be detrimental to Tirana's land and sea forces.

Lixlen was targeting his shockdel guns against the Jorelli missiles and RACs, but his defenses were overloaded—too many targets and too few guns. He saw the shield grid growing weaker and weaker with every hit. The fight was at the five-minute point and the grid was already down by forty percent. They had sustained the first wave. Somehow the weapons on the RACs were seeping through the field and hitting targets inside the grid shield. Lixlen ordered the energy diverted to the chromerion field on the west side to reinforce the field in preparation for the next wave.

Lixlen had ordered the redeployment of his land cruisers to the east side. There he figured they could combat the RLCs and weaken the barrage they were affecting on the shield grid from that quarter. He ordered ready torpedoes out from the underwater piers to handle the Revolutionary Navy, and he gave the order to launch his remaining KACs at the beginning, but KAC leader one had not reported in yet. KAC leader two was in position and wasting valuable time waiting for KAC leader one to call in position.

Lixlen was getting nervous. Then suddenly his console lit up. He looked at the blinking yellow light and breathed a sigh of relief. It was the *'On Station'* signal from KAC Leader One. They had successfully maneuvered nearly three hundred KACs into position.

"Now Tirana, let's see what you got!" he whispered as a challenge.

\*\*\*

Mota veered his RAC skyward, climbing to ten thousand feet and turned back west to set up for another run. He led the first squadron of ten RACs. Underneath him his sensors depicted the fifth squadron of ten RACs releasing fire onto Renard. Five more squadrons would follow and hopefully weaken the shield grid in this sector. Then the beeping noise in his earpiece grabbed his attention. He did a sector scan with his ARIT and saw what caused his indicator to go off.

"There you are," he said to no one in particular.

In front of him was the leading edge of the KAC fleet, coming at him from the sun. Again, the KAC fleet was not where Mota expected them to be. He thought they would be flying from the east to greet him, giving him the sun as the advantage. Somehow they circumvented the fight, and maneuvered to the west and got behind him. Now that he turned to set up for another attack, the KACs faced him. Mota counted twenty formations of twenty, four hundred KACs to his one hundred RACs. He was outnumbered, outgunned, but not outclassed.

"Taiole lead to all squadrons...tars coming in from west A-two–C-four...I repeat...tars coming in from west A-two–C-four. Break off attack...break off attack...engage...engage.

\*\*\*

Xam heard Mota on the secure interlink frequency. Things again, weren't going as planned—at least on the attack portion. A scowl, which was framed by her shiny gray peppered shoulder length brunette hair, came over her face. Xam was thinking. She didn't like how things were turning out. She decided to deviate from the plan, because she had no time to get approval from Tirana. She had to act now.

She walked to the navigational map and keyed the sensor. The holographic display depicted Renard with its twenty-five ring defensive grid hashed in purple. It showed red squares for her forces, depicting the RLCs and RACs. It showed Kie's forces in black. The display was a fraction of a second off from real time, but it was fast enough to give an accurate picture of the battle. Xam knew Tirana was receiving the same holographic image in the command center.

Xam regarded the picture for thirty seconds and formed a plan. She snapped her fingers and a slight smile crossed her lips. Her green eyes danced as the plan played in her head over and over again, trying to ensure she had not missed an issue that could backfire. "This might just work," she whispered. Then she turned to her communications officer and ordered. "Open encrypted interlink to Mota and the northern fleet."

Before the communications officer could comply, the warning horn pierced the normal cacophony of the room.

Xam turned to her defensive officer, "Report."

"Torpedoes inbound," the young officer said, pointing to the black squares on the holographic pad.

"What? How can that be? We demolished his piers and with that his coastal defenses," she recounted.

"I don't know admiral," the defensive officer offered, "but we have torpedoes in the water."

"Decoys out...order the fleet, evasive maneuvers Xam 1A," she ordered, realizing time was of the essence.

Decoy buoys hit the water and steamed toward the torpedoes. Xam's four Jorelli Missile Carriers in the front and to the right of the fleet turned starboard, forty-five degrees. The left four Jorelli Missile Carriers, cut to port, forty-five degrees, while her twelve support ships and loaders slammed into reverse and sped backwards.

"How about the northern fleet?"

"Same," the defensive officer responded. "They are evading torpedoes."

"Kill the sound to the warning, keep the warning light on...run silent...pagenays to bear," she ordered. "Mota, you will just have to wait, I need my pagenays now," she said looking skyward.

***

Slod was a huge man, standing six foot-three inches, with a body of a linebacker. He cut an impressive figure in his dark blue uniform, with its ridged chest and stomach armor. The four lines on his collar, signifying he was a general, were also impressive. His bald, neatly shaven head, magnified it all. The paleness of the white skin on his head seemed to shine when it was covered in perspiration. And right now he was drenched, so his head shone like a lighthouse on a foggy night. The red bandage he wore over the cut he received earlier in the day diminished the shine a little.

Slod listened in dismay as he heard Mota call out the KACs and then thirty seconds later, Xam called torpedoes in the water. It seemed, to Slod, Kie Ritchen planned it all. He was a devious Rox, which made him more dangerous than ever.

Slod had half his regiment training their Kwainique guns skyward in hopes of catching the KACs speeding toward Mota, but they got there some other way. Slod was disappointed, angry and feeling helpless all at once. If he ordered half his regiment to go around the city and help fight the KACs it would take almost thirty minutes for them to get into place. By then the fight would be over, or the damage would be done. Basically, it was too late to do that, but he couldn't stand around and listen to his brethrens die, picked off like vile prairie birds in a hunt. At least the Rox had a chance to escape a hunt, or fight back using their large talons.

He vividly remembered a Rox protecting her young during one hunt; he and Mota went on several years back. The Rox grabbed Mota's pagenay rifle with its talons and flew high in the sky. Then it dropped his rifle from about two thousand feet in the air. The rifle sliced through the air, heading right for Mota's head. And the damn fool idiot stood there watching the rifle fall. The bird had uncanny accuracy. The rifle would have hit Mota and killed him, if Slod didn't push him out of the way.

Later, Mota admitted the bird hypnotized him. Its majestic wingspan, the beauty of its flight as it carried a rifle twice as heavy as it was skyward was just amazing. Mota had a newfound respect for the Rox, the scourge of Kulusk. There was something almost human in the way the bird protected its young. And there was some type of communications between Mota and that bird that day—a type of communication only aviators could understand. The sky was their commonality and they spoke, if just for a split second they spoke. They understood each other. They communicated their fears, and loves all in that split second. As Mota later relayed, he and the bird shared a common bound—not one of like or companionship, but one of respect. The respect two adversaries give one another as they play the game. However, hunting was no game, at least for the Rox. The bird communicated, you can try to kill me, but don't touch my babies. And Mota respected that. Since that day, neither he nor Mota ever went Rox hunting again.

Now Mota was the Rox, trying to protect his children, the other aviators in the sky with him. And the KACs were the hunters, not fearing, not caring who they hunted or why they hunted. It was bad and about to get worse, but all Slod could do was wait and hope—hope that the training Mota received would help him survive the fight.

"Incoming," a voice shouted inside Slod's cockpit.

It was the young navigator to Slod's right. He was watching the sky for KACs and now it seemed he found them. The ARIT recognized two hundred KACs coming from the southwest on an inbound intercept. Slod smiled. At least Mota wasn't dealing with the entire fleet. *Half of them stayed back to have fun with him,* he thought.

"Well Kie…you finally made your mistake," he murmured. "Retool all firing solutions…disengage attack on grid…engage KACs at B-two–C-four. I repeat…retool all firing solutions…disengage attack on grid…engage KACs at B-two–C-four.

***

"Sire, permission to divert pagenay fire on the Kulusk Air Cruisers," asked Colonel Alicia Springs aboard the *Destiny*. The *Destiny* monitored all communications, including the revolutionary's encrypted interlink. Tirana provided them with the knowledge to decrypt the link. The dire situation the revolutionaries were facing had become evident in the few short minutes prior. Springs wanted to relieve some of the pressure off of what she considered newfound allies on an enemy planet.

"Negative," Jackil replied. "Keep all firing solutions on the grid."

"But...!"

Jackil's curt look cut Springs off from finishing her objection. "The Osguard said, 'limited involvement.' We are not to use deadly force unless in protection of our ship." Jackil softened his voice. "I know many of the revolutionaries will die, especially if we don't help. However, it is not our place, nor our duty to help them more than we are."

"Fine," Springs huffed, "but would a warning shot over their heads violate the order?"

Jackil turned to Springs, foaming at the mouth. He squinted his left eye, making a halo effect with his purple colored pupil. It was scary almost devilish when he did this, but Springs had become accustomed to his scowl. Then his scowl evaporated. "I suppose not," he said waiving his hands gesturing for her to make it happen.

Springs smiled, "Tiah!" Then she turned to Sast, who was occupying the Offensive Weapons Officer's seat. "You heard the sire, retool and fire warning shots above the Kulusks' heads."

"Tiah!"

# Chapter 37—The Discussion

Musoto and Stelana drove up to the Allendale Apartments inside Allendale, a subdivision of Shreveport. Delecroix had asked for them to meet him there. It was a few short blocks from police headquarters. Stelana didn't know why. She was ready to go to Dallas and attack the Blue Street Gang. She was sure she would find T-Square there. However, because Delecroix sounded so convincing he needed them both here, she agreed. She was sure she would have another chance at T-Square tomorrow. What was bothering her was she had not heard from Juanita yet. She should have reached Kulusk, retrieved the antidote and administered it to Capitol Station by now. Something was wrong. General Lo had not contacted her one way or the other. She was starting to worry for the first time. She was worried Juanita fell into a trap and that would be the end of USSTAP, as she knew it. The thought made her shudder.

"You okay?" Musoto's voice echoed.

Stelana turned to Musoto and stared at him for a long second, like she didn't recognize him. Musoto looked puzzled.

He repeated, "Are you okay?"

"Yeah...I'm fine," Stelana answered. She shook her head as to wake herself up.

"Good...good...I don't want you zoning out on me." He was becoming worried about Stelana. The comment she made that morning about his justice versus her justice spooked him. He was now wondering if Stelana would summarily execute T-Square on sight. He couldn't be party to any vigilante type justice. Something he never associated with USSTAP, until now.

"Don't worry, I won't zone out," she snapped back.

"What's with you anyway?" Musoto was becoming more agitated than worried now. He was trying to get inside Stelana's head. Something he wished he had attempted when they first met, but he was so overcome with information overload; he had forgotten his training, his instinct and his livelihood. However, he now knew he had to get back to it.

"What do you mean?" Stelana was in no mood to be psychologically probed, especially by an inferior cop.

"I mean, the more we work with the local police, the more you...you...you become agitated. And I would like to know why." Musoto was being honest; he was getting more than a little concerned with her hostile attitude toward the local police. "Have you had a run-in with the police?"

Stelana thought a minute, cocking her head to the side and looking out the window. Her orders were to indoctrinate Musoto...her first real recruitment job. Recruiting took time, and finesse. It took instinct to know when to talk and when to listen. She figured now was the time to talk.

"Musoto, I am Chaktun, born and raised. I've only been on this planet a couple of years." She paused and turned to him, to read his face and to let him read hers.

Musoto stared into Stelana's face. He was studying her, looking for something to tell him she was not of this world. All he saw was a beautiful chocolate black woman, with straight shoulder length hair cropped neatly inward. Her eyes were light brown and sparkling, but also unique in shape, almost Asian or Middle Eastern. However, nothing about her features would scream she was not from Earth.

"Are you surprised?" Stelana asked. She did not need to ask the question, she knew he was surprised. The shock value of her statement was intended to impede any action he was thinking of taking.

"Yeah…quite frankly, I am." Musoto decided to be honest. "But that makes my question that more pertinent. If you aren't from Earth, and you had limited dealings with the police; why are you so hostile? Not just you but why is Osguard Fifty-Five so hostile as well."

Stelana perked her head, debating if she should speak or not. Then she decided she should. Musoto may not need to know what she was about to say, but he needed to hear it.

"Let me tell you a story," she began. "Several years back, the First Osguard was driving with his family in Virginia, scouting out the site for Osguard Gardens. He was on the main road. Back then it was a wooded area, nature had reclaimed the area and the road was the only sign of civilization. Well anyway, he was driving, I think it was a Lexus SUV, and he was pulled over by the local police…

Now the First Osguard didn't think he did anything wrong. He was driving the speed limit, his lights were working, but he was pulled over anyway. You know the right thing to do when the cops stop you. Well anyway…they started hassling him. You know…what is a black man doing out here this time of night? Are you running drugs? Nice car…where'd you steal it? That sort of shit…we have it all on record. He recorded it with his CC…

Well when he realized he was in this situation, he tapped the emergency beacon on his CC. The signal shot to Earth World Headquarters and within two minutes five USSTAP Security guards were in the bushes. They stayed there waiting on the signal from the First Osguard to intervene. Now if they intervened, those cops would have been in some deep shit."

Stelana watched as Musoto's face betrayed his anger at that statement. She knew Musoto didn't understand what she meant.

"We would have taken them, programmed them into forgetting everything and left them somewhere for the police to find later, but that didn't happen…

The cops wanted to search the First Osguard's vehicle. Well first they didn't have probable cause and second, the Osguard had his and his wife's delta belts in the trunk. That would've been hard to explain. So he refused. Well that's when things got hairy…

They pulled the First Osguard from the car and began beating on him. He didn't resist, but he must've felt like shit, getting the crap beat out of him in front of his wife and children by two cops like he was some type of criminal. Remember, his children were about eight and six now. They were crying and screaming in the back, and his wife was full of tears in the front, trying to shield her kids from seeing their father get beat up…

While they are beating on the First Osguard, two good ole boys drive up in a raggedy old pick-up truck. You know the kind. Rebel flag plastered in the back window and on the bumper, gun racks with shotguns in the back

253

window too. They were drunker than a skunk, with beer cans in their hands. They ask the head cop if they need any help in whipping the nigger's ass. The cop tells them no and for them to go on home. He told them they were too drunk to be out on the road and they needed to go home and sleep it off...

Again we have this on record, because the security guards in the woods were recording the entire episode on their PARIT. They were waiting for the go word. Either the First Osguard or his wife could have said it, but neither did.

Do you know how much it must've took for his wife to sit there and know her husband was getting stomped on? I mean they kicked him, they punched him, and they wracked the nightstick across his back. I saw the recording, it was worse than the beating that brother, Rodney King, took in Los Angeles. Blood was everywhere. It was a sight. Remember, this is our First Osguard. Think of it. How would you feel to see your president beat like that on a lonely road at night? It would tear at your heart and choke your soul. I know it did mine...

When they finished with him, they started for his wife. Code word or no code word, General Lo gave the go ahead to intercede. Luckily, the cops received a call. There was an accident up the street about three to four miles. They were needed on the scene right away.

However, before they left, they handcuffed the First Osguard to the grill of his vehicle and handcuffed his wife to the steering wheel. Then they produced a package from their squad car and threw it into the Osguard's car. Finally, they took off down the road...

The security retrieved the Osguard and his family and stepped them back to headquarters. The Osguard had sustained three broken ribs, a broken clavicle and a broken jaw. He suffered some internal hemorrhaging as well. Thanks to our medical technology he recovered fairly quickly...

Unfortunately, the psychological damage to his children was still unknown. They knew their father was the most powerful man in the universe, and they didn't understand why he had to suffer like this. And his wife, she almost went crazy; she blasted USSTAP security measures for allowing this to happen to her husband. Boy was she mad...

Oh by the way...the package, the cops threw in the car, were four kilos of cocaine. They were setting the Osguard and his family up for a drug bust. They were going to take the entire family down...well at least momma and poppa down for drug dealing. Ain't that some shit?"

Stelana cleared her throat. The pain in her eyes, more like the anger in her eyes told the story. Musoto watched and listened. He offered no excuses, but he didn't offer any condolences either. Stelana took mental note of that. She was starting to doubt Musoto's sincerity.

"Later we found out those good ole boys hit a car that had a mother, her two daughters and an eight-month-old son, head own. Killed the entire family—well almost the entire family. The father was devastated. See he was at work that night, and they were coming to see him. The father was a police officer...the same police officer who whipped my Osguard's ass that night...the same police officer who told the drunk drivers to go home...the same police officer who thought it was more important to frame an innocent black man for drugs than to stop a drunk driver from taking a life. Well Jus works in mysterious ways. That cop paid for his indiscretions with his most prized possession—his family."

Stelana looked back out the window. She saw two young girls, no older than twelve walking outside the apartments. She noted it was getting late for them to be outside like this. The night was falling fast and even though they were near a police station, criminals didn't care where they did their deed or whom they did them to.

"UAI lawyers went after the cops with a vengeance. The Osguard Senate did not sympathize with the cop's loss of family. They considered it his fault. They wanted to see him punished for what he did. We had recordings, both audio and visual. The city settled out of court. UAI obtained the land known as Osguard Gardens and the two cops were fired from the force. They were coming up on criminal charges for taking the cocaine out of the evidence locker...no charges stemmed from the little altercation on the road with the First Osguard. That was part of the settlement...

Later, we found out the cop who lost his family, ate his gun before the trial. The other cop got fifteen years in prison, where he ran into some of his old buddies—probably people he framed or set up. Well anyway, he lasted about a year before he got a shank up his ass. They tore him a new asshole—literally. He died two months later from complications. Again, Jus works in mysterious ways...

The Osguard Senate voted on new security measures after this. They gave all USSTAP protectorates on Earth the legal right to defend themselves, even if it meant exposing USSTAP's existence, in a life or death situation of course. Thus, if a cop tried that now, he would be dealt with accordingly."

"What does that mean?" Musoto was somewhat disturbed by the ominous proclamation.

"Don't know...it hasn't happened yet. You were the closest to that happening, and you see what we did with you." Stelana looked back at Musoto, "So there you have it. I don't trust cops." She tapped Musoto on the wrist to ease the sting of her resentment. "Well I do trust some of them I guess. However, I see them as a necessary evil. Someone has to do it."

Musoto shifted in his seat, "Not all cops are bad. It is a small minority of them that are." He was trying to find the right words to justify his statement.

"I know that, and so do the rest of us," Stelana offered, "but it only takes one bad apple."

Musoto nodded. He understood what she was trying to say. Then his mind shifted to his first meeting with Juanita.

"Is this incident the reason Osguard Fifty-Five said what she said about the confederate flag?"

"You have a bad case of cranial anal insertion...don't you," Stelana laughed. "Are you crazy? Like I was briefed before coming to Earth, showing a Confederate flag to an African American is like showing the Swastika to a Jew and I dare say the U.S. flag to a Native American. The atrocities committed under flags like that, to some people, outweigh any virtue or spirit of good intent they represent to others. The division occurs because one side can't forgive the atrocities and the other side...by abstention...condones it. And they think those who do not agree with them are too sensitive. The African American feels the Confederate flag has been twisted and distorted by hate for so long it no longer has any solace in purity or the so called heritage of the South."

Stelana's voice started to rise with anger. "Besides, everything done to an Osguard since Laurona and Nausona stepped foot on this wretched planet has been done in the name of the South's honor. What kind of heritage is that? I mean that flag stands for treating anyone not of white blood as an inferior species when in actuality they are the ones who are inferior. Laurona and Nausona were superior in all respects to anyone they dealt with on this planet and the hate that is called the South's heritage set into motion endless repercussions we are still reeling from today."

"Is that how you think of us white people—as inferior?" Musoto felt a twinge of anger in the pit of his stomach, which was evident in his voice.

"No," Stelana offered, trying to ease the tension she had created. "No one person is superior to another, no matter what his or her race is. I meant Nausona and Laurona were superior in technology and knowledge, but were treated worse than an animal on a farm. What kind of sense does that make? And their descendants were treated worse throughout the years. If you get a chance you can review the Osguards' history on Earth. Their ancestors were murdered, spat on, run out of town and dozens of other things and they were living in the North. Imagine how life would have been if they stayed in the South. Jus only knows if they would have survived to procreate the line."

Stelana squinted and shook her finger at Musoto. "And no...that incident that happened to the First Osguard is not what caused Osguard Fifty-Five to say what she said. No, it is a long history of oppression that directly affected her and her ancestors, which sailed under the banner of that flag that caused her to say what she said. The incident, as you refer to it, was simply the last straw. And let me tell you something, Mr. Musoto. I don't think the Sons of the Confederacy want to challenge USSTAP right now about if the flag is one of heritage or one of hatred. Because, Mr. Musoto, they would lose...they would lose in a big way. So the Osguards chose to ignore it when possible. However, let me tell you, they do take note, as we all do. For those who proudly wave the flag are no allies of USSTAP. As long as they have a constitutional right to wave a flag of hatred, I have a constitutional right to ignore the flag of hatred."

Musoto looked puzzled. He shook his head in rebuttal several times, "But you are Chaktun, not American. The constitution doesn't apply to you."

Stelana observed Musoto with a huff. "You know what I mean."

"Yes, I do. But you have to understand…not everybody who waves the flag is doing it out of hatred. There are some who really believe in the purity of the South and the flag represents that to them."

"I contest, where there were slaves, purity did not exist. Those who think otherwise have blinders on their conscience and are living in a false reality."

"Maybe so, but they aren't the enemies. They aren't professing slavery as a good thing. They are just remembering what was good about the South."

"What was good about the South is a relative term—relative if you were black or white."

"Touché…score one for the visiting team," Musoto said, trying to end the conversation.

"And what is that suppose to mean?" Stelana said rotating her neck. She had copied this body language from watching T.V.

"Nothing," Musoto said backing down. "You made a valid point. Everything is relative. A person's experience, background and upbringing have a lot to do with how they interpret the world around them. What I think is good and moral will obviously be different for someone else without my background and experience."

"Great theory Mr. Musoto, except for one thing—I am Chaktun. My background and experience is not the same as the African American experience. Neither are those from other worlds. And almost by a unanimous vote…I dare say close to a universal unanimous vote, you will find more people agree with the Osguards, and me, than you about this issue. See there have been too many oppressive regimes that rely on heritage as a staple in their existence. We are fighting one now. It is called the Kulusk."

Musoto's mind raced for a reply. He tilted his head and turned away. "So Earth does not have the racist market cornered…it is a universal concept—Right?"

"No…it doesn't," Stelana conceded. "Bigotry comes in all shapes and sizes. It starts from the family unit, which begets tribalism, which begets nationalism, which begets racism, which begets imperialism…whether it is ocean, land, air or space. And finally…it comes down to one simple concept…us versus them. USSTAP has knocked down the barriers to this concept and truly provided the avenue for united brotherhood. But you're right, bigotry, racism or whatever you want to call it remains. It's human nature to be part of a group. Isn't that what fuels the street gangs that haunt your urban cities...the need to belong?"

Musoto agreed. Stelana made sense. He knew this feeling of belonging is what fueled street gangs, and he never thought about it before, but now he imagined it also fueled the nationalism that created terrorists and started wars between nations. The sense of belonging was a simple human emotion, which triggered other emotions such as fear, hatred and the feeling of superiority. Simplified, it was the spark, which started all controversy and eventually all wars. However, things had to be more complicated than that. Life and death decisions should not boil down to one human emotion like the sense of belonging, but it did. Musoto recognized it in an epiphany.

"So the universe boils down to us versus them?" he contended.

"I'm afraid it does," she opined, placing her hand on his shoulder. "The trick is getting a common ground to build us more and them less, until finally there are no more them."

"That is a little too simple," he whispered.

"Simple in concept, maybe...but complicated in practice," she offered.

"Then why not offer common ground to those who wave the Confederate flag?"

"Someday...maybe...someday," she said taking her hand away from his shoulder. She fixed her gaze over the steering wheel outside the windshield ... looking at nothing in particular, but seeing all around her. "But that will have to be done when Earth is accepted into our fold. Until then, we have the Kulusks to do battle with and our own survival. The Kulusks believe in the same concept...diminishing the 'them' ... USSTAP...by attrition...by murder...by war...by any means possible."

Musoto nodded and fell silent. He mulled over what he just heard. It was a simplistic way at looking at things...too simplistic for his comfort. Doubts entered in his mind. W*as USSTAP the great thing he thought them to be, or were they just another political organization after power? Were they fueled by genuine empathy, or were they fueled by a veiled sense of belonging as well, which could be considered racism?* He shook his head to throw these thoughts from his mind as he continued to watch the apartment buildings to his right.

Outside a white woman wearing a short blue skirt and a white tank top caught his attention. She was slender but muscular. Her brunette hair flowed halfway down her back. She wore dark round sunglasses. He thought this odd because it was cloudy and the sun was nowhere in sight. Then he stared at the figure walking across the street. She walked in front of their parked car, about thirty feet away. He sensed he knew her. He studied her gait and her mannerism. Then it struck him. He thought it was Mona—Mona

Richards, the fine young lady he spent several nights with, before he became entangled with USSTAP.

He shook his head. "It couldn't be," he murmured.

"What couldn't be?" Stelana asked.

"Nothing...nothing." Yet, the image haunted him. He replayed the image in his mind. Trying to match the lady in the white blouse with what he remembered of Mona. "Excuse me!" he said, as he opened the passenger door. He was about to step out, when Delecroix stepped up and pulled the door open. Musoto was startled. He looked up and recognized Delecroix. What he didn't realize was his hand was already around his service revolver and a split second from being withdrawn from its holster.

"We got a tip. T-square has a cousin who lives on the first floor over there." Delecroix pointed to the apartment complex half a block down. "Robin and Peter have had it staked out since we got the tip. They called a half hour ago. T-square is inside. I got the warrants. We are a go. I thought you two would want in."

Musoto looked over his shoulder at Stelana. She nodded. He turned back to Delecroix. He stared into Delecroix's blue eyes. The few seconds that passed seemed like hours. Musoto was reviewing all he had said and was weighing his options. Now the conversation he just had with Stelana, played an important part of his decision. Stelana was not a cop. He had pretended she was his partner, but now it was decision time. He nodded at Delecroix then turned back to Stelana.

"You stay here!" he ordered.

Stelana started to object, but she saw the determination in Musoto's eyes. She realized she was an observer and this was his project. After a long pause she agreed. "Don't fail'" she warned.

Musoto looked into her eyes and became frightened. The determination registering in her eyes was scary, almost deathlike.

"I won't. We won't," he corrected.

# Chapter 38—Attack On Renard

He was familiar with his console. He knew every pressure point, every light and every sensor. If the command bridge were dark, Commander Kinl Sast could retool his pagenay guns to within a millimeter of their targets. The burly Lortnoc bustled over his console as his lower forward pagenay ports magically realigned. Then without hesitation he hit several sensors and fifteen short bursts of blue pagenay lights rang from the ports.

Within an instant, the bursts sliced through the Kulusk's atmosphere, without altering or diminishing the deadly power they contained, sailed fifty feet above the KACs and exploded in a brilliant array of lights. The explosion caused a torrential windblast that pushed down toward the surface. At first the KAC pilots were startled, then blinded by the explosion.

The KAC pilots' fright caused them to veer off their intended path— some veered right, and others veered left in a preplanned evasive maneuver. Then the lights from the explosion caused flash blindness. Their KACs' autopilots took over when the pilots released their controls trying to shield their eyes from the blast. However their automatic blast visor clamped down over their glare visors before the blast could do more damage. The pilots blinked several times to aid their vision and grasped their controls once more to complete the evasive maneuver. However, as their hands touched the controls and the KACs released automatic piloting controls, the windblast slammed hard against them from above.

The downdraft pushed three hundred KACs toward the surface. The pilots fought to regain control of their aircraft, but the laws of physics remained constant. Some ships entered a flat spin; others entered into a death spiral. Their true friend at this point was altitude and they did not have much of it to play with.

Mota watched the once tight and valiant KAC formation disintegrate like falling snowflakes. He bit his lower lip in anticipation as he calculated his enemy's rate of descent. He calculated they all would be able to pull out of their death traps, but some would pull out into each other resulting in destruction and more confusion. His heart sank with envy. He wanted to be the one to destroy his enemy, not USSTAP. Then he thought, USSTAP could have hit the formation directly, but they didn't. Why, he wondered. Then it became clear. USSTAP bought him and his squadrons more time; they weren't in it for the destruction. That was his job.

"Taiole lead to all squadrons...we got some help from the heavens, but the rest is up to us. Converge on tars A-two–B-four...repeat...converge on tars A-two–B-four. Use attack Tirana–five...I say again...use attack Tirana–five."

Mota adjusted his controls and put his RAC into a nosedive to intercept the lead echelon of the KACs at the lowest point of recovery. He fingered his Kwainique and let loose with a hail of invisible energy pellets that whined through the air at an ear-bursting high-pitched tone. In his sensors, he could see the Kwainique's reign of destruction take its toll on the crippled KACs. One...two...four...six ships disappeared from his targeting screen, suggesting his Kwainique had destroyed the ships. He acquired more of the faltering ships and activated his Kwainique. The same ear-bursting whine whistled through the air as ship after ship disappeared from his scope.

He caught a glimpse of his rear monitors as he saw his squadron, and the other nine squadrons, line up behind him for the same strafing run. He soon leveled his aircraft and pushed the power to fly as fast as he could through the faltering ships. He held his finger on the Kwainique gun picking off more and more of the helpless enemy. When he had flown to the end of the Kulusk formation he pitched up and climbed ten thousand feet, rolled out heading back east toward Renard. He planned to circle around and execute the same maneuver. He looked down and saw the fifth squadron of ten RACs was executing their strafing run. His squadron and four other squadrons were right behind him.

He nodded his head in slight glee. "Excellent job...I think one more pass should cut them down to a manageable size."

***

General Slod's baldhead glistened with more sweat. He watched on his monitor as the KACs approached his position. His RLCs had disengaged firing onto the grid and now had their Kwainique guns aimed skyward—hopefully in the path of the oncoming KACs. Two hundred blips crowded his screen like sand on a beach, but they still weren't within firing range.

He watched, whispered and prayed for the blips to get within firing range, but they seemed to hover just on the outskirts of his guns' range. Then a flash of blue light darted across the sky. Pagenay fire, he knew at once. The KACs were firing beyond visual range. Then several more blue lights darted across the horizon, crashing into his area. Two RLCs took direct hits and exploded on impact. Fifteen others took minor hits, where their chromerion field took the blunt of the charge. The report flashed in his command RLC ... six men dead and nine others wounded.

Slod closed his eyes in silent prayer, searching his warrior spirit for guidance. He knew if he ordered evasive maneuvers, the Kwainique guns would lose the firing solution and would have to be retooled. This was valuable time he did not want to squander. However, if he didn't move his men, more would die. That was the price of being a soldier, he lamented.

"Steady!" was all he said. He opened his eyes to survey his men. They remained quiet but determined. There was no sign of wavering in their eyes, just professional determination. Slod watched the skyline light up with more pagenay fire.

The hits were more accurate. Four more direct hits, two RLCs exploded and two others were down. The command screen flashed—twelve dead...fifteen wounded. Slod didn't know if he could stand another attack without calling for evasive maneuvers. He started the day with ten battalions—ten RLCs in each battalion—against twelve hundred. The odds were against him, but he had counted on his training being superior. He now realized he counted too much on his training. Now in a short fourteen universal hours and ten minutes into his second battle his total day's loss to his force was forty-five percent—one hundred and thirty-five people. From his simulations, he had counted on losing fifteen percent, and he thought that

261

was unacceptable. His heart screamed for him to call for evasive maneuvers, but his training iced the urge. He just needed the KACs to sail within range of his guns. He just needed a few more seconds...just a few more seconds!

Slod studied the screen as the pixels representing the KACs just skirted the outer barrier of his Kwainique guns' range. He knew he didn't have seconds, he had to act now, or he would lose too much of his force to be effective. *Now or never!* "All guns...fire!" Sixty-five RLCs fired their guns, sending invisible but noisy pellets of destruction skyward.

Even with his ear protectors on, the high pitched whine of the Kwainique guns vibrated his eardrums and sent a piercing pain through his head. He had become accustomed to the pain. He'd almost become addicted to the pain. To him, it meant one inch closer to freedom for every gun that fired.

The sixty-five dots faded from Slod's screen. *Direct hits,* he thought. "Again...fire!" he ordered. The pain echoed in his head, but he greeted it with a smile as he watched more dots disappear off his screen. The running tally at the bottom left hand corner of his screen confirmed, sixty-five more targets either destroyed or disabled.

Victory swelled in his chest, pride danced in his voice and hope rang in his heart as he continued to order his remaining sixty-five RLCs to fire at will. The last pixel flashed off and the running number of targets reduced to zero in the bottom left hand corner. No longer did he see the blue lights of destruction sail across the horizon. No longer did he feel the hopelessness of defeat strangle him. He smelled victory...he smelled freedom!

"Disengage!" he ordered. "Retool firing solutions...target the grid again. I repeat...retool firing solutions...target the grid again."

The order resounded with the authority of a warrior on the verge of a great overarching victory. It resounded with tenacity, grit and honor. For the first time since the beginning of the revolution, Slod felt the conquest Opel had promised so many years ago. "Tonight, Kie Ritchen will die and Kulusk will be free," he murmured.

*** 

Admiral Arual Xam fought the urge to scream. She wanted to hit something. The torpedoes were bearing down on her northern and southern convoys. Sound decoys floated in the water toward the torpedoes as her fleets scrambled to maneuver out of the torpedoes' paths. She felt helpless as she studied her situational map. The pagenays began firing into the water. Although the refractive power of the green water made targeting a little more difficult than atmosphere penetration calculation from space, the pagenay found its mark on the first two torpedoes. However, there were twenty-five of them in the water sailing toward her fleet alone. She presumed the northern fleet had just as much to deal with.

The young weapons officer targeted the torpedoes and sent the retool information to all pagenay bearing ships. His training kicked into high gear as his fingers hovered over the console. His split second decisions traveled from his eyes to his hands without interruption from his brain. His eyes darted up, down, right and left in a sensational crosscheck of his instruments and receivers. His mind was multitasking, tuning all out except the task at hand—twenty-five torpedoes. Then he commanded the ships to fire.

Eight Jorelli Missile Carriers and the command ships fired onboard pagenays. Xam saw nine blue beams of fire pierce the sky, clip the water and detonate their targets. The resulting explosions caused the aqua green mushroom water cloud to lift and rise about thirty feet. The green water froze in time at the apex, allowing the red sky to frame it in a glorious color fest. Then it came crushing down like a dynamited building that lost its foundation, destroying the other torpedoes and sound decoys in the area directly below it.

Xam checked her threat situation holograph board and witnessed on the northern shore, the mirror image of destruction also occurred. The same explosion, the same water mushroom cloud and the same destructive results registered on her board. A sigh of relief filled her lungs, as she wiped the sweat from her forehead. She had never tasted combat before. All her training was accomplished in simulations. However in simulations the human emotions of fear and apprehension were not a factor. Today it had become a factor twice and it tasted sour in her mouth. She swallowed hard, trying to dissolve the taste and wipe it from her mouth, but it still remained. She knew she was not finished yet.

"More incoming," the young sonar officer screamed. The Kulusks had shot twenty-five more torpedoes into the water. "Northern fleet reports the same," he reported in a more civil tone, allowing his training to once again assert itself over his reactions.

"Defer torpedoes to Jorelli Carriers, I want the northern command ship and us to take out the torpedo launchers," Xam ordered. She knew the launcher had to be destroyed first and foremost, because no matter how many torpedoes they destroyed, the Kulusks would shoot more.

Xam swung around to the young man's side and encrypted the order to the ships. "Evasive Maneuver Opel three-A," she called to both fleets.

On both shores, the starboard JMC's cut left forty-five degrees, dropped sound decoys and then cut right seventy-five degrees at full speed. The port JMC's cut right forty-five degrees; dropped the sound decoys and then they cut left seventy-five degrees at full speed. The twelve support ships were still in full reverse from the previous evasive order.

The torpedoes first honed in on the sound decoys, but soon rejected them and altered course toward the JMC's. The young sonar officer plotted the intercept course and pushed to the fleet updated evasive maneuvers. Xam approved the young officer's direction with a simple nod. Then she moved to the forward screen where she calculated they were still thirty rings from shore. She moved to the Jorelli missile operator and watch in earnest as the operator plotted the shoreline and possible torpedo launcher. When she was satisfied she moved back to the forward screen and closed her eyes. In a slow deliberate motion, she raised her hands and with a quick hard cut downwards she gave the order to fire.

She looked into the screen and saw a rainbow arch of blue rays of light slice through the reddish air, penetrate the water and detonate sixteen of the twenty-five incoming torpedoes. Sailing high above the apex of the resulting explosion were two aqua green Jorelli Missiles, screaming toward the shoreline, trailing the characteristic green plume of smoke, both color schemes specifically designed to match the water to aid in camouflage. Her heart raced as she wished the missiles onto the target. The situation board counted down in universal seconds until missile impact—three...two...one...detonation.

The missiles detonated with a forty-foot high orange plume. The explosion generated wild waves into the ocean, reaching ten to fifteen feet in height. The land mass cracked and thirty feet of solid land departed, sunk, slid and melded into the ocean. The launchers were completed obliterated, leaving no sign of any weapon or manmade object under the water line or above it. The wind blast pierced the inlet area tumbling buildings, trees and other weak structures that littered the coastline for at least another two hundred and forty feet.

The Jorelli Missile, the descendant of the Asher Missile, and both belonging to the nuclear family of weapons, had hit and destroyed its target within an inch, leaving no nuclear residue or dirty energy. It was pure, powerful and lethal.

Xam lowered her head and closed her eyes for a moment as she attempted to steady her heart. Then she pivoted around to the holographic situational board to check on the northern fleet. As before, the northern fleet copied the southern fleet perfectly and yielded the same results. The missile launchers on both coastlines were gone, and they were free to execute the plan again.

Xam barked orders for both fleets to rejoin and move toward the coastlines. They had more Jorelli Missiles to deliver and Xam was in no mood for any more interruptions.

***

Tirana sat in the command bunker on the continent of Dijanai. She had watched her air, land and sea forces engage in unplanned and unexpected scenarios and rise victorious. She knew this was due to the expert training her brother had brokered upon his forces. She also knew Kie was clever as much as he was devious. He had not taken any course of action she had expected. Unfortunately, he opted for the most severe and most unexpected course of action during each encounter. There were no words to explain the strategic thinking process motivating Kie. He seemed prepared for all and ready to sacrifice all in his endeavors. Therefore, Tirana had to be the same way, but unlike her wretched cousin, she felt uncomfortable pursuing such a strategy.

She had no words of wisdom or any other brilliant strategies to offer her commanders in the field. She just watched and bit her nails as she witnessed the events unfold on her situation board. While her forces were engaged in battle, Tirana tried to look like she was in command and confident of her on site commanders' abilities. However, deep down she was unsure, frightened and ready to push the retreat button. But her wish for her brother's safe return had quashed her reaction to do so.

She knew the Osguard was alone facing more than her people were, in order to save her brother, and there was no way she was going to forfeit her part of the deal—even if it meant the destruction of her forces. Her brother had to be set free at any cost. Then she felt a sharp pain of shame. Was she so callous she would sacrifice hundreds, maybe thousands of people's lives for her brother? Was he that important to the cause, or was he just that important to her? Was she that much different than Kie?

The calmness, she portrayed, helped soothe the men and women in the command bunker with her. Even in her deep reflection she appeared to have things under control. So her staff continued to push the attack information across all communication regimes in the most professional manner possible.

"Birddog...Birddog...Birddog," Tirana ordered to all forces over the secure interlink.

***

General Tovi Lixlen, the new commander of Kulusk Forces, ran the gamut of human emotion in the few short fifteen minutes the battle had executed thus far. At first, when Maxum Ritchen ordered him to execute the defenses, he was nervous. Then he was frightened when the grid reduced to forty percent and his air defenses were not in place yet. Next he was elated when his air defenses reported in place and ready for the attack. Afterward he was mortified when his air defenses and torpedo launchers were destroyed in seconds. Now he was back to being scared.

He lost five hundred KACs, his coastal defenses were destroyed and his KLCs were still enroute to intercept the RLCs. That would take another ten minutes. His defense grid was down to thirty-five percent and Kie had left for Greenhaven. As far as he knew, Kie had escaped and was on the run. The thirty-man staff looked at him for guidance and he had none to give. He

265

knew even if the KLCs engaged and won the battle with the RLCs, the shield grid would be destroyed and the revolutionary forces would be inside the city within twenty minutes. He could stay and fight, but the defenses were unable to keep up with the incoming barrage of weapons. He knew it would be suicide, and he knew the staff recognized that as well. He swallowed hard and shook his head. *It was hopeless.* Stay here and be killed, or leave and risk the Maxum finding him and executing him were his only options.

"Abandon the city...set defenses to automatic...regroup at alternate command center in Freeport." His voice was forceful and commanding. He was not about to give up the fight, but he was not about to lose it either. He wanted to regroup and fight another day. It was his decision and his decision alone. He knew he would have to bear the wrath of the Maxum, but at least he would be alive to do it. And this way he could save what little forces he had left to build an army again. "Repeat...abandon the city...set defenses to automatic...regroup in Freeport."

# Chapter 39—The Capture

The low-income apartments were called the projects. The brick buildings were connected together by flimsy corridors that made several quads. Most of the inhabitants were black. They included single mothers, large families and the elderly, who either made low wages or were on welfare. The projects had become a staple in the Allendale section of town. City and citizen efforts to clean and maintain upkeep of the area had taken root. In fact the community named it the RAGE project—'Resistance Against Gang Environment.' Most citizens were proud of their living area, but like most areas, there were those who were bent on destroying anything displaying proper pride.

It was a constant battle against the youth and the drug community to keep the area clean. Gang graffiti littered the brick walls of the community, while beer and wine bottles, used condoms and paper bags from fast food restaurants decorated the quads, decreasing the pride and workmanship the honest hardworking patrons of the community had put into the area.

This did not deter them. Every morning, these citizens would wake early and begin the painstaking cleanup process. Many would sweep the walks of broken glass and pick up the trash that the young thugs left the night before. It was a vicious circle, but those who partook in RAGE, felt wonderful about their involvement. Crack houses and street corner drug dealers all but disappeared from these projects. Unfortunately, they moved a block away, but that was okay. The RAGE saying was 'One Block at a Time.'

Musoto and Delecroix moved to the furthest quad from the entrance to the complex. Musoto saw Russell and Allensen maneuver to the back of the complex to cover the rear entrance. A few children were still playing in the quad. It was getting late and he wondered why the children weren't inside. However, it was the last days of summer and he thought they probably wanted to experience the last hours of freedom summer days offered them. However, right now, he wished they were inside. He didn't like them being so close to a probable firefight.

"Delecroix...let's get these kids out of here," Musoto offered.

Delecroix looked into the quad and shook his head like this was the first time he noticed the kids. He was so intent on the object he had failed to survey the neighborhood. This could be the death of any police officer—especially in an operation like this one.

Musoto knew right then Delecroix had been a desk jockey too long. He had forgotten the basic rules of setup for an operation like this. "Forget it...I'll do it," Musoto asserted.

"No...wait..." Delecroix warned, reaching for Musoto's shoulder.

He disregarded the command and brushed Delecroix's hand away. He rushed toward the children who were playing in the middle of the quad. Before he reached them, a young ten year old girl looked up at him.

She smiled at Musoto and pointed at him, "You're Five-O," she screamed. The other children looked up at him.

He put his finger to his lips and motioned them to be quiet, but the children ignored his plea. "Five-O...Five-O," they screamed as they scurried in several directions.

Musoto looked up at Delecroix who was now racing to the apartment door T-square was reported to occupy. The children's chant still rang in the night air like an alarm. Soon doors opened and curious onlookers began gawking at them. Musoto ran toward the apartment door. He hopped two sets of cement steps and lunged to the right of the door. Delecroix was planted to the left. Then he heard it.

Two shots from a thirty-eight caliber rang out, followed by four nine millimeter shots. Delecroix and Musoto withdrew their firearms. Musoto recognized the shots from the police firearms. He surmised it was Allensen and Russell returning fire. Then the radio blared out from Delecroix's belt. "Suspect fired upon us. He ran back into the house...suspect armed...repeat he fired on us."

Delecroix held up three fingers and methodically pulled each finger down. Musoto understood they were going to break the door down at the count of three. When Delecroix reached three, he turned and kicked in the door. The door flung open breaking the lock at the rotten wood frame and tearing off its upper hinge. Delecroix moved back to the side of the door. Musoto crouched low, on the opposite side of the door. Then Delecroix jerked his head to signal Musoto to move. They framed the doorway with weapons at the ready.

"Police!" Delecroix yelled. "Put your weapons down and come out with your hands up," he ordered.

His threat was met with a child's scream, which told Musoto there were innocents in the line of fire. Musoto stepped into the hallway with his gun still at the ready. He stood erect and leaned against the right wall and Delecroix leaned on the left wall. They inched their way down the corridor. Then a shadow flashed in front of them. Musoto's heart jumped as his finger tightened around the trigger. He recognized the shadow as a little girl. He loosened his trigger finger.

"Hey, come here..." Delecroix yelled to the figure. "Come here...police!"

The figure darted into the corridor again. It was a little black girl, no older than five, in her pajamas. She had curly hair and sported a simple smile. In her hands she hugged a brown Teddy Bear. "Come here...honey...please. We need you outside," Delecroix coaxed in the most pleasant voice he could muster. The girl smiled and darted back into the room.

Delecroix tightened his fist, "We may have a hostage situation, Musoto. Thanks for listening."

The words hit Musoto like a ton of bricks. He knew his brash attitude had jeopardized the situation. Delecroix knew the neighborhood, and probably knew how the children would have reacted to a police officer. However, Musoto knew better...at least he thought he knew better. Musoto's eyes told the story, he was sorry and he wished he had listened. Then that split second another shadow darted across the corridor. Musoto recognized it as a man. It was T-Square and he had the little girl in his arms. His gun was pointed to her head.

"Back off...man. Back off, I say...or I'll kill her. I mean it. I'll kill her," T-Square yelled.

Musoto knew T-Square was not bluffing. Musoto regarded Delecroix for an instant, and in that instant he recognized the face of despair. This was not an ideal hostage situation, as if there was such a creature. The surroundings were too confined and the hostage taker was too agitated.

"Now T-Square, you—"

"Shut up," T-Square told Delecroix. "I said back off. Let me out of here...now!"

Sirens echoed in the background. Allensen and Russell must've called for backup, Musoto noted. He knew if they let him out now before backup arrived, he would get away. Delecroix stepped backwards in compliance with T-Square's demands. Musoto looked confused. Delecroix waved his free hand, motioning Musoto to move back.

"He's a killer...we know that Musoto. You already fucked things up. Don't fuck them up anymore. Back off now!" Delecroix ordered.

The look on his face told Musoto he shouldn't push things anymore. He began inching back. Then a woman's voice screamed from behind them.

"T-Square...what the hell is going on here?"

Musoto turned his neck to see a black woman in a black skirt and blue V-neck top standing behind them.

"Momma...momma...Uncle T said he's going to hurt me," the little girl cried.

The shrill of the little girl's voice ran down Musoto's spine. She was scared and the situation was getting way out of hand. Then Russell and Allensen appeared behind T-Square with their guns at the ready. He must have felt their presence because; he turned and placed his back against the wall so he could see them, as well as Musoto and Delecroix.

The woman then tried to dart pass Musoto and Delecroix in a vain effort to grab her daughter. Both men barred her movement with their free arms and shoved her back. She slipped back several inches before she regained her footing and tried to brush by them once more. She howled with a gut-wrenching moan trying to force her way passed them. Musoto wrapped both arms around her and yanked her backwards. He pulled and dragged her outside and slammed her to the dirt ground.

"Look lady, we got this," Musoto warned. "We don't need him to have another hostage. Now back off and let us do our job."

"Fuck you," she screamed. "That's my daughter in there and my drugged out stupid ass cousin is holding a gun to her head. I think it is better if I handle it." She pushed against Musoto's arms struggling to get up.

"Look lady, your drugged out cousin is wanted for several murders and a definite trip to the execution table. I don't think he is going to listen to you."

The mother's eyes widened with fright. The desperation of the situation finally hit her. She realized her cousin was high on crack and the cops were after him for murders that could give him the death penalty. That meant the cops would not hesitate to kill him and he would not hesitate to kill them and her daughter as well. She knew she had to get her daughter out of there. The realization made her struggle more against Musoto. He hung on as much as he could to restrain her without hurting her. The crowd that had gathered near the complex began shouting taunts against Musoto for fighting with a woman. They were unaware of the situation inside the apartment. The crowd just gave the woman more strength to tussle.

\*\*\*

Across the quad, on the roof of a two-story project building, Mona Richards lay in wait. Beer cans, cigarette butts, empty heroin needles and broken crack vials littered the roof. However, this did not bother Mona. She hardly noticed the trash. Her mind was focused on her mission—to discredit USSTAP.

She had followed Musoto from her house in Richmond, to FBI Headquarters, where he met Stelana. Then she used her PGP tracer to follow them to Shreveport Louisiana. She spied and took notes on Musoto's actions and steadfastly reported all she discovered to her superior. The ease in which Musoto fit into USSTAP's regiment was a scary testament to their attractiveness. Her superiors didn't like it and wanted it changed. They wanted her to change it.

She peered down onto the crowd gathering around Musoto. Then she pulled a six-inch chromium and steel rod from her shoulder bag. She twisted the base counterclockwise a half turn. The rod extended to forty inches, wings flipped out perpendicular to the ground, two scopes magically affixed themselves to each end, and a trigger sprang down from the rear bottom. When she was satisfied the instrument was fully assembled, she knelt down and employed it like a high-powered rifle against her shoulder. She lined up the two scopes and fixed her gaze on Musoto. She rested her trigger finger on the trigger and took a deep breath.

***

Delecroix backed out the door with his gun still pointing at T-Square. The crowd of a dozen people saw this and ran for cover. Soon afterwards, T-Square emerged in the doorway, his back to the side and his gun still pointing to the girl's head. The little girl still held onto her Teddy Bear, and she was scared as tears rolled down her face. She saw her mother on the ground struggling with Musoto and started screaming, "Momma…momma."

The shrill in her voice fueled the mother's determination even more. She spat into Musoto's face. He loosened his grip. The woman then kneed Musoto in the groin. The sharp pain shot through Musoto as he collapsed to the side of the woman. Then she got up and raced toward her daughter. She easily brushed by Delecroix, who was not expecting her to be there.

T-Square pointed the gun to the mother and pulled the hammer back. "You better stop LaKisha," he warned.

LaKisha stopped just in front of Delecroix who now began inching his way forward so he could grab the mother. Musoto hopped to his knees as he watched the adventure unfold in front of him. He felt helpless. All they needed was to get the suspect in the open for a clear shot and he let the woman stop that plan.

"Or what…you going to shoot me. Put that gun down and let my daughter go."

"Look bitch, I'm serious, move back." The sweat began beading on his forehead and his hand began to shake.

"Now I'm a bitch. What the fuck is wrong with you. You know better than that. I'll stomp your skinny ass in the ground. Now let my baby go."

"I warned you bitch. It would be fun to put a cap in your ass," he laughed. Then he stiffened his arm to pull the trigger. LaKisha's eyes widened as she saw her cousin was serious about shooting her and about shooting her daughter. Her mouth opened and she began to scream.

What happened next was slowed down by temporal distortion characteristic to any human tragedy. Seconds seemed like minutes and where the human brain in exquisite detail records every factor. A blue pencil beam of light flashed from above Musoto's head, lasting for what seemed like several seconds. Even though Musoto had limited exposure to the weapon he recognized it as a pagenay blast. He followed the blast to a point on the roof across the quad. A feminine figure or what he thought was a feminine figure ducked behind the railing after she spotted him looking. Then he turned back to T-Square.

The blast found root in T-Square's forehead. His body reaction was to pull the trigger. The gun fired, sending a bullet flying. LaKisha's body twisted to her right and she fell backwards into Delecroix who was trying to get a clear shot but could not because of LaKisha's flinging body.

T-Square's eyes widened and his mouth opened as his body wrenched with pain that lasted a split second—not enough time for his brain to register the pain before it shut down. He did not yell, he did not cry, he just collapsed. He was dead before his body hit the ground.

Delecroix laid LaKisha down on the ground. Musoto rushed to them. He checked LaKisha's wound. The bullet went straight through her upper right shoulder. The pain of the wound caused her to lose consciousness. He applied pressure to the wound with a handkerchief from his inside coat pocket.

Delecroix picked up the little girl and shielded her eyes from her mother's body. He ran her past the scene toward a neighbor who grabbed the girl. She was now crying for her mother. Her voice blended into the cacophony of the police sirens in the background. Delecroix did not know if she was dead or alive, but he did not want the small child to have the picture of her mother lying in a pool of her own blood to traumatize her anymore than what just happened.

Allensen and Russell rushed toward T-Square. They checked for vitals and confirmed he was dead. Confused looks washed their faces as they looked at Musoto for an explanation. Musoto shrugged and turned back to his patient.

Stelana pushed through the crowd that had now formed again around the scene. She flashed her fake FBI badge to make several people move to the side. She saw Musoto on the ground administering first aid to a woman. She rushed up to him and knelt down beside him.

"Are you alright?" she asked.

"Yeah, I'm fine. He whispered. "How come you didn't use a stun setting? Why did you shoot to kill?"

"What are you talking about? I just got here."

"Don't play me Stelana. A pagenay blue blast just killed T-Square. I saw it with my own eyes. You were on the roof over there and you shot a pagenay and killed T-Square."

Stelana looked toward the roof and looked over at T-Square's dead body in the doorway. She shrugged. "It wasn't me." She pulled her PARIT disguised as a cell phone and scanned the area. She tilted the screen toward Musoto so he could see it. "See, my pagenay hasn't been fired, but I am picking up a pagenay signature...not USSTAP."

"Kulusk?" Musoto whispered.

"No not Kulusk either," she answered. "It's unknown...I never saw readings like this before."

"What do you mean you never saw readings like this before?" Musoto grilled. "It's got to be USSTAP, Kulusk or Chaktun."

"No...No...And...No! It isn't any of those," she declared. "I have to send these readings to HQ." She then looked into Musoto's eyes, staring into his soul for a moment. "We have company, and I don't have any idea who it is."

# Chapter 40—Enter Greenhaven

The KLC was traveling through the tunnels at a high rate of speed. Juanita was taking readings from her PARIT. She was closing in on Greenhaven and getting closer to Opel. His life signs were weak but readable. Then the yellow light above the windshield glowed.

"What is that?" asked Juanita.

"It is a command change," the young pilot responded. "I need to activate it."

"How?"

The pilot reached for a sensor switch under the light. Juanita trained the coronet rifle on the officer as he moved.

"Like this," he responded as he activated the switch.

The abort order repeated over the cockpit speaker. It was encrypted, but the Kulusk officer ran it through the decryption buffer in the KLCs ARIT.

"The entire fleet will be turning around and heading back west in about two minutes once the fleet commander acknowledges the recall," the Kulusk informed Juanita.

Juanita gasped. She didn't realize Tirana's forces would be so good that they would drive Kie Ritchen to issue an abort order so soon. She calculated she was about twenty miles from Greenhaven. However, with an abort message calling his troops back, her PGP might not set off any alarms. She imagined several PGPs would be activated in response to the order. It was a chance she had to take. She scanned the tunnel system and saw a cutoff tunnel to the right. She directed the Kulusk pilot to take it and stop.

He did as he was directed, still afraid for his life and not knowing who was holding him captive. He just knew she was a USSTP member and she was very determined to get into Greenhaven. He veered the KLC right and allowed it to disappear into the shadows of the cutoff tunnel. He shut the engines down as Juanita directed. When he turned around all went dark.

Juanita had chopped him behind the neck, which sent the young pilot crashing into the console, slamming into unconsciousness. Then Juanita placed sleeper MARITS on both him and the other man. She calculated they would sleep for another four hours—more than enough time for her to get in and out of Greenhaven. She then pulled out her PARIT and tried to fix onto Opel's life signs. The readings were still weak, she could not get a direct fix on the signal, but it was good within twenty yards. She then scanned a point in the center of the readings into her PGP. She double-checked the coordinates with the map of Greenhaven Tirana provided. She wanted to ensure she didn't step into a wall or floor.

It was always dangerous stepping into manmade structures. The PARIT may not pick up certain characteristics and some characteristics may be hidden—especially glass enclosures. The one good thing about a PGP was you could always hit the reverse button and step back from where you started, if the arena it opened into was not safe. It all depended on the oxygen within the chromerion field while you were in inner space.

She had to hurry before the other land cruisers turned back. She did not want to risk being seen by anyone in that long convoy of vehicles. Once satisfied she had proper coordinates, she stroked her PGP and the white door appeared. She took one last glance around the cockpit, for what she did not know. It was a habit to survey the surroundings she was leaving, just in case she had to return in a hurry, she could tell what was out of place. Then she stepped into the light.

The PGP door slid open. Juanita peered out the opening and saw nothing. Feeling confident she covertly entered Greenhaven, Juanita stepped through the opening. When her right foot hit the building's solid floor, a weapon's blast rocked the structure, accenting a poignant welcome to her as the first Osguard to set foot in Greenhaven. She lost her footing and stumbled face first onto the floor. Her rifle flew from her hands and slid several feet in front of her. Dust popped from the ceiling and walls and filled the air like fireflies. Juanita coughed. The dust spurted from her lungs. Behind her the PGP opening hissed closed.

Three Kulusk soldiers stood where the light of the PGP once shined. Juanita's peripheral vision caught the green suited men and she knew she was in trouble. She reached for her pagenay as she shifted to her right. She swung and pointed her pagenay at the three. The middle soldier kicked the pagenay from her hand. The weapon flew up and over her head. The soldier swung his fist down. Juanita blocked the thrust with her wrists crossed, then grabbed his wrist, and twisted it. Then with lightening quickness, Juanita rolled to her left, adding more torque on the wrist. It snapped. She then stood and shot a right side kick to his mid section. The rush of air escaping his lungs told her she had completed the maneuver correctly.

He bent over in pain. She released his wrist, crouched, jumped and rotated over him, just prior to the other two soldiers firing their weapons. She grabbed his neck with both hands and twisted. His neck cracked, bringing instant death. Juanita then pushed the body forward, while still in mid-air, giving her leverage to complete the up and over maneuver. For an instant Juanita felt sorrow, but only for a split second. She wanted to complete the mission without killing, but her presence was compromised and she was now in hand-to-hand combat. Her Sixana training kicked in, in high gear. Survival was now her immediate mission. There were two more soldiers with weapons to contend with.

Juanita landed on one knee behind the other two soldiers. She spun around sweeping her right leg, tripping them. Their weapons flew from their hands as their bodies crashed to the ground. She then crouched and jumped again, twirling three hundred and sixty degrees, multiplying the force of her weight, and landed prone on one soldier's chest, crushing ribs and his heart with her foot. The guard gurgled blood in his throat as the pain of death, brief but extensive, blazed on his face.

Juanita then turned to the other soldier who was scrambling for his gun. Another weapons blast from outside rocked the building. A pillar shook loose and slammed between her and the soldier. Juanita lost her footing, slipped and fell against the wall. In that instant, she lost sight of her prey. She ducked under the fallen pillar, with her coronet gun drawn. Juanita held her breath and listened for any unnatural sound, but the crumbling of dust and debris hampered her efforts. She strained to filter out the noise and single in on the soldiers breathing, heartbeat, or footsteps…anything to help her get a lock on his position.

Then the soldier moved. His foot crushed the dust on the floor. Juanita heard it, but the echo in the large corridor confused the sound. She tilted her head and replayed the sound in her mind. Still she could not isolate where the sound originated. Then he moved again. The debris crumpled underneath his weight and the sound echoed against the vast walls in the chamber.

Juanita strained even more, searching for another sound. Using her enhanced Chaktun senses, she discerned his breathing. It was shallow but brisk. The low sound of the breathing was easier for her to isolate. She calculated his position, counted to three and stood. Juanita fired her coronet pistol several times in the direction of her calculation. The coronet blasts tore through the wall, pulverizing the wall into dust and opening the corridor to the outside. However she did not see the soldier. Juanita paused and scanned the area. Her eyes darted to the left and back to the right. She was confused—until.

The soldier jumped over the fallen pillar and landed behind her. She heard the thud and kicked her left leg behind her, making her body parallel with the floor. Juanita kicked the man in his groin, causing him to bend forward, and then she forced her leg up and kicked him in the chin with the heel of her foot. Juanita then spun around, jumped, kicked and swung her right foot, crashing into his jaw. His jaw broke under the force of her kick, but he remained standing. She raised her elbow, jumped and crashed into the back of his neck, raining instant darkness into the soldier's soul. He fell to the floor, dead.

Juanita took a deep breath and exhaled hard, cleansing her soul and relaxing her muscles. She holstered her coronet pistol and retrieved her pagenay and rifle. She took one more look around the area, and shook her head in disbelief. She heard the walls squeaking and she saw the remaining support pillars start to buckle. The hole she blew in the outer support wall, along with the pounding Tirana's troops were prosecuting on the shield grid had weakened this part of Greenhaven to a dangerous level. She surmised the area was about to come crashing down any minute. She turned toward the corridor leading to the med lab and disappeared into the shadows. Then, as if ordered by God, the structure collapsed behind her, erasing any signs of her presence.

***

Kie was upset at first, but soon realized Lixlen made the proper choice. Things were gloomy and he was out of options. He did not expect an attack from within his own planet, but Opel did attack and Kie knew he was out of assets. Well almost out of assets. He still had Opel and he could still exploit him, no matter what Tirana said.

Kie had stepped back to Greenhaven and was on his way to the medical ward to see his cousin, Opel. The pounding the city's defensive grid was taking, sent jolts through the structure. With every hit the foundation trembled, the walls shook and the floor vibrated, sending loose dust, marble and rock dancing through the air.

Kie surmised the defensive grid was down to about twenty percent. With the pounding the grid was taking, he suspected the entire grid would collapse in ten minutes. He knew he had to move fast. He began running through the marble halls of Greenhaven. His black cape waving majestically in the air behind made him appear as if he was flying through the halls. His breath was labored and his gait erratic. He was not use to physical exertion at this rate. Although he was an expert fighting soldier, he usually dispatched his rival within a short time, never exerting extended energy. His strength was mighty but his endurance was flawed. He paused for rest every few minutes, catching his breath.

For some reason the excitement of the battle had diminished his judgment. He had forgotten his PGP could have stepped him to the medical ward. His thoughts were clouded with revenge and with disappointment—disappointment in his new allies, who have not shown one sign of aid thus far.

He turned the corner to the medical ward and stepped through the doorway as the glass door slid open. In the area were three beds, with one bed occupied. Opel was in that bed—catatonic. Beside him was a black-cloaked individual. The person wore a hood over the head and the hands were folded inside the sleeves of the cloak. The individual turned around and faced Kie.

Kie looked into the eyes of the person. His first expression was one of frustration and then one of elation.

"About time!" he panted. "You were supposed to be here earlier, to take care of those Rox Osguards."

A barrage of explosions rocked the foundation, sending smoke and debris flying into the air like a fine mist. Kie stumbled as did the stranger he was speaking to. However, unbeknownst to Kie and the black-cloaked individual, Juanita used the explosion as an opportunity to step into the shadows of the doorway and slipped into a far corner of the med lab. She was poised to listen to Kie speaking to the stranger. She had her pagenay out and ready with her thumb on the red button. She was prepared to knock both of them out and grab Opel if need be.

"We told you we would only intervene if the ships from USSTAP attacked your planet," the feminine voice answered in Kulusk. Her piercing yellow eyes cut a curt stare unto Kie.

The stranger appeared human. She was tanned but definitely white with brunette hair, highlighted with gold and white streaks. It flowed out from her hood down the front of her black cloak, covering her chest. Juanita thought her somewhat attractive with her high cheekbones and thin nose and lips. Her voice was strong and confident, characteristic of a leader.

"What the Rox do you think they are doing now?"

"This is not the massive attack that you requested intervention against," the feminine stranger scolded. "It is only one galaxy cruiser. We were sure the mighty Kulusk Empire could defend itself against a mere galaxy cruiser."

"Usually it could," Kie said with conviction, "but my space force was destroyed by the galaxy protectors you were to eliminate. My son died, because you did not live up to your end of the bargain." The anger in his voice steamed through his eyes and pierced the civility of the conversation.

"Again, my dear Kie Ritchen," the stranger said attempting to calm Kie. "The Tuits were only to intervene if USSTAP launched a massive attack on your planet. You told us the USSTAP were vile creatures bent on revenge and Kulusk was their next target. However, unbeknownst to you, we have been in your universe for years and we were watching. It was you who orchestrated the attack. It was you who was bent on revenge, not the Osguards. Therefore, it is you we hold accountable for your predicament."

Another barrage rocked Greenhaven as if to put extra emphasis in the Tuit's words. Both the Tuit and Kie stumbled and reached for objects to steady them from a fall. Kie coughed the dust from his lungs and looked toward the ceiling as if he had the gift of X-ray vision and he could see the grid disintegrate. He assumed the grid was down to fifteen percent.

"Nevertheless, our pact states the Tuit are my ally and as my ally I call on your service to help defend my planet," Kie demanded.

The Tuit stranger turned toward Opel. "He is not USSTAP. He is of this planet and my scan tells me he is of your bloodline. Isn't he the one that attacks you this day?"

"Yes he is, but that has nothing to do with the USSTAP galaxy cruiser knocking down my defense grid," Kie roared, waving his hands in front of him and stepping closer to the Tuit in a threatening manner.

"Perhaps...perhaps not," the Tuit interjected, showing no fear. "We were looking for a competent ally in this dimension level. The Kulusks appeared to be that ally, but we were mistaken. You are too headstrong and too stupid to see that your own people, your own bloodline plotted against you. They not only plotted against you, they formed a formidable force, trained and equipped them and they attacked you at your weakest moment...and obviously will succeed in their objective to overthrow you as the leader of this world. The Tuit cannot ally with such a weak entity. You would be a drain on our resources. I regret to inform you, our pact is terminated. You are on your own."

## Malcolm Dylan Petteway

Kie's anger exploded within his soul. His eyes beamed with angst and his muscles trembled with fury. "What do you mean, our pact is terminated? You can't do that."

"We can and we have," the Tuit scolded.

Kie grabbed the Tuit's clothing around her neck and drew his face close to hers. "You listen, you pitiful excuse for a human...you will use your ship and blow the snot out of that galaxy cruiser and then you will help me regain my planet. Do you hear me?"

The Tuit grinned. Her yellow pupils danced side to side as she regarded Kie. Then her smile faded and her eyes stopped dancing. She glared at Kie as if he were crazy. That gaze remained on her face for several seconds, in which time Kie never released his grip. Then she closed her eyes. An orange glow illuminated from her body. It repelled Kie back, shooting him several feet in the air, slamming his back on the floor. The orange glow subsided and the Tuit opened her eyes. Her annoyance was more than evident on her face. She shrunk her eyes by squinting and her neutral expression was gone, replaced by the look of a prizefighter looking for a knockout.

She raised her arm, holding it stiff and pointing it at the dazed Kie. She pulled back the sleeve of her cloak, revealing a double-barreled weapon strapped to her forearm.

Juanita's first impulse was to intervene and use her pagenay to disable the female. However, her body remained still, even though her mind told her to move. Something froze here. In that split second, she didn't know if it was duty that froze her, or her thirst for payback. Nevertheless, she failed to move. She just watched. Anticipating... hoping the Tuit was about to do what she wished she could do...kill Kie.

The Tuit stood over Kie...waiting...watching, with her arm stiff and pointing at him. To Juanita it seemed like minutes, but in actuality only several seconds had passed. The mere expectation became agonizing to Juanita. It also became validation that she was doing the proper thing by waiting. She took in a deep breath as relief filled her soul. She thought the Tuit was only bluffing.

However, the Tuit was not bluffing. As soon as Juanita relaxed, the Tuit fired the weapon. The two barrels glowed red and the weapon fired two beams, blue from the right, and red from the left, that merged into one spiraling beam. In a millisecond the beam shot from her arm and burrowed into Kie's chest, exploding it open, sending blood, bone, cartilage and parts of his lungs and heart spewing into the air in a hundred and eighty degree arc.

The sound of the crushing and exploding flesh echoed in Juanita's ear even after the sound had dissipated. She looked on in horror at the mess the weapon had made of Kie's body. A crater of blood and unrecognizable body parts lay where his chest once was. The look on his face, frozen in time, was one of impending doom. His mouth was open in the conception of a scream. His eyes were wide with fright and the realization of death, but his mouth never screamed and his eyes never saw. Death came quick, painful and dirty.

Juanita turned her head to halt her impulse to gag. The sight of Kie's demise was too much for her to take, along with the stale air and the humidity. She covered her mouth and closed her eyes, hoping not to make a sound. As she turned another barrage of weapons rocked the foundation. Dust, rocks and other debris shook loose and filled the air. The sound of the barrage and its aftermath, help conceal Juanita's choking sounds in the corner. The Tuit did not notice for she was preoccupied finding her footing on the unstable floor.

When Juanita felt sure enough to turn back around, she witnessed the Tuit standing over Opel. Juanita knew if the Tuit lifted her arm she would have to intervene. Opel was the one person she knew who had the antidote, and no harm could come to him. She moved her thumb to the blue button. She had decided death would be the only option if she needed to use her pagenay. This woman was dangerous and unfeeling—a deadly combination to combat.

The Tuit reached down and patted Opel on the forehead. She appeared to be watching him with endearing eyes. This confused Juanita. She didn't know if this Tuit was an ally of Opel's or what. It was like deciphering a soap opera. *Will the real bad guy please stand up,* she wished.

Then the Tuit turned and looked at Kie's body one last time. "You idiot," she scolded the dead man. "We could have ruled the universe together. You could have exacted your revenge without haste. But no…you could not wait until the Tuits were ready. No…you could not stick to the plan. Now because of you, we have to start anew. That's fine. We expected that. Soon this dimension level will be ours, just like the other four we have conquered."

She then pulled a round device from under her cloak. Juanita stood at the ready, prepared to use her pagenay, not knowing what the device was. Juanita's adrenaline was pumping so fast she could hear her own heartbeat echoing in her ears.

The Tuit activated the round device and it hummed. It was a familiar hum to Juanita. It was the hum of a PGP. Her initial thoughts were soon confirmed when an invisible door lifted in front of the Tuit. However, to Juanita's confusion the light illuminating from the door was not white, but red—an eerie red—almost devilish.

The Tuit stepped into the light and the door slammed shut with the familiar swooshes of a gate portal door. Still, Juanita was confused. All gate portal technology she knew used inner-space as a gateway. The portal the

Tuit used did not use inner-space. She did not know what it used, but she was sure it was not inner-space.

*** 

In the *Galaxy Cruiser Destiny*, sailing in space in a synchronous orbit above Renard, the Defensive Weapons Officer, Major Treylo Gnig, noticed a strange anomaly, two hundred thousand kilomarks to the ship's port stern. At first he thought it was a glitch in his console's programming. However his instincts were to record the phenomena before he could dismiss it. Then he executed several diagnostic tests on his instruments. This all took approximately thirty-five seconds. When the test results revealed no known abnormalities, it confused Gnig.

However, in the unfamiliar situation they were in, Gnig thought it best to bring his findings to Jackil's attention. He beeped the sire's chair with a code two find. This meant it was a find not necessarily endangering the ship, but may need the sire's attention at the soonest possible moment.

Jackil took the beep and nodded for Gnig to report. Renard's defensive grid was down and the ship had stood down from firing its weapons. All Jackil was waiting on was word from Juanita.

"Sire," Gnig started. "A moment ago, I recorded massive energy surges two hundred thousand kilomarks to our port stern. They lasted approximately fifty seconds. I recorded the last thirty seconds of it."

"Play it on the main monitor," Jackil ordered.

"Tiah...sire." Gnig pushed his controls and soon he had control of the main monitor. The picture was the mathematical diatribe associated with scans. The numbers streamed seamlessly down the screen then the numbers jumped, revealing several large energy surges.

"What do you make of it?" asked Jackil.

"Don't know, sire," Gnig confessed.

"Any guesses?"

"You may think me crazy, but..."

"But what," Jackil urged.

"It appears like several ships, I dare say as little as six and as many as nine ships...bigger than galaxy protectors...just stepped through a gate portal. However, the gate portal signature isn't of inner-space. It is of something else that I can't quite make out."

Jackil watched the numbers flow across the screen one more time. He applied Gnig's theory and it matched. The numbers did indicate a large number of ships transiting a gate portal. A cold chill rushed over his body as the thought took root in other hypotheses. "Was there another Kulusk armada that just left? If so, where were they going? Did they have IPG engines as well or was this someone else? Was it another decoy or was it another enemy watching them?

# Osguards: Revelations

"Tag and process this data," Jackil responded. "Alert 1…if we have company out there, we need to prepare a welcome for them."

***

In the fields of Tainville, Opel was up to his two hundred and fiftieth Sisle. He sluggishly sauntered to the next row of the white four-petal flower. The pain from his horrendous beating was starting to seep into his mind. He was having trouble blocking it with his anti-interrogation technique. With each step, he felt a twinge of pain shoot through his leg. He adjusted his technique, but he was running out of room in his technique to adjust.

In his mind, he leaned over on the two hundred and fifty-first flower and began smelling it, inviting the sweet biting fragrance to massage his olfactory. He concentrated on the smell. He pushed the pain back as deep as he could, but the hint of pain still persisted. Then he heard it—a spoken phrase from the outside. The phrase designed to automatically push reality into his mind and sweep Tainville out, like a whisper of smoke.

The phrase his mother spoke of in his favorite children's story. The story told to her by her mother and father, and their mother and father before them on Earth ... the old children's story from Earth no one from Kulusk would think of breathing ... the one phrase that summed up his predicament so eloquently—the one phrase—the one name quintessential of his life—Rip Van Winkle.

His field swirled into a tornado and was swallowed up by darkness. Then the pain rushed in like a bulldozer. His jaw hurt, it was broken. His ribs hurt ... several were cracked. It was hard for him to breathe. His right lung was collapsed. He began coughing. Blood spurted from his throat. His eyes were swollen shut from the beating. He couldn't feel anything but pain. Pain had consumed his body. His leg was fractured, his arm was broken and his shoulder was dislocated. The pain was immense, but he heard the name. He heard the name that was his salvation. He heard Rip Van Winkle.

"Opel…Opel. I am Osguard Fifty-Five from the USSTAP. I'm going to get you out of here," the angelic voice pushed into his head.

Juanita then helped Opel to his feet, swinging his good arm around her shoulder for support. She allowed him to lean on her. He was five inches taller than her and a good hundred pounds heavier. However, Juanita was strong for her size due to the Chaktun blood coursing through her veins and the multitude of exercises in her daily regimen.

She activated her PGP with her free hand. The invisible door slid up, illuminating the room with the white light of inner-space. Juanita sighed in relief. She was a little worried the light would be red and the alien had done something to inner-space that would disrupt her comfortable routine of travel. The white light came as a comfort. She recognized and accepted it. She was about to step back to the *USSTAP Galaxy Cruiser Destiny*. There,

281

Opel would receive proper medical attention and she would be able to extract the antidote. Time was running out. She had no more to waste.

She cleared her throat and whisked Opel into the light. The door closed, taking with it the light from inner-space.

# Chapter 41—Revival

The *Universal Science, Security and Trade Association of Planets Galaxy Cruiser Destiny* raced through space at MOP sixty, traveling sixty light years per universal hour, defying the laws of light and physics, whistling on a cloud of unseen particles of gravitational pull. The ship's two large half moon shaped engines, which dwarfed the ship's main body, tore at the fabric of space like a dagger, and magically sewed the seam back in its wake.

Juanita stood behind the command chair biting her lower lip in anticipation. She studied the right screen, backing up the ARITs calculations with her own. Jackil remained in his chair, reflecting on what was happening. The anomaly they experienced just before Juanita stepped back on the ship several hours ago, still worried him. He was waiting on the science corps' report before he mentioned it to the Osguard. Nonetheless, his gut was telling him, he needed to speak up now, especially seeing the deep concern that hovered in Juanita's eyes.

"Osguard," he called.

Juanita turned to him with a raised eyebrow.

"Just before you stepped back to the ship, Major Gnig captured something on his scanners. At first it looked like a portal gate opening, but the energy readings weren't consistent with that hypothesis."

"Yes, go on," Juanita encouraged.

"Major Gnig surmises several ships…large ships…as many as five…maybe more ... pushed into another type of medium."

Juanita sighed and glanced at the ceiling. "Let's talk…in your office."

"Tiah!" he responded. Then he turned to his second-in-command, "Colonel Springs, you have the bridge."

"Tiah!" she snapped.

They then retreated to his office in the long corridor behind the bridge. Jackil took his seat behind his oak desk. Juanita leaned against the wall next to him. She proceeded to explain her encounter with the Tuit in Greenhaven. She explained the devilish red light that emanated from the gate portal the Tuit used.

"So, I believe you are right," she shrugged. "There was someone else out there. And I am afraid they are on their way to Capitol Station."

# Osguards: Revelations

Jackil remained silent for a moment. Inside fright was trying to take over his center of reasoning. He thought the Osguard could be leading them to their deaths in an insane attempt to stop a fleet bigger than the one the Kulusks mounted with one galaxy cruiser. Juanita recognized the doubt in his eyes, and couldn't blame him. Deep down inside she knew it was suicide, but she had no other alternative. Then Jackil smiled. Then the smile turned into a chuckle. Then the chuckle turned into outright laughter.

The laughter was contagious. Juanita giggled with Jackil. Even though she did not know why she was laughing, it felt good. She had not laughed in weeks...not since the Osguard Garden Olympics. The Kulusk attack, her cousin's murder and the biological attack on Capitol Station had left her morose and sour. Somehow the laughter lifted some of those feelings. And she now felt somewhat more human.

Her laughter faded, echoed by Jackil's laughter. When she regained her composure she nodded her head at Jackil. "What the hell is so funny?"

"You," he snickered. Then he saw the confused look on her face. "Not exactly you...it's the Osguard you."

"What?"

"You see, I was on the *G.C. Justice* when your cousin, the First Osguard cut his first tooth in battle against the Moslecks." He shifted in his chair, almost squirming. "I was the young ensign who tried to order him off the bridge that day. Fortunately, he ignored me and took charge." Jackil's purple eyes faded to a distant time as he sat quiet for a moment. "You know, he saved our lives that day. I will never forget it. I was running scared like a little punk, and this teenage boy steps onto my bridge and saves our lives. Right then I knew he was an Osguard. Right then I knew you were all Osguards, and I pledged my life to you. So if it ends today, while I am saving my Osguard, so it ends."

Juanita rubbed the top of Jackil's baldhead. "Thanks," she whispered.

To Jackil, this was all he needed. It seemed her hand soothed his nerves and her voice of gratitude invigorated his command. "Let's do this," he said to no one in particular.

"Sire, Capitol Station...five minutes ahead," came Springs' voice over the intercom. "Should we drop to hypersonic?"

"No," Jackil ordered. "Take her to the porch at present speed. Transmit the Osguard's coded message to deactivate defenses."

"Tiah!"

***

Inside the cryogenic chamber, five gate portals showered the area with white light. The chamber was ten stories high and two hundred yards long, honeycombed with glass bedded enclosures. Railed walkways flanked

283

the enclosures, which contained the sleeping inhabitants. Juanita rushed out of her light first. Springs stepped out next, followed by three security guards. Juanita carried the vaccine in her pouch slung over her right shoulder. She ran to the control board in the center of the honeycomb, and tapped three keys that injected the portal receptor with the vaccine from her pouch. She tapped several more sensors and the vaccine disappeared.

"ARIT…synthesize and administer intravenously…doses of one part per one hundred pounds."

The green light on the board told Juanita the ARIT accepted the command and was executing it. Then she turned to Springs. "Get the vaccine to the cryogenic chambers on the galaxy protectors. We need those crews up, about and in fighting shape as soon as possible."

"Tiah!" Springs tapped her CC and gave the go order for the others to proceed.

Juanita then ran to the ladder and climbed to the fourth story. She then ran fifty yards to her left, just in time to see the glass tube extend out and pop open. The white mist of the cool air fogged the walkway. Then a cough echoed in the air. Juanita looked inside the glass coffin. Michael slowly sat up rubbing his head. He had a cryogenic headache. It was pounding behind his eyes with a sharp pain pushing on his eardrums. He opened his eyes, barely aware of his own existence let alone where he was. Then he saw Juanita.

Instantly, the entire memory rushed into his mind like a hurricane. He just stared at her as he pieced the memory back together. Then he smiled. "I guess you were successful…huh?"

"Yes, but no time to celebrate. We have to get into combat mode now!"

"What? Not the Kulusks?"

"No Michael, it's not the Kulusks, it's someone I fear is more sinister…they call themselves Tuits."

"What the hell—"

"No time, we need everything that can fight out there now, whether it can fly or float, and as long as it can throw a weapon it's got to go."

\*\*\*

Two hours later, sixty galaxy protectors floated from their docking port into a defensive posture in the space surrounding Millmum Capitol Station. Commander Terilela was pushing coordinates to all ships in an eerie reminder of the Kulusk battle several weeks ago.

"This is Millmum Main Capitol Station Control," she advised from the observation deck. "*G.P. Loclam* on port one you are cleared to deport and take heading two–two decimal three–four, mark zero–five."

"This is the *G.P. Loclam*. Copy, two–two decimal three–four, mark zero–five. Tiah," came the voice over the intercom.

"This is Millmum Main Capitol Station Control. *G.P. Nitram* on port six zero, you are cleared to deport and take heading one–two–two decimal one–three–four, mark zero–eight."

"This is *G.P. Nitram*. Copy, one–two–two decimal one–three–four, mark zero–eight. Tiah."

"This is Millmum Main Capitol Station Control. *G.P. Sregaem* on port three-zero, you are cleared to deport and take heading two–two–two decimal two–three–four, mark one–zero."

"This is *G.P. Sregaem*. Copy, two–two–two decimal two–three–four, mark one–zero. Tiah."

"This is Millmum Main Capitol Station Control. *G.P. Sucram* on port one five, you are cleared to deport and take heading zero–zero–two decimal zero–three–four, mark zero–one."

"This is *G.P. Sucram*. Copy, zero–zero–two decimal zero–three–four, mark zero–one. Tiah."

Terilela repeated the command for each galaxy protector, wondering what the threat was, and professionally concealing her fear from her voice. Admiral Toneilk walked the plank behind her. This time he was not nervous. He was anxious. He had tasted battle, and although sour, it tasted good. He was scared, but his fright fueled his resolve. He was ready. And as he looked at his now tested and proven observation deck crew, he knew they were ready as well.

When he was satisfied the perimeter was secured, he called the First Osguard on the interlink, "Osguard zero–one…all ships in place."

"Tiah…here we go again."

Then he saw them. Several gate portals spreading a blood red light. Michael's eyes widened as the ships popped into normal space. The ships were umbrella shaped, pointed in the front and circular flared in the rear. Their engines were embedded in the flare structure and hidden from sight. The ships weren't as wide as the galaxy protector, but they were longer, by at least one thousand meters. Michael saw five ships. They stopped fifty kilometers from the *G.P. Neraka*.

"People, we have company in sector two–G…five battleship sized butches," he announced over the interlink. "Anybody else have company?"

"All ships replied negative," responded Michael's communications officer, Major Best.

"Hail them."

"No reply, sire."

"Activate chromerion field," Michael swallowed hard. "Scans?"

"Humans…each ship has a crew of two thousand." Then Commander John White's mouth dropped. "All female."

285

"What?" Michael coughed.

"All female," the defense systems officer reported.

"Commander Li...ready all weapons," Michael ordered, trying to show he was not fazed by White's report.

"Tiah, all weapons ready."

"Osguard, five of those strange gate portals are opening up again," White reported.

"Commander Li...split your weapons. I want half on those ships and half on anything else that flies out of hell."

"Osguard, the ships are engaging their engine," the defensive systems officer reported.

"Ready our engines, stay with them pilot."

"They're going back in sire...they are going back into the red light. Do you want to pursue?" the pilot asked.

"Negative...I don't want to go into that without knowing what is on the other side."

"Why do you think they turned around?" Best queried.

"I don't think they expected us to be ready for them. Obviously they like their prey half dead. They thought we were wounded already. That's why they only sent five ships."

"Do you think they are going for reinforcements?" continued Best.

"Don't know...I just don't know." Michael sat back into his chair. "Let's get those scans interpreted and sent out to all USSTAP. Stand down Alert One...go to Alert Three."

"Tiah!"

# Epilogue—A New World

"Yes, Mr. President, that is correct," said Musoto for the second time on his secure phone.

Musoto was back in his Washington office backing up his written report to Peters on the events of the previous week. He had spent three full days in debriefings with USSTAP officials and another three days writing his report for Peters. The entire episode seemed so surreal, especially on the heels of the Kulusk attack on Capitol Station. It was hard for him to convince Peters the events were real. He couldn't believe Peters could be so hard headed. Peters was flying to California on Air Force One, for some political activity to endorse some candidate; Musoto neither knew nor wanted to know

"Mr. President, as I said...Osguard Fifty-Five saved USSTAP. She got the antidote back to Capitol Station in time to save all the people in suspended animation. She traveled to Kulusk, rescued this character named

Opel, who is a descendant from the Pathgo clan and bridged an Alliance with the Kulusks. Musoto spent another fifteen minutes explaining that relationship to Peters for the second time. "Kie Ritchen, the character who started the entire mess is dead—killed by some other alien—so Osguard Fifty-Five states."

Peters seemed to understand, but he wanted to see the HVP to support this claim. Musoto had to explain he didn't have access to the HVP. His knowledge came from the debriefing USSTAP afforded him—a debriefing he felt would be his last one. USSTAP recovered his CC and other devices they first gave him to make contact with them. This time, he was under tight security watch and was not given free reign to roam the facility as he was before. Evidently, there was more paranoia on their part toward him. This he also related in his written report, but Peters seemed to have skipped right pass this in the report.

"Mr. President," Musoto called. "I'm not sure my initial readings on USSTAP were correct. I mean the entire thing with T-Square. That was an execution."

"Didn't you say that Stelana said it wasn't a USSTAP weapon?"

"Yes sir, I did…but she also said it was not a Kulusk or a Chaktun weapon. She said the signature was a little off. She showed me the reading, but hell…I could have been looking at a medical readout for all I know. I don't know how to read those damned things. She could have been pulling the wool over my eyes. I really think she killed T-Square and lied to cover it up."

"Why do you suspect that?"

"Just say…I've gotten to know her a little bit better…and by association, I've gotten to know USSTAP a little bit better."

"And?"

"And…let's just say I am not too thrilled about some of their motivation."

"Motivation?"

"I can't put my finger on it, but I think they are driven by…by…less than admirable reasons."

"Stop beating around the bush…just say what you think," Peters ordered.

"Okay sir…I believe USSTAP is the Nation of Islam on steroids. I thought they were the embodiment of Martin Luther King's dream, now I think they are the militant arm of Louis Farrakhan."

"Why do you think that?" queried the president.

"Just the conversations I have had, the feelings I get when I am with them and the gut feeling of a cop. I think they don't like us. I think they are prejudice. They blame all that has happened to their ancestors in this country on us. I think they feel white people are to be loathed."

Peters remained quiet on the other line for some time. Musoto realized Peters was mulling over his words—looking for some sense in what he had just spoken. But as it came out of his mouth, he knew it didn't make sense. He kept his observation out of the report and was satisfied to keep it to himself, but some wild impulse forced him to reveal his observation to Peters. Unfortunately, it did sound wild when spoken aloud.

"Musoto, as president, I have feelings too. And my gut feelings tell me your professional pride was injured on this assignment and you are looking for an excuse to save face. Do you know I had Juanita Genesis-Clark checked out? She is thirty-five years old. She was born and raised in New Haven Connecticut, daughter of Sarah and the Frank Genesis. Her father died of cancer, her brother, Conrad Genesis, died of a drug overdose. She attended public schools, and graduated from the University of Connecticut with a Bachelors Degree in Criminology. She married ten years ago, to a William Ethan Clark. He was killed by a drunk driver, who hit them on I-84 near Danbury Connecticut, on their first wedding anniversary. In that same accident, she lost her unborn child. The man did not serve a day in jail. He paid a hefty fine and was released. Maybe that's the reason she doesn't trust our justice system. She studied Criminology and her first experience with the law left her more than disappointed."

Peters paused. Musoto could hear him sigh through the phone lines.

"Oh, by the way, Musoto," Peters continued. "William Ethan Clark was a white man. I presume the unborn baby Osguard Fifty-Five, Juanita Genesis-Clark, was carrying was half white. So I just don't quite see it like you do. Frankly Mr. Musoto, I am a bit dismayed that I had to use other channels to get this information, when it should have been included in your original report. Maybe if you had done your job you would have a much better insight on the Osguards."

The words slapped Musoto. The sting was painful...so painful he felt rage consume his civility. He opened his mouth to interrupt Peters, but a little voice in the back of his mind told him not to. It told him to be quiet and listen. So he did, swallowing hard to fight back the anger forming in the pit of his stomach.

"Your record is less than pristine and the report I received from the Louisiana Governor says Delecroix was less than impressed with your ability when the action went down. Lucky for you, they are still enamored with T-Square's cause of death. They have no way of explaining the burnt hole in the middle of his forehead. However the Shreveport police are taking full blame or credit...you choose, for his death. No one seems too torn up about it, so they aren't taking too much heat from the civic organizations down there. However, it is written...your action during the standoff was appalling and most likely the cause of the entire episode. Moreover, looking at your past record, I tend to agree with them."

Peters paused, took a deep breath and smacked his lips. "If you weren't the first man to make contact with USSTAP I would pull you off right now, and I am guessing the officials at USSTAP are starting to feel the same way. Perhaps that is why your movement and contact options are now limited." Peters paused once more, knowing he was scolding his only contact with USSTAP.

"I pose to you again...make arrangements for me to meet with any representative of USSTAP and do it the next time you have any contact with them. Do I make myself clear?"

"Yes, Mr. President...I understand."

"Fine." Then Peters hung up, leaving the buzz of a dead line echoing in Musoto's ear.

Musoto slammed the phone down. His anger steamed from his soul as he shoved his computer, keyboard and papers from his desk. The entire mess crashed onto the floor, spreading electronic components, and classified papers throughout the small glass enclosed room. The noise startled several people passing in the hallway who now glanced at the red face Musoto staring off into space, at nothing in particular...just staring, with a rage so apparent it reached outside to them. Those who dare look back became frightened and those who did not look scurried back to their own business.

Either way, Musoto did not notice them. He only noticed Peters had scolded him for doing his job...a job he thought he had done extremely well. But again, he had screwed up.

*\*\**

Her piercing yellow eyes glowed like two suns, almost illuminating the room. She was on the phone but remained silent for several seconds, thinking...dreaming...planning her next move.

"I shot the man Musoto was after with my synthesized pagenay rifle," the angelic voice said over the phone. "I made sure he saw the beam. Even though the USSTAP agent there denied she shot T-Square, Musoto has doubts."

"Good!" said the yellow-eyed woman. "The report he gives the president should not be so flattering after this. Hopefully, this will put doubt in the president's mind about the integrity of USSTAP." Then the yellow-eyed woman paused. "Did he see you?"

"No...I don't think so. When he got back into town he came right over and... Well let's just say, he had another unforgettable night. And I dare say, I had fun as well," the voice joked.

The yellow-eyed woman smiled and let the words linger in the air a moment. "Did you get any more information?" she asked.

"Yes...after he went to sleep, I used the piper like before. This time, I got a lot of information. I narrowed down at least one Osguard and with the computers at the insurance company; I can probably get the names of most of the rest by dinner."

"Are you sure?"

"Yes! It is a wonderful thing, this Internet. I can search almost anywhere. And with your access codes, I can hack into most of the government computers to get any information I want...tax records, birth certificates. Yeah, I will have the majority of these fools by the end of the day. Unfortunately, they know about us."

"What?" the yellow-eyed woman squealed.

"It appears this Osguard Fifty-Five saw Rina shoot Kie Ritchen. She overheard Kie call Rina a Tuit. Rina confirmed we were not from this level in her conversation with Ritchen before she assassinated him. That's how they knew Rina was coming. She didn't know Juanita obtained the vaccine; or that she took it to the station in time for them to get ready for us."

"No matter, it just alters our time table a little bit," the yellow-eyed woman commented. Then anguish framed her face, "What about Musoto?"

"What about him? He doesn't believe the Tuit story, and if he includes that in his report the president will dismiss it. He really doubts USSTAP's credibility right now. And as far as he knows, I am just an insurance agent named Mona Richards...nothing else...but maybe a great lay. That's what keeps him coming back. And every time he does, I will extract what information he knows from his brain with the piper as soon as he falls asleep."

"Fine, I will be waiting for your information," the yellow-eyed woman said. "After you get it, we have to meet up with the mother ship. We have some damage control to accomplish."

"Kiza," Mona Richards replied in Tuit.

Then the yellow-eyed woman hung up the phone and strolled to the bathroom. She opened her contact lens case and put in her blue contacts, covering all signs of her eyes' natural yellow coloring. When she gazed in the mirror, she began her daily make-up routine. When she was satisfied, she smiled and dressed in a black business skirt suit and yellow blouse. She checked herself once more in the full-length mirror, admiring her svelte physique.

*A good-looking body and a sexy smile can go a long way on this planet,* she thought. *Even for a woman my age.* Then Speaker of the House, Representative Joyce T. Eldridge from Texas, exited her bedroom, walked down the flight of stairs, and exited her Washington D.C. apartment to tackle the domestic affairs of the United States of America.

***

The night was unusually chilly for this time of year on Chaktun. However, Michael was happy he was alive to enjoy the night. Two weeks ago he could have died in animated suspension, never having the opportunity to kiss his wife or hug his children again. Now he had that opportunity, thanks to Opel and Juanita. Additionally, he took the special opportunity to show his family his love at every possible moment, because now he had time to reflect and appreciate what he had.

The Senate, the Congress and Parliament were wrapping up after nearly a month's delay. All legislative bills had been passed with an overwhelming majority. Kulusk was accepted into the full USSTAP fold with Opel, as the reigning Maxum and peace once again seemed to loom over the universe...a peace paid for once again by the men and women of USSTAP.

Michael walked along the memorial wall, where he and the other Osguards had just added twenty-four hundred more names—all victims of the Terinolice Virus. Most of the dead came from the Security and Medical Corps. His security personnel were the first to be exposed to the virus when they checked the morgue ships, and as they fell from the virus; the medical personnel who attended to them also became exposed. Another friend, he personally recruited, was now dead—Doctor Susan Tillman.

He closed his eyes in frustration, painfully remembering the circumstance surrounding how he met Susan. It was at Rutgers University during the fall of his sophomore year. Ortho had revealed his destiny to him, he had survived his first space battle and he was floating high on that information. On that night, after leaving the library, Michael was able to use his newfound abilities to save Susan's roommate, Michelle Katherine Goff from being kidnapped by three men. Michael used his Sixana training to kill two men and severely wound the third. Even though Michael had given the order, while onboard the *G.C. Justice* that killed hundreds of Mosleck pirates in his first space battle weeks earlier, the agony he felt about killing with his bare hands threw him into a psychological despair. In his mind, he had taken his first human lives. He had killed. The only saving grace was he had done it to save an innocent person, Michelle—his future wife.

However, there were three other women missing, including Susan Tillman, and the police were hot to find them. Conversely, Michael's actions led the police to believe him more of a suspect than a witness, which endangered his secret identity as the First Osguard. Because of that, he had to choose between finishing what he started thereby saving Susan and the others, and not doing anything at all in order to preserve the sanctity of USSTAP. He chose to use the full technological might of USSTAP to do what the police couldn't. The consequences of his interference threatened USSTAP's security, and forced an attitude adjustment for Michael about USSTAP dealings with Earth. It forced him to support Ortho's policy of placing Earth into protective isolation, which until then he had objected to.

Nonetheless, the bond Michael, Michelle and Susan shared through the rescue, the police interrogation and ultimately the trial of the only surviving attacker was one forged by providence, sealed by destiny and blessed by God, and no one could ever break it. Later, when Susan told him she wanted to study medicine, Michael began the recruitment process. He gave her a card upon his graduation, which she gladly attended. Eight years later, Doctor Susan Tillman was the Assistant Chief Medical Officer aboard the USSTAP Millmum Capitol Station.

This position had caused her to be the first to come in contact with patients with the virus. She worked tirelessly to isolate the virus. She did it at the expense of her own safety. Even in suspended animation, the virus was too far along to be halted. By the time Juanita arrived with the antidote, Susan had died, along with about eight hundred others, whose condition was too far gone to for them to survive.

A tear rolled down his cheek as he read her name. The bond he thought was unbreakable was now broken...broken only by the unseen but undefeated force of death. She was so young, so beautiful, and so full of life. She wanted to marry and have a family. She wanted to have adventure and save lives. She wanted so much, but she got death...death, the unforgiving sleep that all must confront. It was unfair. It was more than unfair. It was unjust, wickedly brought on by a malicious, immoral tyrant.

If Kie were not already dead, Michael would have killed him. He felt he would have traveled to Kulusk and broken Kie's neck with his bare hands, crushed his skull with his feet and ripped his arm from his dead carcass and bashed his brains with it. The man did not deserve to live and God saw to that. Kie had stolen two of his best friends, Sanchez and now Susan. Kie's death was too painless and too merciful. Michael wanted more. He wanted to torture Kie the way he was being tortured, slow and methodical, but he couldn't—Kie was already dead. And you could not kill anyone more than once. It was over...at least the fight with the Kulusks.

From the shadows Michael heard footsteps. He turned to see who it was. When he turned he saw in the light of the orange moonlight it was Jarod Stone, Osguard Eleven, sire of the *G.P. Gentry* and protector of the Siryman Galaxy. He nodded toward Jarod and Jarod waved. He walked up to Michael with the same look of despair in his eyes.

"Hey Mike, what you up to?" he said in a low voice.
"Nothing much, just paying my respects to the wall," Michael said turning back to the wall, staring at Susan's name.

"Yeah, me too," Jarod replied. "I think we all will be out here sometime or another before we leave." Jarod turned to the wall and scanned the names in front of him. "This has been one hell of a month; we lost some good people...some good friends."

"Yeah, I know," Michael said, "but as always, the Osguards survived."

"Yeah, but our number will come up real soon I suspect."

Michael turned to Jarod, "How so?"

"Shit, Michael...the Kulusks are our friends now. You even agreed for Tirana Ritchen to sign on as your Centurion of Operations to replace Sanchez as a final peace offering. However, we still have an enemy; we have a new player in the game—the Tuits. And I'm not sure what their story is. Juanita couldn't get a real good feel for them. So we don't know who they are or where they come from. This reference to dimensional level is kind of creepy."

"Yeah, I've been wondering about that. Reppus said in the ancient writings there is mention of dimensional levels. He mentioned it at dinner tonight. He said he would do some research on it. He thinks the term dimensional level refers to other superclusters in the universe. The Tuits may have found a way to travel through the universal void that separates the Virgo Supercluster from the others." Michael looked skyward and grunted a huge sigh. "My guess is that they are from the Centaurus Supercluster. It is the nearest large supercluster to us...and it is the only supercluster that contains such a large collection of matter that it affects galaxies in the Virgo Supercluster, including the Millmum Galaxy."

"I heard Reppus too," Jarod said, looking skyward as well, "and what you say does make sense. I bet you it is where the other generations of humans ventured. Nevertheless, we just uncovered one revelation that cost us thousands of lives and now we have this bullshit drop right into our laps. Whoever the Tuits are, will be revealed to us soon enough. And whatever, the Tuits have in mind; I have a gut feeling it involves us."

***

# ABOUT THE AUTHOR

Malcolm Dylan Petteway is a military analyst and a twenty-year veteran of the United States Air Force. He flew B-52's as an Electronic Warfare Officer and has 3,000 flight hours and 300 combat hours. In his distinguished career, Malcolm has used his knowledge in the art of war, military weapons and combat defenses in planning over 400 combat sorties. Besides his Meritorious Service Medal with three oak leaf clusters and numerous other awards, Malcolm is the recipient of the U.S. Air Force Air Medal and the U.S. Air Force Air Achievement Medal for his actions during Operation Enduring Freedom. Malcolm Petteway is a graduate of the U.S. Air Force Academy and California State University.

ISBN: 978-0-9843645-1-0

www.ingramcontent.com/pod-product-compliance
Lightning Source LLC
Chambersburg PA
CBHW072223190626
46809CB00016B/217